all fun and games
until somebody loses an eye

all fun and games until somebody loses an eye

christopher
brookmyre

LITTLE, BROWN

A *Little, Brown* Book

First published in Great Britain in 2005 by Little, Brown

Copyright © 2005 Christopher Brookmyre

'Teenage Wristband' written by Greg Dulli. From the Twilight Singers
album *Blackberry Belle*. Copyright © 2003 Kali Nichta Music (BMI).
Lyrics reproduced by kind permission of Greg Dulli.
www.thetwilightsingers.com

A CIP catalogue record for this book
is available from the British Library.

HARDBACK ISBN 0 316 72523 4
C FORMAT ISBN 0 316 72616 8

Typeset in Palatino by Palimpsest Book Production Limited,
Polmont, Stirlingshire
Printed and bound in Great Britain by
Clays Ltd, St Ives plc

Little, Brown
An imprint of
Time Warner Book Group UK
Brettenham House
Lancaster Place
London WC2E 7EN

www.twbg.co.uk

For Hilary Hale and Caroline Dawnay,
without whom . . .

Thanks: Marisa, Greg Dulli, Roger Cantwell and
Duncan Spilling for fitting all those words on the cover.

Special thanks also to Calvin for their song *Supercar*,
which resonated so hauntingly around the time
I conceived this little fairy tale.

I've allowed myself to lead this little life, when inside me there was so much more.

Shirley Valentine, by Willy Russell

The secret of a joyful life is to live dangerously.

Nietzsche

Prologue

Toyz

'It would encourage me, you know, to think ... or rather it would comfort me, no, wrong word, well, maybe the right word, but it would, you know, inspire me but at the same time sort of soothe me in an all-is-well-in-heaven-and-earth kind of way to think, ah, what am I trying to say here?'

Som was sitting on an upturned black flight case, rocking it back ten or fifteen degrees as he rolled his heels on the frosted gravel in front of Bett's mansion. Lex wished he wouldn't do that, *really* wished he wouldn't do that. Okay, it was Som's case, Som's stuff, and maybe he was cool with the contents getting clattered in the less-than-improbable event that his feet slipped and put him on his skinny Thai ass, but that wasn't the point. It was bad practice. There were several black flight cases sitting out there with the three of them in the cold tonight, as on any such night, and Lex didn't much like the thought of Som using the vessel of her fragile, delicately packed and fastidiously inventoried kit as a makeshift shooting stick. Weighing further upon her discomfiture was the fact that Armand's flight cases were occasionally known to accommodate materials sufficient to denude the immediate vicinity of any standing structure, mammalian life, or even vegetation.

'Som, you're 404-ing,' she warned him.

'Sorry. I'm just saying, wouldn't you love to believe that somewhere in this world there really is at least one – just one – hollowed-out volcano containing a super high-tech ops base under the command of a fully fledged evil genius? I mean, I could live with all the havoc the evil genius might wreak simply to know there was a facility like that in existence. It would just make the world a more fantastical place, don't you reckon? In a Santa-really-does-exist-after-all kind of way, you know?'

'Would it need to have a retractable roof for space-rockets and nuclear missiles to launch through?' Armand asked, bringing a measured irritation to bear in the precision of his accented pronunciation.

'I'd settle for a submarine dock,' Som responded, with an equally measured, deliberate guilelessness.

'So,' the Frenchman said, 'the thought of an actual, existent, staffed and fully functioning underground base doesn't, how would you say, blow your hair back? It must be inside a hollowed-out volcano and run by a cackling megalomaniac or it's merely part of the crushing ordinariness of life's relentlessly drab ennui?'

'Not at all,' Som protested. 'I didn't say that. Did I say that?'

'No, but you could be more "up" about it,' Armand complained. 'I've been looking forward to this, you know. Really looking forward to it.'

Lex smiled to herself at the sight of Armand – mercenary, soldier, explosives adept and trained killer – putting on a petted lip and acting like a disappointed child for the express purpose of winding up a scrawny adolescent techno-geek half his age.

'I'm "up",' Som insisted. 'I'm extremely up. I'm looking forward to it as much as you. I'm just, you know, insulating myself against disappointment.'

'A pitifully negative approach to life,' Armand condemned.

'Easy for you to say. When I was a kid, my parents took me to Tunisia, and we went to visit the place they filmed *Star Wars*. I was eight years old, and—'

'Pitifully negative,' Armand repeated. 'And cowardly to boot.'

'I'm just saying, I'd love to believe it'll be all chrome and glass and LED read-outs everywhere, but I'm preparing myself in case it's just a quarry with a roof.'

'Silence, coward. Be gone. Alexis, *ma chère*, when Rebekah gets here with our transport, I'm going to sit up front with our designated driver. Sorry to land you with Som, but I plan on enjoying myself this evening and I don't want him "bumming me out".'

'Yeah, sure,' Lex said, rolling her eyes. '*That*'s why you want to sit beside Rebekah. Forget it. It'll be girls in the front, boys in the back. I've been waiting years for some female solidarity around here.'

Armand waved dismissively at her, but knew she wouldn't

be giving ground, just as she knew he had no intention of sitting anywhere but next to his playmate. There had to be twenty years between them, but as Som and Armand's relationship seemed to be based upon bringing out each other's inner thirteen-year-old, the age gap was irrelevant to their inseparable (and often insufferable) camaraderie. It was the female solidarity she was less sure about. Rebekah had been with the outfit a month now and, despite being the only other female, they'd barely engaged in anything other than the most perfunctory of exchanges.

This was pretty familiar, however. Lex had seen it before, in herself and, more recently, in Somboon. The blasé and cocky figure who was so nonchalantly leaning on easily fifty thousand dollars' worth of electronics, as he bantered about the interior fittings of the underground weapons facility they were about to assault, might fail to recognise the hunched and introverted serial nail-biter who'd barely managed anything more articulate than gaze-averted mumbles for the first month in their company. Rebekah had been less physically withdrawn than Som was during those earliest days, and she looked unused to shrinking from anyone's gaze, not least because she was five-nine and a looker. She was always straight-backed and forthright in her posture, but this struck Lex as a conditioned reflex, a body-language statement of 'no comment'. When she did speak, her accent was American, the delivery a little clipped and forced, like discipline was overruling shyness and more than a little fear. Som had once referred to her as 'the she-bot', a throwaway remark that nonetheless accurately identified something automated about her behaviour.

Rebekah had been unquestionably scared, nervous of her new environment and untrusting of its apparent security; noticeably starting at telephones and doorbells and, rather curiously, at overhead aircraft. Post-traumatic stress disorder, or what used to be known as plain old shell-shock, any observer might reasonably have diagnosed, but Lex could identify the symptoms of a more specific anxiety: that of the fugitive. The girl was still waiting for a trapdoor to open beneath her.

'Lex, you're welcome to sit with Rebekah, far as I'm concerned,' Som said. 'I figure "the Transport Manager" has gotta have some serious driving skillz. She's gonna be throwing that bus around, man. I don't want a front-row seat.'

'I could hear that z, Som,' Lex warned him. 'You've got to drop the leet speak. Seriously. *I'm* the hacker here.'

'I'm so grateful to the American cultural imperialists that they have made English the international language of code-crunchers and keypad monkeys,' Armand said with a sigh, the steam of his breath billowing affectedly in the moonlight. 'It would pain me too much to hear French so vandalised.'

'Ah, bullshit,' Som replied. 'French is just too effete-sounding to be of any use with technology. I mean, listen: *ordinateur*. That sounds like something that runs on steam, with, like, brass fittings and a big wooden plinth.'

'Exactly. You describe elegance and grace, agelessness and finery. That is French. Plastic, fibreglass, coils of tangled cable, porno download, shoot-em-up – English, English, English.'

'Fuck you.'

'*Encore, Anglais, Anglais, Anglais.*'

'Our new Transport Manager.' That was how Rebekah had been introduced by Bett, with their leader's typically cryptic brevity. Each one of them came here with two things: a talent and a past. Everybody would find out the former soon enough, but only Bett would be privy to the latter.

Bett knew everyone's past, but nobody knew his. There were fragments one could piece together, clues in remarks and logical assumptions, but they didn't render a whole that was either coherent or remotely vivid. Some military involvement, obviously. Police work, here in France and possibly further afield. No wife, no children, no siblings or parents ever referred to. Multilingual. First language: pick one from three. Accent unplaceable. Provenance unknowable. A cipher, and yet known in certain influential circles. Private, and yet highly connected. Cold, and yet conscientiously loyal. Solitary, and yet surrounding himself with cohorts, generally much younger, who were energetic and often immature.

Bett collected them, brought to his attention by shadowy contacts and murkily submerged channels of information. Rescued them, no question, from each of their secret pasts, but he kept hold of those secrets too, an unspoken but ever-looming means of leverage. His employees were thus a remarkable raggle-taggle of waifs and strays, who found themselves grateful but beholden, and not a little scared. Lex didn't know anyone else's story for certain, but guessed they would share a number of elements, prominent among them a precipitous epiphany regarding the price a single rash act could exact from what one only now realised had been a bright future.

In her case, she put it down to adolescent impetuousness and misdirected anger. Mistakes we all made on the road to adulthood, lessons we could only learn first hand. Nineteen was a difficult age. Anything beyond twelve, in fact, was a difficult age, but turning nineteen stuck in the mind as being especially tough – something to do with her parents' marriage breaking up around that particular birthday, which happened to be September 12th 2001. Adolescent impetuousness. Alienation. Despair. Misdirected anger. A common enough story. You let your feelings get the better of you and you do something that makes sense at the time, but which will have far more damaging consequences than you have the vision or clarity to foresee from your emotional and immature perspective. Such as getting shit-faced and totalling your dad's car, deliberately screwing up your exams, selling off your mom's heirloom jewellery, or causing an overseas emergency and mid-level international diplomatic crisis from inside your Toronto bedroom.

Yeah. Oops, huh?

Seemed like a compelling idea at the time. Her own private act of post 9-11 anger, prompted largely by the war in Afghanistan and not at all by her parents' marriage disintegrating. Afghanistan. That's where they were bombing. What the hell was there to bomb in Afghanistan? Wouldn't they have to send some army engineers over there to build some shit first, kinda to make the bombing runs worthwhile? Nineteen of the hijackers were Saudis. Bin Laden was a Saudi. The money was Saudi, the ideological pressure was Saudi. So let's bomb Afghanistan. Fuck that.

She shut down a power station near Jedda and halted production in two major oilfields for close to eight hours. It was embarrassingly easy. In fact, if it had been even slightly harder, maybe she'd have stopped to think a little more about just what

7

the hell she was doing. It didn't even take very long, nor was it a particularly cute or elegant hack. She just enslaved a couple of home PCs somewhere in Kuwait and used them as bots to orchestrate a crude, worm-led, denial-of-service email attack. This predictably led the on-site techs to shut down and reboot all but the core operating systems required to keep the station online, conveniently isolating and identifying the masked ports she needed access to in order to *really* screw things up.

There was predictable panic at the business end over motive, perpetrators and what the attack might be a precursor to. Al Qaeda? Iraq? Israel? The US? Calls were made, denials issued, intelligence sources tapped. Fighter jets, she later learned, were put on standby in at least two countries. But while all this was happening, some über-geek in Finland, hastily retained by an oil company, was following a clumsily discarded trail of evidence all the way back to that notorious global aggressor, Canada.

What do you mean you never heard about it on the news?

Embarrassment stings far less if there are fewer observers, and international embarrassment is no different. Neither Canada nor Saudi were ever going to look good over this one, and they knew it would be mutually convenient to write off their losses and cover it up. Countries did it all the time, though it was easier when it was unilateral. A couple of months back, for instance, the US had misplaced a Harrier jump jet, and decided that avoiding scrutiny of the circumstances was worth more than however many million the hardware would cost to replace. Lessons were no doubt learned, private apologies and assurances granted, but, officially, nothing happened, a position that ironically might have been harder to maintain had they actually apprehended the perpetrator.

Nobody heard about it on the news, though that didn't mean nobody knew. Bett sure knew, like he knew oh so many things, and he knew early enough to tip her off that she was hours away from being arrested.

Ah, yes, *there* was a memorable little interlude. Was she ever done wishing she could experience those fun few moments again, as she contemplated what some petulant keystrokes had wrought for herself in the big, wide world. He informed her by email, attaching copies of confidential correspondence, transcripts of briefings, damage reports, estimates of financial implications, projected costs of security upgrading and increased insurance premiums. A lot of very powerful, very important and very serious people would be looking for retribution over this, and that was just at the Canadian end. It looked like the last screaming tantrum of her teen years was going to hamstring her adulthood. She could see college disappearing from the horizon and prison looming up in its place. She could see a weary and crushed version of herself released in five to seven, subject to restraining orders forbidding her access to computers, the one thing in her life that she knew how to make sense of. She could see a long career in waitressing, serving coffee to the people who actually mattered, before slouching home to a shitty apartment filled with laundry and regrets.

Bett had offered a way out. Taking it was only marginally less scary than what she was already staring down the barrel of, involving, as it did, disappearing from her old life with just the clothes on her back (and doing so within an hour of receiving the email), but as far as decisions went, it was a no-brainer. Not quite the career trajectory she'd once envisaged, but things had worked out a lot more colourfully than the future had looked from her old bedroom. She had a great apartment in a beautiful village in the south of France. She had a good job with an excellent salary, plus health and dental. The only niggling flaw was there was no fixed term of contract and nothing in the small print regarding how you went about leaving. Oh, and it occasionally involved killing people.

To Lex's relief, Som at last stood up straight, the flight case gently righting itself as he relieved it of his weight. He jumped up and down on the spot a couple of times and wrapped his arms around himself.

'I hope this place we're hitting has central heating,' he said. 'Wouldn't have to worry if it was a hollowed-out volcano. The top-of-the-range ones have a pool of boiling lava for the evil genius to dispose of dissenters and broil burgers at masterplan-launching parties.'

'This isn't cold,' Lex told him. 'Try winter in Ontario some time. You should have more layers on too.'

'I didn't expect to be standing out here more than a couple of minutes. Plus, we'll have to change when we get there. Bett would have mentioned clothing at the briefing if it was an issue, wouldn't he?'

'I don't know,' Lex replied. 'Maybe he did. I wasn't listening. I thought it was your turn to pay attention.'

'No, I traded with Armand. I have to pay attention next time. Armand?'

'I'm sorry, I fell asleep,' Armand said with a shrug. 'I'm sure he didn't say anything important.'

'Where is Bett anyway?' Lex asked.

'Probably taking a bath,' Armand told her. 'You leave that man unoccupied for any length of time and psshh! He's in the tub.'

'Hey, he's the boss,' she reasoned. 'Guy owns a mansion with half-a-dozen bathrooms. Maybe he figures he's gotta get his use out of all of them or he's wasted his money.'

'Whatever makes him happy,' Som said, stamping his feet on the flagstones.

'He's Bett,' Lex reminded him. 'Nothing makes him happy.'

'Okay, whatever makes him marginally less belligerent.'

'He's got this forecourt bugged, you both know that?' Armand warned, casting his eyes melodramatically towards a nearby fir.

'Seriously, is he around?' Lex asked again. 'Because it doesn't look like anybody's home. Or are we meeting him there?'

'That's a negative,' Som said. 'Nuno's meeting us there. I'm pretty sure I heard Rebekah say we were gonna pick up Bett in Aix.'

'In Aix?' Lex asked, a little dismayed. 'This place is in the Alps. If we're picking up Bett en route, we'll be lucky to get there by lunchtime tomorrow. Are we planning to hit it in daylight, is that the deal? What would be the point of that? Who the hell hits a place like Marledoq in the middle of the afternoon?'

'Maybe that *is* the point,' Armand suggested, smiling. 'Why pay anyone to guard it during office hours if the thieves and marauders only work the late shift?'

'You've been around Bett too long. You're starting to sound like him with that disingenuous bullshit.'

Som rasped his lips and shuddered.

'Day or night, we're not going to get there at all if the wheels don't show up. Where is she?'

'Why don't you wait inside if you're cold?' Lex suggested, prompting him to glance back bitterly at the mansion's sturdily locked storm doors.

'Yeah, very funny. But I'm gonna go sit in my car if she doesn't show soon. What's the time?'

'Seven minutes past five,' Lex told him.

'She's cutting it fine,' Som said. 'You know what Bett's like about punctuality. "Late is what we call the dead",' he quoted.

'She's not late yet,' Lex observed. 'She was only going to Nice, to pick up our ride, she said.'

'She said that much?' muttered Som. 'Favouritism.'

'Our ride?' asked Armand. 'What's wrong with the old charabanc?'

'Maybe it wouldn't stand up to her hot driving skillz,' Som suggested, emphasising the z for Lex's benefit.

'I'm not so convinced about that,' Armand said. 'Have you seen her in that new Beetle?'

'Yeah,' Lex agreed. 'I saw her driving out of here yesterday and it was rocking like it was being boffed by an invisible Herbie.'

'A bit rusty with the manual transmission,' Armand mused. 'Not unusual for a visitor recently arrived from the United States,' he added archly, alluding to the typically shady provenance of Bett's latest appointment.

'Yeah, well, whatever her story, Bett wouldn't be calling her "Transport Manager" for nothing,' Som insisted. 'Hey, what time's it now?' he then asked.

'It's . . .' Lex started, but stopped herself as it occurred to her that Som could not possibly have come out on an op minus a timepiece. 'Why don't you look at your own watch?'

'I don't want to roll up my sleeve. Too cold.'

'You're a pussy, Som,' she told him. 'A shivering, pitiful Thai pussy.'

'Thai pussy *beaucoup* good,' he responded in a hammy accent. 'Love you long time.'

'It's nine minutes past,' she told him, mainly to stop the routine going any further.

'Shit. Doesn't augur well for Rebekah's first op,' he stated.

'She's not late yet,' Lex reiterated. 'Not for fifty seconds, least-ways.'

'Well, I don't see any headlights.'

'Maybe her killer skillz let her drive in the dark,' Lex told him, emphasising the z herself this time.

'Shhh,' said Armand. 'Listen. Do you hear that?'

'What?' asked Som.

Nobody said anything for a few moments, allowing them to hear a low bassy sound, distant but getting incrementally louder by the second.

'You gotta be kidding me,' Lex declared. She stepped further out into the forecourt and looked around, but saw only black night beyond the avenue of trees. Still the noise grew nearer.

'No way,' said Som.

'Thirty seconds,' Armand remarked, standing away from the flight cases and looking towards the house, from which direction the sound was approaching.

Less than ten seconds later, the black shape of a helicopter swooped upwards into sight above the building and circled the property once by way of signalling intention to land on the gravel. The three of them stepped back towards the house, Lex taking a moment to rest Som's flight case down flat before making her retreat.

She looked at her watch again. The chopper touched down at nine minutes and fifty-four seconds past five.

'She's six seconds early,' Lex reported to Som above the storm of the rotorblades. 'Oh ye of little faith.'

'Transport Manager,' Som called back. 'Very funny. I guess she meant Nice as in Nice Côte d'Azure airport, for a charter. Wonder who she hired to fly the thing. Somebody who can keep his mouth shut, I hope.'

The front cabin door opened and out stepped Rebekah in a black one-piece jumpsuit, her blonde hair fluttering untidily in the wind where it spilled from beneath her helmet. She slid open the door to the passenger cabin and strode towards the flight cases. Given their cue, Lex, Som and Armand came forward again and joined her in loading their equipment. Directly underneath the blades, the noise was too intense to allow any verbal communication, so an exchange of gestures conveyed that everything was in place and they were ready to board. Som eagerly climbed in first, followed by Lex, deferred to by the bowing Armand. Rebekah then slammed the cabin door closed and returned to her seat at the controls. It was far quieter inside, but the noise level increased again as the blades accelerated in preparation for take-off. A voice cut across the growing whine, carried clearly over embedded speakers along both sides of the cabin.

'Good evening everybody and welcome aboard this Eurocopter Dauphin AS365N2 travelling to Marledoq via Aix en Provence. We will be leaving very shortly, so please fasten your seat belts and place all personal items, including hand-guns, tasers and plastic explosives, securely in the hatches provided. We ask also at this time that you stow all mobile phones and personal tracking devices, and that passengers with laptops refrain from hacking any mainframe computer systems as this can interfere with our navigational instruments. We would like to take this opportunity to say thank you for flying Air Bett, and that we appreciate you have no choice.'

The stop in Aix was brief, little more than a touchdown. The chopper landed in a car park on the perimeter of a light industrial estate outside the city. A solitary figure stood motionless on the black-top beneath the yellow sodium of street lights, flanked either side by aluminium cases. Frost had enveloped all but one of the four cars lined up closest to the abutting low-rise building, windscreens and bodywork glinting as the chopper's lights passed over them.

Bett began walking forward as soon as the wheels met the earth, leaving the cases where they stood. Without prompt, Armand opened the door and climbed out, moving with brisk but unhurried steps to retrieve Bett's luggage. Bett climbed aboard, ignoring Som's proffered hand-up, and took a rear-facing seat directly behind the slim partition separating the passenger cabin from the cockpit. He glanced emotionlessly at his watch: they were dead on time. As ever, this didn't appear to be any source of particular satisfaction, though Lex had nothing to compare it to. Thus far in her experience, Bett's vaunted displeasure at ever being behind schedule remained at quantum level.

Armand handed up Bett's cases to the waiting Som, who stowed them, as Armand climbed back aboard and closed the cabin door. Then Bett gave the most cursory hand signal through the perspex window panel to the attentively waiting Rebekah, and they were off again.

They were on the ground less than ninety seconds.

Nobody spoke, in conspicuous contrast to the relentless back-and-forth bullshit between Som and Armand on the flight to Aix. It was an observed silence, and slightly tense for it. It was always like this when Bett took his place, like a schoolroom hushed by the intimidating presence of a strict and respected teacher. Nobody would speak until he did first. Once Bett set the tone, other conversation could and would resume, if appropriate. Until he did speak, however, it was impossible to know what that tone would be. He sat silently as they ascended, impenetrable seriousness in his eyes as he stared out into the night.

There had been no greetings, nor would there be any checks or queries as to their preparations. Bett had no need to ask, for instance, whether you had remembered to bring a particular item, or to reiterate any information. Armand couldn't have been less serious when he said he'd fallen asleep during the briefing.

Bett stirred from his inscrutable absorption once they had reattained cruising altitude. He glanced around the cabin at their faces, all three meeting his eye expectantly.

'Alexis, boot up, please,' he ordered, unsnapping his seat belt. He projected his delivery just enough to carry over the ambient noise, which was louder than on a passenger aircraft. Bett didn't like to raise his voice; didn't like ever to consider it necessary. It was said that if you wanted people to listen, you should speak softly. Bett simply assumed people were listening, and didn't expect to have to shout to get their attention.

Lex recalled Rebekah's words over the intercom, echoing the standard in-flight passenger protocols about laptops. On commercial airline flights, that only applied during take-off and landing. She didn't know about helicopters, or therefore whether Rebekah's warning was serious despite its humour, but she sure as hell wasn't going to refer it to Bett. Any sentence that began

'But sir,' was a bad start with the boss. He hated 'whining' as he called it, presumably because it infringed upon his exclusive rights to all grumpiness and complaining within the company.

She unbuckled her restraint and reached beneath the seat for her kit. Meantime, Bett knelt down and slid out one of his cases from the cargo rack, flipping it slightly ajar. She didn't see precisely what he had removed – a flat plastic sleeve, possibly a CD – but did catch a glimpse of a row of identical gun butts nestling cosily in protective plastic foam. A glance at her co-passengers confirmed they were also sneaking a peak. Bett's mission briefings were detailed, but seldom comprehensive. There were almost always surprises.

The first one, this trip, was for her.

'Get into the network at Marledoq,' he said.

'Sure thing.'

Mid-air hacks were not part of the plan; in fact, she hadn't been instructed to do anything more than a covert recce of the Marledoq system prior to the mission, so there was definitely no need to be doing this at fifteen thousand feet. She guessed it must have been a CD-ROM he'd taken from the case, and the contents of it were possibly something that had only latterly come into his possession. Far more likely, however, was that he simply wanted to see her dance. He liked to keep everybody on the edge of their game, always ready to improvise and adapt at zero notice. There was no record in the company of anyone ever complaining about being bored.

'Rough skies ahead,' Lex announced to no one in particular as she tapped slowly at the keyboard and patiently scanned the screen.

'What makes you say that?' Bett asked. 'You scanning Met office websites or are you just . . . channelling?' He paused before the last word to give it emphasis, then pronounced it with a clipped crispness. Bett's scorn was seldom far from breaking the surface, but nor was it ever less than elegant.

'Latency,' she explained. 'Connection's a bit sluggish. Electrical storms tend to do that to these satellite modems.'

'Oh, neato,' ventured Som, gloomily. 'I always wanted to be in a helicopter during a lightning storm.'

'Are you in yet?' Bett enquired.

'General network access,' she replied, 'but if you want me to start tampering with surveillance and security systems, it's gonna take—'

'No, no,' he interrupted. 'I just want you to shut down one of the PCs in the Security HQ. Can you do that?'

'Shutting down a PC isn't going to . . .' Lex stopped herself. 'Yes, sir,' she corrected.

'Good. I want you to script something that monitors when it gets rebooted. Run a clock on it from the moment you close it down. I want a response time.'

'You got it.'

Lex did as instructed, leaving the response-time clock running in a minimised panel towards the left edge of her screen. It would open fully and play an alarm chime when someone at the Marledoq end turned the machine back on. She looked up expectantly for Bett's next instruction, but that appeared to be all for now. He was staring out of the window again, though there was nothing to look at but a few wispy snowflakes dancing across the beams of the helicopter's lights.

The chime sounded and the clock stopped after four minutes and eighteen seconds.

'Log that,' Bett said. 'And shut the same PC down again at exactly twenty hundred hours.'

'Yes, sir.'

The snow grew gradually heavier as the flight continued. There was no lightning, but the wind was picking up and the chopper lurched and dipped with increasing frequency. Lex felt a little nauseous, but wasn't sure whether it was as much to do with the motion as worry. This was only her second time in a helicopter. The first had been eight years ago, a tourist jaunt over Niagara Falls on a sunny July morning, in maximum visibility and nary a breath of wind. Right now it was December, pitch black, there was a snowstorm brewing and they were flying towards the Alps.

'Looks like Lex was right about the weather,' Armand said, looking a little concerned.

'If we don't do this tonight, it'll be at least two weeks before we can reschedule,' Bett stated.

'Only if you're stuck on exposing—'

16

'I'm stuck on all aspects of my plan, yes,' Bett assured him, with the calm of a man who seldom had to stress his point. 'But if the weather continues to deteriorate, it won't be my intentions that prevail. That will be Rebekah's prerogative. In fact, I'll just have a word.'

Bett got up and opened the door to the cockpit, reaching with his other hand into the pocket where he'd secreted whatever he removed from his case. Through the window panel, Lex saw him talk to Rebekah, then hand her what indeed turned out to be a silver disc. He returned to the passenger cabin and took his seat once again, his visage familiarly betraying nothing.

He waited for the next sudden, stomach-knotting surge before responding to Lex's eager gaze.

'Rebekah seems unconcerned,' he said flatly. 'The snow is getting pretty heavy, but she's not navigating by sight anyway.'

'What about the turbulence?' Lex asked.

'Unconcerned,' he repeated. 'I believe her exact words were: "This isn't turbulence." She then added something I didn't precisely catch, but the gist of it was that you'd know what turbulence was once we're above the mountains. Which should be any time now, I estimate,' he concluded, fastening his seat belt with precise delicacy.

Everyone else followed suit, knowing a cue from this bastard when they saw one.

Mere moments passed before the chopper plummeted like a broken elevator, Lez feeling as though her guts had remained at the previous altitude. The descent stopped just as suddenly, the plunge bottoming out, rising and banking into a swoop that seemed to increase their velocity by about fifty per cent.

Those in the passenger cabin weren't the only ones to get a cue. Bett reached his hand behind his head and rapped on the window before gracefully flicking his wrist in a gesture that looked like the proverbial royal wave until Lex realised his fingers were gripping an imaginary baton.

Music. Motherfucker. And a thousand bucks said *Ride of the Valkyries*.

The music began playing over the cabin speakers a few seconds later. It was *Song 2* by Blur. Lex was set to (privately) deride it as old man Bett's idea of cool, but quickly recognised his cold humour at work instead. It was probably a mistake to think he *didn't* know how overused it had been as a soundtrack to such high-adrenaline moments. The man resonated disdain like other people gave off body heat.

Som, being less sensitive to such subtleties, simply went for it, and joined in the 'woohoo's as the chopper dipped and soared through the snow-flecked blackness.

Bett sat expressionless throughout. Lex looked for a hint of a smile or twinkle in his eye to betray just how much the bastard must be enjoying this, but there was nothing. The song played out without him even tapping his feet to the rhythm.

Then came *Ride of the Valkyries.*

The snow lightened off over the final twenty minutes of the flight, down to mere wisps by the time they landed, though it was close to a foot deep on the ground. This proved of no concern to Rebekah, who expertly set down the helicopter on a valley floor, some woodland to the north the only feature of landscape close enough to be visible by what little moonlight broke between the clouds. Lex saw no lights to indicate settlement, though as Nuno was waiting for them behind the wheel of a high-sided container truck, there at least had to be a road in the vicinity. At least, though quite possibly at most.

'Thank you, Rebekah,' Bett said, as the rotors slowed and their pilot joined them on the white surface which was so permafrozen as to compact only a couple of inches under the weight of their feet. Lex had estimated the depth at about a foot, and the chopper's wheels had sunk close to that much, but it could easily be more. Bett sounded, as ever, like his gratitude, while not begrudged, was measured out with microscopic precision to be exactly what was due and appropriate, no less and no more. The sentiment gave off as much warmth as a dying penguin's last breath, but somehow inexplicably avoided sounding insincere or even entirely graceless.

'*De nada*, sir,' she replied.

'Oh, shit, man, it's freezing,' Som complained, while they got busy unloading their flight cases.

'Appropriate clothing will be supplied,' Bett said, signalling to Nuno to bring the truck closer now that the chopper's engines had powered down.

'You are a god,' Som told him, shivering. 'People don't say that enough.'

'No,' Bett reflected, 'they don't.'

Rebekah pulled off her helmet and placed it on her seat inside the cockpit, replacing it with an elasticated fleece cap. Lex approached, flight case in hand as she shut the door.

'Thanks for the ride,' Lex offered with a smile.

'Hope it wasn't too rough. Helicopters aren't really my forte.'

'You gotta be kidding. Not your forte? That was some serious flying.'

'It's all in the technology these days. There's a joke among the civil flyers that future crews will comprise a single pilot and a dog. The pilot's job will be to watch all the computers, and the dog's will be to bite the pilot if he attempts to touch anything.'

Civil flyers, Lex thought. As in what Rebekah was not.

'That's cute,' she said. 'But way too modest. You were hot-dogging up there, and on Bett's orders too, I'm guessing.'

'No comment,' she replied, failing to conceal a smile.

'That's a ten-four if ever I heard one. Where'd you learn to fly like that?'

'Definitely no comment.'

Nuno cautiously brought the truck towards the chopper, the vehicle bobbing and swaying as its tyres traversed uneven terrain beneath the snow. Lex suppressed a smile at the sight of the tall Catalan in this unfamiliar environment, his beloved dark locks all tucked out of sight beneath a tight black ski-hat. She couldn't wait to see how that striding gait of his coped with the underfoot conditions either.

He veered the truck right as he drew close, allowing him to turn in a wide, careful arc, presenting the rear of the container towards the new arrivals. Bett hopped on to the tailgate and flipped a lever, causing the double doors to open and releasing a heavy steel ramp that slid down to meet the snow. Lex felt it bite into the ground with a shudder a split-second after the overeager (and possibly borderline hypothermic) Som skipped backwards out of its way. Nuno

19

trudged cautiously and awkwardly around to the rear and climbed inside behind the boss.

Bett emerged shortly with an armful of clothing, which he tossed to Som. From the flail of sleeves and legs, Lex guessed two fine fleece tops and two pairs of trousers.

'Get these on. That goes for everybody: two layers each. There's a box inside with various sizes. And if you're wearing anything made of cotton, lose it before you put these on.'

Som wasn't about to ask Bett why – you just didn't do that – but his face betrayed a reluctance to shed any of the clothes he already had without a damn good reason.

'Cotton equals death,' Lex told him. 'Cotton holds moisture against the skin and prevents you warming yourself. Trust me, I'm Canadian.'

'Are we talking, like, even my Y-fronts here?'

Lex herself had opted for all-synthetic undergarments, but wasn't sure just how much outdoor work was going to figure on the agenda. She guessed not enough for it to matter if Som's nads got a little chilly. The temptation to lay it on thick was enormous, leavened slightly by the prospect of seeing his scrawny little goose-pimpled butt in the flesh. She settled for: 'That's entirely up to you.'

'Jeez. Just how long are we going to be out in the snow? How far is this place?'

'It's about five miles,' Nuno told him.

'Just get the fleeces on, Somboon,' Bett instructed. 'And if you're still cold, I've got another layer for you here.'

Bett kicked a fibreglass trunk forward across the floor of the truck and flipped open its lid. Kevlar vests. For all the protection they offered, they were nonetheless seldom a reassuring sight.

'Body armour?' Som asked. 'I thought this place was all about non-lethal enforcement technology.'

'If it was a bakery, would you expect the guards to be armed only with custard pies?' Bett asked, with what passed in his case for good humour. 'The parent company also develops laser-guided missiles, so you'll be pleased to know the security personnel are issued with standard Beretta nine-millimetre handguns and none of Industries Phobos' hallmarked product.'

'Don't suppose there's any Kevlar balaclavas in there?' Lex ventured. 'These vests aren't so effective if you get shot in the face.'

'I'll be extremely surprised if any of these people manage to get a single shot off against us,' Bett stated with absolute certainty.

'If it's all the same to you, sir, would you mind if I borrowed Rebekah's crash helmet?' Lex said, only half joking.

'You can't,' Nuno told her. 'It would get in the way of your night-sight.'

Night-sights. Of course. One of the reasons – though far from the main one – why Bett was so confident of not getting shot at.

'I eat lots of carrots,' she protested. 'I'd prefer the helmet.'

Nuno threw her a pair of fleece trousers and a top, both black. 'Get dressed, Lex,' he said.

Once everyone was suited and bullet-proofed, Bett reached for one of the cases he'd brought from Aix. He handed everyone a pistol and two mags. They each slapped one clip into the breech and the spare to their utility harness. It didn't look like a lot of ammo.

'Will this be enough?' Rebekah asked.

'Not if you miss,' Bett replied. 'And on that note, let me just stress that I don't want any of you staying your trigger hand with thoughts of the poor guard's wife and kids tragically impoverished at Christmas. We've got a job to do and so have they. The one who does it best doesn't need to worry about his or her conscience.'

Lex checked the action on her weapon. She didn't need this particular pep talk. These guys were packing Beretta nine-mills: that was all the encouragement her trigger hand needed.

Som distributed earpieces and Pin-Mics that attached snugly and nearly invisibly to the inside of their fleece collars. You pressed down on them to transmit, which was a big improvement on those goddamn sub-vocal things that broadcast every last unwitting word you happened to utter. Once they were fitted, Nuno began handing out night-sights. Gadget-geek Som almost bit off Nuno's hand to get his first.

'These the new LS-24s?' he asked excitedly.

'*Si.*'

'I don't see what's to get excited about,' Lex said. 'Everything looks like green shadows and white blobs through these things anyway.'

'These have a built-in laser range-finder,' Som told her, his enthusiasm undiminished by her failure to share it.

'What's a range-finder?' she asked.

'It tells you the distance to the object you're looking at,' Som explained. 'Lets you know whether the white blob you can see is a tree half a mile away or a boulder ten feet away.'

'Long as the white blob's not a guy holding a gun, what does it matter?'

'It'll matter when you're approaching the boulder on a snow-bike at a hundred kilometres per hour,' Nuno stated.

'We've got snowbikes?' asked Som, who really was going to regret the moisture retention properties of his cotton underwear if his excitement level got any higher.

'MX Z-REVs. What do you think I needed such a big truck for?'

'*Too* cool.'

The new toys were dragged from within the lorry on pallets and slid carefully down the ramp on to the snow. They looked state-of-the-art and expensive, the way Bett liked it. Basic instruction was given, accompanied by some vocal surprise that the resident Canadian and 'expert in all things wintry' should never have ridden a skidoo before. She admitted that she hadn't skied before either, politely explaining that no amount of snow could make eastern Ontario a downhill winter sports paradise due to the place being as flat as a pool table. To this she added that if you gave her a pair of skates and a hockey stick, she'd kick *all* their asses, but by that point Bett was calling them to order with the outfit's most peremptory command.

'A-fag, children. A-fag.'

It was time to get serious.

They rode in darkness. The ZX Rev-Ups, or whatever Nuno had called them, were fitted with powerful headlights, but such luminosity was 'contra-indicated', as Bett put it with understated technicality, when attempting to approach undetected. The noise, he claimed, would be less of a concern as they'd be pulling up a quarter of a mile short, and in darkness no one would be able to determine whether the sound wasn't motorbikes on the nearby road through the valley. 'That's if anyone's listening,' he added.

It was pretty easy, even if viewing by infrared made the sense of velocity seem all the greater. Like their aquatic equivalent, it was hard to imagine a lot of people owning one of these for everyday use. Lex guessed the majority of sales of such machines were for hiring out to tourists, who didn't want to spend a day and a half learning how the thing worked. They just wanted to push a button, twist a handlegrip and go. She got a real fright the first time the sled fully left the ground (range-finder or no, her night-goggles failed to distinguish whether the white blobs of her colleagues in front were gliding on snow or air), but after a couple more such bumps it became a real rush. Her only concern was for her laptop, stowed in a compartment beneath her seat, but with the others setting an unrelenting pace there was no option to ease off. She was already in the rear of the group, trailing even Armand who was dragging a cargo sled behind him. They had left a lot of kit back at the truck, Bett changing arrangements at the last minute as usual, so Lex wasn't sure what the cargo sled was actually transporting, but it was having far less of a braking effect than her caution.

Before folding her laptop closed, she had noted and reported that there was still no response from the PC she'd shut down back at eight o'clock. Bett had nodded dismissively in response, like he always did when you were telling him something he already knew.

They pulled up, as specified, about a quarter of a mile short of the compound, dimly lit against the foot of the mountain by the glow from a few overhead lamps. There were maybe a dozen cars lined up in a tight grid, close to where a counterbalanced barrier and a wooden hut blocked access from the snow-dusted road. The buildings were low-rise and cheap-looking: windowless warehouses, a prefab site office with darkened wire-mesh windows, chemical toilets, an electrical sub-station. Nothing to see here, they were saying to any passers-by. The compound was delineated by a wire-mesh fence, about two metres high. Lex could see a couple of white blobs on top of the wire that she plausibly estimated to be sparrow-sized, meaning it wasn't electrified. Nothing else in her sights appeared to be giving off much heat, apart from the sub-station.

They parked their bikes at the foot of a small undulation, barely a bump on the landscape, but enough to render the vehicles invisible from any range beyond ten yards the other side of it. A heat signature belatedly ambled into view: a guard on patrol, the sight of which prompted Lex to crouch until she noticed that she was the only one doing it.

'Have a look without your night-sight,' Armand reassured her. She did. The compound became little more than glow and shadow. Behind her there was blackness. 'That's what he sees.'

'Gather your goods and chattels,' Bett instructed, and they each unloaded what was beneath their saddles. Armand, she noticed, unloaded nothing from the cargo sled. Lex's batbelt had a specially designed velcro-fastening cradle for her laptop, holding it out of the way, across her back. This meant she was less encumbered by it when moving, but it required detaching the utility harness altogether when strapping the PC in or taking it out, unless someone else was there to help. She was asking for just such assistance when Bett told her to stick the machine back in her skidoo.

'We won't be requiring any remote access from here on in. If necessary, you can grab a terminal directly. You do have your tools on removable storage.'

This last was most definitely a statement, not a question. Indeed, she did have the code she needed on a USB stick, but it wasn't what was on her laptop that she was worried about missing. It was the two hundred gigs of free space on the hard drive. Removable storage was the issue, and whether she'd have room to store what she intended to remove.

Bett set the pace. They advanced slowly, strung out in a wide line, stopping two hundred metres from the fence, or 198.678m according to the range-finder. All but Som got down and lay prostrate, leaning up on elbows to look ahead. Gadget Geek was about to deploy. He placed an aluminium tube down in front of him on the snow, then drew a modified grenade launcher from a quiver across his back. Resting on one knee, he slid the top half of the tube away from the base, inside which nestled six of his self-designed and -constructed Flying Eyeballs. He loaded four, one by one, into the breech and levelled the weapon to his shoulder. Meanwhile, his colleagues were snapping open hand-held LCD monitors, each about the size of a compact make-up mirror. The Flying Eyeballs, as he had explained (at length, in detail and on an unwearied number of occasions), were a means of creating an instant, covert CCTV system without setting foot in the subject area. They consisted of a tiny digital camera, crucially containing no moving parts, and a lens constructed from the same synthetic material as prescription contacts. Crucially, because the device had to withstand being fired several hundred metres through the air by a grenade launcher, plus the effects of rapid deceleration associated with being slammed into its target surface at the end of this flight. For analogue devices and glass lenses, this sort of treatment was largely contra-indicated, to use one of Bett's favoured terms. It wasn't highly recommended for digital ones either, to be fair, and not all of them survived the trip. However, their chances were greatly improved by the round rubber housing that gave rise to the Eyeball part of their name, and more so by being suspended in a thick, gloopy, adhesive resin inside a fragile outer shell. The shell shattered on impact, releasing the resin, which dried instantly on contact with air, theoretically securing the rubber eyeball where it landed, but in practice working better on sloped roofs than plumb walls. The camera was weighted and balanced within the Eyeball so that it would tilt and right itself by gravity up to forty degrees, the lens protected from the resin by a tube-shaped plug that could be popped off by remote once the device was in place. The only thing Som had so far been able to do nothing about was the whole thing hitting a wall or roof lens-side first, which was why he always brought at least a dozen.

He fired off three of the four he'd loaded, readjusting his weight and position as he aimed at different potential vantage points. Then he scuttled around to the side of the compound and began again. Lex checked her LCD, toggling through the views. A lucky night: only one lens-to-wall, one DOA and two nestled on rooftops beneath four inches of snow. Six shots resulting in two functioning cams, giving a pretty good triangulation on the main paths through the compound. There'd been times when Som had cracked off a full complement of those things and they'd still ended up going in blind. She deleted the useless frequencies and toggled between the two good ones. They had views of most doorways, the sub-station and the guardpost at the road barrier.

'Just one guard so far,' said Nuno's voice in her earpiece. 'We don't have an angle into the sentry box.'

'It'll be manned,' Armand ventured. 'It's freezing. If his boss wasn't in the box, don't you think that guy would be in there warming his toes?'

Lex watched the grey figure on her monitor walking slowly and shiftlessly, stamping his feet every so often, bored and cold.

'True enough, Armand,' agreed Bett. 'Assume a count of two. We'll take them separately but simultaneously. Nuno, Alexis, you take . . .'

Bett cut himself off in response to the guard suddenly stopping in his tracks, evidently having heard something. He turned on his heel and began running towards the sentry box.

'Fuck, we've been made,' Rebekah said urgently, unholstering her gun.

'At ease, my dear,' Bett chided, looking at his monitor. Lex couldn't make out what was on his LCD, but it wasn't the same thing she was looking at; there was lots of colour, mainly green, as opposed to grey shadows and snow. 'Quite the contrary, I'd wager.'

The guard disappeared into the hut, from which no alarms sounded, no lights flashed, and indeed from which he did not re-emerge.

'Nuno, Alexis,' Bett said, by way of command.

Lex drew her pistol and flicked off the safety, then back on, then back off. It was an obsessive-compulsive habit, like trying the doorhandle after locking her car, and she'd shown no sign of shaking it, no matter how many times she'd used various firearms. When you were effectively entrusting your life to a device, you had to be damn sure it was functioning.

The snow silenced their footsteps, only the lightest crunch

26

audible as their boots sank gently into the unspoiled surface. As Lex neared the hut, she discovered both that the guards wouldn't have heard a thing anyway, and why Bett was unworried by the sentry's dash to cover. She heard the sound of a crowd and the excited voice of a commentator. They were watching soccer on TV, and Bett had known not only that much, but presumably also which game; that's what he was tuned in to on his LCD. A goal had been scored, and one guard had relayed this to the other – which was why he came running.

They took position side by side, a few feet from the doorway, guns each held in two hands. The commentator's tones got near-hysterical, accompanied by angry and then happy/excited shouts from the two marks. Lex looked to Nuno for the green light, but he took a hand off his weapon and clenched his fist to signal hold. 'Penalty,' he whispered.

There was quiet from the crowd, a collective drawing in of breath. She and Nuno joined it.

'*S'il vous plaît, mon Dieu,*' one guard's voice implored.

'*Ne manquez pas, ne manquez pas,*' pleaded the other.

Nuno smiled and gave the signal.

Ne manquez pas. Don't miss.

They didn't.

Lex and Nuno lay the bodies next to each other on the floor of the hut and patted them down. She found what she was after in a hip pocket, Nuno in a zippered breast-pouch. Swipecards, each with a photo ID thumbnail in the bottom left-hand corner. Low-level security clearance, no doubt, but it would be enough for now.

She checked her LCD, toggling between the two views. No activity from any doorways, no further sign of life.

'Area secure,' she announced. 'Clear to proceed.'

Nuno sprung the mags from the guards' handguns, sliding them into slots on his harness.

'This pair won't be needing them any longer,' he said.

The rest of the team caught up soon after, advancing at a brisk walking pace.

'Which building's the way in?' Rebekah asked.

'We don't know,' Lex told her. 'We're only working from information in the public domain.'

'Yeah, Lex, but I thought when the member of the public happens to be you, the domain gets pretty wide.'

'Ordinarily, sure, but on this job . . .'

'Not in the parameters,' Rebekah finished, nodding.

'There are, I would estimate, at least two, and possibly three, entrances,' Bett said. 'Two cards, two teams. Knock, knock.'

Rebekah went with Lex, Armand with Nuno. They bypassed the prefab site-office and the chemical toilet as these had only conventional locks, making instead for the low-rise warehouses. Each pair approached, guns drawn, keeping an eye on their counterparts to ensure that they acted simultaneously. Lex swiped the card and threw the door open, Rebekah moving quickly inside and levelling her weapon at shoulder height.

The interior was in darkness. Lex found a light switch and flicked it on, revealing a room full of stationery supplies, stocked neatly in six columns of shelves. They were staggered to allow a narrow channel between each, apart from between the fifth and sixth, where there was a wider avenue. She walked along and looked down it. At the end, a few yards short of where the rear wall ran across the rest of the building, there stood two featureless aluminium doors, a swipe slot to their left. Another storey's worth of steel ascended to the ceiling, presumably housing the pulley.

'One entrance located,' she reported. 'And we're cool for Post-its too. How about you guys?'

'*Nada*,' Nuno replied. 'Canteen supplies, I think. Tinned soup. Hey, these guys really like lentil and bacon. Moving out.'

'Hold your position, Nuno,' Bett interrupted. 'Any confectionery?'

There was a pause.

'Yeah, that's a positive on the confectionery.'

'Snickers?'

'Okay, let's see . . . Mars, Twix . . . Snickers. Affirmative.'

'Two please, there's a good chap.'

'Ah, sir, I think that would count as stealing.'

'There's a good chap,' Bett repeated pointedly.

'Yes, sir.'

Som and Bett arrived at the stationery warehouse as Nuno and Armand continued their search. Bett was chewing on one of the appropriated chocolate bars, his face expressionless despite a glow of juvenile satisfaction. If it was giving him pleasure, he was trying to keep that to himself, just like the chocolate.

Lex swiped the card to part the lift doors, holding them open while Som got to work. He had the control panel out in seconds and began expertly stripping wires, splitting and splicing with contacts from one of his gizmos, which he secured to the inside of the panel before replacing it.

'You're cool now,' he told Lex. She stepped away from the doors, which remained open. Som then attached another Eyeball – of the non-flying variety – to the rear interior of the car, this time a remote-controlled, zoom-lens, multi-pivoting device.

'Let's take a peek,' he said, pressing a button on the grotesquely modified gamepad he used as a multi-functioning remote control. The lift doors closed and a deep whine emitted from the housing above. Lex toggled to the newly available channel on her LCD. It showed two closed doors, and it showed them for a hell of a long time.

'Some depth,' Rebekah observed. 'What was this place, a mine?'

'Nuclear shelter,' Bett informed her. 'And before that, once upon a time, a secret Allied operations HQ.'

The whine stopped and the doors opened, revealing a reception area with a desk, a row of bucket seats along one wall, a water cooler against another and two fire doors dead ahead. The lights were on, but there was no sign of human activity. Som twiddled a hat switch, panning right a little and zooming in towards the ceiling. There was a CCTV camera staring back.

'Is that going to be a problem?' Lex asked.

'Only if someone's watching it,' Bett answered. 'But let's assess all our options first.'

Som brought the lift back, undoing his handiwork and retrieving his gadgets with the same speedy but unhurried efficiency as he had deployed them. As he was reattaching the last of his hardware to his harness, Nuno's voice played across all their earpieces.

'Second elevator located. Last warehouse on the right-hand side, closest to the mountain.'

'Received,' Bett acknowledged. 'And what the bloody hell kept you?'

'Thorough reconnaissance, sir,' Nuno replied. 'It took us a while to find the lift, but we now know where these people keep their toilet-roll supplies, so if we really want to hurt them, or this turns into, like, a siege . . .'

'At ease, Nuno.'

Nuno had been part of the outfit longer than anyone bar Armand. Lex used to wonder how many McDonald's long-service stars you had to have amassed before you could talk back to the boss like that, but had learned in time that it was more to do with experience telling you when you could best try your luck. Bett had no favourites and no formal hierarchy beyond the very simple one by which he ruled with supreme authority.

Som repeated his surveillance operation on the other lift, intended for transporting freight going by its greater size, grubbier appearance and wider approach area. The warehouse Nuno called them to had a large loading bay at the front, served by two padlocked vertical roller doors, each around four metres wide, with the card-op entrance separate, three or four yards to the right. Inside there was a lot more space than housed the personnel lift, though there were supplies on shelves around three walls. Much of it appeared to be for general site maintenance – paint, varnish, detergent, lightbulbs, tools – plus, as reported, enough toilet paper to keep them going through a nuclear winter.

They checked their LCDs as Som sent the freight elevator grinding slowly down into the earth. It took even longer than the personnel lift, though most probably because the mechanism was simply slower.

'Must have been some deal to carve this place out,' Rebekah observed, echoing Lex's slightly discomfited awe at the subterranean scale.

'A lot of the caverns and tunnels were natural,' Bett said. 'Magma chambers, lava flows.'

Som beamed, his cheeks aglow.

'What?' Bett asked, with the weary sigh of one who knows he won't be impressed by the answer.

'You've made him very happy,' Armand offered.

Yes, Lex thought. And they weren't short of an evil genius either, though no one was going to say as much.

'Delighted to be of service,' the evil genius muttered, sounding considerably less so.

Lex's screen remained black, despite the mechanism having quit its laboured grinding a few seconds back.

'Open the lift doors, Som,' Nuno prompted.

'They are open,' Bett answered. 'There's no lights on in the freight bay. Which makes the camera issue moot, wouldn't you agree?'

'Unless they've an infrared,' Som suggested. Bett rolled his eyes to indicate how likely he considered this.

'Well, on the outside chance that someone has gone to the bother of monitoring the camera they've got overlooking reception, I think it would be polite to dress for the occasion. Armand, Somboon, retrieve the security guards' jackets from the guard-post and go in through the main lift. Keep your heads down and remember to bin the uniforms once you're past the camera. If I shoot either of you, I'd like to mean it. The rest of us will take the tradesman's entrance.'

No one spoke as the lift descended, the four of them standing with weapons drawn. Lex felt a cold, sweaty nervousness, the like of which she hadn't experienced on a job since the earliest days. No matter how many times she'd gone into situations like this, she'd never lost that feeling of being hyper-energised, like all of her senses were at a level normal life had never asked of them. Time felt both accelerated and suspended, as though standard relativity could not be resumed until events were at a close and this mode was once again set to zero. However, this gnarling, dull fear was something different, a chill terror long-since banished by experience but back tonight, ready to dog her every step. She knew why, and it was nothing to do with those Berettas.

She flipped down her night goggles as the lift doors ground open, infrared describing the room to her in subtle differences of tone and texture, all of it white on green. Shelves, crates, pallet-trolleys and a wide, windowless double door. They stepped forward slowly, Nuno finding his way first to a light switch. He flicked it, turning on strip lighting suspended from a surprisingly high ceiling above. Lex advanced to the card lock and looked to Bett.

Bett signalled to hold, pressing his other hand to his collar-mike.

'Status,' he said quietly.

There was no response. Too much rock. They'd be able to hear Som and Armand again once the pair were down inside the complex.

'Status,' Bett repeated several times, at intervals of thirty seconds.

'Status is we are all troglodytes now,' said Armand's voice at last.

'Acknowledged. We are holding position in the freight bay. Preparing to deploy. Any hostiles?'

'Only Somboon. Ah . . . okay, I've got a layout schematic from behind the reception desk. Freight bay is on the second level, which puts Security HQ upstairs from where you are now, downstairs from us. Back-up generator and power control is in the lowest level. You still want us to . . . ?'

'Proceed with assigned tasks. Remember to smile if you pass us on the stairs. Oh, and Armand, mess?'

'No, everything is very clinical-looking. Som's delighted, I can safely say.'

'No, I meant mess as in canteen, as in dining area,' Bett clarified with barely contained disquiet.

'Oh, *pardon. Oui.* Upper level.'

'Thank you,' Bett said, with all the appreciation one might expect in addressing a stone that has finally yielded 0.01 millilitres of blood.

Bett gave the signal and Lex opened the double door, more strip light immediately spilling into the freight bay from the wide corridor outside. There were doorways along either wall, as well as tributary corridors and a T-junction visible at the far end.

Bett pulled a fire-exit schematic from the wall and they all briefly examined it before moving out. Lex dallied a little, allowing Nuno and Rebekah to head off first, the pair of them charged with locating the staff dining area. She was hoping she could drop behind Bett also, in order to check on something unnoticed, but she had no such luck. Bett ushered her onwards in front of him, making it impossible now to drop back without it being conspicuous. He would be accompanying her in locking down the Security HQ, so she knew her window would be tight, meaning she had to be ready to act when – if – an opportunity presented itself.

The four of them walked briskly on soft feet, proceeding down the corridor to the end, where they turned right towards where the fire plan had indicated the main staircase to lie. Nuno went a few paces ahead of the rest, stopping short of the final stairs to extend a mirror into the corridor on a telescopic handle. He checked the view in both directions, then gave the signal to advance. They split into their pre-assigned pairings at the top, approaching each bend silently and with guns at the ready.

Lex and Bett found themselves at one end of another long corridor, more doors and passages leading off along the puce-painted walls. The decor was cleanly and uniformly slapped on to bolted gypsum panels, making it impossible to distinguish where the façade was covering mere partitions or live rock on the reverse. A grid of white tiles above indicated a suspended ceiling, housing vents, pipes and cables. It wasn't much different to a corridor in any modern hospital or school, she thought, but there was something about the way it swallowed sound, far more than any lack of a view, that emphasised the inescapable isolation of the place. Som, she was sure, wouldn't be disappointed, and like her would be regretting that they couldn't freely explore every last bend of this labyrinthine oubliette.

The thought reminded her of what else her itinerary didn't officially have a space for. They took another corner, observing cover protocol, though she could tell Bett was going through the motions for the sake of good practice. This next passageway took them past banks of glass on either side, allowing views into darkened laboratories, in which only the shapes of computer monitors were distinct. She stopped by a door and swiped the card, figuring blatant was less suspicious than furtive. It remained locked.

She had her answer prepared should Bett enquire why she

had done it: she was checking to see what level of security access was on the cards they'd lifted from the feckless gumbies top-side. Bett didn't ask. His lack of enquiry made the ensuing silence seem an intolerable vacuum, which meant she had to force herself not to guiltily volunteer her explanation.

She felt like she was scattering pointers the whole time, and that he must be seeing her guilty intentions in widescreen. That was merely fear. She had to hold her nerve. Truth was, she had no idea whether Bett was so difficult to keep a secret from; this was just the first time she'd tried.

Bett signalled to move swiftly around the next corner. They'd been able to see into the adjoining passageway through a bank of windows perpendicular to the ones they were passing, but Lex suspected Bett was getting fed up playing it by his own book.

'We could be waltzing through here naked, playing trombones,' he said, confirming as much.

'Permission to discount that image, sir.'

'Granted. Ah, here we are. At last.'

Lex skipped ahead and took position against the wall outside the Security HQ doors, one of which was wedged open. She waited for Bett to do likewise, but instead he marched past her and straight on in, miming playing a trombone as he did so.

Lex followed him into the room, a split-level office with a bank of CCTV monitors along one wall of the upper area, and a row of computers facing the same direction on the lower tier. Identical screen savers played on all but one of them, depicting a three-dimensional animation of the Deimos logo. The odd one out was blank, being the PC Lex had shut down at eight o'clock, meaning no one had been in here since. She looked at her watch. It read 21:43. The CCTV cameras all looked across empty corridors, apart from those that were looking at complete blackness in rooms where the lights remained off. Bett sat down at the control suite and brought up some different views. More corridors, more blackness, and one 'Error: Camera Offline, Lev1/secNW3/cam1'.

'Also known as the mess, I'd wager,' he remarked drily.

The strip lights overhead flickered briefly as she took a seat at one of the machines.

'Smooth,' Bett noted approvingly. He meant the near-seamless switch to auxiliary power just effected somewhere below them by Som and Armand. If the main power went down, there was an average three-second delay before the back-up systems kicked in, which would be enough to put even this sorry mob on alert that something was amiss. Their trick was to bring the auxiliary power online first and make the transfer before killing the main grid.

'Very,' Lex agreed. It hadn't even rebooted any of the PCs, which made a change. The corollary of Murphy's Law dictated that she *wasn't* midway through an elaborate script the one time a power switch *didn't* crash the computers.

Lex restarted the blank one, then glided in her chair along the edge of the long desk, nudging mice to bring the rest of the screens back to life.

'I want the duty roster for tonight, Alexis,' Bett announced, looking at his watch. 'And we're going to need it in approximately two minutes plus injury time.'

'Yes, sir,' she answered with genuine enthusiasm, though not for Bett's request. The machines all had users logged on so that if anyone checked the records it would look like they'd been working – and one of them had high-level security clearance. The roster was located in seconds. There was no need to share this with Bett quite yet, however, so she had a brief window of plausible hacking time while she ostensibly 'retrieved' his request. Instead, she went straight to the access setting and killed the maglocks on all the security doors, then jacked in her USB stick and ran a probe through the network in search of her target.

'Sir, it's Nuno,' whispered a voice in one ear. 'We have recce'd the mess. Six guards and three, I think, lab techs. One plasma screen, one Champions League match in progress, two cases Amstel beer. Nice to see them getting into the spirit with a named sponsor. Are we good to go?'

'This is Armand. We are good to go, awaiting command.'

'The order is on your command, Nuno,' Bett advised. 'But let's give them until the final whistle. Unfair not to let them find out how it ends.'

'You're all heart, sir. Too kind sometimes.'

'I know. Hang on, how many did you say? Nine?'

'I can't be sure. Using the mirror, I couldn't see all angles. But nine at least.'

Lex knew what he was thinking. It was Rebekah's first mission.

She held her breath. Opportunity might be about to knock if Bett opted to go help out.

'Could do with another gun to be on the safe side,' he said. Oh please, oh please. 'Alexis, you got that roster yet?'

Shit.

She was past the point of no return regards sneaking around behind his back, but she wasn't ready to lie to his face yet. Especially not when it was lying about a small thing that was most suspicious if you got rumbled.

'Printing it now, sir.'

He looked it over, nodding, as it wafted from the printer.

'Get upstairs to the mess. And don't stop to smell the roses. Go.'

Damn it.

She grabbed the memory stick from the USB port as she got up, daring a glance at Bett to see whether he had noted this. He wasn't watching, still toggling through security cameras. What was he looking for?

Injury time, he'd said. He was referring to the end of the soccer game the guards were watching, but it was both literal and metaphorical in this instance. 'Injury time' was the term they used when they were tight up against the clock but didn't know exactly how long they had left. No one knew precisely when the referee would blow the final whistle.

Lex charged up a staircase with greater concern for haste than stealth, then found herself barrelling down more corridors, Nuno giving her a running commentary of directions as she went.

You are in a maze of twisty little passages, all alike, she thought, wryly. Hacker-speak for lost and confused, recalling a phrase from early, text-only adventure games.

Nuno warned her she was getting close, so she traversed the last corridor silently, the sound of the soccer game and accompanying anxious shouts at the TV spilling from the nearby mess. Nuno and Rebekah were crouched on the near side, weapons ready.

Lex approached the doorway and gestured with her mirror to indicate that she was taking a look for herself. She could go sight unseen into a tiny hut with two guys in it, but nine targets in a large room meant she needed a first-hand take on the layout. The plasma screen was against the right-hand wall at ninety degrees to the corridor, the targets sitting around in two rows: one on aluminium chairs, the other behind, and more elevated on tables. Unused chairs had jackets thrown over them, holstered guns resting on other table tops next to the beer crates. It was midweek party night. On the far wall, at the end nearer the TV, was a long panel of sliding shutters. The assembly sounded increasingly anxious, calling encouragement in near-despairing tones. Time was running out, in more ways than they knew.

Lex withdrew and took her place alongside her companions. Nuno got to his feet.

'On my command,' he whispered, standing up.

Lex gestured to hold.

'Did you see those shutters?' she asked.

'We tried,' Nuno replied. 'No access.'

'Not any more,' she assured him.

'Okay, cool. Let's go.'

Thirty seconds later they were in position inside the kitchen, standing behind the canteen's serving hatch.

'Stand by, Armand,' Nuno ordered, pulling down his night goggles. Lex and Rebekah followed suit.

'Standing by,' came the response.

Three whistles sounded from the other side of the sliding shutters, accompanied by cries of deep disappointment.

Time to put them out of their misery.

'Go.'

There was no panic when the lights went out, which was helpful. There were groans and ironic cheers in response, suggesting it was a far from unprecedented occurrence, and a remark bemoaning that the power hadn't gone out earlier and 'spared us watching that bunch of clowns tonight'. Amid this hubbub, no one much noticed the sound of the shutters being opened.

They all stayed still, probably in accordance with a safety

protocol, and waited expectantly for the back-up system to restore the light. Down here, the darkness was total. It was pretty spooky to be standing so close (3.278 metres, according to the range-finder) to people, to be looking at them, levelling guns at them, yet to remain utterly invisible to them. Once you got over the ghostly feeling of disconnection, the sense of power was enormous.

Nuno nodded, and in less than three seconds, every man in the room was down. Rebekah, as it turned out, found her marks flawlessly. Theoretically it was no great shakes to hit blind, unmoving targets from close range, but when it came to the moment and those targets were live flesh, anyone might choke the first time. No one could predict it for sure, not even Bett, which was why he'd sent Lex as back-up.

Lighting was restored on Nuno's order. They angled up their night-sights and climbed over the counter into the mess.

'I want a body count,' Bett ordered redundantly in their ear-pieces.

The total verified Nuno's estimate: six guards, three other staff. He relayed the news to Bett with a concealed satisfaction his boss would have been proud of.

'There should be ten,' his boss informed them all, cutting it short. 'According to the duty roster, we're one lab-rat light. I'm checking the cameras, but no dice so far.'

'Shall I cut the power again?' Armand asked.

'No, that'll only make him scurry. We're looking for a lab-geek who's neither interested in football nor beer. He'll most likely be happily back over his Bunsen burner now that the power's been restored. Nuno, Rebekah, Alexis, take a floor each and find him. Armand, Som, back to the script.'

Nuno sighed, but Lex didn't share his disappointment. This was the chance she was hoping for: free rein to wander, nobody on her shoulder.

'I'll take the bottom level,' she volunteered, before Nuno could send her elsewhere. The brief search time she'd had upstairs before Bett dispatched her on gun duty had been sufficient to locate which lab she needed, though not enough to crack the security, otherwise she could have downloaded the files over the network.

'Okay,' he agreed. 'Rebekah, you take this level, I'll go . . .'

Nuno was interrupted by the sound of an alarm, its electronic pulsing reverberating around every corridor in the complex.

'Sounds like our lab-geek's more spooked than Bett thought,' Rebekah observed.

'Yeah,' agreed Nuno. He pinched his collar-mike. 'Maybe we should rethink the lights,' he suggested.

'That's a negative,' Bett replied. 'Armand and Som have work.'

Back to the script, Lex thought. She headed out into the corridor and down the nearest stairwell, the noise bouncing around the place in an incessant blare. Not highly conducive towards concentration, but she'd zone it out, same as she'd background the possibility of the spooked stray getting hold of a piece and taking panicky pot-shots about the place. It was now or never.

'Alexis, I need you back here ASAP,' Bett ordered.

Shit.

'I want this alarm shut down and I need the authorisation codes to stop the cops coming down here.'

Learning from the main man, and though there was no one around to see, Lex concealed both her initial angst and her subsequent delight behind a neutral expression.

'It'd be quicker if I just grabbed a machine where I am, sir,' she relayed, continuing past the floor Bett was speaking from and making for the deepest level. Now, she not only had a window to work, but a reason to be at a PC if the CCTV cameras happened to spot her doing it.

'You can get the codes from another machine just as easily?' he asked.

'That's why you pay me the medium-sized-but-entirely-reasonable bucks, sir.'

Lex sprinted towards the specified lab and sat down next to the nearest PC, waking it from its screen-saver snooze with a nudge of the mouse. She doubted she could get the auth codes anything like as easily from here as from a terminal that was already logged on at high clearance, but the fact was she didn't need to. She'd systematically – you could even say reflexively – logged all the auth codes and passwords immediately when she found them, in the same directory as the duty roster.

Lex plugged in her memory stick and called up the files. She could buy herself more plausible keyboard time if she held off relaying them to Bett, but the alarm sound was proving more brain-meltingly unbearable than she'd anticipated. Presumably in a facility such as this, the intended effect in an emergency was to make the staff stop at nothing to evacuate.

She told Bett the codes. The alarms ceased a few seconds later, and she wouldn't need to worry about his next order for a little while either as he'd be on the phone to the local fuzz telling them to stand down their response. The ringing in her ears faded into the deep, still silence that once again enveloped the complex. There was nothing to hear but air vents and PC fans. Lex took a breath, blinked her eyes clear and got to work. It took less than a minute to locate what she was after. The files were encrypted, but she didn't need to worry about that just now. She just had to get them on to the memory stick. She initiated the copy process and sighed deeply as she watched the blue line slowly grow, crudely measuring the transfer's progress as file names whizzed in alphabetical order, too fast to read, across the bottom of the window.

The huge DivX files were last, naturally.

'I need as many of the research and development files as you can get, but the videos are crucial. If you don't come back with those, don't come back at all.'

Those were his words, the non-negotiable terms of the deal.

She cursed the slowness of the USB port as it drip-fed the data, but she knew she should have copied the DivX files first, on their own, before anything else. However, as she was in injury time, she had opted to select everything and just blob the whole lot at once. Her anxiety was irrational, she knew. No one was coming down here, certainly not in the couple of minutes it would take to complete the transfer, but it was the stakes that made it excruciating.

'Come on, come on, *jeez*,' she muttered to herself.

Her ante: going behind Bett's back.

On the table: walking free of him forever.

'Bett's not the only man in the world with contacts. You do this for me and we'll see whether the Canadian government still cares so much about isolated acts of teenage exuberance.'

The transfer finally completed, the event unnecessarily

announced by a dialogue panel with typical Microsoft self-satisfaction. Lex dismissed it then knelt down and reached behind the box for her USB stick. She heard the metallic click of a gun being cocked somewhere behind her, and froze, feeling her insides turn to concrete.

'Don't fuckin' move,' said a male voice, angry determination not quite masking tremulous fear. The accent sounded close to her grandfather's, though the choice of vocabulary was not. He sounded close, only a few feet away, and yet she hadn't heard him approach because she had all interrupts locked out, so intent had she been on her business. Her first thought then, upon hearing the voice, was relief at whose it wasn't.

'Get up. Back away from the desk. Keep your hands up.'

She complied, looking along the desk to where she'd left her weapon – not far out of reach but far enough.

'Turn around. Slowly.'

She turned, keeping her hands visible but close to her head. She let one drop slowly to her collar, grimacing as though nursing a strain to disguise that her fingers were pressing the mike.

'Who are you people? Hands up where I can see them, I said.'

Lex removed her hand from her neck and faced him. It was the lab-geek, no question: a little older than her, sandy fair hair, complexion hacker-sallow from being cooped up in here and not spending much time in the Big Room. He held his weapon in both hands, a stubby device with a bulky black-plastic stock and the widest muzzle she'd seen outside of Elmer Fudd's arsenal.

'*No hablo inglése*,' she ventured, by way of procrastination.

'Aye, right,' he retorted. 'That's why you were saying "come on" to the computer? What are you doing here?'

'Computer *no hablo español*. Me doing *nada*.'

His eyes flitted restlessly, their focus pinging around between the multiplicity of factors he needed to control: Lex's gun, his own weapon, Lex's hands, her face, her batbelt and the countless possibilities beyond the periphery of his vision.

'Answer me,' he said, his voice lowered to a whisper by dryness in his throat. He was very scared and for that, very dangerous. 'Why are you here?'

41

'I'd find it easier to answer questions if that thing wasn't pointed at my face,' she said calmly.

'Yeah,' he replied, beads of sweat forming around his temples. 'But I've a sneaky feeling you'd be disinclined to answer altogether if it wasn't.'

'Could be right,' she conceded. 'But just stay cool right now, okay? You gotta think very carefully about your next move, dude, and I'd advise you against anything that might seriously preclude making friends with me.'

'Why the hell would I want to do that?'

'Because you may have the drop on me right now, but I got buddies coming and you don't. The alarms have been deactivated, the call-out to the cops has been cancelled and we already took out all the security guards.'

'In which case why would you spare me?'

'I could tell you, but you wouldn't believe me. In fact, you'd think I was just trying to sell you a line that might get you to put the gun down.'

'Well, there's a quality double bluff if ever I heard one. I've no idea whether I'd believe you, but believe this: nothing you say's going to make me put this gun down. Though seeing as we're standing here, why not try me anyway.'

'Okay. We're here to . . .'

Lex never got to finish her sentence as her eye was drawn to Armand, stealthily opening the door six or seven yards behind the lab-geek's right shoulder. Her pause betrayed him. It wasn't much, but with her captor's eyes locked on hers, it was enough. He turned in response to the noise, swivelling his shoulders and firing the weapon just as Armand was levelling his. Armand's right hand recoiled and slammed into the wall next to the doorway, driven there and stuck, together with his gun, by an issue of thick white goo.

The lab-geek spun back to face Lex, but he'd blown it the second he took his eye – and his aim – off of her. Lex had changed her stance immediately, her weight shifted and her hands already in position to grip as he brought the gun around. Her right hand took his forearm, holding it straight, as her left pushed the gun firmly and smoothly, his own despairing grip causing his arm to twist and his balance to lurch in compensation. After that it was a matter of merely taking one step away to drop him on his back to the floor, that same step taking Lex closer to her own weapon. She gripped it in her right hand, still holding his with her left, and pointed it at his chest.

'Told you you should have made friends, dude,' she said.

Her knuckles curled around the trigger as a voice sounded in her ear.

'Don't shoot, Alexis. Just bring him to me.'

It wasn't only Lex's fingers that froze. She glanced away from the sprawling lab-geek and scanned the room. A camera spied down at her from one corner of the ceiling. Bett was watching. But how much had he seen?

'Yes, sir,' she said, pressing her collar-mike.

'What is this stuff?' Armand asked, as he tugged his arm from the wall, his fingers and sleeve entangled in stringy, elasticated yuck. It resembled a gigantic gobbet of bubblegum, or 'the world's biggest come-shot', as Som vividly remarked when he arrived to assist.

The lab-geek said nothing, but the words 'non-lethal enforcement' came to Lex's mind. She unplugged her memory stick and slipped it into a velcro-sealed pouch on her harness, then helped the lab-geek to his feet.

'A moment,' Armand requested, as she prepared to escort her prisoner away. He gestured that it was for her ears only, so she drew close. 'Keep his eyes front,' he stated, indicating with his own which direction she ought to be leading him.

Lex didn't ask why; it wasn't a priority. She marched the lab-geek into the corridor a couple of paces in front of her, her pistol pointed at his back. This allowed her to steal a glance in the proscribed direction. There was a pallet-trolley parked further down the tunnel, in the direction of the cargo bay and the freight elevator. Grey fire blankets were draped over whatever Armand and Som had been transporting, so Lex didn't get to see what it was, but at least she now knew what that extra sled was for.

Lex was grateful to be walking behind her charge, because that way he couldn't see that she was almost as nervous as him. Once again, she had to rationalise. This was just her fear lending Bett absurd powers of interpretation. There was little he could have seen that would have caused him suspicion: Lex at a PC, tapping away. Even if it was after she'd supplied the codes, it wasn't unusual that she'd be curiously poking about inside the system; that was what she *did*. Besides, if he'd been looking at the right monitor at the time, he would have given her a heads-up that she was about to be ambushed.

Still, the rush of arguing voices and conflicting possibilities was growing cacophonic inside her head, which was why she ended up making small talk with the geek.

'We're not going to hurt you,' she assured him. 'Just taking you to see the boss.'

'Aye, right,' he doubted.

'Hey, it could have been worse, man. You could have been watching the game with the others. You not a fan?'

'I was taping it. Planned to watch it when I got home. That's if nobody told me the score.'

'No danger from me. I don't know it. But I do know what-ever happened, it didn't end well for your security guys.'

'So I gathered,' he said bitterly. 'And how's it going to end for me?'

The Security and Surveillance HQ doorway stood only yards ahead.

'You're just about to find out.'

Lex overtook him and ushered him inside, where Bett was waiting next to the monitor console, a telephone ready in prepa-ration. He offered the lab-geek an outstretched hand, which he shook half-heartedly with near-dazed uncertainty, then Bett told him what he wanted him to do.

Bett hit dial. They heard the tones sound out twice from the speaker before it was answered.

'Hello,' said a voice: male. English accent. 'Nicholas Willis here,' he identified himself. 'Who is this?'

'Sir,' the lab-geek started throatily. He swallowed and began again. 'Sir, this is Ross Fleming at Marledoq. I'm calling to inform you that it's twenty-two eighteen hours and I am currently being held at gunpoint by intruders who have complete con-trol of the facility. Sir, I'm sorry, they just came from—'

'Yes, thank you, Mr Fleming, that will be all,' Bett said, taking the receiver from him and turning the speakerphone off. 'Hello, Mr Willis. Yes, reckoned I'd better do that in case you thought

44

I was making this call from my living room. For the record, we had complete control at twenty-two eleven, that's twenty-four minutes after entering the subterranean complex, forty-one minutes after first point of contact at your exterior perimeter and sixty-seven minutes after landing our helicopter. Indeed. I'll be putting all of those details in my written report, along with my full list of recommendations and, of course, my invoice. No, I agree, it's not good at all, Mr Willis. Well, that's at your discretion, but, personally, my first step would be to fire anyone who is right now literally sleeping on the job. I'll be in touch.'

Bett put down the phone.

'Who are you people?' Fleming asked.

'What's called a Tiger Team,' Lex told him. 'We were brought in to carry out a Defence and Integrity test on the Marledoq complex. If you don't mind me telling you the scoreline in advance, it didn't pass.'

'No kidding.'

'I'd anticipate seeing a lot of changes around here, Mr Fleming,' Bett said. 'Your employers are about to seriously upgrade this facility's security. I'm sure you know more than I about precisely why, but from precedent my guess is you're working on something that certain people might be prepared to go to extreme lengths to procure.'

Lex felt her hand move unbidden towards the pouch on her harness where the memory stick sat safe, storing her stolen digital cargo.

Extreme lengths indeed, she thought.

Sports cars and casinos

Jane stopped dead in her tracks when she saw him approaching hurriedly in the smir under the low, grey, mid-morning sky. It was eleven in the morning, but passing cars still had their head-lamps on and there had been no improvement in natural visibility since the street lights went off two hours before. He was in uniform, grim-faced as he clutched his gun. She stared, the consequences hitting home, and in that moment her hesitation cost her the option to hit the deck. He looked up and saw her. Eye contact had been made, so he knew she was there.

If she'd been more alert, she could have spotted him earlier, she knew, and taken steps accordingly: changed her itinerary, used her time on areas his intrusion wouldn't affect, or possibly just hidden her presence altogether. Kill all the lights, stay low, wait it out, and he'd move on; then a simple phone-call to relay the appropriate information would prevent his coming back. But all of that was moot now. She no longer had any choice but to let him do his worst.

She walked reluctantly to the front door in her stocking soles, the delicacy of her imprint seemingly pointless in the face of what was about to be wreaked.

'Morning. Here to read your gas meter,' he announced.

'Oh, sure, come on in,' she said, faking a smile. It wasn't his fault; he was only doing his job. It was just bad timing, really bad timing. If she'd held off on the hall for five minutes, it wouldn't have made a big difference, or if she hadn't just mopped the kitchen floor, she could have called him round the back door and let him in there.

She led him down the full length of the hall to the cupboard under the stairs, at the far end next to the living room, where he pointed the gun and took his reading.

'That's me, thank you,' he told her, then she escorted him back out again. A matter of moments, that was all it took.

Jane closed the door and turned around, surveying the damage. Two sets of bootprints, one in each direction, tracked the meter-reader's passage up and down her just-hoovered hall carpet. He'd not been particularly tall or heavy-set, but that didn't matter: it was all in the soles. Flat spread the weight and left minimum markage, but his chunky, patterned rubberware had bitten into the pile like a Dobermann, and that Dobermann had drooled, too. Almost every step was damp on the inwards journey, and nearer the door there were dark streaks, an abrasive seasonal compound of earth, decayed leaves, gritter-salt and bark.

She should have let him in the back door anyway, she thought ruefully. At this time of year, she should always and only let them in the back door. Mopping the kitchen again would take a fraction of the time, though at the cost of damp stockings (bare feet not being an option due to leaving prints that remained visible against the tiles after the floor was dry). The damp stockings were going to be unavoidable anyway as she had to get to the sink and the cupboard under it in order to begin working on the damage. Jane looked at the glistening kitchen tiles. Why was it they only looked that clean and shiny when they were wet, and why was it that you always had to go back into the kitchen for something as soon as the floor had been mopped? She could wait ten minutes for it to dry, she considered, already anticipating the feel of the cold wet on the soles of her tights, but that was ten more minutes for that sludgy compound to be drying into her carpet.

Damn it. She took a step forward, bracing herself for the ick factor of that cold, spreading sensation, then stopped and remained at the edge of the carpet. For the resourceful operative, there were always other options. Jane leaned inside, her left foot still outside the door, her right held in balance in the air as her hands met the island worktop. She tipped herself further until the edge of the Formica pressed just beneath her chest, then reached her hands towards the far edge and pulled, her centre of gravity shifting all weight forwards. Both feet left the ground as she pivoted on her front on the edge of the worktop, before hauling herself and turning in one movement to leave her sitting on the island. Good to know all those aerobics sessions at the gym had a practical pay-off. Drawing her legs up to her chest and spinning on her bottom, she manoeuvred to the other side of the island, from where she was able to reach out with her right leg and hook a dish-towel off the radiator with her big toe before transferring it to her right hand. Thus armed, she let the towel unfold and dropped it gently to the floor, then stepped down on to it with both feet. After that, it took only half a yard of the tied-foot shuffle to get her to the sink, the dish-towel providing a priceless protective membrane between soles and floor.

Jane ran a basinful of hot water and added some washing-up liquid, before unlatching the cupboard below, where her heavy-duty chemical arsenal was stored. So many abrasives, detergents, poison warnings, death-heads, bio-hazard decals. She often wondered whether, if you put all these cleaning agents together in the right quantities, you might create something that could blow half the neighbourhood to Kingdom Come, or even just to Busby.

They should never have gone for self-coloured, she thought, working carpet-mousse into the fibres with a sponge. It showed up everything; not just dirt, but each wisp of fluff from Tom's socks, each discarded snippet of thread from clothing. Plus, they should have definitely, definitely chosen a twist rather than a pile that becomes churned-up and streaky if walked upon in anything more substantial than M&S nylons – and even that is enough to make it look bumpy and mottled after a while. What use was a carpet if it doesn't look good after any modicum of pedestrian traffic? On occasion, she found herself watching visitors arrive and wishing she hadn't invited them because they were about to violate this expanse of laboriously cultivated neatness. Then, once they were inside, her mind was drawn impatiently throughout their conversation to thoughts of combing it neat again as soon as they left.

She finished with the mousse and returned the basin to the kitchen floor, then made for the hall cupboard and her trusty Dyson. Within a couple of minutes, most of the meter-reader's tracks had been erased, with only the damp patches near the door testifying to his having visited. She surveyed this with the satisfaction she always enjoyed when it had been freshly combed: no streaks, no imprints, just an unspoilt virgin purity. If only people didn't then have to go and walk on the damn thing.

Okay, all of this was daft, she knew. The guys who painted the Forth Bridge understood that there was no end; like the river below them, their work was a constant flow. She understood that too, most of the time. Today, for goodness' sake, she was hoovering every speck, and rendering the place immaculate when she knew Michelle was bringing Rachel and Thomas over in the afternoon – the pair of them capable of turning the place upside down in minutes. But she needed, every so often, to restore a kind of equilibrium. It reassured her to achieve this – the untrammelled carpet, the sparkling kitchen tiles, the empty laundry basket, no clothes on the horse or in the pile – because if that equilibrium had been restored, even for a short while, it meant that no matter what the subsequent disruption, it could be restored again.

And this also, she knew, was daft. Very daft. She had to take a step outside herself to see it, however, which was a rarely glimpsed perspective, and sadly not one revelatory enough to free her. It meant she was still obsessive-compulsive, but self-conscious and embarrassed about her lot into the bargain.

Obsessing over carpets and laundry. How on earth had it come to this? Tom said she was suffering some kind of mid-life crisis, though that was in response to her Private Hire work and her abortive mature student foray into academia. He didn't really mean it. It was merely his way of discounting what she was doing as a phase he was impatiently awaiting her to get past. Men were good at that; Tom was anyway: filing your activities and enthusiasms away under Silly Female Behaviour, transient notions of a feeble and ditzy mind. Bide your time and she'll be back to normal soon.

But what if this 'normality' *was* her mid-life crisis? If so, she'd be extremely disappointed. She'd always imagined it would take a form considerably more dramatic than involuntary emotional investment in the condition of her floor coverings, and be precipitated by something significant, remarkable and halfway interesting. But maybe normality *was* what precipitated it. What bigger crisis was there at this late juncture in your life than finding yourself asking: Is this it?

The ironing, dusting, hoovering, mopping, sponging and re-hoovering complete, Jane moved on to cleaning the bathroom and the downstairs toilet – temporarily gleaming china representing a few more brief licks on those river-spanning girders – before continuing her rich, full day with a jaunt to the shops.

Apart from the major milestones of marriage, parenthood and bereavement, other people marked the passing phases of their adult lives by the cities they had lived in, stages in their careers, lovers they'd been with, projects they'd worked on. 'Ah, yes, the Barcelona years. Those summers with Theo, before we grew apart. That controversial tenure with the Philosophy Department. My Impressionist period.' Jane could break hers down by supermarket. Early Eighties: Presto. Late Eighties to mid-Nineties: Tesco. Late Nineties: Safeway. Early Twenty-First Century: her J Sainsbury period. This last she considered something of a *belle époque*, but strictly in terms of the shopping.

Jane had never had a career. A succession of jobs, yes, interrupted by child-rearing, but never a career. She'd known only one city, and having lived on its periphery in East Kilbride most of her adult life, she couldn't even claim to have known it that well. For more than twenty years she'd lived in the same house, and for longer than that had had the same lover. Well, the same man anyway. Projects? At least on that score she could say there'd been two. But they had both left home now, indeed one of them had left the country, and neither gave the impression they believed she'd done a bang-up job. On the plus side, one of them *was* still speaking to her.

Being just up from Whirlies Roundabout, the Kingsgate retail park was yet another node in the EK traffic-generation-and-recycling system, but it was worth tolerating the congestion to shop in a comparatively calm and spacious environment, especially when you spent as much time in supermarkets as Jane did. Also, for Lanarkshire, they boasted more than the average number of aisles not selling oven chips and frozen pizzas.

Jane enjoyed trailing along the shelves and counters, daydreaming about what she'd like to make if she wasn't going home to cook for Tom, who thought that alternating between Indian and Chinese for his Friday-night takeaway meant he had an adventurous appetite. Tom's favourite home-cooked dish was stovies, though ideally it would have been cooked in his previous home by his mother, whose culinary expertise had inexplicably failed to grant her international acclaim and whose secret recipe for her signature dish had gone with her to the grave, along with close to a hundredweight of rosary beads. It said a great deal about why Scotland was perennially referred to as the Sick Man of Europe that Tom considered home-made stovies a healthy and wholesome option, as opposed to, say, a deep-fried pizza supper or an intravenous injection of lukewarm, but rapidly congealing, pork-fat. Consisting of reheated Lorne sausage swimming in a watery stew of boiled carrots and disintegrating spuds, Tom's-Mammy-recipe stovies looked like what you might find swilling at the bottom if a butcher, a greengrocer and a pet-store shared the same wheelie bin. Jane was of the belief that Lorne sausage was something people would get into trouble for feeding to animals in ten years' time, and was pretty sure that in other countries, they wouldn't even let you store stovies in the same wheelie bin as normal domestic waste. So, it being Thursday and her not having cooked it so far this week, guess what was on the menu tonight? A fillet of that tempting-looking sea bass on a bed of wasabi mash, with a spinach-and-coriander salsa? Some of that Gresham duck breast nestling on crisp salad leaves and drizzled with an orange-and-mango reduction? Or . . .

'Half a pound of square sausage, please.'

'Square? Right you are, missus.'

Jane's efforts at tempting Tom with more exotic fare had long since been abandoned. Minor variations on familiar dishes were met with queries as to whether she'd not been able to get the standard ingredients, and more ambitious undertakings had frequently been forsaken at the preparatory stage; Tom suspecting experimentation was afoot and venturing into the kitchen to inform her: 'I'll just have my steak/chicken/fish plain, with a few totties. Save you all that bother.'

She should have spotted it from the start, and looking back, the evidence was all there, but when you're young you sometimes project more than you actually see. The teen magazines of her youth should have offered less advice on make-up and period pain if it allowed space to pass on more useful wisdom, such as a warning that you were kidding yourself if you thought your young suitor's less desirable traits would fade with time, while allowing the fairer ones to bloom. An old-fashioned streak in an adolescent can seem endearing, single-mindedness a sign of character. Add twenty years and the effect is considerably less charming.

It wasn't that he was cantankerous or miserable with his stone-set ways: what truly alienated Jane was that he was so satisfied by them. 'Philistine' was a term people used too freely to describe individuals they considered less cultured than themselves, even just people who didn't share their tastes. (The supreme irony of this, she had learned, was that the original Philistines were about five hundred years more culturally advanced than the Israelites.) If Tom preferred stovies to a Nick Nairn creation, that was his shout. It wasn't his taste that made him a Philistine. It was that he seemed, as one of her favourite books put it, content to live in a wholly unexplored world.

The book, *The Lyre of Orpheus*, was about staging a new opera, from conception through to opening night. She'd read it no fewer than five times, savouring every word, its pleasures, like all of the best novels, bittersweet that it was a fiction. What wouldn't she give to be part of something like that? Any part: a seamstress working on the costumes; a line-prompt; the librettist's assistant, transcribing his flights of idea. To be working in concert with committed, remarkable people, giving the best of themselves to create something of such excitement and beauty – a fluid, living testament to the peaks of human aspiration. Who wouldn't want to swap reality for the world between those pages?

Answer: someone who'd rather be further advancing his attempted symbiosis with a leather armchair while watching endless repeats of Celtic games on satellite pay-per-view.

She toured the store methodically, threading her trolley along every aisle apart from the pet-food section, briefly skirting the alcohol selection last, to pick up more cans of Export for Tom. The shelves of wine bottles glinted colourfully as she passed them, but, as ever, she wasn't tempted to lift any. She also felt a little intimidated by the vastness of the selection, reckoning you really needed to know what you were doing when it came to that sort of thing. She didn't drink wine. She'd had the odd glass of fizzy stuff, but it gave her a headache, and on the very rare occasion they'd been out for a meal, Tom just drank beer with his food. She remembered he had once or twice (more probably once) opted for sharing a jug of sangria with dinner when they were on holiday in Spain with the kids, but she wasn't sure whether that counted. It had tasted like medicine.

Her friend Catherine drank wine. She'd often have a glass or two, sometimes more, when they met up for lunch. Jane never quite caught what she was ordering, unless it was Chardonnay; she'd heard that mentioned enough to remember, and had even tried some once. It tasted worse than medicine. She knew you had to 'train your palate' to appreciate it, but couldn't imagine herself doing so. Catherine only ordered Chardonnay occasionally, so most of the time what she asked for sounded like some arcane code, worse than when Ross started to talk technical. Every so often she would urge Jane to have a glass, but as they usually met for lunch in Bothwell, where Catherine lived, Jane would have to drive afterwards. She liked the idea of drinking wine, but it was the same as she liked the idea of learning to play piano. She suspected it was a bit late to start, and besides, you'd need to go to night school or something to learn your way around all those bottles.

Jane headed for the checkouts, habitually scanning along the row. It wasn't busy, but she'd have to own up to queue length not being the only criterion for her choice of conveyor belt. Embarrassing as it was to admit, she preferred not to be served by a certain cheerful elderly lady, identified as 'Margaret' on her name badge. Margaret was pleasantly chatty and entirely efficient, and had done nothing to Jane that any rational person could complain about, but had nonetheless meted out the greatest offence in a passing remark, all the more wounding for it being an inescapable truth.

Jane had often been at the supermarket in charge of one or both of Michelle's kids, for whom Margaret always had a smile and a wave; and when Jane was there on her own, the sight of a few bags of chocolate buttons on the conveyor belt would prompt an affectionate enquiry after the wee ones. It was on one of the latter such occasions that Margaret committed her great oblivious sin, in response to Jane's relating her recent success in getting the weans to take a nap one afternoon while she got on with the ironing.

'Aye, us grannies ken the score,' she had said.

Jane could still feel that moment, the sensation of paralysis as disbelief and denial crumbled, leaving a shattering revelation amid the broken shards of the illusion with which she'd been deceiving herself. All right, maybe that was laying it on a bit, but she'd never experienced such a sense of life having ambushed her since the first time she found out she was pregnant.

Us grannies. She and Margaret, this white-haired and birdlike woman with false teeth and wrinkled fingers, who was old enough to be Jane's mother. It was intended as a show of solidarity, even sorority, but in that moment Margaret had held up a mirror and let Jane see how the world saw her. In that mirror, she looked like Margaret. *Us grannies ken the score.*

Jane had technically become a generation older the moment her first grandchild was born, three years ago, but Margaret's remark was the moment when she belatedly felt it. At the time of Rachel's birth it hadn't meant anything: she knew she hadn't got any older and it was still the same face in the mirror. Her thoughts had only been of joy at the sight of her granddaughter, tinged admittedly with a few concerns about Michelle, only twenty-two and following in the missteps of her mother, who'd found herself in the same position at nineteen.

She was forty-six now, forty-three when Rachel was born. There'd been lots of jokes about her being a granny and applying for her bus pass, but she'd happily laughed it all off because she still considered herself young. Being a grandmother at forty-three didn't change the fact that she *was* forty-three, any more than it had altered the status of her school friend Jennifer when she became an auntie at the age of nine. Forty-three was still young. Forty-six was still young. You're only as old as you feel, ran the cliché. She'd known people who'd been in their fifties since they were adolescents – she had in fact been foolish enough to marry one. Age was merely chronology. She knew what being young meant. It meant that life still had plenty in store for you; maybe even that it still had more in store for you than you'd already experienced. It meant there was still time to do all those things, whatever all those things might be.

Margaret's remark hit her so hard because it forced her to realise that by this, her own definition, she was no longer young, nor had she been for some time. She felt pulled forward in some temporal vortex, at the end of which she was sitting there, white-haired, bird-like, with false teeth and wrinkled fingers, never having done any of those things. There was no time, and life had little in store but more of the same. Suddenly she was in the third act, the beginning of the end. Us grannies ken the score: we've had our whack. This *is* it.

When Jane was a girl, it felt like the greatest treat when there was a James Bond film on TV on a Sunday night, an epic adventure that made school the next day seem a long way off. The Sixties ones were best, with Connery, but even *OHMSS* was a fantastic escape. It didn't matter about Lazenby because, unlike her brothers, she wasn't watching them for James Bond. She was watching them because they were like a two-and-a-half-hour holiday, a tour of enticing locations and a vicarious glimpse of a lifestyle that was a world apart. Scuba-diving in the tropics, skiing in Switzerland, chateaus, mansions and hotels. One day, Jane Bell had always dreamed, she would go to a casino on the French Riviera, dressed in something you'd get lifted for in Glasgow, and she'd arrive there in a convertible classic sports car. It wasn't a yearning for riches, for money (although, as her mother used to say, it came in handy when you were paying for the messages); it was a yearning to prove she could be that woman, who could wear that dress, drive that car and walk into that casino. And Jane Bell could have been that woman, she was sure, but she wasn't Jane Bell any more. She had become Jane Fleming, and Jane Fleming ken't the score.

Jane got pregnant when she was nineteen. She'd wanted a lot more from life than even her Riviera fantasies before that happened. It was just before the third-term exams in her first year at Glasgow Tech, two generations and a lifetime ago. She was studying engineering, one of very few females doing so at the time, but having grown up in a house with three older

56

brothers, she was used to the ratio and all that went with it. They were exciting days, and not just for the usual reasons of adolescent liberation. The cultural insurgence that was Punk was well under way, and with it a sense that nothing couldn't be changed; everything was finally up for grabs in an ailing and long-stagnant society. The meek acceptance that everything was in the clutches of an older generation and a higher caste was being noisily trashed. That's what the purple Roneo-copied fanzines said, anyway. Almost everyone she knew was 'starting a band', even if for many the declaration of intent was as important a statement as any music they may or may not ever get around to playing.

Jane wasn't much of a rebel. She got on well with her parents, for a start. They were kind to her and she liked to please them in return, liked to see them happy with her, their one little girl after three rowdy boys. She liked pleasing them as she liked pleasing people in general, hideously uncool as that was to admit. She'd been brought up to endeavour to do what was right, whether that be working hard at school to get good results or going the messages for old Mrs Dolan next door. John Lydon would have had her ceremonially thrown out of that SPOTS gig if he'd had any idea of what was in his midst. Jane wasn't out to change the underlying social order. She was just intoxicated by the energy of it all, of youth fearless and unfettered. She cropped her hair short and dyed it blue. She mutilated this old red tartan frock of her auntie's to make a two-part tabard and mini-skirt affair. The top half was barely held together down the sides by safety pins and hairy string, while the bottom provided minimal cover but maximum contrast against her preferred Day-Glo green tights. She still had a photo somewhere. She looked shocking, awful, ghastly. But in a truly magnificent way.

There was a comic song around that time, the B-side of Andy Cameron's doom-tempting World Cup single, called *I Want to Be a Punk Rocker but Ma Mammy Wullnae Let Me*. Jane guessed that could well have been her, had it not been that her mammy did let her. Her mum had already been through a few pointless losing battles with her eldest brother, Billy, over long hair, a skinhead, long hair again, flares, platforms and Slade gigs. If

Jane had stopped going the messages for Mrs Dolan or tidying her bedroom of a Saturday morning, that would have caused more censure and concern. She feared she was, in the words of another song of the time, a part-time punk, but in that she was hardly alone. It being Glasgow, a familiar cry around the family hearth of a Saturday afternoon would have been: 'Haw Maw, gaunny iron ma bondage troosers fur the night, pleeeease.' It wasn't about changing the world; it was about being nineteen.

She called herself Blue Bell, in reference to her hair. She and her pals all had these punk names for themselves. Suzi Spiteful, Tina Toxic, Corpse-Boy, Venom, Bloodclot. She remembered two old punters behind them on a bus into town one night, listening with growing amusement at their names. 'Whaur's Biffo?' one asked the other. 'Is that Biffo next tae Korky and Gnasher?'

She saw The Clash, The Damned, The Buzzcocks, and of course SPOTS – Sex Pistols On Tour Secretly – this last via a very drunken six-hour transit-van trip to Middlesbrough. Casinos and sports cars weren't high on her wish list at that time, any more than a newbuild in EK with a husband and a baby. But guess what?

For someone with dreams of distinguishing herself, of living a life that was remarkable, was there any greater failure, anything more embarrassing, then ending up a cliché? There were various ways of relating the tale, slants and spins that could be put upon the details, but the most important facts didn't change: she got pregnant, had to drop out of college and was railroaded by her circumstances into marrying the guy. The only way she could have topped that would have been if the fateful encounter had been her first time, but it wasn't. It was just her first time with Tom and her first time without a condom.

Tom was a friend of her brother Steven, who knew him from the College of Building and Printing. He was twenty-one but seemed older, certainly more mature. He'd gone to college at seventeen so by twenty-one had graduated and was working in his first job as a surveyor. He had disposable income and his own car, which would have made him an attractive prospect even if he wasn't good-looking, but he was, albeit in a rather serious way.

He wasn't a punk (a real waste given that Flem was a ready-made nickname), but he did seem to like the music and could

58

afford to buy more of the records than Jane or her crowd. He came along to a few gigs and discos, dressed in drainpipes and a leather jacket, but could hardly go the full bhoona, with hair and piercings, he explained, because he still had to turn up to places in a suit on Monday morning. Jane suspected Tom would never have been going the full bhoona anyway, but didn't particularly mind. Going out with him, she felt she was getting the best of both worlds. She had her punk pals to be daft, outrageous and generally irresponsible with, and, on the other hand, she had a sensible and mature boyfriend, with prospects and money in his pocket, who made her feel grown up in a way every young woman enjoyed. His serious side was a welcome contrast with her other crowd, and it actually felt quite flattering that someone like that didn't see her as a silly wee lassie. What he did see, she wasn't so sure of, but she didn't give it much thought. At that age, you don't ask these things of yourself. You just go out until it stops being fun. When you're truly young, you feel like the present is forever. That's why you don't see the future careering towards you like a runaway eighteen-wheeler.

Before going out with Tom, Jane had sex with two boyfriends plus two one-night stands, both times drunken 'friend-sex' encounters with guys in the punk crowd. The punk scene had been derided as sexless and John Lydon's withering remark about 'two minutes of squelching noises' was often quoted in support, but only, Jane suspected, by green-eyed chroniclers on the outside looking in. Sexless? Take adolescents in ripped clothes, add music and liberal doses of cheap alcohol. What do you think you're going to get? The tabloid reporters with their hackneyed seaside-postcard idea of what constituted sexy couldn't get their heads around the fact that they weren't dressing to attract the opposite sex. They were – girls and guys – dressing to express themselves, and as far as she was concerned, nothing was sexier than that.

Sex at that age felt like another youthful freedom, another new area for exploration, for expression, for *fun*. Meaningless? Maybe. Serious? Never. Then along came Tom and it suddenly became a psychological minefield, each minor advance in how far she could tempt him to go followed by a ghastly spectacle of guilt and self-recrimination.

59

Jane's family were nominal Prods but actually not religious. Perhaps if they had been, she'd have known a little better what she was dealing with, before Catholicism notched up another pyrrhic victory by punishing ordinary human behaviour.

Tom wouldn't accede to her request, even couched in his own words, to wear a condom 'in case things go too far'. His otherwise cautious and sensible rationality was obliterated by a combination of primitive superstition and plain old denial. The logic ran thus: the big beardy punter in the sky forbade contraception, and wearing a johnny 'just in case' would only make going too far that bit easier. This part she couldn't argue with; indeed was counting on to get him past this stupidity. His counter-logic, however, was that not wearing a condom would therefore constitute an insurmountable deterrent.

In the words of the wee schoolboy, upon being told by his teacher that there was no example in the English language of a double positive expressing a negative, 'Aye, right.' When religion attempted to play the immovable object to human sexuality's unstoppable force, there could only ever be one result.

The A word loomed large in her head, filed under Easy Way Out. Toxic Tina's older sister had had one. She could get it done before anyone found out. But 'before anyone found out' was always going to be a short window of opportunity, and it proved not to be one she was decisive enough to take. The catch-22 was that aborting was something she could only go through with before anyone close to her found out, but she couldn't go through with it before talking to someone close to her. She wasn't the most politicised student, but she knew where she stood on a woman's right to choose: she'd signed the petitions, been to the meetings, worn the badge, and she'd do the same today. But at that most lonely and vulnerable time, her squeamishness at the thought of something growing inside her was topped only by her squeamishness at the thought of somebody taking it out.

Her parents were as supportive as she could have possibly hoped, and in that respect she knew she'd been extremely fortunate. Matters were discussed openly and pragmatically, but she still got the sense that summit meetings had been taking place above her head. Marriage, therefore, was more arrived at by consent than proposed. There was no going down on one knee and, then at least, no ring. Tom offered because he was dutiful, responsible and caring, and because he believed it was the right thing to do. There was also the fact that his parents would rather see him burned at the stake than be father to an illegitimate child – and a Proddy one at that – but her own mum and dad made it clear to all that it would be Jane's decision and hers alone.

She was so, so young. Marriage was for proper grown-ups, not kids like her. But then so was motherhood. Tom was decent, attractive, had a good job, money in the bank and she knew he'd look after her. What more could she ask for, in her circumstances? It wasn't how she'd pictured this moment in her life, but it wasn't the end of the world; just the end of *a* world and the beginning of a new one.

Fast-forward three years and it was a far better world than she could have imagined. She had two lovely children, Ross then Michelle, fourteen months apart (she had her tubes tied after the latter given that Tom still wouldn't countenance any form of birth control), a nice house, holidays abroad, even her own car, Tom's promotion earning him a company one. A glimpse at how her old pals were doing showed her where she could have been had she finished her studies, and it looked like she had been the one who struck it lucky. It was the early Eighties, Thatcher was in power, nobody had a job and everyone was skint, still living like students in bedsits or in many cases back with their folks.

On the whole, she knew she had it good; but though she had few complaints, that didn't mean she was without regrets. There wasn't much prospect of a career, for one. Even once the kids were both school-age, the hours between dropping them off and picking them up were rapidly filled with shopping, cleaning, ironing and cooking, leaving no scope for anything other than part-time work. It was something she accepted, but never entirely made her peace with. She enjoyed being a mum and she loved her kids, but from time to time felt this guilty admission that she still wanted something more. Not something else, just something more. Was that such a heresy, to admit that your love for your family wasn't sufficiently all-consuming as to extinguish all other desires? Did it mean she wasn't cut out for this?

And did any other mothers feel this way too? None that were owning up to it, but that didn't mean she was alone.

As the years passed, though, she found herself rationalising many of her own dreams away, and having dreams for her kids instead. These proved no less a source of frustration, but at least helped her see how daft some of her own notions had always been. Sports cars and casinos were just a wee girl's fantasy, but they had endured in her mind as icons that had come to represent another self she could yet aspire to be. They symbolised her belief that she was still young, that she could still do something more with her life, one day.

Going back to college, for instance. That was meant to be the big new beginning. She had no inclination to resume her original studies, instead deciding that someone who had read as many books as she ought to have a crack at English Literature. She applied to Glasgow Uni and received an offer conditional upon topping up her qualifications, including an improved and more up-to-date Higher English. This meant a year of night classes, which was no hardship as it regularly got her out of the house and away from half-man-half-armchair and the relentless tyranny of Sky Sports. Having waited this long to restart her life, what was another year? Well, another year was time enough for Michelle, who'd graduated from Strathclyde in Pharmacy and was working at the Royal Infirmary, to meet Doctor Right, marry him and conceive their first child.

Jane tried not to dwell on the rather mocking sense of déjà vu when she calculated that Michelle was due around about third-term in her first year as a mature student, and pressed ahead with her studies. She sat – and passed – her exams, amid the considerable distraction of Rachel being born, then enjoyed a long summer, during which it became clear that she was indispensable to her daughter. And if there was any doubt in her mind where her responsibilities lay, Michelle getting pregnant again, before the autumn leaves fell, dispelled it utterly.

This time she had no regrets. It put into perspective what was important, and besides, she told herself, there was still time for . . . whatever. Michelle planned to go back to work after the second baby, so both the kids would be going off to nursery when they were two. Jane was only forty-three that autumn.

She was still young; life had plenty left to offer. She'd resume her degree one day, along with whatever else she wanted to embark upon. Broadened horizons, new beginnings. One day.

Michelle did go back, taking a job at Hairmyres Hospital once Thomas had started nursery. That was about six weeks back, just before Margaret laid down that inescapable truth which, deep down, Jane had known all along.

There is no 'one day'. There is only *to*day, and today wasn't about sports cars or casinos or degrees or new beginnings. Today was about hoovering the carpet, trailing round the supermarket and cooking stovies, before vegetating mindlessly all evening in front of the TV next to a man she still lived with only because neither of them had anywhere else to go.

Us grannies ken the score.

Aye. We lost.

The specialist

Lex was stirred from her daydreaming by the sensation of the chopper losing altitude. She'd been watching the rain streak the window to her left, there being nothing else to look at as they'd been flying through cloud for the past ten minutes.

'I've always wanted to ask, how do pilots know where they're going when they can't see twenty feet in front?' she enquired of Rebekah, sitting to her right at the controls.

'Navigational instruments and the altimeter let you know where you are. You don't think in terms of what's directly in front – it's not like driving a car. You think in terms of what's five miles in front. It's all about vectors and trajectories.'

'Yeah, I got the navigational concept. But how does thinking in terms of five miles in front help you avoid some other sky-borne object that's a hundred feet ahead inside the cloudbank, or when it's pitch-black outside?'

'Oh, that's generally where air traffic control comes in. Flights are all logged, airspace allocated – you got corridors at different altitudes.'

'Generally? What's the exception?'

Rebekah smiled. 'Unofficial, unauthorised aircraft flying at ultra-low altitude to evade the ATC systems and thus remaining off the charts.'

'Damn, I hate it when I know what you're about to say. And what do those aircraft use?'

Rebekah laughed. 'Radar, what else? You see that panel there?'

Lex looked at the little LED screen where Rebekah was pointing. She understood the principle but was neither impressed nor assured by the lack of detail. There was a white triangle in the centre, picked out against the blue background, two arrows flanking it, each above two decks of numbers.

'Anything in the sky within range will show up, with its altitude and velocity cited beneath the blip. Quit worrying just because you can't see tail lights or lines on a highway. You're only seeing clouds because you're only looking at clouds.'

'I think I'd want something more than a tiny blinking light to let me know there was a Seven-Forty-Seven bearing down on us at five hundred miles per hour. What are you seeing?'

'Clear passage to our refuelling stop, ETA three minutes.'

'Okay. Just as long as you're also seeing pylons, steeples and cliff faces.'

'Relax. We're not as low as you think. Just wait for the second leg if you wanna see low.'

Lex slammed her head back against the seat and sighed. 'Scroll up to my previous entry re knowing what you're about to say.'

'Oh, grow a spine, girl. We're still in French airspace. We haven't even done anything illegal yet, never mind dangerous.'

'What about flying unlogged and unauthorised below ... etcetera etcetera?'

'I was pulling your chain. This part of the flight is logged and authorised. It's the next part that won't be.'

'So we haven't flown below ATC radar yet? Oh God, don't answer that.'

'Scroll up yourself, I already did.'

'And you actually relish the prospect of flying over the North Sea at roughly the same altitude as a skimming pebble?'

'Not a whole bunch, but I relish it more than the prospect of being escorted to an airbase by RAF fighter pilots armed with heat-seeking air-to-air missiles.'

'Copy that,' Lex agreed.

They touched down on schedule. Having descended through a grey abyss of cumulo-nimbus, it was a relief to finally emerge into clear air, even if there wasn't so much of it between them and terra firma. Rebekah landed the bird close to a hangar at a small private airfield, then killed the engines and waited for a fuelling truck to make its way across the runway from next to the flimsy-looking office building.

Lex stepped outside to get some air. There was a light drizzle blowing around so she didn't stay long, but she needed a few moments' wandering where it was cool, with some wind in her face and her feet on the ground. She'd never been scared of flying before, nor would she say she particularly was now, but her perspective upon it had changed in recent months since riding up in the cockpit with Rebekah. She'd never felt quite so safe again in any car after her first driving lesson, suddenly bereft of the protective illusion afforded by complete ignorance. Obviously she'd never been allowed to take the controls of the helicopter, but simply being up in that thing with Rebekah had caused the same effect: the magic spell had been broken.

That, however, only accounted for a fraction of her anxiety about this trip. In fact, the moments of visceral terror awaiting her on their low-level scoot across the English Channel and the North Sea would at least provide momentary vacations from worrying about everything else.

'You okay?' Rebekah asked, having docked the fuel hose and given the go-ahead to the truck-driver to start the pump.

Lex nodded.

'It'll be cool,' Rebekah assured her. 'These things practically fly themselves. So much technology. One pilot and a dog, remember?'

'I remember. And it makes me think about what we in the computer world call the Airplane Rule: a twin-engine airplane has twice as many engine problems as a single-engine one. Complexity increases the possibility of failure.'

'Good job we aren't flying in an airplane, then, huh?'

'Oh yeah. I'm sure the principle doesn't apply to egg-beaters. How many engines does it have?'

'Two,' she admitted with a naughty-little-girl grin.

'Figures. Tell you the truth, though, the aircraft and the sub-radar low-jinks don't have me worried as much as the reason we need all that.'

'Well, I know the etiquette about personal questions, but I'm guessing you don't want to end up being questioned by the British authorities any more than I do. The sub-radar low-jinks are the price we pay for secrecy. What's wrong with that?'

'The secrecy angle is covered. Look at the documentation we're carrying: fake passports, drivers' licences, credit cards – complete ID work-up. We could both make this trip on commercial transport under assumed identities and no record would show that Alexis Sinclair Richardson or Rebekah Kristine Bardell were ever here. The reason we're doing it under the radar is that Air Bett is less antsy than the commercial carriers about itty bitty things like toting handguns and live ammunition on board their aircraft.'

'Maybe you'll tell me different, Lex, but I can't imagine you'd feel better about walking into this thing *without* a gun.'

'I'm pretty certain I'm carrying it for more than reassurance. That's what I'm nervous about. It would have been cheaper, simpler and safer to stick me on a plane. Bett sent me this way, with you, on a private helicopter, under the radar, so that when I got there I'd have a gun in my hand. That's a lot of trouble for just-in-case.'

'No, Bett sent you this way, with me, on a private helicopter because he has a private helicopter and a trained pilot at his disposal. He did it because he *can*, and thus it's the simplest solution. No disrespect, Lex, but if Bett really thought we were heading for a shooting match, do you think he'd have sent you and not Nuno?'

Lex had to concede the point. Rebekah was right about this, just like she was right that the flight would be cool; terrifying, but ultimately cool. Unfortunately, it was actually neither of these things that had Lex's guts in spasm, her brain dropping packets and her eyes looking over her shoulder. They were merely plausible explanations to offer Rebekah when she noticed.

Truth was, Lex had been suffering from a feeling of impending disaster since the moment this mission began, and nobody could reassure her over her fears because for anyone to know what she was afraid of would require the worst of them to have come true.

In fact, the feeling had started before she even knew what the mission was, when Bett turned up unheralded at her apartment. Bett, to her knowledge, never turned up unheralded at anyone's apartment. If he needed you *tout de suite*, he paged you and you went to him, right that second, no matter where you were, what time it was, who you were with or whether you'd come yet. If for any reason he needed to visit you at home, it was the same drill, and you had, on average, about ten minutes to get ready. Whether you spent that time putting on some clothes, tidying the place or improvising an explanation to erstwhile lovers and inebriated houseguests as to why they had to leave the building at four in the morning was entirely up to you. For him to just show up and ring the doorbell was unprecedented and uncharacteristic, both of which she took as surely indicative of only one thing.

She had been working on the procurement of some electrical schematics and architectural blueprints pertaining to the vault and safety-deposit box galleries of a bank in Lisbon. They weren't planning any practical demonstrations; she just had to report on how much technical information she was able to acquire and what level of expertise had been necessary in doing so. The answers at that point would have been, respectively, 'Not much so far,' and, 'More than this lamer has been able to exercise,' with a rider that things might look different in a few hours if she could get this crufted-together code she was wrestling to do the needful. Consequently, she was in what real programmers called deep-hack mode – interrupts locked out – when Bett rang her bell. This, in fact, meant he had to ring her bell four times before she was drawn sufficiently close to the surface as to be able to hear it. Naturally, he was not delighted by the delay, though the displeasure in his face was nothing compared to the revulsion he must have seen staring back in hers. Happily, he'd seen the depressurisation-trauma effect of her being peremptorily yanked back from deep-hack mode before, and assumed that this was all he was seeing, thus failing to register her genuine terror and conspicuous guilt at the mere sight of him standing in her lobby.

There'd been a number of 'This is it' moments since her act of moonlight freelancing on the Tiger Team job at Marledoq. The instances had depleted with time, beginning with the paranoid expectation that Bett's every greeting was an overture towards challenging her about her deception; then graduating towards making the same assumption only when he did something slightly unusual, such as compliment her work or offer her a smile. With three months having passed, her more rational side was starting to hold sway in its bid to convince her that if Bett knew anything, he'd have done something about it by now. Her less rational, but defensively cautious, side was nonetheless still aware that Bett was the kind of calculatingly twisted individual who might keep his powder dry – and his transgressor in excruciating suspense – before finally meting out punishment just when she thought she was in the clear.

Up until then, Marledoq had borne no consequences, least of all the ones she'd bargained on. Yeah, why wasn't that a surprise. She'd been way too eager to grab at the bait, and once the deal was struck had thereafter been more worried about how she was going to pull off her side of it than about whether she was ever likely to see the reciprocal back-end. Man, did she ever walk into that with her pants down and her wallet open. She'd known it, truly, deep down: face it, girl, when she went to that hand-over she'd have been surprised if she was sent away with anything more than 'Thanks' and 'I'll call you'. But still she'd needed to try. Maybe it was an act of faith and maybe it was just an act of defiance, but she'd been compelled to give it a shot.

And she'd done it, too. That was what made her feel so dumb about walking away empty-handed. She'd been smart enough to acquire the files, but not smart enough to make the most of it once she had them. Why did she just cough up like a good little girl? Why didn't she play hard, or even halfway cute? 'Sure, I got the memory stick, but you don't get your hands on it until I see something more than a promise in return.'

Yeah, right. Like she could have pulled that shit off. He'd have laughed in her face, then probably killed her and raided her apartment to get what he needed. In that respect, she was actually kind of relieved that nothing further had come of it, that it was over and she wasn't going to hear from him again. She had no idea who she was dealing with – or even what his name was, or how he knew what he did about her. From the moment she agreed to steal the files, she had a real sense of getting in over her head, and, coming from someone who worked with Bett, that was saying something.

So she hadn't played hard and she hadn't played cute, but she hadn't played it entirely stupid either. She didn't give up the stick before making copies of the files, albeit as much out of habit as any kind of strategic thinking. Lex was an obsessive when it came to backing up data, and the harder it had been to

70

create or acquire something, the more insurance she required against it being wiped. Given what she'd gone through to swipe the Marledoq files, there was no way she was going to entrust their integrity to a flimsy USB stick. She'd copied the portable memory to her laptop immediately when she got back on the chopper, then transferred the data to the PC in her apartment as soon as she got home.

It had just been a matter of back-up, nothing more under-hand, and nothing he hadn't anticipated anyway.

'I've no way of knowing whether you've copied these files and you've no way of proving you haven't,' he said. 'But if you do have copies, I'd advise you to erase them right away and to do so without looking at them. What's on them won't mean much to you anyway, but as I always say, what you don't know, you can't be tortured to reveal.'

She hadn't examined them, not even the DivX audio-visual files, not having needed any dire warnings to reason that it was best for her own protection to be only the courier. She was para-noid enough about saying something that would give her away to Bett, a danger that would be greatly exacerbated by a burden of knowledge she wasn't supposed to have. One wrong word – or rather one informed word – and she might have a lot of explaining to do.

Nor had she felt remotely comfortable about storing this stuff on her hard drive at home, despite the data being re-encrypted, the file-extensions altered to disguise their nature and the whole cache buried somewhere so deep in the hierarchy that nobody would ever stumble across them unless they really knew what they were doing. Erasing the files seemed like the most logical and sensible thing to do because, once they were gone, so was the evidence of what she'd done, meaning she could draw a line under the whole thing.

However, logic and sense were not enough to overcome Lex's instinct and compulsion: when it came to data, she only erased what she was sure she'd never need again, which had thus far included only mislabelled MP3s and emails offering to make her penis twice as long. For Christ's sake, she still had a CD up on a shelf, full of save-game files so she could pick up where she left off if she ever felt like reinstalling *Doom II*. There was no way she was trashing the Marledoq files for the sake of most probably only fleeting peace of mind.

There was a compromise: if she wouldn't be remotely comfortable storing the files locally, then she would be comfortable storing the files remotely. She copied them to an FTP server and committed its address to memory, before wiping all trace of the server and the Marledoq files from her system. After that they were out of sight and increasingly out of mind.

Until Bett rang the doorbell.

'Grab what you need – absolute basics and essentials,' he said, once she'd sufficiently recovered from her shock to step aside and let him stride through the door into her hall. 'Something's come up, time-sensitive. Rebekah's prepping the Little Prince.'

'Do I need overnight stuff? I mean, like, how long?' she managed to mumble.

'Just put on something you didn't sleep in and bring whatever brain capacity isn't currently online, which doesn't appear to be much. Come on.'

'I'll be right there,' she said, going to the bedroom to change her underwear and pull on a fresh T-shirt and some jeans. She was indeed still wearing what she'd slept in last night, or fairer to say she'd slept for a while in what she was wearing when she started work. 'I just need a second,' she called out. 'I didn't know you were coming. Why didn't you page me?'

'I did,' he replied, with testily over-pronounced patience. 'Twice. After that, I had ascertained you were likely to be Glasgow Coma Scale four in front of that monitor and was on the verge of calling Armand instead, but as you were the first person I thought of when this thing came up, I set off in the hope of having greater success via your doorbell. For your information, you had approximately twenty more seconds before I kicked the door in and dragged you physically away from the computer.'

'Sorry, sir. It was the Lisbon project. I figured out a way to get beyond this impasse between—'

'Relevance suspended. Get your laptop. We're going back to Deimos.'

That last word echoed around Lex's head as she descended the stairs and followed Bett out to the street, where his Porsche was waiting. She'd no idea what this was about yet, and no rational reason, therefore, to make any assumptions, but merely hearing the name again was enough to unsettle her. Marledoq hadn't gone away. She may have cached the evidence and covered her connection to it, but there was no way of knowing what might have been set in motion when she handed over those files.

Bett's other remarks did little to quell her unease, and she was wary of how they piqued her curiosity. *You were the first person I thought of when this thing came up.* Why, she wondered, though her desire to vocalise this question was tempered by the returning fear that in doing so she might give something away. Would it sound strangely defensive for her to ask this, or would a lack of curiosity be more suspicious?

She wasn't cut out for bare-faced deceit. Stealth and subterfuge, sure thing, but not this. Trying to remember what ought to be natural, what she should or shouldn't appear to know, was never something she'd enjoyed much of a facility for. Not offline, anyway.

Happily, Bett saved her from making the decision; less happily, his words did anything but allay her anxieties.

'We're not going back to Marledoq itself,' he explained, pulling away on to the quiet, narrow street, 'but to Chassignan, where a lot of the workers live. However, the job should nonetheless provide you with an opportunity to redeem your little lapse there in December.'

'Yes, sir,' she said, as neutrally as her acting talents would allow, then remained silent, not because she reasoned it the best policy, but because she'd be struggling to keep the tremble from her voice if she said anything else.

This was one occasion when it was definitely the right stance to sound like she knew what he was referring to, even though she didn't. If by her lapse he meant her spot of privateering, then it was wisest to play it straight and thus play it down. 'Oh yes, that, sir. I was wondering when you'd bring it up.' But realistically, he wouldn't be this calm if that was what he was talking about. Not unless he was being truly, dispassionately sadistic, a thought too frightening to contemplate. Her stilted answer precluded finding out what other lapse he could mean, but to do else would alert him that there was more than one lapse to consider; or, almost as suicidal, suggest she couldn't immediately think of any flaw in her performance that she needed to make up for.

They arrived in Chassignan a few hours later, Rebekah on air-chauffeur duty and evidently not much else given that Bett had begun briefing Lex in the passenger cabin and thus excluded their pilot from the discussion. Lex lapped up the information, sparse as it turned out to be, because every detail was further reassurance that Bett's agenda was something other than that which she feared.

'One of their staff has gone missing,' he said. 'And not the janitor, as I'm sure you can guess.'

Bett told her the name and she nodded, disguising the fact that it meant nothing to her. This in itself was not significant. Names were seldom the thing that stuck about people Lex met; stories, yeah, mannerisms, sure, hair, relative height. Not names. Everybody had one. Online handles were a different story, because at first they were all you had to remember someone by, but out in the Big Room, other aspects usually proved more memorable. In this case, then, it was no surprise she was drawing a blank. She'd only been to Marledoq for less than two hours three months ago, and as her principal interaction with most employees had been shooting them with tranquilliser darts, none of them had much time to make an impression, far less tell her their names.

Except one. Ah. And now she had it: not just who Bett was talking about, but what her 'lapse' had been. The feeling of relief – that he meant the lab-geek who'd got the drop on her – lasted for roughly the time it took to remember why the guy had been able to catch her off guard.

'He's in Research and Development, presumably working on something rather important. In my experience, there are few companies sufficiently concerned about employee welfare as to bring in professional help when one of their wage-slaves takes an unannounced mental-health day, and weapons manufacturers would be well down that list. If he was replaceable, they'd already be hiring.'

'So how missing is missing? Has he been gone long?'

'Details are sketchy, and I wouldn't expect them to get much clearer any time soon. What you'll have to keep in mind throughout this business is that we are dealing with the arms industry. These people are secretive and disingenuous when they're asking you to pass the milk over breakfast. Just because they need our help and they're paying us doesn't mean they'll actually tell us what we need to know in order to get the job done.'

'And why do they need us to get the job done? I'm guessing they don't want the police involved—'

'Very good, you're learning.'

'But this isn't exactly our speciality either.'

'Quite. The police won't get involved in a missing-person case unless there's firm evidence of criminal activity, and if there is firm evidence of criminal activity, you can be damn sure Industries Deimos won't want the police getting involved. They came to us because we are a known quantity. We have a relationship with them and they trust us. Two seconds to identify the error in that statement.'

'Arms companies trust no one.'

'Correct. So in this context, by trust I mean they believe they can control our involvement and remunerate us sufficiently to guarantee our discretion after the fact.'

'And would the cache of gizmos we stole from them in December for Som to play around with constitute a down payment on this remuneration?'

'Not as far as Deimos are aware. The loss of such items merely highlighted the prevalence and ease of pilfering from the facility under such lax security conditions.'

Lex blanked out the more paranoid interpretations of this remark.

'I guess they wouldn't have called if they knew otherwise,' she said, thinking of the true extent of that night's theft.

'Oh, they might, they might. In the grand scheme, quite probably. If they needed us enough, they wouldn't let something as trivial as that get in the way. And they do need us. However, the main reason they've come to us pertains to the main thing we need to know and the last thing they're going to tell us.'

'Which would be what?'

'Whatever they're afraid of. Locating a missing person is, as you said, not our speciality. So I'd be surprised if Deimos haven't also engaged the services of others whose forte it most certainly is; freelance investigators, maybe the odd cop who's on back-handers. But I would predict that tracking down the missing scientist will prove less than half the battle. They came to us because they suspect that even once located, their quarry won't be easily retrieved. And retrieving what is guarded and hidden, my dear Alexis, most definitely *is* our speciality.'

They landed in a field outside of the village, and were met by Nicholas Willis, who'd been waiting for them by a large silver Mercedes. Willis was a tall, gaunt, middle-aged guy, bald of pate with trimmed patches of white hair above his ears. He was dressed in a suit and a greatcoat, but Lex pictured him wearing a cravat and frilly cuffs on his days off. He looked like 'Old Money', as her monetarily preoccupied (and not a little snobbish) grandmother would have approvingly observed.

Rebekah killed the engines but stayed with the helicopter while Lex followed Bett to the car. Bett got into the passenger seat, Willis chivalrously opening the rear driver's-side door for Lex. Bett and Willis exchanged pleasantries but avoided the matter in hand, like they didn't want to prejudice the experiment. Willis would have already told Bett all he could, or all he was prepared to, leastways, so there was nothing much to add prior to seeing the apartment. They spoke in English, Willis sounding even more Old Money than he looked.

Some people's accents altered in response to certain others': hardening and running to the colloquial, softening to accommodate an unaccustomed ear, stiffening in formality. Sometimes it was a relaxation, other times a courtesy; it could be a posture or a statement, and it could be entirely subconscious. Bett's accent did not alter one micro-nuance. This at least provided some suggestion that English wasn't his first language, but no further clues to his provenance. Chalk another one up to Mr Impervious.

The journey took less than three minutes. Chassignan was a pleasant but mousy little place, not so much sleepy as in chronic stasis. A small gas station was the only immediate exemplar of twentieth-century construction on the tree-lined main street, otherwise flanked by tall, well-maintained and uniformly shuttered apartment buildings. Lex's own place dated from the early nineteenth century, and these looked of a similar period or older. Closer examination of a few shop windows broke the fairy tale spell: recent DVD posters in the tabac, Microsloth and Macintrash logos looking out through the glass of an internet café. They had broadband ISPs and they had Vin Diesel flicks, so the village knew there was good progress and bad progress, but she couldn't imagine much had really changed around here in a couple of centuries. Had to be an abduction, she thought, sarcastically. How could anybody leave all this?

Fleming's apartment was one street back from the main drag. It was on the fourth floor of five (or the *troisième étage*, the way the Europeans counted it), up a bright and airy stairwell with broad stone steps and wide, solid landings. Willis led the way on long, spindly legs, the hard leather soles of his shoes tapping loudly on the stone with each step. They looked and sounded expensive; the gait and footwear of a man unafraid to announce his approach. Lex glanced at her scuffed training shoes, their impacts dampened almost apologetically by chunky man-made grips. There was a good reason people called them sneakers.

Bett walked at the rear on Doc Marten patent Airware. The soles cushioned his steps, but his frame carried enough muscle for his footfalls to reverberate with a formidable sense of presence she could feel as well as hear. He was looking around as he ascended, scanning, analysing, evaluating, filing. Lex knew she could look in the same places and see no more than a staircase, which made her wonder what use Bett expected her to be when they reached the flat.

Willis pulled a set of keys from his greatcoat pocket, delicately undoing the lock before turning the handle with a grimace, as though he was opening a wound.

'Where did you get the keys?' Bett asked.

Willis stepped aside from the door.

'Oh, from our property manager. It's a new lock. He put it in to replace the other one, which was ruined.'

Bett had a look at the doorframe. 'It wasn't forced,' he observed.

'No, drilled, he said. Drilled through.'

'And you told me on the phone that nobody in the building heard anything?'

'Property manager believes it was a . . .' Willis mimed turning a crank. 'You know?'

'Yes. Stealthier, but slow. You own the building?'

'We own the apartment. We have a few dotted around. If you want to headhunt gifted staff, you have to be able to accommodate them immediately. Some stay just until they find a place themselves, but others . . .'

'How long was Fleming here, then?'

'Two years. Shall we . . . ?' Willis invited, with visible reluctance and distaste.

They stepped into the small hallway, which was little more than a conduit between three rooms, the largest of which was an open-plan kitchen and living area.

'Have you been in here before?' Bett asked. 'I mean, since . . .'

'Yes. We tried not to disturb anything. I don't find it particularly comfortable, to be frank, being in someone else's home without his say-so, but the buck stops here, as they say.'

Lex could sympathise. It was not a comfortable place to be. The feng shui was all off. The sofa, for instance, was at a psychologically jarring angle (upright was more calming), and, in her judgement, pot plants worked best when they weren't lying sideways across the floor.

'Alexis, the camera,' Bett reminded her. She pulled it from a pouch on her laptop satchel and began taking shots of the scene, snapping as she picked her footsteps carefully amid the mess. The only clutter-free areas were the shelves and bookcases, because all of their contents had been scattered about the floor. CDs lay fanned-out like fallen dominoes, next to books, DVDs and magazines. Pictures had been pulled from the walls and left on the floor, though Lex noted that the glass was intact on each of them. The only wall-hung decorations remaining were glossy pin-ups in two clusters: one in the kitchen and one next to the computer. Soccer players, tour posters, some movie stills.

A flat-screen monitor sat on a desk by the farther of two broad windows, the PC itself nestling underneath, surrounded by piles of blank and used printer paper, stacked like kindling. A pale green light indicated activity.

The kitchen area was a real treat. Rice, pasta, flour, salt, breakfast cereals, washing powder and dishwasher tablets had been emptied out on to the floor and their containers discarded on top. Pots and pans had been pulled from cupboards and now lolled like grounded ships upon the banks of powder and grain. Supermarket ready meals lay around the foot of the fridge-freezer, contents spilling out where the plastic film had broken, their cardboard sleeves dotted randomly about the floor. Four bottles lay undisturbed on a wine rack atop the work surface next to the sink, and Lex noticed also that no crockery had been broken.

In the compact little bathroom, the contents of a mirrored cabinet had been dumped into the basin directly below, bottles of shampoo and shower gel tipped into the bath. Again, the shelves and surfaces were clear, including the cistern lid, which was slightly askew.

The bedroom was the same deal. The place had been tossed, not trashed.

'How did you find out he was missing?' Bett asked.

'Didn't you ask me this before?'

'For the benefit of Miss Richardson here, and to refresh my memory.'

'Rather undramatic, initially. He failed to turn up for work, although that was fairly remarkable for him, I suppose. He'd seldom lost a day before that. When the road has looked like being closed in the winter, he's often slept at the lab because he'd rather be stranded that end. When he didn't call in by midday, somebody phoned here, to no reply. Couldn't get him on his mobile phone, either. Then the property manager got a call from one of the neighbours who'd noticed the door was ajar and the lock damaged. She'd rung the bell, then stuck her head inside when there was no answer. When she saw what she saw . . .'

'And you came here yourself? Right away?'

'I realised that Mr Fleming could have been incommunicado because he was with the police, reporting a burglary, but if that wasn't the case, I knew there was no time to lose. I had to see for myself.'

'Who spoke to the neighbours? You said nobody heard anything.'

'I did. I mean, I didn't go round the whole building, just, you know, next door, above and below. Nothing.'

'What did you tell the woman who noticed the door? She'll be wondering why she hasn't seen any police, to say nothing of not seeing her neighbour.'

'I think she thought I *was* the police, to be honest.'

'You didn't tell her you were,' Bett said, with a note of caution.

'Oh, no. I see where you're going. No. I just didn't tell her I wasn't, if you know what I mean.'

'Sure.'

Bett knelt down and picked about among the mess. He opened a couple of CD cases, revealing the silver discs to be in place within. Then he lifted up one of the pictures, a photo collage.

'This is Fleming, right?'

'Yes. That's him with the little girl.'

'Not his, I assume.'

'No. Family.'

'Can I take this?'

'Yes, certainly. I mean . . . I don't like giving . . .'

'I understand. But so will Mr Fleming.'

'Indeed. I've also got some personnel file photos of him in the car.'

'Alexis, can you have a look at the computer?' he ordered.

'Yes, sir,' she assented, her gratitude at having a recognised purpose only marginally diminished by having no idea what she should be looking for.

Functionality would be a start, she decided, so she gave the mouse a wiggle to see whether the system would wake up or required a full boot. It proved to be the latter; the absence of fan noise had suggested this, but you could never assume. Not every machine was cursed to sound like a Spitfire readying for take-off, just every machine she'd owned. She paused over the switch, considering whether there might be a logic-bomb in the start-up folder, primed to trash the hard disk whenever the machine was turned on; in fact merely booting the thing up normally would obscure a few of the previous user's tracks. Instead, she undertook a little hardware surgery, connecting her laptop to lift an unadulterated image of the hard disk.

That done, in the absence of any specific request from the boss, Lex went about some basics. 'First thing to remark is that the machine is intact,' she told Bett, hoping he'd respond with some form of cue. 'They didn't smash it and they didn't steal it.'

Bett said nothing, simply went about his recce; stepping slowly and precisely around the room, stopping to examine certain items, sometimes just staring. It looked like detection by osmosis.

Lex scoped the system. She checked the boot log first to see when the machine had last been up and for how long, then began looking deeper. The first thing to stick out was the directory access records, denoting which folders had been opened during the last session. The answer was most of them, right down almost every branch of the hierarchy, even into the murkiest depths of application sub-directory temp folders. This was not indicative of normal usage. If it was your own machine and you couldn't remember where a file was, you'd use a search facility to locate it; someone would only go through the folders manually if they weren't sure what it was they were specifically looking *for*. This was the electronic equivalent of all the open drawers and cleared shelves elsewhere in the apartment.

'It's been sifted,' she announced. 'Systematically, from top to bottom.'

'Care to hazard a guess at what they were looking for?' Bett asked Willis.

'If you mean do I think it's to do with Marledoq, then no. He wouldn't have material relating to his work here.'

'Wouldn't or shouldn't?'

'Both. I mean, yes, theoretically there's no reason why he might not have some files relating to work, but, well, the thing with Ross is that he's seldom out of the place. If he wants to work on something, night times or weekends, he stays on-site. He was there the night you hit the place, remember?'

'I understand. But that doesn't mean that what they were looking for wasn't related to Marledoq. Someone interested in Ross's work wouldn't necessarily know whether he had material at home.'

'My take is that he didn't,' Lex offered, warding off thoughts of a more successful theft from Marledoq of work-related data. 'And I'd say that whatever they were looking for, they struck out. This thing's just a media toaster.'

'Would you translate, please,' Bett insisted, 'for those of us with a less neological vocabulary.'

'Fleming uses this thing for comms and entertainment, nothing else. And he doesn't do a lot of that either. This machine must be two years old if it's a day and yet the hard drive's only about a quarter full. Mostly vanilla apps—'

'Alexis,' Bett warned.

'Standard retail applications. The bulk of the used disk space is JPEGs, MP3s and AV . . . sorry, that's picture, music and video file formats, sir. Going by what's on the floor, the music's mostly ripped from these CDs, so the PC's just a conduit for a portable player. The majority of the video files are archived webcam captures; after that it's downloaded clips, mainly soccer, going by the tags, and they're all in the temporary cache, nothing older than thirty days.'

'Why?'

'Files in the temp cache are automatically wiped after a while so you don't end up with twenty gigs of last year's web content clogging up your HD. Default setting is thirty days. It tells me this guy doesn't tinker much with this thing, just uses it to keep in touch. He's got a mike here and a webcam above the monitor, see? Archived webcam captures are all labelled the same: "mich" then a date.'

'His sister's name is Michelle,' Willis informed them.

'Let's see one,' said Bett, eyeing the photo collage he'd lifted.

Lex opened the most recent file. It was small spec but decent frame-rate, though no sound. It showed a young woman sitting with a toddler in her lap, a slightly older child standing beside her. She urged the older kid to wave, which she did. Junior waved too, though he was looking at his sister instead of the camera.

'Moving postcards from home: sis, niece and nephew. It's the same kids in most of his picture files, too.'

'And you've transferred *all* these files to that laptop?' Bett asked.

'Yes, sir. They took up less than a quarter of his HD space.

I'll remove the hard drive itself too. That way I can check for residual data from files that might have been erased.'

'You can do that?' Willis asked.

'Sure,' she told him. 'But I wouldn't hold out for any big secrets. Like I said, it's a media toaster. This thing's on light duties. He doesn't even have any games apart from vendor pre-installs.'

'You'll have to forgive Alexis,' Bett said. 'English isn't her first language. Go ahead, remove the hard drive. I'll have a look on the laptop during the flight back. Mr Willis, anything else you have by way of background would be useful. The more we know about him, the better chance we have of working out where he might have gone.'

'That's assuming where he's gone is his own choice,' Willis suggested.

'Everything I've seen so far points to flight rather than capture,' Bett replied. 'Despite the mess, there's little to suggest any of it was the result of a struggle. No blood, no breakages. If there'd been a fight in here, one of the neighbours would have heard something, to say nothing of taking an unwilling subject down three flights of stairs.'

'There wouldn't be a fight if they took him at gunpoint.'

'And yet if they took him at gunpoint, they wouldn't have needed to rifle through the place looking for whatever they were after. They could simply have threatened to shoot him unless he told them where it was.'

'How do we know it's "they"?' Lex asked. 'Or is that just a figure of speech?'

'It's they,' Bett answered. 'Two different sets of footprints spreading that mess from the kitchen floor. Well, four sets, actually, but I'm eliminating the ones Mr Willis's shoes left on a previous visit and the ones you made when you were taking pictures. There were two of them, and Fleming wasn't here when they searched this place. Abduction, whether at gunpoint or not, is about getting in and getting out as quickly and quietly as possible. Whoever was in here took their time. They were careful, they were quiet and they were thorough. They looked behind paintings, inside CD cases, they even searched rice and flour hoppers. Someone spent how long looking through his computer?'

'Last session was forty-eight minutes.'

'Time they knew they had, because they weren't expecting Mr Fleming to walk in and disturb them. They knew he was gone. They may well have been coming to abduct him, and most plausibly at gunpoint, but when they arrived, they discovered he'd been one step ahead. He knew they were coming for him. It could have been mere moments' notice – maybe something fortuitous he saw or heard – or it could have been hours; but the main thing is, he knew they weren't there to sell the *Watchtower*. Ross Fleming ran, and not to the police. We need to work out where, but equally important, we need to work out from whom.'

Bett looked down at the photo collage, then around the diligently strewn chaos of the room, before zeroing in on Willis again.

'If I were to ask you,' he said, 'just off the top of your head, worst-case scenario or merely the first thing that leaps to mind: what would you guess this is about?'

Willis paused, sighing with discomfiture. 'I . . . I'm sorry, I hate this kind of speculation. It seems so disrespectful, like we're working for the tabloids, digging up dirt.'

Lex caught a concealed glance from Bett, a brief roll of the eyes conveying a weary but arch frustration at this squeamishness. Here was a man whose company made instruments of violence and destruction, recoiling from a task because it seemed impolite. Yes, Willis and her grandmother would definitely have got along.

'Worst-case scenario?' Willis resumed. 'I suppose that would have to be that he's been murdered. If they knew he was already dead, they'd be guaranteed all the time they needed to search his apartment.'

'But why?' Bett pressed, forcing him back to the point.

'I really don't know. The first thing that comes to mind is, well, drugs, I suppose. I hate to say it, and it's probably just one generation's prejudice.'

'And is there anything more than prejudice to support that notion?'

'Not specifically in Ross's case. But I'm not entirely naive in these matters. I've seen a lot of very dynamic, very driven young people working with us, working extremely long hours, sometimes in isolation. Stimulants are not unprecedented.'

'Is Fleming well paid? I mean, he doesn't appear to have

much of a social life, so would a speed habit have him in that much hock?'

'I can't say I know the going rate for any given controlled substance, but you make a fair point. I can't imagine him racking up debts to dangerous people without giving off signals that something was amiss.'

'Drug addicts can be most resourceful at concealing their problems,' Bett observed, 'but I can't envisage the local whizz dealer quietly and meticulously doing this to the place over an unpaid debt. "Pay up or we de-alphabetise your CDs." Nor would he be likely to turn up any unused drugs or unpaid cash inside Fleming's My Documents folder. So rack your brains a little harder, Mr Willis, dig deep and dig dirty. What do you think this is about? What do you *fear* this is about?'

Willis sighed again.

'I fear it's about work. *That*'s my worst-case scenario and I'd prefer it to transpire otherwise. I'm aware of how selfish that sounds; but if we're digging dirt, then I suppose I shouldn't flinch from appearing grubby myself. I'll admit it, I'd be relieved if this was to do with some matter personal only to Mr Fleming, though that wouldn't make him any easier to replace.'

'What was he working on?'

Willis paused, wincing a little. 'I know this is frustrating, but that's not something I can freely comment upon.'

'Can you comment on whether it would make him any kind of target? Can you comment on whether someone might believe he had materials or information that he could pass on via bribery or coercion?'

'I can say this much: I brought you people in last December to tighten up security at Marledoq precisely to prevent those possibilities. Deimos is not a gun manufacturer launching a new line of automatic pistols. When you're in the business of innovation, there is nothing more potentially damaging than industrial espionage. It's not just that we can't afford to suffer the theft of blueprints or prototypes: it's that we can't afford to let anyone know what we're developing full stop. If this was the pharmaceutical industry, what do you think the other drug companies would do if they found out we were working on a cure for an ailment they sold remedies for?'

'You're saying what Mr Fleming was working on poses a threat to the arms industry?' Bett asked, with a quiet calm that Lex had learned to recognise as masking grave concern.

'Of course not. But we're developing a number of projects, any one of which might pose a threat to someone's profit margin, and this is not an industry renowned for its scrupulous practices in defending the bottom line. I don't wish to impugn your own integrity, Mr Bett, but the fact is, this kind of information is so sensitive that I can't tell you what Fleming was working on just in case his disappearance turns out *not* to be related to it. However, if some of that information is already out of the box, then yes, bribery and coercion might potentially have been applied to procure materials and information, and yes, he is potentially a target. As would be anyone who got between him and his pursuers.'

'Which is really why you came to us,' Bett stated. 'You need people who can look for Fleming but who are capable of watching their own backs while they're about it.'

'Yes. That and the fact that if this is what it looks like, then it's down to a breach of *your* security system. I'd need to check the fine print of the guarantee, but—'

'User error isn't covered, Mr Willis. No security set-up can offer contingency against individual indiscretions on the inside. If sensitive information got out of Marledoq, it wasn't because an intruder walked in and took it. For one thing, the intruder would need to know there was something specific worth looking for in the first place.'

At this point, Lex was grateful to be under the desk disconnecting the hard drive, her colour-drained face and reflexively gawping eyes hidden from view. Up until then, she hadn't been absolutely sure. Marledoq was a huge place. Fleming had already noticed something was amiss and had set off the alarms, so he could have tailed her, or been hiding out near where she happened to appear: just because he'd snuck up on her there didn't mean that was specifically his lab or his machine, she'd told herself. But now she could have no reasonable doubt that it *had* been his machine, and that this was therefore the second time she was swiping data belonging to the same man.

'We'll track down Fleming for you,' Bett assured Willis. 'But in the meantime you'd better ask yourself who knew enough to set this in motion. If you've got a leak, then you'd better find it fast, and don't trust anyone until then.'

'I won't, Mr Bett. I never do. Occupational hazard, I suppose.'

'Personally, I'd classify it under Health and Safety.'

Lex couldn't decide whether it was scarier flying with her eyes open or closed. Open, she had the full benefit of watching the sea pass so close beneath that they had to be leaving a wake; closed, there were the combined anxieties of vividly imagining the same sight anyway and of not being able to see disaster coming. Like it would make any difference.

They were heading for a trawler, collision course, she was certain. She assumed Rebekah could see it with her bare eyes as well as with the radar, but she didn't appear to have imminent plans for evasive action. Lex wanted to say something; actually, she wanted to scream something, but could tell from Rebekah's minutely detectable smirk that this might be a counter-productive action.

They passed directly over the trawler, which turned out to be further below than Lex had gauged, but not by much.

'Rebekah,' she said with Bett-like overstated calm, 'I just saw what that fisherman was having for lunch. He had a mug of coffee and a triangular sandwich. I could *see* what shape his sandwich was. We are too fucking low.'

'Alexis, you have got to chill,' Rebekah responded, grinning with despicable pleasure at her passenger's dismay. 'Did I hit anything yet? Did we ditch and I missed it?'

'No, but you'd only need to do it once.'

'Believe me, I've flown lower than this at, like, five times the speed.'

Lex turned her head to stare at Rebekah, fully taking her eyes off the water for the first time since they left dry land.

'What the hell kind of helicopter flies five times as fast as this?'

'Oh, it wasn't a helicopter. I guess it might not be the best time to admit this, but I'm not actually a helicopter pilot. Not licensed, anyway. I mean, I can fly this thing; hell, *you* could fly this thing.'

'So what are you licensed to fly? Oh shit,' she said, making a connection. 'Fighter planes. You're USAF, aren't you?'

'Well, that's my personal business, isn't it,' Rebekah stated, reminding Lex of the unwritten protocol.

'I'm sorry.'

'It's okay. But for what it's worth, I'm not USAF.'

Rebekah had grown considerably less withdrawn as the months passed, though she remained the most private when it came to what had brought her under Bett's wing. Everyone else was periodically given to less guarded allusions or even, occasionally, outright admissions, but, to be fair, these had all come after having been around a lot longer. Lex, for one, had taken her own time to accept that it would make no odds to her fortunes or reputation if the others knew of her place in the annals of either hackerdom or international diplomacy. However, even after reaching that understanding, she'd still felt protective of her past for reasons she couldn't quite nail down. Perhaps it was simply due to it being the episode that had made her most scared in her entire life, and exposing it at all tapped into a little of that fear.

Rebekah was markedly more relaxed after Marledoq, her first real mission, though it had hardly been the most taxing exercise. Perhaps it had helped for her to have a defined, indeed indispensable, role, in order to feel she was somewhere she could belong. She'd grown conspicuously less jumpy about overhead aircraft too, a trait Lex had considered all the more curious once she learned what the role of Transport Manager truly entailed. Lex had come to realise that this nervy reaction was not in fact startlement at the sound of the engines, but simply that the sound acted as a prompt to be looking over her shoulder. Like Lex, and now like Ross Fleming, Rebekah had run from something, and in the place she'd run from there must have been airplanes.

It wasn't, she now insisted, the US Air Force. So where the hell else would she be flying jets at five times the speed of this chopper?

Then Lex remembered some of the illicit data Bett had taught her to sift for. A Harrier jump jet had gone missing, the US considering the embarrassment more costly than the hardware, and thus concealing the incident. It had been a few months back, just about the time, now she came to think of it, that Bett introduced his latest recruit.

Jump jets flew off aircraft carriers.

I'm not USAF.

No, girl. You're a swabby. And you're damned well used to flying above water.

Lex sighed upon making this deduction, her posture slumping as the tension lifted a little.

'You finally chilling?' Rebekah asked, taking note.

'No. I'm practising holding my breath for when we inevitably splash down and go under.'

'Come on, admit it, you're starting to dig the ride. Beats the shit out of Space Mountain, don't it?'

'I think I'd be enjoying it more if we were on the way back.'

'I hear ya,' Rebekah replied. 'But you need to chill about that too. Bett's got faith in you, and he doesn't strike me as leaving much to chance and just *hoping* you do okay.'

'Sure, but that would be a bigger vote of confidence if I thought Bett's judgement was flawless.'

'You think his judgement is flawed because he has a higher estimation of you than you have of yourself?'

'It's not his estimation of *me* that I've got reservations about. And I don't believe I'm the only one. Nobody's said anything, but . . .'

'But they're thinking it, I know,' Rebekah agreed, nodding. 'He's one hell of a smart guy, and I'd hate to have him as an enemy. Jeez, being on his side is hard enough. But yeah, I'll hold my hand up, I've got my concerns about this one. He's normally got all the bases covered, so I can't help worrying that this time he's putting all his eggs in one basket.'

Lex managed a small laugh at this.

'What's funny?'

'Oh, just an alternative perspective. Remember what I was telling you about the Airplane Rule?'

'Yeah, two engines means twice as much can go wrong.'

'Well, there's a corresponding argument that the best plan *is* to put all your eggs in one basket – you just gotta make sure it's a really *good* basket.'

'So maybe Bett's judgement isn't so flawed after all.'

'We'll soon see.'

She remembered Bett sitting opposite her in the cabin most

of the flight home, poring over the laptop like it was a dossier, formulating, processing. If he'd been a computer, his drive access light would have been blinking faster than the beat of a hummingbird's wings. Every so often he had a question, but it felt like he was accessing her just as functionally and impersonally as he was accessing Fleming's copied C-Drive; his own pronouncements not so much thinking out loud as the verbal equivalent of printing a hard copy of what his brain generated.

'Your take on Fleming,' he'd demanded, for instance.

'My . . . I . . .'

'Come on, first impressions, one word, no hesitation.'

'Okay, geek. Geek like me.'

'Geek. Nerd.'

'No, just geek. Geek isn't necessarily pejorative, in certain contexts. Nerd is.'

'Do geeks do a lot of drugs?'

'I'm not saying they don't, and I can't speak for the genus, but Fleming's drug of choice wasn't proscribed. You saw Chassignan, sir. You don't settle there for the nightlife. He's a lab-rat. He lives for work.'

'My thoughts too. So what else does a geek want? I'll rephrase that: what would tempt you enough to go behind my back in search of it?'

Lex's mouth fell open, but no words spilled out.

'Money?' he suggested, closing the trap door again.

'Two years in that little apartment? I didn't get a picture of a guy after a fast buck. He's young, driven, probably brilliant. Money would come in time.'

'Yes. Willis didn't tell us his salary, but, let's face it, it's the weapons business. You could say he's already sold out, and yet his motivations did not appear to be material. If he was trading secrets, it was coercion, not bribery. In which case, why not go to the police?'

Lex offered no answer, knowing none was being sought.

'Why did they shut down his PC?' Bett had later asked, yanking Lex back from window-staring introspection as to whether they could possibly get to the bottom of this without her own crucial role in it emerging.

'Huh?'

'Why bother? They didn't go putting anything back on shelves or in drawers, so why power down when they were done looking there?'

'To hide what they were looking for. Shutting down wipes certain temporary data from the OS, sorry, operating system. They went through the hierarchy manually, but, I'd guess, only after running automated searches. The keywords in those search strings would have been recoverable if they'd left the machine running.'

'And are they still recoverable? You said you could restore deleted files.'

'Sure,' she said. 'Of course, if you really want to know what they were looking for, the quickest solution would be to download the files from the FTP server where I stashed them,' she didn't add. Instead, she told him: 'They opened his email application and they checked through all recently generated text documents, too. They wanted to know who he'd been in touch with and what about.'

'They won't have found much, going by what I've seen. Willis can rest easy about that. It was, as you say, a comms device, a media . . . what was it?'

'Toaster. Though, to be honest, until I can get a closer look at this hard drive, we really won't know what they found. And even if I recover deleted files, there'll be no way of knowing who deleted them: Fleming or his pursuers.'

'Granted, but I think this has to be as much about the man as the motive. They were after more than secrets. He wouldn't run just to keep Marledoq data out of their hands. Otherwise the first place he'd run to would be his employers.'

'Unless he got into this mess because he'd been up to something he didn't think his employers would be too happy about,' Lex suggested, with acutely vivid personal insight.

'Well worth bearing in mind, yes. But his value to his employers is key. Willis came down to handle everything himself, didn't delegate. That should tell us something. He didn't come out and say that Fleming was irreplaceable, but I'll wager it's close to the truth. The data probably isn't worth much without the man. To come back to Willis's pharmaceuticals analogy, if it was my drug firm whose remedy was going to be rendered obsolete, I wouldn't resort to dirty tactics merely to halt its development. If I was going that far, I'd want to steal the development for myself outright.'

'And to do that you'd need more than the secret formula.'

'Call it extreme headhunting. And the inducements won't be options on stock and the promise of a corner office. They'll be the option to stay alive and the promise of removing the electrodes.'

'Shit. I guess we'd better make damn sure we get to him first.'

'Indeed. And make no mistake, Alexis, we'll be competing with some very dangerous people to do so. People who already have a head start, so we're going to need an edge of our own.'

Lex wondered what could give them an edge against people Bett described as dangerous. She'd never heard him say that before, no matter what they were dealing with. These people are organised, he'd warn. Ruthless, paranoid, trigger-happy, efficient, vigilant, well-trained. Never dangerous. Given that he was easily the scariest person she had ever met, Lex seriously didn't like the idea of taking on anyone he considered a worry. No shit, they'd want an edge.

She was going to ask what he had in mind, but knew that Bett was never inviting a cue. If he knew, he'd announce. He returned to his scrutiny of the laptop and the hard-copy files Willis supplied, nodding occasionally as he flicked through them, sometimes staring out of the window at the blue sky and the clouds below. Then, a while later, he looked up from his reflections and spoke.

'We're going to need to bring in a specialist.'

'In what?' she couldn't help but enquire. Given that they had computers, weapons, electronics, surveillance, air transport and God knows what else covered, she was genuinely puzzled as to what Bett thought they needed to 'outsource'.

'We need an operative with expert knowledge in the field,' he told her. 'Someone fearless, someone who can adapt and improvise, someone resourceful and cunning, stoical in the face of pain and danger, ruthlessly uncompromising in pursuit of the objective, and utterly merciless in eliminating anyone who stands in the way.'

'Tall order. Who do you have in mind?'

Ride, then

Jane looked at the woman before her: familiar, but not entirely recognisable, no stranger, but not a particularly welcome sight either. She couldn't honestly say who she was expecting, but was inevitably disappointed every time this hacket shambles showed up, and this hacket shambles showed up every time. Impostor. Where the hell did you come from? she wanted to ask her. What did you do with the girl who used to come around?

When did you last see her? the impostor would rightly reply. Was it recently?

No, she'd have to admit. It's been a while. So long, I can't remember.

There were ads all over the Sunday supplements boasting about the technological properties accommodated within flat-screen plasma tellies just a couple of inches deep, but they had a long way to go before they caught up with the average bathroom mirror. Hers was only half a centimetre thick, yet provided clarity of picture that was sharp to the point of cruelty, and boasted Residual Image Sustainment, a capability far in advance of anything Sony considered state-of-the-art. This was the feature whereby no matter how many times you looked at yourself, you saw the same face, apparently unaltered and unchanging over years and even decades. Unfortunately, this feature very occasionally went on the blink and the glass presented you with an image of someone far older than you were expecting, providing a startling comparison with the face you once knew. It never lasted for long, but when it happened, it reset the system and only showed you the older face from then on. You got used to that one, and the RIS meant the older face didn't appear to change much either, but this was merely a special effect. An optical illusion.

Jane looked at the greying hair, hanging dry and limp where it wasn't haphazardly kinked. She saw the deep-etched lines around her eyes and her mouth, once-taut skin draped gauntly over cheekbones like ill-worn upholstery. The mirror never showed this happening, merely proved that it had. She just couldn't remember when. Further down she saw off-white underwear that had been through the machine a thousand times with Tom's socks, the closest thing to intimacy between them in an age. Behind her on the bed lay trousers and a top that were among three outfits in permanent rotation, pulled from the wardrobe because they were the first to come to hand, eschewing conscious selection because that merely reminded her of the paucity of what she had to choose from.

Her hair was seriously in need of colouring and a whole lot more TLC besides. Merely some committed effort of a morning would be a start. Those straighteners Michelle had bought her for Christmas – she'd used them a couple of times over the holidays and had been pleased with the results, but they'd lain in a drawer since Ne'erday. It wasn't even like she could claim she was too busy or in a rush to get out of the door each day. There just never seemed any reason to make the effort, which was why her visits to the hairdresser had grown further and further apart. Who was going to notice? Not Tom, anyway. Once upon a time there'd been a punk named Blue Bell who dressed just for herself, but these days it seemed Jane Fleming was even less critical or at all noticing of her appearance than her husband.

There hadn't come a day when she consciously decided, sod it, I'm past caring about clothes and hairstyles and make-up, but the evidence suggested she'd reached that position nonetheless. She and Catherine used to have a good bitch about the Bothwell ladies of a certain age, with their panstick foundation, their gold shoes and their Couture d'Agneau designer suits, lunching in a tiny village whose main street nonetheless housed six hairdressers. Scornful of the aesthetic that equated all beauty with youth, Jane had always believed a woman should aspire to look good *at* her age, not *for* her age. The woman in the mirror, however, couldn't even charitably be described as looking either. Maybe she should embrace the future by investing in a twinset and pearls. At least it would be a consciously constructed image, not simply a pot-luck payout from the bedroom's MFI equivalent of a one-armed bandit.

If there was a human-interest upbeat kicker at the end of the mirror's daily bulletin, it was that what lay below the neck and under her clothes was in decent shape. This, she gloomily predicted, only meant she'd soon be one of those lean and bird-like old women rather than the round and dumpy model. Jane had always been skinny, her slimness accentuated by being comparatively tall, but her father always put her figure down to the fact that she 'couldn't sit at peace for five minutes', constantly driven by a compulsive, nervous energy to forever find something useful to be getting on with. And if there was nothing useful to be getting on with, she'd get on with something anyway, such as hoovering the hall carpet for the third time that day.

There was, however, a difference between being slim and being fit, as she'd learned the hard way when she joined a gym a couple of years back. She remembered thinking she was going to spew all over the lycra-wrapped-sinew-with-a-ponytail in front of her at that first aerobics session, and had been so sore in so many places afterwards that she'd been unable to eat more than a mouthful of dinner before retiring to bed for a painfully sleepless night. Catherine had bought her a month's trial subscription as a birthday present and, for a few days after, Jane had been thinking of polite ways to say thanks but no thanks with regard to joining her in long-term membership. But, once the aches subsided and she was satisfied she'd suffered no permanent harm, she found herself surprisingly determined to return, and persevered because she believed this was precisely the kind of thing she should be able to handle if she was indeed young enough to change her life.

She wasn't so sure she'd have made it back for that second session if she'd joined after learning that *us grannies ken the score*. But then maybe next time she thought of Margaret at the checkout, she ought to remind herself there were women and men ten years younger alongside her at the boxercise or body-pump classes each week, many of them visibly feeling the pace more than she was.

The slow-puncture to her pride in this particular achievement was that while it made her feel physically healthy, she nonetheless couldn't shake the lingering notion that you should be fit *for* something, rather than as an end in itself. Being more lithely capable of dusting in awkward spots, or being able to vault around kitchen units in order to avoid stepping on a newly mopped floor seemed a slight return for hours of arduous training.

Jane went into the kitchen and crouched down to have a look at what the fridge had to offer. There was some leftover pasta that would do; she only wanted a bite, as she was going to the gym and then on to a late lunch with Catherine at the Grape Vine. She stretched some cling film over the small bowl of penne, taking care to keep her fingers clear of the box's serrated plastic strip, one of the most highly lethal cutting edges known to man. It could slice effortlessly through human flesh, and in fact could probably saw through just about any material if properly applied. The only thing it wasn't much cop at cutting was cling film, but no design was ever perfect.

She placed the bowl into the microwave and gave it a spin on full power. God knows how anyone ever got by before these things. She thought of her mother's kitchen, everyone sitting down for a regimented meal because it only got served hot once, and, with a grimace, remembered oven-dried reheats (to say nothing of her older brothers eating the cold remnants of fish suppers washed down with Irn-Bru when they got up around noon after a late Saturday night). She wondered whether the Christian Right had ever pilloried the role of the microwave in disintegrating the nuclear family unit. Maybe they could boycott Comet in the name of Jesus, Mary and the *Daily Mail*.

Ross had explained to her how they worked, something to do with the microwaves causing water molecules to vibrate, but Jane reckoned she had her own, more practical command of the principle. As far as she could make out, the microwave oven super-heated crockery until it required asbestos gloves to touch it, and as a by-product of this process, any food on the said crockery would be warmed to just above room temperature.

She poured herself a glass of grapefruit juice and was reaching for the oven gloves when her doorbell rang. As she walked down the hall to answer it, she looked out of the front window through the open living-room door to see Michelle's Espace parked in front of the driveway. She also saw a black Vectra parked a few doors down on the other side of the street, the engine off but the driver still in his seat, looking at a folder or clipboard. She felt her hackles rise. She was sure she'd seen another one prowling around earlier, which was why she wanted to check outside before responding to the bell. Oily lizards asking you to change your gas billing to an electricity firm or vice versa. Very slimy, very persistent. 'So you're telling me you don't want to save money? Seems a bit daft to me,' one of them once said. She had come very close to heading back to the kitchen and fetching the basin full of dirty dishwater to chuck at him.

She opened the front door and was almost knocked down by the unexpected impact of Rachel diving into a hug around her thighs; unexpected because she should have been in nursery. Michelle was behind her, on the path, with Thomas in her arms. Jane reached out to take him for a kiss and a cuddle, but he shrank back and whimpered, as he did when he was out of sorts or just woken up. Michelle looked harassed, not managing much of a smile by way of a greeting.

'Gran!' Rachel shouted delightedly. 'Nursery's closed. Is that good?'

Jane laughed, but it didn't look good for Michelle.

'Come on in, all of you,' Jane said.

'I'm sorry, Mum, I'm in a bit of a guddle,' Michelle explained redundantly. 'They've had a burst pipe at the nursery. Just as well I was off today anyway – I was supposed to be taking Thomas to the dentist's and then to get his feet measured for new shoes. Turns out I'll be taking him to the doctor's as well. He's a wee bit hot, just not himself. Probably only a wee bug, but with us going away at the weekend, I want to make sure he's not brewing anything nasty.'

'Do you want me to take him? It's no bother.'

'Not at all. You've seen what he's like when he's a bit ill – won't let go of me. Can't imagine the dentist's is going to be a barrel of laughs, but it took ages to get an appointment that coincides with my day off. Otherwise I'd have cancelled.'

'So do you want me to keep Rachel here while you . . . ?'

'Do you mind? I'm really sorry it's such short notice.'

'Not at all. It's no bother.'

'Are you sure? Did you have plans?'

97

'No, no,' Jane told her, grateful that her gym bag was still upstairs on her bed, and not lying in the hall next to the front door. It wasn't a vote of confidence in her outfit that it didn't announce 'lunch date' to Michelle, but then anything she wore out to lunch with Catherine would look frumpy by comparison. She'd wait until Michelle was gone before phoning Catherine to say she couldn't make it. Jane had been there often enough to know a harassed mum could do without feelings of guilt and obligation on top of everything else. It was one of the more constructive ways in which grannies ken't the score.

It was no great loss. She got out to lunch with Catherine every couple of weeks or so, and she generally went to evening sessions at the gym these days anyway. It would have been more of a blow if she'd had to cancel her plans for the next day, when she was down to do some voluntary work at an assistance centre for asylum seekers. She'd been going there two, sometimes three days a week, as many hours as she could spare, for just over a month. Mainly she worked the phones, chasing and coordinating donations of food, clothing and furniture, as well as helping those struggling with English to fill in the masses of paperwork.

She'd done voluntary work in the past, when she didn't have paying jobs to occupy her, but her duties as a grandmother had always got in the way. Both of Michelle's kids were in nursery now, and though she knew there would still be emergencies such as this, they were likely to be fewer and further between. Places like the asylum centre needed you to be dependable, no matter how much or how little time you said you could spare, and just because they weren't paying her didn't mean she owed them less than her full commitment.

'Do you want me to bring Rachel over to yours later, then? Tea-time?' Jane asked.

'Och, no, I'll come and collect her.'

'It's no bother.'

'No, honestly. I'll only need a couple of hours.'

'Can we go to Kaos Kottage, Gran?' Rachel asked.

'No, Rachel,' Michelle interjected. 'Gran's got things to do. You'll have to be a good girl and play here for a wee while.'

'Aw, but Mum . . .'

'I don't mind taking her.'

'I know, but she shouldn't just ask the minute she's in the door.'

'Ach, she's only a wean. I'd have probably suggested it anyway. Looks like it might rain. That would get us out the house, at least – it's indoors.'

'Yes!' Rachel celebrated. 'That's brrrilliant. I love Kaos Kottage.'

'Well, tell you what, Mum, I'll meet you there once I've done my rounds, and I'll take Rachel home after that. I can go to the chemist's in the supermarket next door if Thomas needs an antibiotic.'

'Sure. Just take whatever time you need. I'll meet you there, when? About three?'

'Two should be plenty of time.'

'Well, don't rush. I'll take Rachel over there in a wee while and I'll see you when I see you.'

'Thanks, Mum. And again, I'm really sorry to just dump on you like this.'

'Not at all. Do you want a wee cuppa before you go? A biscuit or something for Thomas?'

'No, he's not touching a thing at the moment. Only milk. I think I'll just get my skates on. I was lucky to get a doctor's appointment, so I'd better not be late.'

Michelle left again without having ventured further than the downstairs hall, and without Jane getting even a kiss from Thomas, who was clinging on to his mum like a baby ape on a wildlife documentary. Jane watched Michelle return to her car and strap Thomas into his child-seat, staying in the doorway, with Rachel peeking around her legs, hoping against probability that she'd get a wave from the wee man as they pulled away. She didn't. Instead, she could tell he'd started crying, quite probably because they hadn't stayed at his gran's even though he hadn't wanted anything to do with her. The black Vectra pulled away shortly after them, executing a three-point turn to head off in the same direction. Just as well for him, as Jane had been considering getting Rachel to fill her potty, never mind dirty dishwater.

She closed the door.

'Now, what are *we* going to get up to?' she asked.

99

Rachel just grinned.

Looking after Rachel was an easy shift. It would have been a lot tougher had it been Thomas she was left alone with for a few hours, without the distraction and assistance of his older sister. There was a big difference in that year between them, Thomas still sufficiently early in his toddlerhood to occasionally remind her he was little more than a walking baby. Everyone talked about the joys and the hardships, but for most of the first three years, as Jane remembered from Ross and Michelle's infancies, motherhood mainly consisted of gaping aeons of numbing tedium punctuated by sudden, heart-stopping moments of panic. After that, the weans got a lot more interesting and far easier to handle. You could negotiate with them, for one thing, which was how she procured Rachel's cooperative assent that when they went to Kaos Kottage later, it would be via Sainsbury's (it being crucial that you saw your side of the deal honoured before the welching little buggers got theirs).

The supermarket was actually one place Thomas tended to be better behaved than his big sister, as he was usually content to sit and watch the shelves and shoppers go by. Rachel, these days, insisted she was too big to go in the kiddy-seat, and so trailed around hanging on to the trolley, deluding herself that she was the one pushing it. This more than doubled how long it took to get in and out with even a handful of items, but one thing Jane couldn't complain about in her life was that she was short of time. It was also far preferable to wrestling a struggling wee madam into the trolley-seat and listening to her whines and protests echo around the aisles.

On this occasion, Rachel was impeccably behaved, possibly because even a trip to the supermarket with her gran was a result when she'd been expecting another day at nursery. Impeccable behaviour, of course, didn't mean the trip passed without incident. Jane had sat her shoulder bag on the unoccupied kiddy-seat as she guided the trolley and its hanger-on around the store. Her non-passenger being such a stated impediment to swift progress, she occasionally parked the thing and told Rachel to stay put while she nipped further along an aisle to quickly retrieve an item from a shelf. The milk shelves were always busy with shoppers, so she'd left Rachel a few yards back, next to the cheese, while she grabbed a two-litre carton. Milk in hand, she turned back to see a young woman stretching across Rachel and the trolley to reach some Parmesan.

'Let me get that out of your way,' Jane said, hastening back.

'It's no problem, honestly,' the girl replied. She sounded American, which made her pretty exotic in EK. 'I don't mean to hurry you.'

'Lady dropped her phone,' Rachel said. 'It's in your bag, Gran. Let's phone Mummy.'

'Have you?' Jane asked.

The girl hurriedly patted a pocket and produced a mobile, glancing at it with relief. 'No, pleased to say. Gave me a fright, though.'

'She likes to keep everyone on their toes,' Jane remarked. 'Don't you?'

'She dropped her phone. Ring, ring. Ring, ring.'

'Report status.'

'*Pardon?* Oh, *d'accord.*'

'Yes, they speak English here. English, remember?'

'Shoh thang.'

'Your accent is a major point of witness identification. Bear that in mind.'

'Difficult to get by with just mime. I could try a Scottish accent.'

'I fear that would be an even greater point of witness identification. So, to repeat, report status.'

'Status is I have the vehicle in sight, two car lengths ahead, still in the car park. They've just left the supermarket and are indicating right.'

'Two car lengths is good. Just don't get close enough to arouse suspicion.'

'I'm not tracking a professional here. Nothing is going to arouse suspicion. Ordinary people do not expect to be tailed. Have you ever travelled with a child in the car? She's got enough distraction to keep her thoughts off who's in the rear-view mirror.'

'So what happened in the supermarket? You said . . .'

'I know. I thought I might have an opportunity, but it was too risky.'

'Understood. But the longer we wait . . .'

'The more risk we may have to take, I know. But I assure you, it wasn't right, not when pursuit is a factor. I'm still queuing to get out of this car park. Are you still where you said last?'

'Yes. Ready to move out.'

'Oh, but wait wait wait. This looks promising. Yes. *D'accord.*'

'What?'

'She's headed for, em, I don't know what you'd call it. An indoor playground. 'Kaos Kottage'. Lots of cars outside, looks busy. Movement, crowd, distraction. Could be ideal.'

'Roger that. Where do you want me?'

'Stay where you are. Seclusion for the vehicle switch is worth more than shortening possible pursuit time.'

'Okay. Standing by.'

Rachel was bouncing up and down in her car-seat as Jane pulled her Civic into the road leading to Kaos Kottage, the wee one having caught sight of it as soon as they came over the brow of the hill. It was hard to miss, being the size of an aircraft hangar, its colourful sign huge enough to be recognisable from the main road two hundred yards away, and no doubt, there-fore, the occasion of a million tantrums as kids were driven past on the way to less desired destinations. Rachel had got into quite an energetic rhythm by the time they neared the car park, though it was unlikely to prove a significant draw on her energy reserves.

'Boing, boing, Kaos Kottage, boing, boing, Kaos Kottage,' she chanted.

Parking was side-by-side either flank of a cul-de-sac that ran in front of the hangar, ending at a low-rise concrete warehouse she presumed to belong to the abutting Safeway, recently usurped by the new Sainsbury's as her supermarket of choice. She couldn't see any spaces, which was bad news. She'd have to turn, go back around the roundabout and then down the other side of the hill to the corner of the supermarket car park remotest from the store but closest to the play-house. From there, a short path led directly to the cul-de-sac, so it wasn't the distance that was the issue. It was the fact that a full car park meant a full house, which meant her ears would be ringing far worse than if she'd been to see Motorhead. A few of the cars might belong to customers at the adjoining hairdressing salon, but it would be a tiny ratio, even smaller than the corresponding proportion of floorspace the two businesses incongruously occupied within the cavernous building. Jane had always wondered about the juxtaposition, what conglomerate economy they were thinking about, or whether they were thinking at all. Maybe the idea was that a pair of young mums could take turns amid the pandemonium while the other enjoyed a bit of adult pampering. The flaw was that it was a bum deal if you got first shift in the salon, given what your hair could look like when you emerged from the indoor jungle.

She drove into the cul-de-sac, intending to U-turn on the T-shaped apron at the end, but before she got that far she noticed someone pull out at her back, right in front of the doors.

'We're in luck,' she told Rachel, before reversing a dozen yards or so and swinging the Civic neatly backwards into the vacated space.

She spotted Michelle's Renault over on the other side and checked her watch. It was just coming up for two. She wasn't late, but she had intended to be here a good bit earlier. Who knew where the time went? One minute it was eleven o'clock; she'd made Rachel some lunch and then been coerced into playing at tea-parties with every non-breakable utensil in the kitchen, and whoosh, two hours had evaporated.

She held Rachel's hand tightly after lifting her out of the Civic. Rachel was straining on her arm, desperate to get across to the play-house, and the possibility of oncoming traffic would not be uppermost in her little mind. Jane did an exaggerated demonstration of looking left, right and left again, before declaring it safe to proceed. A man walked briskly past on the other side, approaching from the far end of the cul-de-sac. He reached the door a few seconds before them but neglected to hold it open.

Jane had to stop herself muttering anything that Rachel might repeat, denying herself from even observing 'what a rude man', as she knew he'd be directly in front of them at the reception desk.

Oh well, let he who is without sin, she thought. He was

probably running late to pick someone up, juggling several commitments at once. She'd been there herself, so stressed over the kids that you lose all perspective until a three-second wait holding a door for someone becomes an unaffordable delay.

The noise came at her as she held open the glass door for Rachel. It was muted by a further wall of glass beyond the foyer, but this merely served to emphasise what level of volume was being contained. A tug on the next set of glass double doors unleashed it. Bedlam.

The reception counter was flanked on either side by magnetically locked, waist-high gates, entrance on the left, exit on the right. The staff noted your surname and number of kids as they took your money, checking the details off on the way out before they let you leave. Given how hard it was to keep track of the little daredevils once they were inside the place, it provided a welcome reassurance to the adults that their charges couldn't escape, particularly so given that staff often deserted the reception counter to provide assistance elsewhere. The downside, as Michelle had joked, was that you couldn't leave any behind, either.

A woman was edging a double-wide pushchair through the entrance gate as Jane and Rachel came in, leaving Mr Unchivalrous at the front of the queue. Jane, as ever, had to restrain Rachel from scurrying forward and ramming the barrier.

'Are you together?' the girl behind the counter asked.

The man turned briefly to glance at the pair of them. 'No,' he said. 'I am meeting someone inside. My wife – she is already here.' He sounded foreign, possibly French, though it was hard to make out much above the din coming from the play area.

'The name?' she asked.

He looked past the receptionist for a moment and waved, though Jane didn't see at whom. The girl looked back inside also. As she did, the man glanced at the register-sheet lying atop the counter. He put his index finger down on the clipboard. 'Mackie,' he stated. He put a hand into his trouser pocket and proffered a fiver.

'Oh, no, we just charge for the children,' the girl explained, smiling.

'Okay,' he said.

She hit a button under the desk and buzzed him through.

Jane, a seasoned visitor, had the exact change ready in her hand.

'Hello again,' the girl said. 'Fleming, isn't it?'

Jane nodded, managing a slightly bashful smile. Other people got recognised by the staff at their local, their favourite restaurant, maybe their golf club. Her face was her passport in supermarkets and soft-play centres.

She kept hold of Rachel (with some difficulty, it had to be said) once they were beyond the gate as she wanted her to note where Granny was sitting before haring off into the multi-coloured jungle. Jane was having trouble enough spotting Michelle in the throng. The accompanying adults were mainly accommodated around rectangular picnic-style tables with built-in seats, though there were also a few round tables with individual chairs, as well as benches hugging the walls. Every last one of them appeared to be taken, with the corner housing the snack bar particularly mobbed. The main attraction was an enormous, labyrinthine climbing structure combining ramps, ladders, chutes, tunnels, webbing, ropes and swings. Underneath it there was space for pits full of soft balls. There was also a bouncy castle and a cushioned, miniature adventure zone for the smallest visitors. Rachel's experiences of the place had begun down there, but she had soon graduated – an initially heart-stopping experience as adults were not permitted (and seldom physically able anyway) to accompany the kids beyond ground level. Once your little one took off up that first ramp or ladder, it was out of your hands, which you would thereafter be needing to cover your eyes as you watched through your fingers. It was scary enough when the place was quiet, but with kids swarming all over the structure like ants, you just had to take a seat, maybe grab a coffee, and simply hope your wee treasure reappeared at some point.

'Mummy!' Rachel called out, zeroing in instinctively as Jane continued to scan the tables.

Michelle was kneeling down on the foam flooring of the toddler zone, staying close to Thomas, who was scrambling the wrong way up a ramp that led into a pit full of soft balls. Rachel bounded over to her mum, slaloming tables and benches, then gave her a brief hug before tearing off up a cushioned staircase. A man stepped across Jane's path to lift a proffered baby from his breast-feeding partner, and when he stepped back out of the way, Rachel had disappeared from sight.

'Miraculous recovery?' Jane asked, indicating Thomas.

Michelle looked up.

'Hi, Mum. Yeah, bloody typical. He perked up about ten minutes after we left you. By the time we were in the doctor's waiting room, he was bouncing off the walls. Then I've to stand there going: "Well, he was looking a wee bit hangy earlier on, Doctor."'

'Och, the doctor will have seen that often enough,' Jane assured her. 'You and Ross were both masters of the two-hour fever.'

Jane looked at Thomas and waved. He smiled and waved back, causing him to lose his grip on the slope. He slid back down into the balls with a giggle, which confirmed a return to full fitness. Any hint of feeling sorry for himself would have turned that little setback into a major trauma.

A table became free soon after as an elephantine pair of women vacated with an equally rotund brood.

'Must be genetic,' Michelle whispered. Jane knew Michelle was trying to get a rise out of her, provoke her disapproval, but she wasn't biting. She didn't like to dwell on whether Michelle's bitchy streak was a genuine reaction to her own chronic preaching of tolerance, respect and general politeness. The more benign explanation was that it proved Michelle had absorbed all of the above and that the joke was in knowing her comments were unacceptable, but as far as Jane was concerned, the jury was still out. The only thing it had ruled on was that you didn't stop worrying about your children's upbringing even when they were bringing up children of their own.

She circled the supermarket car park once more, following the one-way system until she reached the furthest corner, which abutted the cul-de-sac. The rear of the blue Civic was visible through the slatted wooden fence, unlikely to be going anywhere for a while, even in the implausible event that the driver had gone into the little hair salon. Lex picked a space further up the slope, with a clearer view of the play-house's front doors, reversed into position and killed the engine.

She reached across to the passenger-side footwell and lifted a briefcase on to the seat. From it she removed the nine-millimetre and silencer attachment, screwing the two together in her lap. Both parts were for 'insurance'. She hated the idea of using the gun, but knew that if it came to it, she had no choice, and it would lead to fewer complications if there were no reports echoing around the area.

Discretion was an underlined mission parameter. She had to acquire the target without being conspicuous, without either of them drawing attention to themselves. Tough gig. Forcibly rip a human being from their everyday life and demonstrate to them how the world is a far more evil and dangerous place than they ever feared, but please do it quietly and without anyone noticing.

She wouldn't be easily separated from the kid; Lex was under no illusions about that. It would therefore be all about choosing the moment. Unfortunately, she knew the number of moments from which she could choose was ever diminishing. Patience had to be allied to judgement, but patience against the clock meant judgement had to be allied to nerve.

Their seats were close to the action, a row of tables back from the toddler zone. Jane stayed with Thomas for a while to let Michelle rest her feet, then tempted him over to the table with the promise of some chocolate buttons. He sat on Jane's knee and smeared contentedly while she and Michelle had a coffee. Every so often, they'd make out a familiar voice calling 'Mummy!' or 'Gran!' amid the dozens of unfamiliar ones calling out the same thing, and look up to see Rachel wave at them from some vertiginously elevated part of the climbing structure.

'It's as well she does that now and again,' Michelle remarked, 'otherwise I'd lose track of her completely.'

'In my experience, she comes back approximately every ten minutes for a drink of juice. I'd only worry if she exceeded that.'

'This place is just mental. Too busy, too many weans. There's a wee girl in here with the same dress as Rachel. I waved to her soon as I saw her through the crowd, a few minutes before you got here. Felt like an eejit.'

'Glad it wasn't me that waved, then,' Jane said. 'You'd have said I was having a "senior moment".'

'I'm telling you, you're the one that must have your wits about you, taking Rachel to this place so often. I cannae handle it. She goes haring off and disappears, then my heart's in my mouth when I do see her, because she's hanging off something or diving head first down a slide.'

'You'd better just accept it, Michelle, because it never ends. One minute she's heading up that ladder, the next she's asking for driving lessons.'

'Please no motorbikes. Please no motorbikes. If I believed in God, that would be my prayer every night.'

'Just don't let them hear you saying it. Somehow they always find a way of doing the opposite of what you want for them.'

'Well, that depends on whether what you want for them is reasonable or consistent, doesn't it?' Michelle replied, a slight edge coming into her voice. Jane immediately regretted her last remark. It was the kind of thing you could comfortably say to any mother on the planet apart from one who also happened to be your daughter.

'I'm not having a go, Michelle. Just saying it'll come to you.'

'I'll be ready. Donald and I talk about this all the time. You can have your hopes, but don't have expectations. The fun's not in guiding them, but in what they do on their own.'

I'll quote you on that a few years hence, Jane kept to herself. 'Wise words,' she said instead.

'And anyway, Mum, I don't think you can cry foul too loud. I must be about the only daughter whose mother complained about the fact that she quit playing in a rock band in order to study hard and get a good degree.'

'I never complained,' Jane protested. 'I was just surprised you didn't take it a bit further, see where it led.'

'Take it further?' Michelle asked, raising her voice, but laughing with it. She could have been screaming her lungs out and it would have attracted no more attention amid the din.

They'd been over this umpteen times, Jane perhaps subconsciously picking at the scab as she so often found herself bringing it up. Michelle got less aggressive in response these days, but there was a tone of tired exasperation to her voice, asking the same question as Jane was right then asking of herself: why couldn't she let this go?

'Mum, it was a student band. We were called The Giorgio Marauders, for God's sake. How far did you think we were going to take it?'

As far as a mother's daft dreams, was the answer; a mother who wanted her daughter to have the things she never had, whether her daughter wanted them or not. Sports cars and casinos, or maybe just the path less travelled by. It wasn't about the band, it was about the marrying and settling down when Michelle had other choices that Jane didn't.

'I know the band was just a bit of fun, Michelle. I never complained,' she reiterated. 'I was just a little surprised – not disappointed, surprised – your choices at that age were, I don't know, so conventional.'

'The apple doesn't fall far from the tree, Mum,' Michelle replied, shaking her head. Michelle reached, too late, to grab Thomas's hands before he could wipe them on Jane's jacket, leaving her with three chocolatey streaks around either breast. 'Sorry. Is it dry-clean only?' she asked, with a wince.

'No, no,' Jane assured, lying. 'But what do you mean, the apple doesn't fall far from the tree?'

Michelle laughed again, and Jane knew she was sugaring a pill.

'You're saying you're surprised I've been conventional? Well, wherever did I get it from?'

'You mean your father,' Jane stated, relieved to divert but feeling slightly disloyal.

'No, I mean you, Mum. You've never exactly been the essence of urban rebellion, have you? You keep a house so immaculate you could eat your dinner off the bathroom floor, you drive five miles below the speed limit at all times and when you're not bailing me out at zero notice, you spend your spare time doing work for charity. You're the soul of dutiful and responsible behaviour. What kind of an example is that to give your children?'

Jane laughed to convey that she was taking it in the lighter spirit Michelle intended. Inside, part of her wanted to weep.

'I'm not that responsible,' she insisted, a little bashfully.

'Oh come on, Mum. I don't think you've ever had a parking ticket. How many times did you give us that speech about how respect for other people and respect for the law are one and the same thing, and that's why you've never broken it?'

'There's nothing to be ashamed of about—'

'I'm not ashamed of it, Mum. But I'm not so sure about you. Just because you stuck by the rules doesn't necessarily mean you're happy about it.'

Out of the mouths of babes. It was hard to take when your kids thought they knew you better than you knew yourself; harder still when they were right. On this form, she should ask Rachel to attempt a Jungian analysis.

'And what I really don't get,' Michelle continued, the pill getting audibly more bitter, 'is why you act like I was a mug for settling down when I supposedly had the world at my feet, yet you're in the huff with Ross because he dumped his fiancée over that job in France. How does that work? He gets a hard time for breaking the rules and I get a hard time for sticking by them? Make up your mind.'

'I'm not in the huff with Ross,' Jane insisted, turning suddenly defensive to protect a vulnerable spot. 'More like he's the one in the huff with me.'

'What's the difference? When did you last speak? Ages, I'll bet. You should call him.'

'I do call him. He's never in. I always get the answering machine.'

'Do you leave a message? You don't, do you?'

'I hate those things.'

'That's a no.'

'I have left messages,' she said, which was true but only just into the plural, and the last had been several weeks ago. 'He never calls me back.'

'No, and knowing Ross, he's not going to say he's sorry, either. But one way or another, you need to talk, and I mean properly. Not five minutes with Dad about Celtic and then you asking him how the job's going.'

Jane winced. More preter-generational wisdom, Michelle describing fairly accurately most of their telephone exchanges with Ross even before their falling out.

At that moment, Thomas climbed down from Jane's lap and began tugging on his mum's hand, indicating his desire to return to the toddler zone.

'Balls, Mummy,' he said, pretty much echoing Ross's sentiments the last time they'd had a discussion of any substance.

'Duty calls,' Michelle said, allowing herself to be dragged from the bench. 'But I'm serious, my last word – you need to talk to him.'

'I will,' Jane said, unsure whether this was a statement of intent or merely an optimistic prediction.

She watched Michelle walking away, bent over Thomas, and reached for the last of her coffee. It was still just about warm enough to drink. She knocked back a big gulp and looked around the climbing structure for Rachel. So many little bodies, clambering, sliding, pushing, so many tunnels and barriers. She remembered bringing a camera here once, and trying for a frustratingly long time to get a picture of Rachel in action. She ended up with a few blurry shots of her bolting away from the end of a chute, and several of completely different children. Eventually Jane spotted her. She was up on the highest tier, her back visible through a grid of safety webbing, waiting – but not queuing – for her chance to slide down the big yellow tube that curved its way gently to ground level. Jane knew she'd wait there for ages, if necessary, not quite confident enough to take her shot while there were bigger kids around, nor understanding that the more polite of them were deferring right of way.

Jane took a last mouthful of now barely drinkable coffee, and was about to look up at the structure again when her attention was distracted by a sudden outbreak of howling, a little voice frenziedly shrieking 'Mummy! Mummy! Mummy!' This was hardly unusual, and Jane was two generations adept at channelling it out, but it was accompanied by a flurry of movement at the corner of her eye, which involuntarily drew her gaze.

It was the little girl Michelle had mentioned, wearing the same dress as Rachel, having a force-nine tantrum as she was carried towards the exit by the stressed man with the foreign accent. He was holding her across him, her face into his chest as she beat her arms and kicked and yelled. The man wore a weary and stoical smile to mask a familiar embarrassment most

111

bystanders knew it was politest to look away from and ignore. Jane dutifully observed the etiquette herself, returning her attention to the structure.

It took a moment to find Rachel again, and when she did Jane saw only a brief flash of her back before she disappeared down the tube. Jane looked down to where the slide exited on to a bank of soft mats. A couple of seconds later the child emerged, sliding out on to her tummy. She sat up and waved to someone nearby, finally facing Jane's direction.

She felt the world freeze for just a moment.

It wasn't Rachel.

Jane turned around and looked at the man carrying the struggling girl towards the gate, now approaching the woman working the counter. She still couldn't see the girl's face. Her mind raced, balancing rationale against fear, logic against instinct. The dress came from Next; it was hardly unique. She could stand up and scream for him to be stopped, but it really would be a 'senior moment' if Rachel appeared looking for juice just as she made her hysterical accusation of abduction.

The woman buzzed him through. Jane still couldn't see Rachel anywhere, still couldn't see the tantrumming girl's face. She remembered him standing at the counter, pointing to his name on the list. Pointing to *a* name on the list. Mackie, he'd said, in that French-sounding accent.

Mackie. How French was that?

Jane got to her feet and began running for the exit.

'Stop him,' she shouted. 'Stop him right now.'

The woman on the counter looked bemusedly at Jane as she approached. The man was through the first set of double doors and into the foyer, where he looked back, caught sight of Jane and began to run. He turned around to back his way through the outside doors, changing his grip on the girl as he did so. Her head came up as she continued to squirm and flail. Jane saw her face: flushed, tear-soaked, howling, hysterical. Rachel.

She hurdled the gate, putting one hand on the counter to give her more lift, then barrelled through the double doors and into the glass foyer. She could see him running diagonally across the cul-de-sac, heading towards the dead end where the only exit was the path leading to the supermarket car park. Ahead of him the lights flashed on a black Vectra, signalling its being remotely unlocked.

Jane got to the front doors a crucial moment *after* a chubby couple in matching Celtic tracksuits began negotiating their way through them with a double-wide buggy and two sleeping kids. It must only have taken a few seconds, but their awkward and lumbering movements were excruciating enough for Jane to consider throwing herself through one of the plate-glass windows for a quicker exit. Jane squeezed around them as soon as there was a gap, barely registering the indignant tut this drew, and charged out on to the pavement, almost flattening one of the next-door hairdressers who was outside having a cigarette, scissors and comb tucked into his breast pocket.

She looked to the black Vectra and felt her heart jump as she failed to see the man or Rachel. Then the top of his head became visible above the Audi next to him. He was leaning over an open rear door. The bastard had a child-seat or some other restraint, and was strapping Rachel into it. She heard the rear door slam and saw him pull open the driver's one in front. Jane thrust her hand into her jacket pocket and gave thanks that she hadn't taken it off when she let Thomas sit on her lap with his packet of melting chocolate buttons.

She ran for the Civic, had the doors unlocked by the time she got there and turned the key in the ignition even as she climbed into the driver's seat. She could see the Vectra moving as she put her car in gear and released the handbrake. It was gathering speed, but it wouldn't be fast enough. She released the clutch and rolled the car forward across the single lane of tarmac, then ratcheted the handbrake and dived across the gearstick to the passenger side as the Vectra impacted.

She fell into the passenger seat and cracked an elbow against the door as the driver-side airbag inflated, billowing out from the steering wheel into unoccupied space. The optional five hundred quid for the passenger-side airbag proved money well saved, as Jane was able to exit the car unencumbered. On the far side of the Civic she could see that two airbags had detonated inside the Vectra, temporarily pinning the driver to his seat.

'Are you all right?' the hairdresser asked, stepping towards her.

'He's got my granddaughter,' she screamed, barging past him to get to the Vectra. 'He's got Rachel.'

The Vectra's bonnet had crumpled, its nose partially embedded in the Civic's SIPS-galvanised driver-side door. Through the windscreen Jane could see hands grapple with the deflating airbag, and could hear Rachel's muted screams from inside. She ran around the back of the Vectra to the rear passenger-side door and tugged at the handle. It was locked. She balled her fingers into a fist and drew back her arm. Caution should have told her that she would shred and mangle her hand, but something deeper was overriding all personal concerns. It was, however, the same instinct that stilled her fist, as she envisaged the spray of glass that would cover Rachel. In that moment, the Vectra began to reverse at speed. The man remained obstructed by the airbag, but his feet still had control of the pedals. Jane stepped clear just in time before a wing mirror could clip her middle. The hairdresser began to give chase, and she was about to follow until she realised what the driver intended to do.

She ran across the tarmac and pushed the hairdresser between two parked cars as the Vectra leaped forward again with a squeal of hot rubber. It shot past, blind, clipping the fronts of several stationary vehicles before slamming once more into the Civic, which was spun ten or fifteen degrees, but still presented a sufficient barrier to prevent the Vectra from getting past. Standing between the parked cars, Jane was only feet away from Rachel, who was thrashing hysterically in the child-seat. In front, she could see the driver's arms flailing and tugging, and the grey glint of a blade. He was ripping the airbag with a knife, and once free of it would be better able to guide the Vectra for another ramming charge.

Jane turned to the hairdresser.

'Gimme the scissors,' she demanded.

'What?' he asked blankly, clearly too dazed to respond. She reached to his chest and grabbed them from the pocket, then scrambled to the side of the Vectra and plunged them into the rear tyre. At first the blades just bounced off the tread. Then she remembered that the side wall was less protected. She dug the scissors in with both hands, her fingers white and her arms

114

taut as she applied all the pressure she could summon. Suddenly the tips burst through and air came rushing from the gash. She pulled the scissors out and was about to make for the front tyre, but by this point the driver had completely extricated himself from his airbag and began to reverse once more. The car was already listing as it drew back, but it would still be able to jolt the Civic again, maybe this time enough to open a gap wide enough to escape through.

Jane ran back to her own car, threw open the door and plunged the scissors into the airbag, following his lead. It worked considerably faster than the automatic deflation process, but the Vectra had already ceased reversing and there was no way she'd be able to get behind the controls in time. Instead she reached across the seat, under the folds of the bag, and released the handbrake, then gave the steering wheel a sharp turn. The camber of the road sloped gently towards the building, causing the car to roll forwards and thus reclose the gap.

Jane turned to see the Vectra roar towards her. She saw his face, determination in his eyes, blood streaming from his nose from the impact of the airbag. He was focused not on the Civic, but on her. Whichever way she ran, that's where he was going to steer, and there wasn't time for her to get back between the parked cars.

She turned, placing both hands on top of the Honda, and vaulted on to its roof a fraction of a second before the Vectra smashed into the side for a third time. Jane felt the impact with a shudder that came from inside as much as the jolt from without. She was bounced off the roof on the passenger side, but was able to correct her fall so that her feet hit the ground before she tumbled to all fours. The palms of her hands were skinned pretty raw but, crucially, there were no impact injuries to her wrists.

She got to her feet and looked to the cars. In trying to kill her, he'd ended up hitting the Civic straight on, which had maximised the damage to his own vehicle and failed to spin the Honda any further out of the way.

People had begun to emerge from the building to investigate what all the noise was about: the woman from the counter, the male half of the podgy tracksuit-Tims, clients and staff from the salon. They stood in a line as though there was a glass pane separating the spectators from the combatants, their faces a mixture of curiosity and confusion. They didn't yet know enough to evince due shock or concern, but mere caution prevented them rushing into involvement before they had a handle on what was going on.

Jane heard a whine from the Vectra, which let her know the last crash had stalled it and that the driver was struggling to get it going again. She could also hear Rachel's glass-muted screams, which served to clear her mind of all shock, all pain and all distraction. She knew only one thing: she had to get Rachel out of the car, and she couldn't do this while that man was inside it; not while the bastard was conscious, anyway.

Jane stepped to the rear of the Civic and popped open the boot, from which she removed Rachel's buggy, neatly folded for transport, then ran around the back of the Vauxhall. The driver was hunched over the steering wheel, turning the ignition key and frantically pumping the accelerator. He looked up and to the side as Jane launched the buggy through his window, two wheels shattering the glass and continuing into his face, with all the strength and fury she could bring to bear. She pulled the buggy back and sent it in again, but this time he deflected it and pulled it right inside, Jane letting go before she could be dragged against the door towards that knife.

'Here, that's enough, calm it doon,' said a male voice, and Jane felt hands gripping her shoulders tightly from behind to restrain her. 'Just calm it doon, missus,' he reiterated forcefully. The grip tightened as she struggled. She couldn't see him, but he was pulling her against his ample body to hold her in place, while in front of her the driver resumed his attempts to restart his engine. It burst into life with an unhealthy sounding snarl, repeated twice as he gunned the revs to make sure it stayed alive. Jane could see his shoulder shift as he put it into reverse, this vigilante halfwit's arms now around her chest. She sent her head back with a full-blooded jerk and felt the crunch at the back of her head as she broke his nose. She then sent a foot stamping hard into his instep and broke free of his embrace.

The Vectra reversed laboriously along the cul-de-sac, its engine whining and its rear driver-side tyre grinding metal on concrete, accompanied by a flapping wup-wup-wup noise. She went after it, not running, but striding along the centre of the lane, keeping her options open. She looked him in the eye through the windscreen. He looked at her, then at the Civic, then at the gathering crowd.

The car stopped, but this time it didn't come forward again. He opened the door and stepped out, brandishing the knife: no Saturday-night chib from mammy's kitchen drawer, but a long, thick, serrated weapon that looked like it was specifically designed and intended for killing people. Jane reached into a pocket in her jacket and pulled out the hairdresser's scissors. They stood fifteen, maybe twenty feet apart, close enough to see into each other's eyes. He continued to scan his surroundings, but never lifted his gaze from her for long. She saw desperation but not fear, anger but not rage, and his expression was coldly dispassionate.

Jane gripped the scissors, curling two fingers and a thumb around the steel loops. She heard a voice bellowing with fury, with fire, with certainty, its words echoing off the walls.

'I'LL KILL YOU. I SWEAR I'LL KILL YOU.'

It took a moment to realise it was coming from her own mouth.

The man looked at her for one more cold second, then looked away. He opened the rear passenger-side door and pulled a briefcase from within, then turned and began to run. He held the case in his left hand, the knife and a mobile phone to his ear with his right as he headed for the path to the supermarket, before disappearing out of sight behind the fence.

His retreat had barely begun before Jane was sprinting towards the car. She dived in through the still-open rear door and clambered across the upholstery to where Rachel was strapped into the child-seat.

'Gra-an, Gra-aaan,' she was howling, tear-streaked and terrified.

Jane unclasped the buckle, yanked the straps free and hauled her into her arms. She let herself collapse against the leather of the back seat, held her granddaughter tightly to her chest, breathed in the smell of her hair, then cried and cried and cried.

Abduction: how to do it properly

Lex had sat up that bit straighter and felt herself tense as she saw the man emerge carrying the little girl. At that point and from that distance, she couldn't identify the child (and an adult hurriedly toting a raging kid through a car park was not in itself a remarkable or alarming sight), but the very possibility that it was Ross Fleming's niece presented every last ramification she had feared about this job. The emergence of her target a few seconds later told her she didn't have to worry about what might happen any more: her worst-case scenario was now thoroughly in progress.

Bett's instructions, often infuriatingly elliptical, had been extremely clear on one thing: she was not to intervene in any situation involving the target unless, as a last resort, it was the only way of preserving the mission. Nonetheless, her first reaction upon seeing this situation unfold was to grab her mobile. There was a two-button speed-dial combination that would get her Bett immediately on a dedicated line that he kept clear for when any of them absolutely needed to speak to him. She now had confirmation that another party most definitely was involved, and they were in the process of abducting a three-year-old, either as bait or leverage, proving them to be as direct and ruthless as Willis had implied.

Her finger hovered over the keypad as she watched Fleming's mother dash across the cul-de-sac, the kidnapper pulling out of a parking space further along the lane. She remembered Bett's typically stern advice regarding the speed-dial 'White Line', as he called it.

'As a rule, in any given situation, the first three times you want to use it, you'll already know the answer. Don't waste my time.'

Lex watched Jane Fleming's car drive across the kidnapper's path and stop dead, then moments later the black Vectra buried its nose in the Honda's flank. She put the phone down. She did already know the answer. Things were nowhere near last-resort stage, particularly if Bett was right about this 'specialist'; and as she knew only too well, Bett was always right.

His description echoed around her as she remained in the hire car and witnessed the duel unfold. A man began trotting after the Vectra as it reversed. Fleming ran across the tarmac to push him clear as the car shot forward again.

Someone fearless . . .

The woman grabbed something silver from the bystander – looked like scissors – and began digging it into one of the car's tyres. Moments later she would be using a child's pushchair to smash the window and bludgeon the kidnapper.

Someone who can adapt and improvise . . .

With the Vectra revving up for another attempt to barge past the Honda, she managed to roll it back across the path, despite the encumbrance of an airbag.

Someone resourceful and cunning . . .

Then she dived clear just in time, bouncing off of the Civic's roof and down on to the tarmac, where she didn't even dust herself down before charging back on to the offensive.

Stoical in the face of pain and danger . . .

With the Vectra limping backwards like a wounded beast, the kidnapper climbed out, holding a hunting knife. Fleming faced him down, brandishing a pair of barber's scissors.

Ruthlessly uncompromising in pursuit of the objective . . .

'I'll kill you,' Lex heard, the words reverberating around the entire area with a mortal conviction. 'I swear I'll kill you.'

. . . and utterly merciless in eliminating anyone who stands in the way.

Chalk another one up to that son-of-a-bitch: it looked a hell of a good basket.

Lex watched the kidnapper emerge from the path and into the supermarket car park. He had a briefcase in one hand – couldn't leave evidence of his true purpose when he bailed – and was already on his phone, calling in the bad news. She could see him scanning the cars as he jogged. He needed an out fast and jacking a passing driver was his best shot in the short-term.

Lex realised that a valuable opportunity was presenting itself, but it was way, way outside of mission parameters. It was a chance to get a handle on who they were up against, but would only come at the expense of dropping the target. This window would not be open for long, she knew. The question of deviating from the mission was ordinarily a no-brainer, but nobody, not even Bett, could have anticipated a potential break like this. She reached again for the phone. Again, her finger stalled above the keypad. Again, she already knew the answer. The target wasn't going anywhere, and anyway, Lex had already made the principal drop back at that other supermarket. She slipped the nine-millimetre into a pocket on the inside of the door, put the car into gear and pulled away.

In a few seconds she was parallel to him, one row distant, as he jogged between the lines of parked cars. She descended the passenger-side window with a touch of a button.

'Get in, now,' she called out.

He looked around to see where the voice had come from.

'*Allez, allez,*' she insisted impatiently.

At that, he bolted for the Renault and pulled at the front door, which he found to be locked.

'In the back, you fucking idiot, and keep down.'

He clambered hurriedly across the rear seats and pulled the door closed as Lex accelerated towards the exit.

'*Et qui êtes-vous?*' he asked, nestling uncomfortably across the rear footwells.

'In English, dipshit,' she answered, figuring they wouldn't send someone who couldn't speak it. She knew also that it was harder to lie in another language; or harder to hide it, at least.

'I said who are you?' he revised.

'I'm back-up. I'm the Seventh goddamn Cavalry. Certain parties weren't so confident you could pull this off without a hitch.'

'What parties?'

'Informed parties, it looks like.'

'What's your name?'

'That's on a need-to-know basis, dude, and, right now, you don't need to know. In fact it's best if you don't.'

Lex negotiated the car park's one-way system quickly but without any conspicuous haste. She kept her eyes on the road, but did grab the occasional glance at her passenger, who remained curled across the cramped channel. She wheeled around the roundabout, then accelerated as she finally hit open road.

A glance down behind her revealed that he was no longer on the floor. She suddenly felt cold steel held across her neck.

'Now, how about you tell me who the hell you are, yes?' he demanded.

'Look, I gotta warn you, driving isn't my specialty, so I'd appreciate it if you didn't put me off, okay? Less of the fucking theatricals, jeez.'

Still he kept the knife in place, pushing it a little harder against her skin.

'Answer me,' he growled, a throaty hiss.

'I told you. I'm back-up, and my name is strictly need-to-goddamn-know. You want credentials? Look in the briefcase on the front seat. The folder,' she directed.

He tried grasping for it with the knife still in place, but didn't have the reach. Lex tutted, like this was all a real drag to her. She reached a hand across and opened the dossier, revealing photographs of Fleming, his parents, his sister and her husband and kids.

'Okay,' she said, 'so I'm working the Fleming job, you're working the Fleming job. Or rather you're fucking up the Fleming job.'

He withdrew the knife as he leaned over to try and pick up the folder, but she slammed shut the briefcase.

'Hands off, *ami*. You don't have that kind of clearance, believe me, and I ain't telling you any shit that I'm not certain you're authorised to hear. So how about we establish *your* credentials, find out what you do know and then I'll decide whether it's worth us trying to help you redeem this situation. We'll start with where you're headed.'

'This way is good,' he said, settling back into the seat. He looked slightly relieved, slightly pissed off, which was what she wanted. He was grateful that someone had saved his ass from the authorities, but was beginning to contemplate that no one could save it from his bosses. 'I have someone waiting. We were supposed to change cars. It's secluded. Woodland. About three miles.'

'Then you'll meet as planned and we'll work out the next move from there. The important thing right now is to get clear of this mess.'

'*Oui*,' he grumbled.

'So what's with the big blade? Don't they trust you guys with guns?'

'We had to move at short notice. Can't take guns on a flight and the alternative was to drive. Takes too long.'

'Plus you figured you wouldn't need 'em, huh?' she chided. 'So when did they scramble you? Yesterday? Or have you been on this from the start? Was it you guys went for Fleming at his apartment? Made quite a mess.'

Lex checked the rear-view to see his expression. It was irritated.

'Someone else handled that. Our job was just the child, after they didn't deliver.'

'So who's supposed to bring Fleming in once you've got the kid?'

'I don't know. Lucien, I guess. It was he who went to Chassignan.'

'Lucien?' she bluffed, turning around and taking her eyes off the road for dramatic effect. 'God help us,' she continued, braking as she approached another roundabout. She was actually finding it easier to handle driving on the left during this discussion because it kept her from thinking too much about what she was doing. 'Please don't tell me Lucien's supposed to bring in the other stuff too.'

'What other stuff?'

'What this whole thing is about. The goods, man.'

'As far as I know, Fleming *is* what this whole thing is about.'

'Hmmm. Well, yes and no.'

'You know different?' he asked, sitting up.

'Keep your head down, man. I can't discuss it, but it's to do with the Marledoq materials, and I don't know how much you're authorised to hear. I mean, have you seen the video files, for instance?'

'Jesus, yes. Of course. *Everybody*'s seen the video files.'

'Well, exactly. I can only talk about what everybody already knows, so what's the point, right? Unless . . . hey, what name do you call your boss, the main man?'

'You don't know who my boss is? I thought you said . . .'

'I know who your fucking boss is, I asked what name you call him. He has more than one. What you call him denotes your level of clearance; it's shorthand code.'

'I call him Parrier. And I've never heard of this different name shit.'

'Which, unfortunately, tells me exactly what level you're cleared to. Sorry.'

'Hey, who the hell are you anyway?' he snarled, sitting up again. 'You look like you're just out of fucking high school and you're talking to me like—'

'Yeah, yeah. Just remember who came to whose rescue back there if you need a sense of perspective. If you had done your job properly, you wouldn't have even needed to find out I existed. But we're both here now, so let's just deal. Hey, we're coming up on another roundabout. Straight on?'

'No, right,' he told her, looking up again.

She turned and accelerated on to a dual carriageway.

'Where the hell's secluded around here?' she asked.

'Woods. You'll see. Left at the next roundabout, and then another mile. One minute it's town, the next it's countryside.'

Lex drove on, holding in the left-hand lane despite being stuck behind a slow-moving dump truck. A silence began to grow between them, which she knew would make her uneasy. So far she'd succeeded in practising what Bett had taught her about situations like this, the first trick being to get the other party to justify himself to you and establish *his* credentials, rather than the other way around.

The second trick was to keep him talking, preferably answering questions, so that he couldn't dwell too much on who you were and how little you were giving back.

'Shit, what a mess,' she said, shaking her head. 'I don't think there's been a video clip that's caused such a stir since Pammy and Tommy, huh?'

'No kidding,' he agreed grumpily. 'And you're asking why I'm carrying a knife?' he added archly.

'Point taken,' Lex said, bluffing that she had any idea what his point could possibly be.

As he had indicated, the buildings and houses along the carriageway soon petered out into countryside. A left turn took them up a potholed side road towards woodland, then a further turn between two no entry signs brought them on to a rutted single track winding uphill and deeper into the trees. It was secluded, all right. Dim, claustrophobic, secret. A place for shameful deeds. Lex started to feel sick. She thought of that little girl who should have been in the back seat of the guy's car at this point, but that wasn't what was doing it.

They came to a clearing, barely more than a passing place, really, but wide enough to accommodate two cars and the pile of stripped, narrow pine trunks that lay to the right of the track. There was a dark blue Ford sitting motionless ahead, dull and treacherously anonymous. The figure behind the wheel got out as the Renault approached.

Lex stopped the car ten yards short. This was where it got tricky. Stringing two guys along with a charade like this was a lot more than just twice as difficult. Besides, the disadvantage of a bluff based on superiority of rank was that she had to give the impression she already knew all of the information she was able to elicit, making it all the harder to pry without raising suspicion. Information, Bett had frequently impressed upon all of them, was instantly devalued the moment the enemy knew you had it.

'Okay, here's what's gonna happen,' she told her passenger as she killed the engine. 'I gotta make a quick call. While I'm doing that, you go fill your buddy in on who I am so we don't have to go through all the same shit again.'

'Sure,' he grunted, climbing out of the back seat.

Lex reached for her mobile for the third time. Yet again, she already knew the answer; she'd known the answer the second she rolled the window down and told this asshole to get in her car, but she dialled the number anyway.

She was prepared to do a lot of things for Bett, but one of them wasn't sparing him the burden of complicity in this. She wanted to hear him say it, wanted him to explicitly speak the words. Five hundred miles away from this shit, it was the least the fucker could do.

He answered in less than five seconds. She explained the situation in less than ten.

'Execute them,' he said. 'Put the bodies in the car. Burn it.'

The line went dead.

Monster.

Fucking monster. That was what he was, and what he made you.

Lex looked ahead through the windscreen. Her passenger was standing next to his partner, an older man with close-cropped grey hair, also in an inconspicuous business suit. The younger was gesticulating, miming what had befallen him at the play-house place. The older man cast a couple of glances Lex's way, but she'd made sure not to catch his eye. Casualness was her disguise and her shield. She retrieved the nine-millimetre from the pocket in the door and tucked it into the rear waistband of her trousers, the silencer attachment nosing between the tops of her buttocks. She flapped at her jacket to ensure it covered the handgrip, then got out of the car and walked towards them. The older man turned first, inviting her into an ongoing discussion about how they planned to proceed. He seemed intent to impress upon her both his seniority in the pairing and his initiative in taking matters forward. Either way, he was taking her at face value because he assumed anything else would waste time and lose him points with people further up the chain.

'Doing it in a public place was always risky,' he said, heavily accented. German, maybe Dutch. 'Too many variables. We should reacquire the child at the house, after dark, where we can control the environment.'

'I don't know,' the younger man argued. 'They're going to be extremely vigilant now. What about the cops?'

'The parents will be shaken up,' grey-hair agreed, 'but they won't think the girl was specifically targeted. The police will assume it was a random attempt, and that's what they'll tell the family to put their minds at ease. The cops won't be watching the house, and the parents won't think that lightning is about to strike twice.'

'They won't be letting the kids out of their sight, though.'

'That's not going to matter. We're not talking about a snatch job any more. We'll do it like we should have in the first place: hit the house at night, take what we need and silence what we don't. Kill everyone but the older kid. She'll be worth more to Fleming that way – she'll be all he has left.'

Lex listened to this matter-of-fact discussion and remembered that there were degrees of monstrosity.

'It's a bit of a leap from child abduction to what you're talking about,' she observed, with a fragile façade of calm.

'So, do you have a problem with that?' the younger man asked, still wrestling with those hierarchy issues. 'Are you going to tell us it's not "authorised"?' he added nippily.

'Oh, I'd authorise it in a New York minute. I just wanted to check you guys aren't squeamish about this kind of thing. But you're okay with the idea of killing people, just like that, if it cuts down on risks?'

'Anything that makes it easier to get the job done,' grey-hair told her.

'Cool,' Lex said, reaching behind her back.

Unsafe building

The sting of antiseptic on Jane's palms was the first sensation her nerves had managed to get through to her brain since the moment she realised it wasn't Rachel coming out of that yellow chute. She was beginning to notice a duller, deeper ache around the right side of her pelvis, the site denoted by a thread-dangling rip across the material of her trousers. She couldn't quite remember where or when it had happened – whether it had been as she bounced on the roof, or perhaps when she hit the ground just after.

She was sitting upstairs in the Kaos Kottage's private party room, where groups of kids were taken to get filled up with Coke, chips and E numbers (just in case they weren't high enough) in a brief respite from their physical activities. Jane had to make do with a cup of tea, but she imagined, even without a slice of birthday cake, that her experience must be much the same as the weans': a moment to sit down and refuel, her legs starting to tingle in testimony to their efforts, her mind trying to replay and digest what had passed in a blur of excitement. One of the staff was in attendance with a first-aid kit, and was dabbing at her grazes with cotton wool and Dettol. A police-woman was downstairs waiting to talk to her, but was busying herself with other witness statements in the meantime.

Michelle had already gone, taking both the kids home on Jane's insistence. She'd offered to hang around, but Jane knew it was just a gesture of gratitude. They all needed to be back where they felt secure, and as soon as possible. Michelle's husband Donald had been called and was on his way back early from the hospital. Jane, for her part, needed to know they were home and safe more than she needed any solidarity. She felt strangely apart from everybody in the aftermath anyway; every-body except Rachel.

Mercifully, Michelle had missed all the fun. With the place

129

being so mobbed, the noise inside had meant the crashes were only audible nearest the entrance, which was why merely a trickle of observers had come to investigate, many of them from the salon. With her attention taken by minding Thomas as he clambered clumsily around the toddler area, Michelle hadn't noticed Jane make her hurried exit, nor even heard her calls above the din of excited young voices. She was understandably shaken up when she learned exactly what she had missed, but Jane was greatly relieved her daughter had been spared the most of it, and by far the worst of it.

There was a sensation that seized you suddenly like a cold steel fist in the pit of your stomach when you realised you didn't know where your child was. It happened all the time – wandering mere feet away out of sight in a shopping centre; slipping unnoticed to the toilet, leaving you staring in horror at an empty back garden – and usually resolved itself in moments, but frequency never diminished the impact. The worst of it, the thing Michelle had been spared, was what followed when the next few moments didn't bring resolution. The worst of it was the helplessness. The worst of it was the paralysing realisation that your child's welfare was out of your hands – the hands your child looked to for all ministrations, the hands that would in that moment give anything to touch your child's living flesh again.

Michelle had been spared, and, in this case, Jane had been spared too.

There had been no helplessness, no paralysis, and matters had been in her hands like they'd never been before. Nothing had ever felt so compellingly instinctive. There had been no fear, not for herself. There had been no choices, no decisions: only actions, only necessary deeds. It had seemed as though she was a passenger inside her own body, and someone else, someone tens of thousands of years more experienced, was doing the driving.

She sipped her tea and obliged her first-aider with the politest minimum of conversational responses necessary to convey that she didn't much feel like talking. The police might get more, but they'd need to wait; she wasn't ready, and nor did she feel like she would be for a while yet. At this stage she was still struggling to assemble her memories coherently. They were like jumbled snippets of film and audio footage that still had to be correctly juxtaposed in order to create a linear narrative. Some of them told of events, some of them only of thoughts and feelings, and while she could dwell on them individually, she couldn't yet work out how they all fitted together. One element in particular jarred discordantly with the rest; or perhaps it was fairer to say that the rest was consistently discordant and thus rendered this one, oddly harmonious element out of place.

Moments played in loop-back, over and over, out of sequence. Sounds echoed, words repeated. She knew the story and knew that it had worked out in the end, but knew also that it was not a happy tale. Rachel's terrified screams cut shrilly through her and would do so forever in her memory (though Rachel herself would be over it by bedtime thanks to that kiddy resilience that helped ensure the very survival of the species). Jane had felt a horror, a wrenching fear of loss like nothing she'd experienced in her life, and in each of those looping moments there was danger, violence, destruction and pain. All of which, she could, given time and enough tea, just about fit together.

The jarring element was the hardest to isolate, the most difficult to expose and consider, never mind find a place for, because it wasn't supposed to be there. It had taken her a reluctant while to acknowledge its presence, but there it undeniably was, hidden deep and secret as any other uncomfortable truth about herself. It didn't fit, it didn't belong, and people would say it wasn't right, but she couldn't pretend it didn't exist either.

She looked at her hands, the grazes minimal now that the blood and dirt had been washed away. The backs of her fingers stroked the rip in her trousers, felt the tender skin and pulsing ache below. Her heart still thumped like after her first ever workout, and her limbs sang in the afterglow of their exertion.

'You poor thing,' the first-aider said yet again, repeating the sentiment she'd heard from just about everyone except Michelle, who'd stuck to thank-yous. 'How awful for you.'

But she didn't feel like a poor thing.

Jane took a mouthful of tea and nodded, but her wordless assent was to herself, not the woman with the cotton wool.

It hadn't been awful for her.

She'd enjoyed it.

That didn't alter the many, many ways in which it had been one of the most horrible experiences of her life, and her fear for Rachel was something she never wanted to feel the like of again. There was anger, also hatred, still simmering from the act itself, and a fierce burning outrage that he had got away, which she knew she would draw upon when it came time to talk to the police. But despite it all, there was a part of her that had never been so alive as in those blurred, extreme, insane moments: so in control, so defined, so consumed, so full of purpose, so unstoppable, so bloody, utterly magnificent. And that part of herself wanted to feel that way again.

Instead, she was facing a slow come-down towards mundane reality: this cup of tea, questions from the polis, then home for a change of these torn trousers, and time to make the dinner. What night was it? Tuesday. Mince and tatties followed by live Champions League football. Haud me back.

It struck her that this was the first she'd even thought of Tom since the incident, and now that she had, it depressed her. Unlike Michelle, it hadn't even occurred to her to call her husband. She didn't want his comfort, nor did she even much want to tell him about it. He would only patronise her and belittle what she'd been through. He'd inevitably make her feel like a victim, almost wilfully misinterpreting what she told him in order to edit out the parts that didn't fit in with his image and expectations of her. But perhaps more icily than that, she didn't want to tell him because she felt that this was hers and she didn't want to share it. Not with him. Not with anyone yet, but definitely not with him. This was hers and he would only ruin it.

'I've a needle and thread downstairs if you want me to fix that tear,' the first-aid woman offered.

Jane looked again at her trousers, pulled automatically from the wardrobe that morning because she knew no single pair in there had any more style than the rest. She was a whole mountainside beneath the height of fashion, but even she drew the line at breeks with a stitched-up rip down the side.

'It's all right,' she said. 'I'll just change when I get home.'

'Can I get you another cuppa or anything?'

Jane was about to answer in the negative, when the woman's mobile began ringing. Or rather, Jane assumed it was the first-aider's until the woman said: 'I'll let you get your phone.'

'I don't have a phone,' Jane replied.

'Well, it's not mine. Mine's downstairs in my jacket.'

The ringing continued: a standard, electronic double chime as opposed to a melody, accompanied by a faint pulsing buzz. Jane looked down next to the table and realised that the sound was coming from her bag. She bent over and reached into it, feeling vibrations against the leather as she moved aside her purse, a short umbrella, a packet of baby wipes and a copy of the *Big Issue*. Her fingers found it before she saw it, feeling it pulse through a towelling bib right at the bottom of the bag. She lifted it out. It was silver, sleek and compact. Jane held it in her palm as it continued to chime, regarding it with the same puzzlement as though it was an alien artefact dropped from the skies.

Then she remembered: at the supermarket, the girl with the American accent, Rachel pointing to her bag where it lay in the trolley seat.

Lady dropped her phone. It's in your bag, Gran.

But the American girl had denied it and held up her phone to demonstrate. Held up *a* phone to demonstrate. What the hell?

She dropped her phone. Ring, ring. Ring, ring.

Ring, ring, it chimed on.

'Are you going to answer it?'

'I'm not sure how.'

'I'll show you.'

The first-aider took it between her forefinger and thumb and unfolded the device with a snap. She held it out to Jane, saying: 'Press the green button to answer.'

Jane took it from her tentatively, pushed the button and held the phone reluctantly to her ear.

'Hello?' she ventured delicately.

'Good afternoon,' said a male voice, relaxed and confident.

'Ehm, before you say anything, I have to let you know, this . . .'

'Isn't your phone, I know. It's mine.'

'Oh, right. I see. It's not stolen, just so you know. Well, maybe it was, but not by me.'

133

'I know that too, Mrs Fleming.'

'If you're wanting to come and get it, I'll tell you where I am, but it's not exactly the best time. Mind you, there's police here. I could give it to them and . . .'

Jane stopped talking. Her cognitive abilities were understandably a little out of synch, given everything they'd been processing over the past hour or so, so it took an extra couple of seconds for her to deduce what was wrong with his last remark. By that point, however, he had trumped it.

'Not the best time, I appreciate that. And quite an understatement given that you're talking about the attempted abduction of your granddaughter. Are you alone, Mrs Fleming?'

Jane now had the phone clamped to her ear, staring blankly at the open door to the stairs. She blinked and glanced at the first-aider, who was looking expectantly towards her for news.

'No,' she stated.

'Then please ensure that you are before we continue this conversation.'

Jane instinctively placed a hand over the mouthpiece, though it wasn't the man at the other end she wished to prevent from eavesdropping.

'I'm sorry, would you mind leaving me a minute, please?' she said.

The woman gave her a look of puzzlement which Jane met with a stern nod. The first-aider then withdrew with a shrug and closed the door.

'Who are you?' Jane asked immediately. 'And how do you know about—'

'About Rachel? Believe me, this is *not* about Rachel.'

Jane felt a surge of anger.

'Was it you?' she demanded, though the very idea posed a cascade of questions, none of which she could concentrate to focus on.

'No. I have no interest in your granddaughter. But neither did the man who tried to take her.'

'So what is this about?'

'Have a look at the screen.'

'What screen?' she asked, looking around the room, her paranoia reasonably extending to assume he could somehow see where she was sitting. He seemed to know everything else.

'On the phone,' he clarified.

Jane took the phone from her ear and felt that cold steel fist for the second time. The little LCD window showed a photograph of Ross. Jane tried to speak but found her throat blocked.

'Now press the right arrow key on the keypad.'

She complied, accidentally doing it twice. She saw a photograph flash past, replaced immediately by another. It showed a room in disarray, utterly ransacked.

'These were taken yesterday morning at your son's apartment in Chassignan.'

She pressed the left arrow key. The previous image was restored: a kitchen in a similar state of chaos. She'd never seen Ross's place, never visited him in France. There seemed no reason for the man to be lying but no reason why she should believe him either. She pressed forward again. A third picture of the trashed apartment appeared. On one wall, tiny though the image was, she recognised a Celtic poster.

'Oh God,' she whispered.

'Your son is missing, and if you wish to help him, you're going to have to accede unquestioningly to my requests.'

She swallowed, fighting tears. 'What do you want? Money? My husband and I don't have much, but—'

'No, I don't want money, Mrs Fleming. I want you.'

'Me?' she asked, her incredulity undisguised. 'In exchange for Ross?'

'I'm not offering an exchange, but if you want to see him again, you're going to have to stop asking questions and start following instructions.'

'And I take it the first of those is not to talk to the police?' she stated acidly.

'You may talk to them if you wish, but they will not be able to help you. They will only waste your time and your son's time, and I cannot stress this enough: time is not something you can afford to lose. Neither is your temper.'

'Okay,' Jane said. She composed herself, silenced her questions, calmed her indignation. 'Okay, what do you want?'

'I need you, and you alone, to get to the address shown on

the final image and I need you to get there by this time tomorrow. That's twenty-four hours starting now.'

She toggled through the pictures until she came to one showing a black, wrought-iron double gate. Beneath it, there was some text superimposed:

Rue Marisse
Le Muy
Region La Var
France

'France? Tomorrow?'

Jane immediately began thinking about flights, trying to recall how much money she had in her current account, how much credit on the Mastercard. Then she remembered something dreadful.

'But I don't have a passport. It's away being renewed. I don't even have a car. It's just been written off.'

'Then you can't help your son. Goodbye.'

'No, wait,' she implored, but the line had gone dead. She stared, bereft, at the phone, wishing she knew how to redial the last number, wishing she could believe it would make a difference.

There was a knock at the door. The first-aider opened it a little and stuck her head through the gap.

'Eh, the police were just wondering if you're ready to talk to them yet.'

Jane nodded, holding up a finger to say she'd be a minute.

They will not be able to help you. They will only waste your time and your son's time.

The cold steel fist had gripped again when she saw Ross's picture and heard the words: *Your son is missing.* Now it was ready to develop into its full-blown state: the helplessness, the paralysis, the agony of not knowing and the indignity of not acting. Through the door and down the stairs lay a conversation with the police, a deliverance of matters into their hands. It would not be an interview: it would be an abdication, a resignation, and beyond it lay a seat on the sidelines next to Tom to endure an endless, excruciating, impotent wait for other hands to act. It would be the very antithesis of that which had seized her, propelled her, *electrified* her as she fought to rescue Rachel. Today, she had experienced what it was to feel truly alive, and, despite the circumstances precipitating it, she'd found herself wishing for more. That wish had just been granted. What on earth, she asked herself, at this moment, in this life of hers, did she have to lose?

Only time.

She slipped the phone into her jacket breast pocket, picked up her bag and headed for the stairs. There were two police waiting for her, one male, one female, standing next to a table around which several members of staff were seated. The place had been evacuated apart from witnesses, some of whom were still waiting to give statements. The place was strangely still and quiet, the climbing structure looking somehow smaller now that it was denuded of its regular swarms.

The policewoman stepped forward as Jane came through the door leading up to the 'party room', but Jane fended her off.

'I've just got to nip to the Ladies,' she told her, turning a hundred and eighty degrees to go through an adjacent door.

Jane looked back to check whether she was being watched. Through the wire-meshed glass panel on the window she could see the policewoman had returned to conversation with her colleague. Good. She walked around the L-bend beyond the Ladies and the baby-changing room. The Gents was on the left, and dead ahead was an emergency exit. There was no question that this constituted an emergency, but she knew it couldn't provide her exit as the door was alarmed, principally to prevent someone doing precisely what had been attempted upon Rachel earlier. On the right was a third door, marked Staff Only. Her long-earned familiarity with the building's layout told her that it must be the entrance to the kitchen, which she banked on being unoccupied as all of the staff were out front continuing the group self-recrimination exercise they'd embarked upon as soon as they learned what had happened.

She turned the handle and, to her relief, the door opened. As she entered, she had it in her head that there was an outside door at the rear of the kitchen, but couldn't be sure whether this was something she had noted on her many visits to buy coffees, juice and lollipops; something she had deduced logically from considering a commercial kitchen's health and safety requirements; or something she had merely decided from raw, desperate need. Jane kept her head low as she entered the room. A tall, stainless-steel shelving unit formed the only screen between the cooking area and the serving counter, from beyond which she might be visible. She darted behind it and was relieved to see that there was indeed an outside door, exactly where she had envisaged it. She notched that one up to memory. For some reason, it seemed important not to attribute it to a lucky break, perhaps because she, more than ever, needed to believe she knew what she was doing.

The outside door was neither locked nor alarmed. She opened it quickly, wincing a little as it squeaked, then pulled it behind her. She had a mind not to close it fully, in case the noise brought any investigation, but there was enough of a wind to threaten that it might bang shut on its own. She delicately pressed it to, released the handle and began walking briskly along the side of the building, heading towards the path that led to the supermarket car park. A snidey voice in her head asked whether she had any idea where she was actually going. It sounded a bit like Tom. She was slightly surprised to already have a firm answer. That other, thousands of years older woman was telling Tom to shut up and turn back to the football. This was women's work.

She knew exactly where she was going: the airport. She didn't have a passport, but it was the quickest way to get to the south coast of England where she might exploit softer options than air travel for crossing the Channel. Other means might be less security conscious, especially going in that direction; nobody was particularly worried about the threat of people illegally sneaking *out* of the country.

First, however, she needed wheels, and her own car wasn't quite in showroom condition right then. That was why she was heading to the supermarket, where she could call a taxi; she had forty or so in cash in her purse, and reckoned twenty-five or thirty would cover it. Then that particular train of thought derailed as she realised that paying her fare should barely be registering on her list of priority considerations. In fact, if it appeared at all, it would be categorised as an unnecessary and therefore unaffordable expense, and not merely of money. She only had a few minutes before the police came looking for her, and she of all people knew that at rush-hour a taxi could be at least a quarter of an hour in responding to the call-out. To say nothing of the fact that the driver would later be able to tell the cops where he'd taken her, and she might well be caught up with again before she had the chance to get on a plane. Not having broken any laws, they couldn't physically restrain her, but she felt it imperative to extricate herself from official interference, not least because she wouldn't fancy answering questions about what the hell she thought she was doing.

She needed a car of her own and she needed it immediately. Her first notion was to head for the supermarket's petrol station, near the entrance to the car park, but it was on the side of the hill and its forecourt in direct sight of Kaos Kottage. It was also a rather conspicuous spot to be hanging around on foot, even if she didn't look a standard photo-fit for the type of potential twoccer of whom most drivers were likely to be wary. Besides, who left their keys in the ignition when they were filling up? She looked around. There were dozens, acres of cars lined up in all directions. But not a drop to drink, she thought ruefully. Then her eyes alighted upon the front of the supermarket, and she knew exactly how to slake her thirst.

The car park was enormous, and even at busy times there were plenty of spaces to be found if you drove a few rows back. Immediately to the left of the entrance there was a row of specially reserved spaces for disabled drivers, denoted on the tarmac by yellow badges; while *directly* in front of the entrance, there was a specially reserved space for four-by-four drivers, denoted by two thick yellow lines.

She didn't have to wait long, only a few minutes, and there was certainly nothing conspicuous during that time about a lone woman standing expectantly outside the doors of a supermarket, other than perhaps her lack of shopping. A black BMW X5 soon pulled up, and as it approached she was pleased to note that the driver was not hanging off the wheel and looking searchingly into the shop. This was the explanatory body language offered by those who were picking someone up, though it failed to also explain why they couldn't do this by simply

139

finding a proper space and walking twenty yards. Such inconveniences were presumably for lesser members of society without such hectic and important lives, who could better spare the few seconds it took to perambulate from those parking bays surely intended only for the proletariat and their normal-sized vehicles.

Instead, she hit paydirt, seeing the hazard warning lights flash even before the vehicle had come to a complete stop. The hazards were oscillating a unique form of Morse code that Jane had learned to decipher thus: IN A BIG HURRY STOP JUST NIPPING IN FOR ONE THING STOP CAN'T EXPECT ME TO PARK THIS THING ALL THE WAY OVER THERE AND WALK JUST FOR THE SAKE OF A PINT OF MILK STOP FOR GOD'S SAKE I'LL ONLY BE A MINUTE STOP LOOK I'VE EVEN LEFT THE ENGINE RUNNING STOP.

Oh yes, you even have.

Jane watched the driver get out and jog through the automatic doors. She quickly checked the rear for unseen junior passengers, then opened the vehicle and climbed in. It was an automatic, which would make things simpler. Just two pedals, one steering wheel and several tons of unnecessary bulk. She wished Michelle was here for this moment.

You've never exactly been the essence of urban rebellion, have you? I don't think you've ever had a parking ticket.

Yes, honey, but that was the old me. You might prefer the new one. She's a car thief.

Jane put the beast into drive and hit the accelerator.

She got a bit of a fright when music suddenly started blaring at her from all sides, and realised the stereo must have been changing CDs, like Catherine's Merc which had that thingy in the boot. It was an old punk-style number that began playing, everyone in the band not so much trying to stay in time as each trying to play faster than the rest. An angry, defiant and so very, very youthful voice sounded insistently over it, entreating her to declare herself an unsafe building.

'I think I just did,' Jane said.

'Hey Lex.'
'Hey Reb.'

'You doin' okay?'

'You ever shoot two people you'd just met, twice each in the head, and burn their bodies?'

'Not that I can recall.'

'Well, that's how I'm doin'.'

'What's your twenty?'

'I'm currently headed north-west on the A-seven-twenty-six. I don't have eyes on the target, but I know where she's headed.'

'How's she doin'?'

'Oh, pretty good. She just aced grand theft auto on the first attempt. Availed herself of a nice SUV, so she's travelling in style.'

'Where's she travelling to?'

'My money says GLA.'

'So she gets on a plane to NCE and we take Air Bett back to base?' Rebekah asked optimistically.

'Afraid not. She doesn't have a passport – latest heads-up from Bett.'

'Shit. So why aren't we taking her? What's the point in having your own private chopper if—'

'I know, I know. That's exactly what I said to him.'

'Yeah, right. Sure you did.'

'He said the parameters hadn't changed. No intervention. I guess he wants to see if she got game.'

'Figures. If she can't manage something as simple as evading border security, she ain't gonna handle the hard stuff too well. But if it doesn't alter the parameters, why the heads-up on the passport?'

'So we'd know she couldn't just jump on the first flight to the Côte d'Azure. You know the deal: where she goes, I follow, and it looks like I'll be taking the long way around.'

'Well, if you glance up from hurling your guts over the side of a ferry, I'll give you a wave as I pass.'

Jane had to steel herself to ward off the potentially debilitating paranoia that everyone on the road could see she was driving a stolen car, and that the police would be forming road blocks right then somewhere around Rouken Glen. Keep the heid, girl, she told herself, suspecting she'd have to get a lot more comfortable with criminality if she was to reach her destination in time, or indeed at all. Thinking rationally, the only possible outward indicator that she didn't own the X5 she was driving was that she wasn't driving it like she owned it, which would of course entail driving like she also owned the road.

She hit a bit of a tailback around Clarkston Toll, and came to a stop behind a silver Saab as a telephone sounded inside the car, accompanied by a blinking light to the left of the steering wheel. She noticed for the first time a tiny black Nokia clamped to a hands-free unit. Tentatively, she reached out and hit the green call button before remembering who the call would be intended for. She was wrong, however. For the second time that day, a call on someone else's phone was intended for her, though this time the caller was a little less informed.

'Hello?'

'Hell . . .' he started, a little surprised perhaps to have got an answer. 'Now listen here. This is the person whose car you've just stolen. I don't know who the fuck you are, and I know you think you'll get away with this, but I'm tellin' you, I'm gaunny fuckin' find you, and when I do—'

'Excuse me, sir,' she interrupted. 'I don't believe there's any need for that language, and I don't think your threatening tone is very constructive either.'

'Very cons— Who the fuck are you?'

'I work for Safeway car-parks' management. Your car hasn't been stolen, it's been towed. We've removed the phone to my office here for security reasons.'

'Towed? But I was only in the bloody shop two seconds.'

'We're having a crackdown on people parking in highly inappropriate and inconsiderate places. We're hoping that if you have to walk a few miles to retrieve your vehicle, you'll consider it a shorter walk in future if you just park in one of the many clearly marked spaces we provide.'

There was an enormously satisfying silence.

'Sir?'

'So where do I go to get my car back?'

'All towed vehicles are impounded at our main depot in Bellshill.'

'Bellshill? How am I supposed to ... Okay. Right. Jesus. What's the address?'

'I'm sorry, sir, you're breaking up. I think the power's running out on your ...'

With which she hung up, giggling. That felt good. Damn, that felt good. At the back of her mind – well, actually a lot nearer the front than that – there remained the hollow, cold knowledge of why she was doing this, but its sheer imperative compulsion was liberating her from all of her normal concerns and compunctions. Right now, for once in her life, everybody else could ... God, it had been so long since she'd said that word ... Everybody else could ... parenthood and grandparenthood had disciplined her out of using it, and she'd even started *thinking* in the more guarded and polite terms that she could tolerate the weans repeating. Everybody else could ... she'd said it all the time, and worse, when she was younger, before she became Jane Fleming. But today, she wasn't Jane Fleming, not any more. She was Jane Bell again. Blue Bell. And everybody else could fuck off.

She dumped the X5 in the short-stay car park nearest the terminal. It had been tempting to slew it in front of Departures and just walk away, thus ensuring that it really did get towed and impounded, but she knew from her taxi experience that there would be plenty of polis patrolling up and down, and didn't want to run the risk of being stopped on her way into the building. Nor would it be wise for the registration to be noted for any reason, given that the owner would by now have ascertained from Safeway that they had nothing to do with his vehicle's disappearance.

The first plane to London was to Heathrow. She had it in her head that Gatwick would be closer for getting to the coast, but it certainly wasn't ninety minutes closer, which was how much longer she'd have to wait for a flight there.

It was the first time she'd ever just walked up to the counter and bought a ticket, most of her previous flights being package charters booked months in advance by Tom.

'Return?' the girl had asked, with unknowing poignancy.

'No,' Jane stated firmly. 'One way.'

She paid with her credit card. It went through her mind that the transaction was traceable, but it was only a ticket to London, and besides, the guy hadn't asked her to disappear, only to get there. She was starting to think like a fugitive, perhaps even a criminal, and was surprised to consider this was no bad thing.

She had about forty minutes before boarding, which she put to use planning the next leg of the journey. Ten minutes or so on a walk-up internet terminal outlined her options for crossing into France by train, either on foot at Ashford via Eurostar or by car at Folkestone via Eurotunnel. The good news was the services ran late enough that she should be able to make the trip that night. The bad news was both websites' boasts about passenger screening and security. Neither option was going to be simple without a passport, which was the issue she addressed during the remainder of her wait.

She went to an autoteller and lifted the maximum two hundred pounds in cash, figuring the next fare she paid might present a discrepancy between the card-bearer's name and that of the passenger, especially given that she didn't know what that passenger's name was yet. Then she went back downstairs to the check-in area and looked at the screen listing international departures. She took position by a pillar and watched the queue for a Tenerife charter, carefully observing each party as they approached the desk. Looks and age wouldn't matter, as nothing she could effect was going to withstand close scrutiny. It was all about opportunity, and she'd know it when she saw it.

It came in the form of four pensioners, all women, who took an unfeasible time to accomplish the relatively simple process of depositing their luggage and handing over their documents. Jane checked her watch. She'd have ten minutes at the most, and at this rate the group she was watching would still be arguing over who would sit where well after that had expired. Nonetheless, patiently but anxiously she waited, because they represented the best chance. It was nothing to do with their disorganisation or any prejudiced notion that their age would make them a more distractible target for pocket-picking. It was quite simply their hand-luggage: three of them were carrying open-topped, twin-handled bags, presumably all the better to tote

144

more duty-free, into which they had popped their tickets, boarding cards and passports.

Jane watched them bumble their way up the escalator and then followed at a distance of a few yards. They made their way predictably to the shopping mall on the upper level, where one of them broke away in stated search of the toilets, leaving the others, as Jane had hoped, to browse in John Menzies. The three of them tarried around the women's magazines, all but blocking the lane, which provided plausible cover for Jane to edge past, close-up against each of them, looking down for the most attainable glimpse of burgundy vinyl. The unlucky candidate had her bag slung over her shoulder by one strap, rather than held at arm's length, which put it at a convenient height for Jane to reach inside as the woman stretched for a copy of the *People's Friend*.

She walked unhurriedly out towards the domestic departure gate, unable to stop herself thinking of the fact that her actions had just denied some poor old wifey her holiday. There had been a horrible couple ahead of them in the queue, a wee nyaff in unacceptable grey slacks and an absurd beige canvas jacket, haranguing the check-in girl with affected incredulity about there not being a smoking section on the plane, while his wife stood with her arms folded, nodding her 'aye, aye, that's right's in torn-faced agreement. Jane would have been happy to torpedo *their* holiday, but the wee nyaff had taken both their passports and zipped them into one of at least a dozen pockets on his appalling outerwear. It was a pity, but pity was one more thing she was going to have to get over. Before this thing was through, she feared she'd have to be a lot more ruthless than this.

Jane stole her second car within forty minutes of touching down at Heathrow. It would have been half that time, but she had an important bit of business with a photo booth she'd needed to conclude before moving on. She acquired herself a rather tasty green new-model Volkswagen Beetle on the first floor of the Terminal One short-stay car park. A quick recce having established that it was a pay-on-foot arrangement, she was not surprised to observe that, in keeping with practices in Lanarkshire, most drivers who had forgotten to pay opted not to re-park and walk to a machine. Instead, they generally drove to the nearest pay-station and left their cars on the yellow chevrons in front while they nipped behind the glass partition – engines running to emphasise the intended brevity of their stop. Jane had waited less than five minutes for her chance, bearing her own ticket that she'd gone downstairs to the entrance barrier to procure before nipping up a level and paying, as the signs instructed, on foot. On this occasion she'd seen the owner re-appear in the rear-view mirror, running hopelessly after her stolen pride and joy, before disappearing from view as Jane accelerated down the curving ramp.

'Hey.'
  'Hey.'
  'Where you at, fly girl?'
  'Somewhere close to the sea, either Norfolk or Essex, not sure precisely. I followed the coast, kept me away from the busiest ATC flight paths. Right now I'm in a field, so there ain't much to see.'
  'What are you doing in a field?'
  'Waiting. Air Bett doesn't fly as fast as a BA 757, but nor does it require one-hour check-ins and it doesn't need to circle in the stack above LHR.'
  'Tell me about it.'
  'How's our girl?'
  'Oh, so far so good. She's now standing at two counts of GTA, plus one of larceny. Given it was a passport, that probably comes into a higher category than petty theft. Pretty clumsy lift, to be honest, but she got away with it. Need to hope they don't go checking the CCTV tapes from the store where she made her move, but that's not likely. The old lady she swiped it from probably thinks she dropped it someplace.'
  'She's robbing old ladies now, huh?'
  'Yeah. What *have* we created here? She's a one-woman crime spree. And to her running total I think we can probably add forgery. She stopped at a twenty-four-hour supermarket a ways back. I didn't follow her in, but she was pretty busy in the car for a while before hitting the freeway again.'

'I think they call them motorways here.'

'Well hark at you, Lady Rebekah. One day in England and you're an expert.'

'Where is she now?'

'Folkestone. Channel Tunnel rail terminus.'

'You called that right, then.'

'Easy enough. I logged on to the web terminal she'd used at the airport and checked what she'd been looking at.'

'Can you do that?'

'*I* can do that.'

'Figures. Easy for some, huh?'

'Tricky part was Heathrow. I booked a hire car online before boarding the flight, but I couldn't collect until I knew what she was driving. Had to stand right by and watch while a vehicle was stolen in front of my eyes. The scandal. Good job she helped herself to something distinctive. I caught her up after about forty minutes. She was sticking to the limit to avoid the cops. But so far so good, and now we're going underground.'

'Only if her forgery skills pass muster.'

'A condition that couldn't be more prominent in my mind right now, Reb. Or hers. Looks like they examine your docs at a drive-through checkpoint. She's two cars away from finding out. Correction, one car now.'

'You got a contingency if this goes belly-up?'

'Yeah. I'm gonna step in as a Scottish cop and say she's already wanted north of the border.'

'They got a lot of Canadian cops over here, then?'

'I'll fake the accent.'

'Sounds like her forgery skills really are our best hope.'

'Thanks for the vote of confidence. Oh, hang on. Here we go. Her turn.'

'Fingers crossed.'

'Come on, come on, come on. Drive forward, girl, drive forward. Go on, man, wave her through. Wave her . . . oh shit. Oh fuck, this don't look good. She's getting out of the car. He's coming out of the booth. Reb, I gotta go.'

Jane had done a lot of scary things already that day, but none of them had made her feel as anxious as this, because none of them had made her feel so literally hemmed in. At all other junctures and dilemmas, there had been options, the safety net of alternatives. That, in fact, was really why she'd driven past the Ashford off-ramp and carried on to Folkestone. Ashford was for walking passengers only, and the literature promised airport-style security measures. Passport control was these days the least stringent aspect of such regimes, but it would most likely still be enough to rumble her *Blue Peter* effort, and the means of distraction she had in mind could only be pulled off if she had space and privacy to work. Folkestone and its drive-on channels offered that, but the moment she entered one of them, it felt very much like a last resort.

There'd been one final alternative before this, which she'd also had in mind as she ignored the Ashford exit on the M20, one that might eschew the need for a passport at all. With it being a popular alternative to the 'booze cruise' (the Chunnel funnel?) she reckoned there would be a few transit vans with empty storage compartments on their way to the Calais hyper-markets. Stow away in the back of one of those, then get driven on to the train and she wouldn't even have to spring for the fare. On the other hand, she didn't know whether the first thing the officials did was throw open the doors and check there weren't six fare-dodgers inside. In the event, the opportunity hadn't arisen. She'd only encountered a single such van that was parked, and didn't think she could sneak aboard one waiting in the queue without the driver hearing noises from the back. The stationary one was outside the terminal complex, and she had given the doors a try as she passed on her way to buy a ticket, but they were locked. It was unsurprising. People were bound to be extra vigilant these days, everyone terrified of returning to HM Customs and finding half-a-dozen Somalians lying in the back, pished out of their faces on your Euro-bevvy.

So that had left her exercising her final option, here at the terminus, the end of the line. She knew it was all or nothing when she guided the Beetle into the approach lane, but the real ice-in-the-gut sensation had come when a car pulled up behind her, meaning there was no way out but forward.

She waited until there were only three cars to go before

opening her bag and removing some of her recent purchases. There had been an all-night Tesco just off the motorway, where, in addition to some clean knickers and a toothbrush, she picked up some scissors, a transparent plastic wallet and some Pritt-stick, as well as clearing their entire shelf-stock of red food colouring. The photo page on the passport wouldn't bear any kind of close inspection, though she hadn't done too bad a job of switching the pics. The first thing they were there to establish was that you were carrying a passport at all. After that, the degree of vigilance could be reduced under the right circumstances, or at least that's what she was relying upon.

She removed a couple of hankies from the packet and then began emptying some bottles of food colouring on to them. She surveyed the results. It had been a veritable cochineal-beetle bloodbath, but not bloody enough for her satisfaction. The stuff just didn't run properly, and looked too damn pink as soon as it hit any kind of material, even under the artificial light of the terminus' floodlamps. Worse, on the flesh of her hand, it looked like nothing other than dye. She'd thought about beetroot back at the store, but the smell was potentially too much of a give-away.

The Audi two places in front moved on, taking her one car length closer to the booth.

There was only one way to do this properly, and it wasn't going to be pleasant. She bent down out of sight, balled her right hand into a fist and drove it against her nose.

Ow.

It hurt like buggery, bringing tears to her eyes but no blood to her nostrils.

Shit. She tried again. Sorer, cumulatively, but probably more tentative than the first attempt and thus no more successful. She looked up. The car in front was being waved forward to the window.

Jane bent forward again with renewed determination. She'd been through a sight more pain than this for Ross: thirteen hours' labour to deliver just over eight pounds of baby, most of it head. This was nothing.

She remembered accidentally bursting Margaret Heron's nose at netball in third year, her horrified insistence to the victim and the teacher that she hadn't thrown the ball hard. Don't worry, Miss Kane had said. It wasn't the force, it was the angle.

Jane turned the heel of her right palm towards her and brought it upwards on to the bridge. The running sensation commenced almost immediately. Her nose began streaming blood from her left nostril, dripping messily on to her hands and the bunched-up hankies. She lifted the passport and tickets and let it trickle on to those too, then looked up to see her car being waved forward by the man in the booth, an older bloke with white hair and a matching moustache.

Jane brought the Beetle in line with the window, holding the hankies up to her nose with her left hand, gripping the steering wheel with her right. She gestured with a single finger – give me a minute – then held her head back against the seat. The man in the booth was mouthing 'Are you all right?', which reminded her that her window wasn't wound down. Instead of reaching for the button, she undid her seat belt and climbed right out of the car, holding the passport, tickets and hankies together against her face with her left hand as her right worked the handle. Blood continued to drip from her face and hands as she stood next to the Beetle.

'Are you hurt, madam?'

She shook her head.

'It's okay. It just came on like that. Usually an early warning sign of a bad cold, with me. Typical timing.'

She offered him the ticket and passport, blood still running among her fingers and on to the documents as she held them out. His hand hesitated visibly, signalling his queasy reluctance to even touch them, never mind take hold. He delicately pinched the passport at a blood-free corner, the ticket falling to the ground. They both went to lift it, but he got there first.

'No, no, keep your head back,' he advised.

She did, but tilted it slightly to look down as the inspector bent to retrieve the ticket. He pulled it partially out of its paper wallet as he stood up again, gripping both parts where there were no smears. The passport remained pinched between his left forefinger and thumb.

'Maybe I should get someone to take a look at you.'

'I'll be fine in a minute, honestly,' Jane assured him. 'Besides,

I don't want to hold everybody up.' She glanced back along the queue, as did the passport inspector, still holding both documents extremely gingerly.

'All right, well, just take your time, dear,' he said. 'If any of 'em toots their horns, I'll sign 'em up for full body-cavity searches.'

Jane laughed through the hankies, eyeing the passport. He still hadn't checked it.

'I think it's easing up,' she said, pinching her nose with her right hand. She offered her left to take the documents. 'Sorry about the mess.'

'Just you look after yourself,' he told her. He seemed about to hand her the documents, then pulled back. A well-practised flick of the wrist opened the passport at the photo page, at which he grimaced, blood having been splattered across both sides of the hinge like a Rorschach test. He let it close on itself and placed it into her waiting hand with another queasy grimace.

'Thank you,' she told him, and took a step back towards the car.

'Have you got your vehicle papers, madam?' he asked.

Jane felt her eyes widen before she could do anything to compose herself.

'In . . . in the glove compartment,' she recovered enough to suggest, though she had no idea what, if anything, lay in there, only that none of it would be in the right name.

'Okay. It's just a reminder in case people have forgotten. Going to the continent and all.'

'No, I'm all present and correct.'

'All right, then. I'd say mind how you go, but it looks like I'm too late,' he added with a little laugh.

Jane got back into the Beetle and dropped the documents on to the passenger seat. Her instinct was to put the foot down and drive away immediately, but she had to quell it. Instead, she sat with the hanky at her nose for another few seconds, offering the man a smile and a thumb-up gesture, then pulled slowly forwards, one hand still pinching her snib, towards where a girl in a brightly coloured jumpsuit was waving cars into slots aboard the train.

In her rear-view she could see the passport man, back in his booth, leaning out to greet the next driver. Sigh was too short a word for the exhalation that followed.

Jane opted to stay in the Beetle rather than take a seat on the train. She could have seriously done with a coffee right then, but considered it more circumspect to remain out of view. A sudden, in-progress nosebleed explained her condition to the passport officer, but her appearance might prove disturbing – memorably, remarkably disturbing – to her fellow passengers.

Weird. There'd been clothes at the all-night supermarket, but it hadn't occurred to her to lift any, just the spare undies. All her thinking was pared down to essentials. She didn't know how much money she might need, and was even less sure how much she actually had, liquid or credit, so spending any of it on even cheap jeans and a T-shirt seemed an unaffordable luxury and possibly a reckless financial gamble.

She had a look at herself in the sun-visor mirror. Blood still rimmed her nostrils and smeared her top lip. Her hands were sticky with it, her clothes dotted by it. She definitely, definitely wouldn't be getting those trousers repaired.

Yes. Best to remain hidden right enough.

Some chamber in her mind echoed with a recall of the last time she looked in a mirror. Was it really that morning? It already felt like years ago, some memory of an earlier time in her life.

Even in the insulated and suspension-cushioned capsule of the VW, she felt the train begin to decelerate, prompting another quickening of the pulse and tightness in the gut. She hoped to hell the website had been right about clearing all officialdom at the English end and simply driving clear at Calais.

An announcement over the PA announced their imminent arrival and informed her that the local time was an hour ahead of GMT. She looked at the dashboard's digital clock, which read 11:05: only eight hours since she'd been watching the weans play at Kaos Kottage in East Kilbride.

The train stopped and only a few seconds later the huge side doors slid back, allowing cars to begin filing out. She started the engine and pulled away slowly. There were no booths, no officials, no customs checks: just an overhead sign reminding her to drive on the right, and, beyond it, open French road. She

152

put her foot down and enjoyed a moment of blessed relief, which turned very soon into fatigue. With the pressure off – for the time being, at least – her aching body was able to get a word of protest heard above the rest of the voices clamouring in her head.

She had already decided to drive all the way rather than flying to Nice. A look at the road atlas she'd bought at the supermarket told her she could probably manage it in about ten hours. A flight would be far quicker, but not if it turned out that the first one out of Charles De Gaulle wasn't until three in the afternoon. Plus, she'd still need a car when she got there, and saw no point in taking on the risk of stealing another one.

A neon sign in the middle distance advertised a roadside motel. It was a chain name, a modest, low-rise and low-frills kind of place, conveniently anonymous. She came off at the next exit and drove into the car park, where she spent a few minutes cleaning herself up, employing the practised-mother's hanky-and-saliva method every daughter naively swears she'll never use herself. She checked her reflection again. It wasn't a pretty sight, but at least only for the usual reasons. It would do. She didn't want to attract anyone's interest or solicitations, and a lone female looking bashed-up would do precisely that. They'd think she must be on the run from someone scary and dangerous, but the truth was worse. She was on the run *to* someone scary and dangerous, and she couldn't afford to have anyone prevent her from doing so.

The room was clean and basic, though it did have a phone, which prompted a reminder that there were people back home who'd be very worried and not a little confused by now. She lifted the receiver, then placed it back down again without dialling any digits, before pulling the mobile phone from her jacket. No point in having the charge go on to her room bill; she'd let the mystery caller pay for it. In fact, she'd half a mind to dial her cousin Grace in New Zealand and leave it connected until the batteries ran out.

Instead, she called Michelle, finding it engaged. She tried her mobile instead, but it was switched off, probably for recharging given the hour. Jane remembered hearing Donald chide Michelle over this unnecessary practice, but she had retorted with something about not actually wanting to be phoned at that time of night, especially as the chances were it would be a confused Junior House Officer who'd misread the rota and phoned the wrong pharmacist.

Jane waited five minutes and tried again. Still engaged. Reluctantly, she dialled her own number. She'd hoped to have Michelle pass on the news to Tom, but she couldn't wait all night. She'd just give him a few bullet points and get off before he could start the histrionics.

That line was busy too. Reason told her they were most probably on the phone to each other. She could get through on Tom's mobile, she knew, which was when she was forced to admit to herself that she really didn't want to talk to him right then; only Michelle. She looked at the clock, calculating how much sleep she could hope to get before she'd need to be on the road again. It wasn't a lot, and it was ticking away against the pulsating sound of engaged tones.

Forget it, she thought. They'd be worried, sure, but she had to focus, prioritise. Their worries weren't her biggest concern. Sleep was more important.

She got undressed and climbed into bed. Twenty minutes later, she knew she had no chance of sleep without letting them know she was okay. That, whatever else she told herself, was immediate priority number one. She gave Michelle's number one more try.

'Mum! Where the hell are you? What's happened?'

'I'm okay.'

'The police have been round. They said you just disappeared. Dad's up to high doh. Where are you calling from?'

'Never mind about me. Is Rachel okay?'

'Never mind? Rachel's fine, but the rest of us are worried sick. Nobody could find you, and we didn't know what to think, after what happened today, and then . . . it was on TV about two burned bodies being discovered out by Calder Glen, and we were terrified that . . .'

'I'm sorry. I should have called sooner, but I never had the chance.'

'Why? Where are you?'

'I can't say. Look, I can't talk long. I just wanted you to know—'

'You can't talk . . . Mum, what's happened? Oh God. Are you . . . Is someone else there? Are you under some kind of duress? Just say "I'm fine" if that's the case.'

'There's no one else here, honey. Keep the heid. There's just something I have to do.'

'Like what? Why can't you tell me? What's going on?'

'I have to go now, honey. I'll be in touch. Call your dad for me, would you, please?'

'Me? Why aren't you calling him? What the hell do you want *me* to tell him?'

'Tell him . . .' Jane took a breath. 'Not to wait up.'

The sensation of coming around to the sound of the telephone's automated alarm call was the only evidence Jane had of actually having been asleep. It seemed like she'd just lain there all night feeling sore and beat, her head whirring as it processed memory and prepared for what was to come. There was no moment of bleary disorientation, no waves of reality crashing in to wash away the merciful oblivion of her dream-state. The second she was conscious, at exactly five a.m., she knew exactly where she was and what she had to do. She got up, pulled her clothes back on and checked out, before grabbing breakfast from a vending machine in the lobby: a styrofoam cup of bad coffee and a cellophane-wrapped *pain au chocolat*. She placed the coffee in the Beetle's cup holder and the pastry on the dashboard, beginning to consume both only once she was on the autoroute south.

Dawn broke some time after six. A crisp blue sky was revealed above, spring sunshine lighting the fields and bringing up the temperature on her instrument panel. Jane had always wanted to drive through France, and had, in her fantasies, imagined a sunny day just like the one that was shaping up, but she wasn't going to be stopping to take the air and see the sights. She just drove, eyes on the tarmac and the traffic, singularly and tirelessly mowing down the miles towards her destination, though it seldom left her thoughts that she had no idea what awaited her there.

I don't want money, Mrs Fleming. I want you.

What on earth did she have that this person could possibly want?

She tossed their brief conversation around and around in her head, trying to assess what could be inferred, what differences there might be between what he was saying and what she had interpreted him to mean.

I'm not offering an exchange.

She didn't know who this man was or what he had to do with Ross. What she did know was that he had taken pictures of Ross's ransacked apartment, and had been the one who broke it to her that her son was missing.

It hit her with a sudden chill that maybe she was in the process of delivering to this man the very thing that Ross didn't want: a weapon to use against him. What if the guy wanted Ross to do something, give him something, tell him something, but he wouldn't comply?

Believe me, this is not about Rachel.

How better to force his cooperation than to get hold of someone close to him? Rachel in the first instance, then, when that didn't work out, get his dear old mother to hand herself over.

But then she remembered: the phone had been secreted by that girl at the supermarket, before the attempt on Rachel. In any case, right then it didn't matter what it might or might not be about, what she could interpret or deduce. All that mattered was the one thing she knew for certain: if he said the only way to help her son was to get to this address, then she was going, as he put it, to accede unquestioningly to his request.

She made a couple of stops to fill up the tank and to stretch her legs, but she wasn't feeling the long haul as too much of a strain. Jane had always enjoyed driving, especially long distance on open roads like this, or in the city at night when the streets were quiet, these being the times you could really buy into that romantic notion of the car being an instrument of freedom. It was a good deal harder to believe that the road could take you anywhere when you were stuck on the M8 at Shawhead, the traffic moving slow enough for you to read, 'Wash me, please' and 'No hand signals – driver having a wank' scrawled on the grimy rear of the artic in front. Having provided an on-call, zero-notice free taxi service for Ross and Michelle for the best part of two decades, it was perhaps inevitable that it would occur to her to give it a go for real, especially when the alternative of an evening was sharing the living room with Vegetable Man and Henrik Larsson. That was arguably the greatest factor in her decision to start private-hire driving: avoiding the tandem isolation of two people who lived alongside each other rather than together; driving around in the darkness because it was too late to truly run away.

They weren't meant to be joined at the hip, and they weren't meant to share all of each other's enthusiasms, but at the very least they were meant to be pals, weren't they? She and Tom weren't pals. They were like workmates with nothing else in common but this shared occupation, speaking without saying anything other than the necessary technical discussion that the job in hand entailed. Right now, the job was living together and sometimes being grandparents. In the past, as mum and dad to two kids, there had been more to it, and for that it had been easier to ignore what was missing.

Of course, there was a lot more to being a taxi driver than having a set of wheels at her disposal or merely a passable knowledge of Lanarkshire geography. For example, you didn't just need to know how to get somewhere, you had to know how long it would take in the prevailing traffic conditions, so that you and the dispatcher could think two or sometimes three jobs ahead. It required an ability to read customers and situations, to anticipate the obstacles and delays and to understand the crucial differences between what the fare told you and what he or she actually meant. Most of this she learned the hard way, such as how a call-out to a pub at eleven o'clock didn't mean the fare had any firm intention of leaving the establishment at least until he'd finished the round he'd got in at last orders. Some of the drivers seemed to have a sixth sense, always managing to be in the right area as a fare came up, thus avoiding idling or long, passenger-free jaunts between pick-ups, but really this was all down to experience.

Her first fare was the most nerve-racking, even though it was just picking up some old wifey outside Safeway and taking her home with a boot full of messages. All the way there, she'd felt disproportionately apprehensive and could feel her cheeks redden in anticipation of being somehow found out. Tom's encouraging words – 'You're kidding yourself on and you'll be back here in an hour' – rang in her ears, in the end providing ample motivation through spite. It also reminded her that while she might be kidding herself on, the fares wouldn't know that she hadn't been doing this for ten years. In the case of her debut, the old wifey gave no indication of suspecting she was in less than experienced hands, though the fact that she proffered a fiver unprompted once Jane had dumped the last of her bags on her doorstep did save Jane from walking away without remembering to ask for payment. After that, she just relaxed and got on with it.

She went out four or five evenings a week, sometimes more. At first she'd start after dinner, just as Tom was reattaching the armchair's umbilicus, but in time she progressed to eating earlier on her own and leaving a portion for him to microwave. She enjoyed it, on the whole. There were times when it was boring, but never as boring as being stuck in that living room, and even on the quietest nights, she still got more conversation than she would had she stayed home.

Some talked from the minute they climbed into the car, others said no more than their destination. She could usually tell what she was in for from the off. If they sat up front, they wanted company, and you were in with a better shout of a tip too, as they weren't going to treat you like you worked below stairs. There was no code of client confidentiality as guarded the consulting room, the couch or the confessional, but there still seemed an assumption that what was said in the car was sacrosanct, as she'd been party to the most unguarded and indiscreet personal revelations from people who'd only met her less than ten minutes back.

The fares didn't actually need to speak to grant her glimpses into their lives, and often they were lives you wouldn't want any more than a glimpse into. Poverty, squalor, desperation and so much loneliness. Destination Hairmyres or Wishaw General, ferrying worried and sometimes bereaved relatives to and from their last hours with loved ones. Angry wee men, seething all the way home from the pub, no amount of drink enough to anaesthetise their grudge against the world at large, turning Jane's thoughts to the poor dear who would be opening the door to that in a few minutes. Young women, out of their faces despite the bumps swelling their waistbands. A moonlight flit while an abusive partner is out of the house, Jane being treated with a reverent gratitude like she was one of the emergency services, and pleaded with not to disclose her destination to anyone.

It certainly afforded her a sharp perspective upon where her own complaints ranked in the grand scheme, though humility and consolation were not the same thing. In her grandmother's words, 'There's always somebody worse aff than yoursel'', and there was a difference between being grateful for what you had (or hadn't) and settling for it. Jane had a comfortable home and an honest, dutiful husband, even if she didn't want to be there spending time with him. She wasn't abused, she wasn't bereaved and she wasn't dying a slow, painful death.

Just a slow, numb one.

She got glimpses into better lives, too. Having brought up Ross and Michelle, she'd long ago made her peace with the younger generation being the ones who had all the fun, but it wasn't them she was jealous of. She drove people who were her age or older to restaurants, bars, hotels, theatres, the airport, and it wasn't the good times they were in for that made her envious; at least, not entirely. It was the good times they were having before they stepped into her car, before they dialled the cab firm's number, before they booked the table or the tickets.

And then there had been that one, most haunting night that had stayed with her such a long time after, like a secret stolen treasure, and yet one that ached to recall. The fare was a guy in his mid-forties, going to King Tut's Wah Wah Hut in town. She didn't get much of a look at him in the few seconds the inside light came on before he closed the door and extinguished it. He had a full head of flecked salt-and-pepper hair, she saw that much, and was wearing jeans and a leather overcoat.

As predicated by his choice of seat, they talked, or rather, mostly he talked. He was off out to see some band Jane had never heard of, though it was twenty years since that distinction would have put the said performers into any exclusive percentile of obscurity.

'Me and the missus don't go oot much any mair, just the odd restaurant a couple of times a month,' he said. 'But I'll be staunin'' in these places wi' a Zimmer, because it makes me feel the same as it did when I was my weans' age, you know? The atmosphere, the smell of drink and smoke, the posters on the walls, folk gettin' aff wi' each other in the corners. That rush when the lights go doon. Pure magic. It never changes.'

Clearly, he didn't ken the score.

He was still blethering away enthusiastically as they reached his destination. When Jane put the overhead light on to take the fare, she finally got a good look at his face and confirmed her growing suspicion that she knew him. Ferguson, had been the job name. Iain Ferguson. Ferret. That's how he'd been known, though only as a convenient corruption of his surname and no reflection upon his physical appearance or libidinous conduct. This was worth stressing given that Jane remembered having sex with him, in a drunken and barely competent, but nonetheless enjoyable, one-night stand.

He paid the fare, giving her a twenty-pound note to cover a seventeen-pound ride. She thanked him and told him she hoped he enjoyed the show. He hadn't recognised her and she chose not to jog his memory.

She was idling in town when the call came for the return trip. It was often worth hanging around in the city centre at that time of a Saturday night if a fare had taken you in there already, but she knew not to be kidding herself. She had waited because she wanted the job.

She walked down the basement steps and into the bar, which was deserted but for a couple of staff and a girl in goth garb placing club flyers on to the empty tables. She could hear the thrum of the music from the venue proper upstairs, could feel the bass vibrate around the building.

'Taxi,' she explained as a barman approached, ready to take an order. 'It's for—'

'On you go up,' he said, nodding to the door that led to the stairs. 'Band's no' finished. Or you can stay here if you prefer. You want a drink?'

'I'll go up,' she decided, enticed by curiosity and a desire to revisit the scene of a cherished moment.

It had been less than half full on that occasion, the audience less than half enthusiastic, which was to be expected given that

160

the headliners weren't due on-stage for another ninety minutes at the time. None of that had diluted Jane's sense of electrification, because the rest of the crowd didn't see what she was seeing. They were watching the first of two unknown support acts; she was watching her baby girl on bass guitar.

Tonight, however, it was packed to the rafters and late in the proceedings. She shuffled further inside to get a view of the stage, her vantage point also affording a clear perspective on the exit, in case her fare should walk out past her. It only took a few moments watching the band to know that wasn't going to happen until they had finished. The singer clutched a mike stand, guitar slung around his neck, an imposing bear of a man, grinning wickedly as he spoke. Jane was confessedly out of touch with this kind of thing, but she could still tell that he had the whole place eating from the palm of his hand. They'd listen to him if he sang until dawn, and a glint in his eye said he might just stay and do that. He even sang as much: 'I've fifteen hours to burn and I'm gonna stay up all night.'

When he sang, his voice *was* a nightclub: smoky, sultry, seductive, intoxicating, sleazy, euphoric, threatening, dark, dark, dark and an irresistible temptation. Jane thought of the old legend about the blues guitarist waiting at the crossroads to do a deal with the devil. This guy would have dragged the devil to the nearest bar, drunk him under the table, fleeced him and then laughed him out of town.

Jane was soon under the spell too. She knew that what she'd brought with her was a factor. Memories and forgotten dreams, echoes of a girl she'd once been and perhaps the other women she might have turned into. 'It's Saturday night, baby,' the singer kept calling out. Sometimes it seemed incorporated into his lyrics, and at other times it was simply a spontaneous, ecstatic exclamation. 'Hey Glasgow, it's Saturday night!' He did it with such rapture, such a sense of celebration that Jane realised she had long ago forgotten why. Saturday night was meaningless when every day was the same, when you were never going to do anything special with it anyway. But this was a stirring reminder of what it used to mean. Saturday night, Saturn's night. The night of misrule. The time when you threw off cares and conventions and thought, the devil take tomorrow – right now

I'm going to live for me. When had she last looked forward to Saturday night? When had she last thought: I'm gonna stay up all night, fifteen hours to burn or not?

She dropped Ferguson off, finished her shift and went home to bed, where she utterly failed to get to sleep. At first this was because her ears were still ringing from the music and she was still a little too exhilarated to switch off and let her fatigue pull her under. But as she lay awake, she found herself thinking about Ferguson: daft, desperate projections. The two of them going out to a bar where music was playing, maybe before a band took the stage, talking about the old days, talking about where life had taken them since, talking about what they still wanted, talking, talking, talking. That could happen, couldn't it? That was plausible: each of them finding a companion to go to places neither his wife nor her husband could be dragged along to. That was how it could begin, maybe, and then per- haps they might find themselves doing other things their spouses weren't interested in any more.

No, that was silly, wasn't it? It was just a fantasy, but the pleasure of it told her something about herself that she couldn't unlearn. She hadn't simply been fantasising about sex, nor even simply fantasising about having an affair. She was fantasising about being in a different marriage.

She didn't see Ferguson again, and the chances of doing so were seriously diminished by being forced to give up the private- hire work. Circumstances had forced her to give up plenty of things down the years, but this was the one that really rankled. She was let go by the cab firm.

She knew trouble was on its way when she was told there had been complaints about her driving. She was too slow, the manager said. Customers expected her to put the foot down at times and she hadn't been prepared to do so. This not only made customers late, it made for unacceptable delays between jobs.

A few passengers *had* complained to her that she was too cau- tious while she was driving, but neither they nor the firm could seriously expect her to break the speed limit or blaze through amber lights in the name of the job. She had a clean licence and hadn't broken any laws since her last under-age tipple or possibly her last illegally taped LP. Nobody could demand that she change that, she told the manager, but despite a protracted exchange of views on the subject, they both knew that it was nothing to do with the real problem. The real problem, about which this was a coded ultimatum, was that she refused to do 'drops'.

The cab firm had recently come under new ownership, not that its previous owner had any intention of selling until about six hours before the paperwork – and a baseball bat – were put in front of him. The new proprietor was one Anthony Connelly, who was building a monopoly of private-hire companies in Lanarkshire, the better to control and distribute the drugs from which he made his real money. He'd started with the biggest firms in the area, but not even smaller outfits like the one Jane worked for were immune, and she quickly learned why. 'Drops' were passengerless fares, door-to-door deliveries of all Class-A varietals. Connelly didn't need every outfit in the area in order to meet logistical demands; he needed every outfit in the area so that the drivers would be forced to comply, cutting off the option to quit and go work for an untainted firm.

Jane considered quitting anyway, both on principle and as a matter of personal safety, but a more defiant part of her didn't want to just melt away for the convenience of these people. If they wanted rid of her, they would have to come out and blatantly admit why.

After the 'slow driving' warning, she expected to be binned outright the next time she refused to respond to a drop call, but it didn't happen like that. Rumours were rife of the threats and coercions that had been applied to drivers by Connelly's foot-maggots, so she got pretty jumpy at the ensuing lack of consequences. Almost a week passed, and it felt like too long a silence. But it turned out that this was a courtesy, and she was a special case.

Connelly, she knew, had been in Tom's year at both primary and secondary school, and, while it wouldn't be fair to say that Tom refused to hear a word against him, his own words about the man were far from condemnatory. He was a decent enough guy at school, Tom told her. Not one of the nutters. Could look after himself, but never a bully, never gave Tom a hard time, stuck up for him once, blah blah blah. Nor did it hurt Tom's estimations that the duplicitous creep went to Mass every Sunday at his parish, to maintain his respectable public face.

It was probably true of every little clique, coven and insular community on earth, and therefore unfair to single one particular sect, but Jane found it sickening that Connelly's charade was indulged by the likes of her husband on the rationale that he might be a drug-dealing gangster, but at least he's a Catholic drug-dealing gangster.

She came home one night to find Connelly's Mercedes parked outside the house, and as she walked up the drive, Tom was showing him out the front door, the pair all joking and genial. He patted Tom on the back as he walked away, but barely looked Jane in the eye as he passed.

'What did *he* want?' she asked Tom accusingly.

'You'd better come in and have a seat,' he said.

Then he laid it down, not that any of it was news. Connelly had used allusion and euphemism, Tom indulging him the moral cowardice of his language like he indulged him his pillar-of-the-community fantasy on a Sunday. There was trouble in the air, dangers Tom wouldn't want his wife exposed to. The minicab business wasn't what it once was in this neck of the woods, no place for a lady. He'd come as an old friend and fellow parishioner; a courteous letting-down-gently but an unquestionable letting-down nonetheless.

Tom had indulged Connelly, but Jane didn't indulge Tom. She spelled out what was really going on and demanded to hear Connelly's every word and nuance. Tom looked regretful and exasperated.

'I don't approve of what he does, but we don't want to be on the wrong side of a guy like that, do we? And you don't want to be involved with all this, surely? Let it go, Jane.'

She knew she had to, but it stung, and she hated Tom for letting himself be Connelly's instrument. She couldn't have expected him to defy or antagonise such a man, but she did expect him to have a little dignity, on both their behalfs. Tom had let the guy patronise him, kid him on that he was treating him with respect. It made her sick, and it felt like such a betrayal, something not helped by the fact that Tom got what he wanted from it, too. It brought an end to this latest daft dalliance; and there would be no more microwaved dinners to tolerate, either.

She reached the village of Le Muy just after three o'clock, having missed the turn-off the first time and then doubled back to approach from the opposite direction. It was just a daft over-sight, a misreading of the right-hand exit lane, and it probably only cost her five or six minutes, but it told her how tightly wound she was that every second the autoroute took her away from her destination felt like miles.

It looked a quiet little place. In fact, for the most part, it looked shut, and it was only when she located the local *poste* that she found an establishment open for business at this sleepy time of the day. She knew practically no French, but for a few phrases still rattling around her head since sitting her Higher at the age of seventeen. The teller didn't know much English either, but, fortunately, giving him a look at the address on the phone's LCD was enough to convey what she required. He started bab-bling lots of *à gauche*s and *à droit*s before remembering how little any of it meant to her and, more helpfully, drawing a map. She thanked him and returned to the Beetle.

She'd have thanked him more if he could have told her what the place she was looking for actually *was*, but, as it wasn't iden-tified by anything more than a tiny image of some black gates, it was perhaps a little much to ask. Rue Marisse, when she found it, began a couple of streets north of the village square, before snaking its way right out of town. She drove along it slowly, flanked at first by tall terraced buildings, uniformly shuttered, before these gave way to lower walls and eventually bushes and trees. After her recent experience overshooting the autoroute, it occurred to her to go back and look again in case she had missed something: perhaps the gates covered a passage between buildings, and they were unseen for being opened inwards against the walls.

Instinct and reason overruled. It made sense that the place be out of town, isolated. If this guy's reach was long enough to hand her a phone in EK, then she somehow couldn't picture him living up a close. She drove on, the windows down to let in some cool air as the afternoon sun warmed the car. She passed

165

fields, vineyards, walled orchards. She wished she could bank how it looked, how it smelled, the feeling of the breeze through the windows of the VW – save it for a time when she could enjoy it.

A blue Citroën passed in the opposite direction, the only other car she'd seen since leaving the village. The desire to turn around and retrace her route returned. How far out could this place be and still have Le Muy as its address? Then she saw it, maybe a quarter of a mile ahead on the right. Not the gates, for she was too far away yet, but a sight that she was certain denoted what she was looking for. It was the trees. Conifers. Lots of them, tall and thin, standing like a line of sentries, conspicuously distinct from the indigenous arbour in their regimentation and their dress. They stood in rigid perpendicular ranks, clothed tightly and slim in thick green, masking whatever was beyond them from the road. As Jane drew nearer she could see a low stone wall supporting iron railings in front of these looming guards. The wall skirted the trees for a considerable distance in both visible directions, broken only, she observed with a mixture of accomplishment and dread, by two black wrought-iron gates.

Jane gently hit the brakes and pulled in, indicating despite there being no other drivers anywhere in sight to be indicating to. She pulled out the phone and toggled to the image, though she needed no confirmation. Those were the gates. This was the place.

She stepped out of the car and walked towards them. Up close, she could see that the ironwork formed an intricate mesh of thorned creepers around supporting rigid spars, like some metal parasitic weed had overgrown the place. The effect was less than welcoming; nor, did she suspect, was it intended to be. In the centre, where the gates met, there was wording incorporated into the interlacing design.

Maison
— Rla —
an Tir

Through the ironwork she could see only more trees, with a narrow, dust-covered avenue snaking between them before itself

166

bending out of sight. She stood there a few seconds, wondering whether there was any angle she could play here to give her some kind of leverage, and more pertinently, how she was actually going to get in. That was when she noticed the intercom built into the wall on the left-hand side of the gatepost, a grey panel of buttons with the cold circle of a glass lens above it, ready to remotely examine the caller. She reached tentatively for the buzzer, but before she could touch it, the gates began to swing open with a near-balletic grace; noiseless too, but for a faint buzz of the electrical mechanism.

Jane stood and waited to see whether a person or vehicle was approaching. None did. Having tarried long enough to convince herself that their unlocking was not a coincidence of timing, she climbed back into the Beetle, took a very deep breath, then drove through the gap.

The land of do as you please

Most people, happily, never had occasion to give any thought to what going on the lam for their lives might feel like. If they dwelt upon it for a moment, they would probably imagine an obvious checklist of fears and insecurities, physiological and psychological symptoms. They might even consider a few practical and logistical elements: money, transport, bicycle clips to stop the shite running out the bottom of their trousers – that kind of thing.

And they wouldn't be very wrong, as far as they went, but as far as they went would in most instances only cover the initial sprint. Running for your life, as Ross Fleming was in the process of discovering, was a marathon. Flight and concealment? Fine, done, covered. The more demanding part could best be summed up by merely two words: now what?

The closest thing he could think to compare it to was dogging school, though the metaphor wasn't exactly based upon an abundance of experience. He'd only actually dogged school once, which meant he could speak more authoritatively about being on the lam, but there was sufficient overlap for it to be valid. It hadn't even been a full day, just an unexpectedly sunny spring lunchtime when his pal Davey had even less expectedly suggested they head literally for the hills rather than back to face double Chemistry and double Physics.

What he mainly remembered was a disorientating absence of purpose. They just wandered around the paths, fields and slopes, the welcome warmth of the sun on their shoulders – all pleasant enough, but Ross had felt that he was doing nothing more valuable than killing the hours until he could feasibly walk in the front door without his mum asking why he was home early. Purposelessly marking time was the driven over-achiever's idea of hell.

The problem, now as then, was of not knowing what to do

with himself, all the while knowing there were things elsewhere that he could otherwise be more constructively getting on with. The problem, now as then, was having more freedom at his disposal than he had the detachment to appreciate or the imagination to use. This was something he was going to have to remedy pretty quickly, because killing the hours until he could go back to Mammy wasn't an option.

He could go wherever he wanted, other than home, do whatever he liked, apart from show up for work, and he had, right then, a responsibility only to himself. Who wouldn't fancy some of that? Who hadn't wished it for themselves as they slogged out another few revs on their own personal hamster-wheels? Yet it didn't feel like any kind of freedom. Nothing did, nothing could that was enforced, because freedom began with choice, and his had been suddenly very restricted the moment he knew Project F was compromised. Actually, maybe his choices had been restricted earlier than that: pick any point on the line right back to the moment he gave it voice and let the very idea out of the safely contained environment of his head.

There was a fine line sometimes, not a molecule wide, between the best idea you ever had and the absolute worst. Just ask Alfred Nobel. Or Joseph Guillotin. Perhaps it was a flaw inherent in the inventive mind to have vision but not foresight. Was it that so much concentration went into developing the idea that they could not see beyond it? Or was it an inhibition of the urge to see beyond that allowed them to develop ideas before they could be dismissed as folly? Any eejit could have told Alfred that stabilising explosives and thus reducing the risk to their deployer was only going to lead to an awful lot more things being blown up. Any eejit could have told Joseph that a quicker and more humane way of executing people would inevitably lead to more – albeit quick and humane – executions. Someone spying that wee bit further might even also have wagered that, as an aristocrat, Joseph might have to be light on his feet to ensure the last sound he heard himself wasn't 'whoosh – clunk'. And any eejit could have told Ross that attempting to implement his own bright spark would be roughly equivalent to donning a T-shirt with a large concentric-circle target on it above the legend: 'Please kill me'.

But not one of these three non-eejits had caught a glimpse of what they were heading towards until they were on the other side, until the idea was out there, at which point they couldn't believe how blind they'd been, and at which point their deeds were, unfortunately, irreversible.

Boom. Whoosh – clunk. Please kill me.

It was no mitigation to be able to state that he hadn't as yet actually succeeded in inventing the bloody thing. That only made him even more of a tube for being in this situation and failing to anticipate that it was exactly what was bound to happen.

Precautions had been taken at the behest of those at Deimos happily blessed with any eejit-level foresight. But it was Ross's belief that those precautions had themselves been the instrument by which he was placed in danger, like some Escheresque loop or self-fulfilling prophecy. Security at Marledoq was seriously beefed up, in accordance with the assessments and recommendations of this shadowy and faintly sinister consultant outfit Willis had brought in, beginning with their 'Tiger Team' phoney assault on the facility. But by the time the first trip-laser or optical-recognition scanner had been fitted, as far as Ross was concerned, it was already too late. The Tiger Team themselves had been the source of the leak, he was sure. Why else would that girl have a removable-memory device plugged into the back of his PC?

He'd expressed his concerns to Willis, but the old man was in typical ostrich-mode. He trusted this firm implicitly. Mr Bett traded on the utmost integrity, honesty and discretion, wouldn't tolerate any duplicity, reputation worthless if there was ever any question of blah blah blah.

Aye, right. So honest and reputable that they'd fucked off with a shedload of kit, some of it still in Beta. The stock inconsistency had been blamed on cumulative staff pilfering, exacerbated by guys helping themselves to souvenirs out of spite after being canned for their abysmal performance on the one night they were put to the test. Ross reckoned otherwise. Those clowns had proven they barely knew which way to point a pistol; what the hell were they going to do with a Sonic Blackjack or a Resin-Cannon? And even if his crew hadn't stolen the gear and this Bett guy was as straight as Willis believed, it wasn't robots he had working for him. Any firm could have a traitor in their midst, something of which Ross had become acutely aware the second he saw that girl hurriedly tapping away at his machine.

The single greatest security precaution they had in place prior to then was the simple fact that nobody on the outside even knew what might be there to steal. And yet she had known not only what, but specifically where to find it, too.

Willis, being this buttoned-up old-school (tie) fossil, had seemed almost as disturbed by the very impoliteness of Ross's accusation of Bett as by the substance of it. It was as though he found the idea of dishonesty and underhandedness so distasteful that he recoiled from dealing with it, much like how Ross felt when faced with removing someone else's hair from a plug-hole. The extrapolated implication that it meant they had some unknown, duplicitous defector on their own books therefore appalled Willis so much that it sent him sailing many more miles down the river in Egypt, further entrenching him in the self-comforting belief that all of Bett's people were beyond reproach. Sometimes Ross wanted to ask him what he thought people got up to with the missiles his company sold, and where he reckoned the collateral damage of taking out twenty civilians in a bread queue ranked on the scale of impoliteness.

'Why,' Willis asked him, 'if there was a leak at Marledoq, would a double-agent on Bett's team be required to sneak out the files? Why wouldn't the traitor simply copy them himself?' Ross conceded that he didn't have any firm answers, though distance and deniability were two that sounded pretty plausible.

However, on Ross's insistence, Willis did ask Bett about what the girl was doing with a portable memory interface jacked into his computer. The answer, Willis reported, was that it contained her own tools of the trade and allowed her to manipulate the system from whichever terminal was handy; in this case a machine in Lab Four because she was down there as part of the search for the one unaccounted staff member: him.

This sounded neatly plausible and had satisfied Willis, but Ross remained of the opinion that it was a hell of a coincidence her part in the search took her straight to that lab, where she logged on to that particular machine. Nonetheless, he had to leave it at that. Nothing could be proved, and Willis wasn't the type to aggressively pursue it. Under the circumstances, Ross thought it best not to also enquire of Willis whether he'd asked Bett about all the missing gear. The embarrassment level for that would have been potentially life-threatening: Willis's cravat might have intervened and strangled him rather than allow him to commit such a social faux pas.

He kind of felt sorry for him, to be honest. Willis was a gentle old soul, naturally shy (with which Ross could certainly identify) and tending to give the impression he'd been born at least thirty years too late. It was hard to picture him offering much in the way of parry-and-thrust in the modern era of boardroom warfare, and with rumours constantly rife about Phobos selling Deimos or even just shutting it down, it was generally expected that he'd be bowing out gracefully in the not-too-distant future. It seemed incongruous to think of the guy as an arms dealer, but in another way, Willis represented the quintessence of the arms industry. Suits and friendly faces, meetings in suites, lunches on yachts, deals and contracts, just high-spec commodities and large cheques changing hands, like any other business. Presumably it was easy to think of it that way when you were never around to see what happened next. And besides, it wasn't the arms industry, or the weapons industry, it was the 'defence' industry. Nobody *ever* bought weapons to attack anyone. What a horrid thought that one's merchandise could ever be so irresponsibly abused.

Ross had seen the missiles lined up in storage, partially assembled for safety. It was easy to see what Willis saw: sleek shapes, precision engineering, cutting-edge technology, gleaming steel. Fetish objects of a very male aesthetic, lined up, cold, clean and glinting like Porsches in a showroom. But he knew never to lose sight of their purpose, like he ought never to let Willis's being a crusty old duffer cause him to forget he earned his corn flogging bombs. And he knew never, ever to forget that just because he worked in developing non-lethal weapons, it didn't change that he was in the employ of the most deadly, amoral and untrustworthy business on earth.

It was something he'd tried to bear in mind since day one, though inevitably it did fade into the background for considerable periods. Every job became comfortably familiar, if not exactly routine, given enough time – even jobs located inside a weapons research facility hidden under a mountain. However, there had been plenty of incidents that restored his cautiously stark perspective, not least the Tiger Team incursion, after which he had prudently assumed it merely a matter of time before his video clips were playing before certain alarmed and influential eyes.

No expense had been spared to improve security at Marledoq (and to be fair, anyone who could get past the provisions installed upon Bett's recommendations *deserved* to make off with their prize), but that only protected the goods. If someone decided to go after the source, there was only one inch of cheap front door to negotiate. Ross might be an untreatable workaholic, but even he wasn't inclined to move a bed into the lab and live in the bloody place. Nor could he consider the facility as secure as everyone else did, because somebody there had already sold the jerseys once. On top of that, given the kind of kit that was lying around, it wouldn't be hard for that same traitor to arrange a tragic but unsuspicious little industrial accident. He'd therefore made it a personal priority to meticulously – but inconspicuously – watch his back. So when it finally happened, when they came for him, he had a start; it wasn't much, but it was enough, because he'd long been ready to run.

As an early precaution, he'd long ago wiped all sensitive files from his home PC, and wiped them properly, not merely deleted them: the appropriate memory sectors had been overwritten nine times by strings of randomly generated numbers. Nobody tossing the flat would find anything more controversial than a few illegal movie downloads, but just as important was to be sure that neither, if they came uninvited, would they find him.

He had tenaciously persuaded Deimos to authorise the purchase of a video-phone entry system at his apartment block, but as their property management people continued to show no sign whatsoever of actually installing the thing, he'd made a few unauthorised installations of his own. One of them was a hidden camera pointed at his front door, motion-activated because it was wireless and ran off a battery. The other, more vital, was a dual-sensor, motion-activated alarm system that sent a signal to a vibrating pager. The first sensor merely detected motion and 'woke up' the system's second stage, which detected whether whatever had triggered stage one now remained in front of the door; in effect a lack-of-motion detector. Thus, a neighbour walking past would cause the system to return to sleep, but someone pausing for more than a second sent a signal to the pager. Most times it was the postman, or Monsieur Torcy from the flat above coming home pished again and forgetting he still had another flight of stairs to climb. All of this was veri-fiable via the remote camera, though the hour on the clock was usually enough: the postman always came between seven and quarter past, while Monsieur Torcy usually tried his key in the wrong lock ten minutes after chucking-out time at Café Colette.

So when the pager woke him at four in the morning, he knew before checking the miniature monitor on his bedside table that it wasn't a Jehovah's Witness with a fucked wristwatch. He saw two men in heavy coats, one of them crouched at the lock. He didn't wait to check whether the guy was just shining it up with Brasso. Within seconds, Ross was gone, out his bedroom window in just his T-shirt and boxers, along the ledge like he'd prac-tised, then up the external fire escape to the roof.

Once up there, he uncovered the bag he had stashed beneath a tarpaulin, and proceeded to pull on a pair of black jeans, a black jersey, a warm jacket (*noir*) and a pair of grey running shoes. Even in times of peril, there were still certain minimum standards to be observed, and he drew the line at black trainers; after all, if things went okay, people would get to see him again in daylight. Also inside the bag were his passport, five hundred euros and two lip-balm tubes containing something more than lip balm.

When packing the bag he'd considered more heroic measures and the items appropriate to carrying them out. He could have at his disposal an arsenal of temporarily debilitating devices, as well as the drop on anyone who came calling. He'd have an unseen elevated perspective, or the option of an ambush when whoever it was left the building afterwards. Trouble was, chances were a million to one *on* that such late-night gentlemen

callers would have their own arsenals of permanently debilitating devices, and the steel to use them in the chaos of the
moment.

As Ross stood there, shaking from more than just the cold,
he knew how much he'd understood himself when he made his
provisions. He wasn't cut out for that, never had been. The only
martial art he was trained in was putting one foot rapidly in
front of the other. Shanks's pony, ninth dan. He'd learned it at
school and kept up the training ever since that first time he'd
been made to appreciate that getting your sums right did not
always reflect well within your peer group.

Boffin. That was the least pejorative term he remembered, the
only one that had any trace of compliment or acknowledgement
to it. Funny word, he'd always thought. It did contain that trace
of acknowledgement, but there was something disrespectful
intended by it too. Brainy sub-genus of freak, but freak nonetheless. It was the word the tabloids patronisingly used to describe
scientists whose findings they approved of or whose work in
some way amused them. (Scientists they disagreed with, of course,
were 'so-called experts'. Just because you were the world authority
on something didn't mean you knew more about it than a gin-
soaked and pish-stained leader-writer.) So at school, sometimes
he was described as a boffin, but mainly the term for someone
of even slightly elevated intellect was 'fuckin' poof', and his feet
had rapidly developed a Pavlovian response to hearing it.

He made his way across the rooftops, travelling along the
street and around the corner, climbing where the abutting buildings were higher, carefully lowering himself where the level
dropped. When he reached the end of the terrace, he trotted on
soft feet down the fire escape and into the narrow alley between
the tenement building and Jarry's bakery. As he jogged quietly
between the walls he recalled his dry runs of the route. It wasn't
the more physically demanding or potentially dangerous parts
that stuck in his memory, but the easier, more straightforward
stretches such as this, because that was when his mind had been
more free to doubt the wisdom – or more pertinently the necessity – of what he was doing.

You're kidding yourself, pal, he'd thought. It felt daft, scut-
tling about in the dark. What the hell was he going to say to

anyone who caught him at it? He could always tell them he was trying to screw a few flats, at least it would sound more plausible and less embarrassing than the truth. Rehearsing a getaway in case big bad men come to get him. How fucking ridiculous did that sound? Who the hell did he think he was? He was just some wee geek from East Kilbride, getting carried away with himself.

But it was always seductive to think of yourself as insignificant, that the true principals will play out their drama centre stage as you fade into the background, fifth business, a role without repercussions. What was he doing all this time at Marledoq if it wasn't an attempt to create something hugely significant, and how had he envisaged its impact if not as the heart of a drama that would have massive repercussions?

No point playing the innocent civilian. His dream of success was a whole industry's nightmare, and if he represented just a potential threat to it, then the threat to him was real and immediate. These fuckers didn't play the percentages. Even potential threats could wipe points off share prices, regardless of whether they ever came to anything, and there was no length to which they wouldn't go to make *damn sure* they never came to anything.

That was why his car was parked not outside his building but close to the end of the alley, as close each night as he could find a space. He'd been doing it for nearly three weeks, fending off the self-consciousness he sometimes felt about it. It was crazy, egotistical paranoia, he'd chided himself. It starts with this shit and before you know it, you've got Geoffrey Rush and Russell Crowe fighting over who gets to play you in a biopic. But egotism was not something Ross could be accused of, nor had there ever been much chance of describing a slightly introverted workaholic 'fuckin' poof' as crazy. As for paranoid, well, that was moot now; the moment that pager went off, it proved beyond all reasonable doubt that they really were out to get him.

He remotely unlocked the black TT and jumped in, slinging his bag on to the passenger seat before turning the ignition. As the engine growled into life, the thought belatedly occurred to him that they could have booby-trapped the vehicle. He stayed his right hand for a moment, resting it on the gearstick, his left foot on the clutch. In the movies, it was always turning the key that did it: that was what had sparked his fear; but in reality, the possibility remained. In reality, nobody wired a bomb to the ignition – it was too much bother. They stuck them underneath with a mercury switch: it was the motion that triggered the explosion. He got out and looked under the car, conscious of how crucial the seconds were as they ticked away without him travelling. He couldn't see anything, but the street lighting was dim, and to check properly he'd need a mirror to see right underneath.

Something moved between two parked cars further along the street, causing him to spring up and rattle his head off the TT's wing mirror. It was just a cat, but it got his heart thumping and, it appeared, his scalp bleeding. He had to get out of there. The last ten minutes had told him he was right to be paranoid, but he still had to trust his judgement, and right now his judgement told him two things: that these people would want him alive, initially at least; and that if he didn't want that to happen, he'd better stop fannying about and burn some rubber.

It was about two miles out of Chassignan that the 'Now what?' question first hit him, though at that stage merely in dilute form. The pure strain would come later. He'd concerned himself so exclusively with the immediate practicalities of escaping that he realised he'd given only the vaguest thought of where to escape to. Paris was about as specific as he'd managed. Bustling, sprawling, anonymous: somewhere he could just disappear into the crowd, and, for a couple of days, that would be what he did.

He took a circuitous route to get there, however. Once out of Chassignan, he headed east towards Switzerland, stopping at the small border town of Demerin just as the earliest cafés and patisseries were opening up for the day. He had breakfast while he waited for certain other businesses to open, parking his car up a side street off the main drag, from where he knew it would be impounded as an obstruction. Local police would take note of this, including make, model, registration, time and date, and his intention was that this information might make its way along certain channels. In case that wasn't enough, he then went to the local Credit Gironais and lifted the three hundred euro maximum from a hole in the wall. It would be the last he could afford to make from that account for a while, as any subsequent withdrawals would flag up his movements to anyone connected enough to take a look. This wouldn't leave him with only what cash was in his pocket, however, as he had in recent weeks been steadily moving sums to a long-dormant Royal Bank of Scotland account set up back in EK when he was a student. Since moving to France, he'd run all transactions, including his salary, through the new account Deimos set up for him with CG as part of the resettlement package. Deimos knew the account number, and Deimos was compromised; thus, anything through CG was potentially traceable, including his credit card. The RBS account was less accessible to prying eyes, and still carried Maestro and Cirrus facilities, though his Mastercard would be used to cover one last, deliberately transparent transaction here on the Swiss border. His coffee downed, he took a walk to the railway station, queued at the booth and bought a one-way ticket to Toblerone Country. Half an hour later he returned and paid cash before boarding the next train to Paris.

Ross had never been to the capital before. He'd always fancied a wee trip there, maybe of a weekend, but somehow there had never been the time, and nor had there been any hurry. When you're in a country for two days, you try pretty hard to see the sights. When you're there several years, you figure you'll get around to everything eventually.

Once he got there, he felt more like a ghost than a tourist. It didn't feel like free time to do what he wanted, it felt like he had opted out of his life, faded from society, drifting unseen. He checked into a small hotel near Les Halles, paying cash up front and giving a false name so that his real one didn't get fed into any databases.

Time dragged. Two days felt like a week. That was when 'Now what?' really gave him both barrels. He walked the museums, ate cheaply away from the hotspots, tried to lose himself in the movies after dark, when he most needed escape and distraction. Paris was stuffed with cinemas. There were the big multiplexes on the Champs Elysées and around Montmartre, but it was the little independent ones that really gave the impression of profusion. These were crammed and crowbarred improbably into the tiniest little spots, showing an amazing diversity of fare, and fortunately, little of it dubbed. He was tempted by a few rarities, but some unspoken need for comfort caused him to succumb to a place off Rue du Louvre showing a new print of *Dr No*.

He'd only ever seen Bond films on the telly. Proper Bond films, that was, not the Pierce Brosnan shite that was even more of a spoof than Austin Powers, though not as funny. He remembered watching them at home as a kid, his mum making a big fuss, turning it into a bit of an occasion. In their heyday the Bond flicks probably weren't intended by Mr Broccoli as family entertainment, but in Ross's household they were a sight more likely to gather both generations around the box than any Disney effort. When his dad was finally persuaded to buy a VCR, the first time his mum showed any interest in learning how to work the thing was when *Thunderball* was on. She did love her Bond movies. Ross even wondered whether his dad's surname being Fleming was what had attracted her to him; there certainly didn't seem to have been much else, not that had survived. It was one of the few enthusiasms he remembered his mother giving much expression to, though he was sure there were others that, for whatever reasons, she kept to herself. He had been planning to buy her the Connery DVD box set back when he got his first salary cheque, but by that time she had started digging him up about breaking it off with Maureen, so his good intentions were the first casualty of his huff.

It wasn't exactly like he'd ditched Maureen at the altar or anything. They hadn't set a date, they were just 'engaged'.

'Let's get engaged.' That's what Maureen had said. Not, 'Let's get married.' The implicit awareness of doing it by increment must have told them both there was something missing. Marriage was an all or nothing deal, surely; something you wanted absolutely. You didn't say: 'Let's move up to DefCon Two and see how it looks from there.'

When something came along that he *did* want absolutely, he could see clearly how much the pair of them were kidding themselves. By declaring their engagement, they'd just been hoping their relationship would turn into something it was not. Too many people thought the same thing but weren't smart enough to get out in time. He only had to think of home to see what those people looked like a few years down the line.

That said, he missed them. For all he knew how much they'd be doing his box in after five minutes, he missed them: Dad

cocooned in his deluded patriarchal fantasy world and intel-
lectually sedated by his religion; Mum fed up listening, tuning
the conversation out when he was holding forth. It was probably a form of emotional self-defence when there was so much
aggro. Watching Michelle with Rachel when she was being difficult brought home how aching it could be to watch parent and
child at loggerheads, and Ross was just the uncle. His mum had
spent years watching her husband and her son locked in permanent ideological conflict, and he felt guilty that he'd never
considered how much it must have hurt.

As he walked back out into the Paris night, he felt suddenly
very alone and very vulnerable. For the first time since moving
to France, home seemed an achingly long way off. He couldn't
return, though. It would be the first place they'd look, and he
didn't want to bring any danger there either. He guessed one
consolation of him and his parents being in an ongoing cream-
puff was that at least he didn't need to worry about them being
wound up over not hearing from him for a while.

Disgorged from the cinema, he walked beneath the street lights,
where the post-movie sense of disconnection was far more acute
than normal. Paris was looking alien, dangerous, untrustworthy.
He was starting to feel conspicuous amid the crowds, like his
own alienation was making it externally manifest that he was
a fugitive who didn't belong. It was irrational, but it was irresistible too. He felt a need to get away again. Being on the move
had felt right: transit as procrastination, putting off 'What now?'
for a while, but travelling hopefully only worked when you had
a destination to arrive at. Otherwise, travelling itself would
become part of 'What now?'.

He wished he could be somewhere he felt less alone. He had
the means and the freedom to go anywhere he wished, but none
of the places he'd daydreamed about held quite the same allure
under his current circumstances as they had when he was
driving to work on a cold grey morning. He'd always fancied
a few days in Prague, for instance, but now it would just be
another unfamiliar place to feel lonely and exposed in.

His hotel was in sight, but there was too much going on in
his head to let him sleep. He decided to stop at a little *tabac* for

181

a nightcap. He had a *pression* and a brandy, sitting at the bar. Someone had left a copy of *L'Equipe*, the sports paper, lying next to a plastic water jug advertising the Ricard pastis it was there to top up. Ross flicked through it idly as he sipped his brandy, then happened upon something that truly startled him. It wasn't the content itself, but the fact that it referred to a matter which would have dominated his thoughts in recent weeks had his life been carrying on as normal.

He hadn't even known it was happening.

It still meant precious little in his current scheme of things, but it made up his mind where he ought to go. Home, he knew, was not an option, but a city imminently playing host to twenty thousand Glaswegians would do in the meantime.

Ross left his drinks unfinished and headed back to the hotel, where he packed his bag. As soon as he had a new destination, he knew he couldn't wait to begin travelling. Staying where he was, even just until morning, would feel like needlessly hanging around somewhere he could be caught. He'd have more chance of sleeping on a train than in the hotel now that he'd made up his mind he was leaving. He made some calls and found out that he could get a train departing just after one in the morning. There was a connection in Marseille, less than an hour's wait, then onwards again. He'd be in Barcelona by early afternoon.

Him and twenty thousand Celtic supporters.

He thought of his dad, of being taken to games at Parkhead as a kid. It was the only thing he could say he'd ever really seen his dad passionate about, and, in time, the only thing they truly shared, the solitary conduit left through which they could communicate.

He had to talk to him, had to talk to someone. He looked at his watch. It was late, but not too late. Dad usually stayed up past midnight, and it was only twenty to. He'd give him a ring. They'd trade platitudes, awkwardly as ever, then get on to talking about the game. His dad's voice would change, and he'd again become the man who used to throw him up in the air and play cowboys with him out in the back garden. The man who used to make him feel safe, like nobody could hurt him, whether they be monsters, Alsatians or bad boys from Blantyre.

Dislocation

Jane eased the Beetle along cautiously in second gear, following the winding track through unbroken shade amid tall trees and clustered shrubs. The S-bends negotiated a needlessly indirect path through the wood, ruts and tyre-marks at the edges testifying to past impatience with the route, which could have easily featured as a rally stage. As she tugged the steering wheel sharply around another hairpin curve, she reckoned the only thing she was more likely to encounter than a souped-up Subaru was a little girl in a red hooded coat on her way to grandma's with a woven basket. Except that she was the one heading for a rendezvous with the big, bad wolf.

The track finally emerged at the border of quite the most enormous gardens she had seen without paying the National Trust for parking. Here there were more trees and shrubs, but smaller, and very precisely located upon rolling, immaculately kempt terraced lawns. A gravel path and a short stone staircase bisected the greens, leading at the top to an expanse of flag-stones as wide as Buchanan Street and not much short of half as long. More arbour stood amid the stones, as did several short lamp-posts and a fountain. And behind all of that, there stood a structure grand and imposing enough to suggest that calling it *Maison* Rla an Tir was an act of seriously piss-taking false modesty. *Château* would be nearer the mark.

He'd said he didn't want money. He should just have sent her a photo of the place, that really would have said a thousand words.

It was three storeys tall, all hewn dark stone and shuttered windows. She took a guess there'd be twenty rooms in there, but really she had no idea; it could be twice that. There were out-buildings too, two of them, neither of which looked modest enough to fit the word 'garage'. Small hangars was closer, but in her mind that word normally described flimsy-looking aluminium shells, not such sturdy, stone-built constructions. Perhaps 'hangar' popped into her head because, as well as there being a number of cars parked on the gravel, there was also a helicopter tailplane visible behind the near side of the house. Jane reckoned it safe to assume that the remainder of a helicopter was indeed attached, tailplanes on their own never having caught on as a garden ornament.

Besides the size, the other thing that most struck her was how perfectly and precisely everything had been maintained, from the paintwork on the shutters to the flush edging of the lawns; from the pointing and slatework to the absence of moss or weeds between the flagstones on the forecourt. It was unnervingly disciplined. Even the ivy gripping trellises on the house's front edifice looked like it had been warned not to stray, on pain of a sharp smack on the fronds. The attention to detail was not so much loving as slavish, as much painsfearing as painstaking. She got a sense of absolutely nothing having been missed or overlooked, no corner cut, no compromise ever made, rendering an effect that she found coldly inhuman. The only place she'd ever observed anything like it was Disneyland. This was only marginally less sinister.

She parked the Beetle alongside the other cars – a Clio, a Megane, a BMW Z4 and another Beetle – and sat for a moment to see whether anyone would emerge to greet her. From the house, nothing stirred. Most of the windows had their shutters opened flat against the wall, but she could see no movement inside; in fact, the way the late afternoon sun was reflecting off them rendered the glass all but opaque.

'I've come this far,' she muttered to herself. She climbed out and walked to the front door, up a short staircase guarded on either side by statues: a griffin on the left and a wereworm on the right.

Here be dragons, right enough.

She reached for the doorbell, barely able to believe that was what she was doing. Ding-dong. Is the criminal mastermind of the house in?

As at the gate, her hand didn't reach its target before being pre-empted. The door swung inward slowly, into a dark entrance hall, wood panelling visible only as far as the sunlight spilled.

Jane saw merely an elbow around the outside of the frame as the door opened, before the figure behind it stepped to the side and revealed herself to be the girl from the supermarket.

Jane gaped for a second.

'How the hell did you get here?' she spluttered. 'Who are you?'

'My name's Alexis. I got here the same way you did, though by more legal means. Come in. You're expected.'

'That would be one way of putting it,' Jane said, stepping inside.

Alexis closed the door. Jane stood on the spot upon a marble floor, her eyes adjusting to the unlit interior after the brightness of the sunshine. She smelled furniture polish and wood oil. It was pleasant enough on the nose, but it made her think of museums; add apple and wet parka and it would be redolent of her old primary school. It did not smell like a home.

She looked up and around. A wide staircase lay ahead, climbing two storeys in a wide, straight-sided ascent of steps, galleries and marble balustrades.

'This is just like mine at home,' Jane said, aware that Alexis had noted her gawping.

'I'd give you the ten-cent tour, but we've things to do. A lot of it's off-limits anyway. Come on.'

Jane followed Alexis along a corridor to the left. The marble gave way to polished wood, the panelling to painted off-white walls, but the sense of being in a museum did not diminish. She passed a suit of armour – an actual suit of armour – standing upright like a sentry in a corner. Antique weapons festooned the walls: pistols, muskets, swords and daggers.

Alexis opened a door on the left-hand side of the corridor and led her into a broad sitting room. Sunlight streamed in through the windows, but served only to contrast with the dark wood of cabinets and rich colours of upholstered armchairs and sofas. There was also room – plenty of room – for a large oak table and eight chairs, the sight of it suggesting to Jane board-room rather than dining room. A small log fire burned in the hearth beneath a marble mantelpiece wider than the frame of Tom's garden shed.

The room felt warm, but not uncomfortably so. Jane guessed

185

the fire had been recently lit, in advance of a drop in temperature as the sunlight faded.

'Take a seat,' Alexis offered. She smiled with politeness more than warmth, the girl looking distinctly uncomfortable, and not a little embarrassed, in Jane's immediate presence.

'Thank you, but I'll stand,' she replied. She was stiff and tired from the journey, and the sofas looked inviting to stretch out upon, but sitting felt wrong. The need to remain on her feet was compelling, instinctive.

'How about a drink? Coffee?'

'Some water would be great.'

'Sure thing,' she replied, eager to retreat.

'Oh, before I forget,' Jane called out. 'I've got your phone.'

'It's not mine. I was just the courier.'

'Whose is it?'

'You'll see,' she mumbled, biting her lip.

Jane stood in front of the fire, her eyes drawn to the flames. She'd have loved to have a real fire at home, but there seemed something daft about it in a standard Wimpey place, even if you had a working flue. The dance of tongues and colours was hypnotic and soothing, made all the more attractive by comparison with the view above the mantelpiece, where a huge mirror hung. Jane looked exactly like she felt.

She noticed a flash of movement in the glass as the door opened, the dryness in her throat suddenly accentuated by her anticipation of the water Alexis had gone to fetch. When she turned around, however, it was not the girl who stood before her: it was him. She didn't know how many people were in the building, nor did she have any firm expectations of who the voice on the phone would belong to, but when she saw the figure standing there, she had no doubt whatsoever that this was the man who had brought her here. Never in her life had the phrase 'looking like he owned the place' been anywhere near so apposite, and not just because he did.

It wasn't an arrogance, nor a proprietary air. It was a confidence, an absolute certainty. She couldn't picture him strutting or indulging any kind of ostentatious gesture to underline his status. He looked so utterly sure of that status that he had nothing he needed to prove to anyone.

Jane tried to summon up anger, but felt only anxiety; defiance withering by the second. She'd had fantasies of slapping his face, whatever that face turned out to look like, but now that she saw him she knew she might as well ball her fist and punch the solid stone walls.

He wasn't big, not particularly; maybe five-ten at the most, built solidly and athletically but not muscle-bound. He wore a crisp white shirt and camel-coloured trousers that she'd have described as chinos if they didn't fit so perfectly as to appear tailored. His hair was dark, matched below by a tight beard, both thatches flecked unapologetically with silver-grey. His skin was tanned and weathered, the light copper shade testament to years in the region's climate as opposed to a recent fortnight on the beach. The face was coldly daunting; not aggressive or severe, but as indifferent and impregnable as the walls outside. If she had to age him, she'd guess late forties, maybe early fifties, but while he doubtless had the body of a man half that, his eyes suggested they had witnessed more than a man twice those years.

'Mrs Fleming,' he said simply. She expected a redundant platitude, a 'good of you to come' or a 'glad you could make it', but none was issued.

'Yes,' she responded, economically in kind. 'And you are?'

'Bett. My name is Bett. If you'll take a seat, I will tell you what I know first, and then I imagine you'll have some questions. As time is of the essence, I'd recommend that you keep the rhetorical, petulant and just plain stupid ones to a minimum.'

Jane's indignation caught in her throat as she replied: 'Under which category would you file "Where is my son?"' She feared her words would choke in tears, but her voice held out. Her eyes didn't quite manage as much.

'Under unanswerable,' Bett replied. He turned a hand as a gesture for her to sit. 'So let us move swiftly from that which I don't know to that which I do.'

Jane remained standing. She didn't want to concede anything to this man, but more importantly, she feared that if she did sit down, the last of her composure would collapse and she'd be reduced to a blubbing wreck.

'As you wish,' Bett said.

He took a seat as he talked, turning one of the wooden chairs away from the table and sitting cross-legged. His accent was unplaceably neutral, certain inflections suggesting either that English was not his first language, or that if it was, he didn't always speak it as often as he did others. If she had to hazard a guess as to where he was from, Jane would have said Europe, or maybe just Earth.

He talked calmly and concisely, in a manner that indicated he was used to rapt attention and was thus only going to say this once. Jane didn't need him to repeat a word of it in any case. The natural interjections of dismay and incredulity – 'Are you sure?', 'I don't believe it' – did not get past her lips. He most unquestionably was sure, and after the past twenty-four hours, she quite definitely did believe it. She stood and listened, sipping the cool water Alexis had brought in, the girl wordlessly depositing two glasses and an earthenware pitcher on to a low side table before taking position by the door like some Edwardian servant.

Her head swam. She had so many questions that she was perversely grateful for Bett's abrupt words of caution, for they forced her to sift, evaluate and prioritise.

'I'll give you a moment,' he said, rising from his seat. She thought he was about to leave the room, but he merely took a short walk to one of the huge windows and stood, looking out, hands clasped behind his back.

'I'll start with just one,' she said, allowing herself the compromise of half-sitting, half-leaning against the back of a sofa. Bett turned around. 'What am I doing here? I mean, as you've explained, your people are all experts and professionals, and you guys swim freestyle in a pool normal people don't even dip their toes into. I've been asking myself this for twenty-four hours and I thought that when I got here I'd find an answer, but nothing you've said so far gives me any inkling what it is that you're expecting from *me*.'

Bett walked across to the side table and poured himself a glass of water. He took a drink and stood a few feet away. She caught whiffs of shower gel and deo, a light, soapy aftershave, freshly laundered clothes. Smells of cleanliness and order. If it was a marketed scent, it would be called Discipline or Precision. He looked her in the eye.

'What would you be prepared to do to get your son back alive?'

'I'd say your question should be "what wouldn't I be prepared to do?" Since learning he was missing, I've stolen two cars, forged a passport and violated international border controls, and that was just logistics. I'd do anything. I'd do anything it takes.'

'Then anything it takes is what I expect from you. But we'll begin with what you can tell us about your son.'

Bett pulled out a chair for her around the big table and nodded to Alexis. She exited the room, returning momentarily in the company of another girl, a blonde who carried her tall frame slightly inelegantly, a tomboy all grown up. She had a natural, unaffected prettiness about her, but Jane somehow couldn't picture her in a dress and heels. She looked the type of girl who'd played with all the boys, then didn't quite understand why they suddenly got shy around her sometime after her fourteenth birthday. She looked mid-twenties, slightly older than her companion.

'This is Rebekah,' Alexis introduced.

Rebekah smiled shyly and took a seat.

They were followed into the room shortly by three males. First was a boy – he barely looked twenty – of South-East Asian aspect, skinny and awkward, cheerful but restless. He introduced himself as 'Somboon, but call me Som'. Then came a tall and chiselled-looking young Catalan called Nuno, who carried himself gracefully and lightly on long legs, exuding almost as much effortless confidence as Bett. The undone top buttons of his cornflower-blue shirt revealed shaven skin across taut muscle. In contrast with Rebekah, here was someone who was *always* aware he looked good.

Finally came a balding and grizzled individual, of similar height and build to Bett, though perhaps more tending towards squat. He was also the only one of the group close to Bett in years, and in the company uniquely rugged-looking in contrast to so much fresh-faced youth, the only one who could lay claim to a hard paper-round. Jane anticipated a voice to match his swarthy appearance, from a throat conditioned by a hundred thousand Gauloise, but when he spoke it was smooth, mellifluent.

189

If he read female erotica for audio-books, he'd be a millionaire in six months. He was the only one to approach her before sitting, walking around the table and briefly taking her hand as he announced himself, 'Armand, Madame Fleming.'

All of them seated, Bett commenced his questions. His team didn't have notepads, but they paid such close attention to Jane's answers, it was as though they expected to be tested on it at the end. She reckoned they'd all score full marks, though she wouldn't rate so highly. She felt horribly put upon. Bett's questions were, to begin with, fairly general stuff about Ross, but she couldn't see where they were going, other than ultimately towards the admission that these days she knew little of any use or relevance about her son. The worst of it, however, was the sense of being on the spot, all these bright and inquisitive faces hanging expectantly upon her every word, so many pairs of eyes focused upon her – and she looked *like this*. Jane felt old and ugly, scruffy and sore. Every so often her nostrils caught the smell of her own sweat, turned stale and musky from so much heat and effort in the same clothes, and she guessed if she could smell it herself, it must be rank to the others. What did she look like to these people? And what would they do once they found out she was just another redundant, alienated mother, stranded on the far side of the generation gap?

She stared across the table at Bett. The feeling of intimidation was wearing off, fatigue, sorrow and embarrassment starting to overcome more transient emotions. She felt like a rag doll with the stuffing hanging out of it, and he was still talking away, oblivious to her suffering, indifferent to her state. She was just business on the agenda, the subject at hand. There was a moment when tears might have come again, but it passed. She'd bottomed out, and now her fragile feelings of self-pity were being transmuted into anger and resentment.

'Did Ross mention anything to you recently about what he was working on?' Bett asked.

'What he was working on?' she replied, trying to calm the incredulity in her voice. 'No, we've never talked much about his job, it would be fair to say.'

'Just an allusion, perhaps. Even a flippant remark.'

'I'm trying to remember. What was that you were saying about time being of the essence and not asking stupid questions?'

'Mrs Fleming,' Bett appealed calmly, 'it is always possible that the most fleeting—'

'He doesn't talk to me about his job, okay? I know he works for Deimos, I know he's in research and development of non-lethal weapons. That's it. He doesn't send me any blueprints. In fact, these days I'm doing well if I get a birthday card. Do you talk to your mother about your job?' She threw this last question in a rage, and the words were out before she could consider whether he still had a mother to talk to. He didn't answer, but there was a brief flash in his eyes, just a milli-second's glimmer of reaction before discipline restored the veil of his assured composure. He opened his mouth with a smack of the lips, then paused, as though changing his mind about what he was next about to say.

'When exactly did you last speak to him?' he asked.

Jane sighed. 'Exactly? I don't know. Maybe three weeks ago.'

'Three weeks?' asked Bett, trying not to sound surprised and, she suspected, disappointed. 'And how did he sound? Was he worried?'

'He sounded the same as he always does. Uncommunicative. We exchanged the usual formalities, skirted around the things we ought to be talking about but never do, and then I passed the phone to his father. Forgive me if I failed to interpret any-thing crucial from minor nuances in his speech patterns.'

'Do you know what he spoke to your husband about?'

'Not in detail, no. But I doubt it would be of any greater per-tinence. Not unless you can detect any coded message in whether Chris Sutton is best deployed as an out-and-out striker or played deeper behind Larsson and Hartson.'

Nuno shifted in his seat at this. He looked like he wanted to say something, but reluctantly swallowed whatever it was. Jane had detected a growing tension around the table as she failed to provide any salient information, sighs and traded looks that Bett's admonishing glances were having a diminishing effect in reining in. She felt under increasing pressure to deliver, and thus more resentful that she had been put in this position.

'Does he . . . do you have any relatives on the continent, or friends that he might contact? People or a place he might consider familiar?'

'No. No relatives. As for friends, I don't know.'

'Does he have a girlfriend? Or boyfriend?'

'He was engaged, but that's all off now. Two years ago, in fact.'

'Two years ago is a long time. What about now? Did he ever mention seeing a girl?'

'I'm the last person he'd talk to about that. He's still sore at me because we had a bit of a falling out over him breaking it off with his fiancée.'

More sighs, rolled eyes, a tut.

'Look, I'm sorry if I'm not a fount of knowledge here, okay?' Jane hit out, staring fiercely around the table. 'But I never volunteered myself and it wasn't me who thought I would be.' She looked last at Bett, as did everyone else. The dynamic was beginning to become a little more clear. It wasn't her they were frustrated at.

'Mrs Fleming, please don't allow yourself to become flustered,' he stated flatly. He couldn't have been less solicitous about it; his concern was all for the success of the interrogation. 'This is not a test of your knowledge or of your relationship with your son. What you don't know may prove as relevant as what you do, and what you do know may not be immediately apparent to yourself.'

This sounded like rubbish. Maybe it wasn't her he was trying to convince.

'If you had to take a guess, just on sheer instinct, where would you say Ross might go? Pure gut-reaction. He's alone, he's anxious, he needs to hide, needs to feel he's somewhere he knows, an environment he can control. Where would he go?'

Jane sighed, venting her own frustration. 'I haven't a clue. I'd guess home. That's the only place that fits the bill as you described. Maybe he's there right now and we just missed each other yesterday. Shall I call?'

Bett continued, his tone betraying no response to her sarcasm. He was singularly undistractable. 'Home is too dangerous. Too obvious. He's smart, he wouldn't take the risk. Nor, I imagine, would he want to bring his pursuers anywhere near to his loved ones.'

'Yeah, thank God that didn't happen.'

'Is there another city he's familiar with? Somewhere he's frequented, a regular family holiday destination from his youth?'

'We went to the Canaries mostly. Tenerife, Lanzarote a couple of times.'

Bett shook his head. 'The police impounded his Audi TT after it was left illegally parked in Demerin, near the Swiss border. He also lifted a lot of cash from an autoteller there, according to records obtained by Deimos.'

'So you think he's in Switzerland. We've never been there, not the family.'

'I don't think he's in Switzerland, but I believe that's what he wants people to think. He knew his bank records were traceable and he had no shortage of inconspicuous places to leave his car. He wanted it found. So I ask you again, one guess, but mainland Europe. Where would he go? First thing that comes into your head.'

'Paris.'

'Why?'

'It's big and impersonal. It's comparatively close. Lots of transport options. He speaks French.'

'Does he know it well?'

'I don't know. I don't know if he's ever been, to be honest, but you said first place that comes . . .'

'Okay.'

Nuno shifted restively again. He and Bett stared at each other for a tense couple of seconds, then, with an irritated tut, Bett returned his gaze to Jane. 'Barcelona,' Bett said, with the merest hint of weariness.

'What about it?'

'Does it mean anything to you? Can you think of any reason Ross might go there?'

She looked back blankly and shook her head. She tried to remember whether Ross had ever expressed any interest in the place, but no bells rang. Hadn't he once . . . no, she was pretty sure that was Prague. Or maybe Budapest. Christ, this was hopeless. Bett looked to Nuno with a thin-lipped expression and a fleeting twitch of his brow. Though wordless, it said 'Told you, now shut up,' more witheringly than words could have expressed. Part of her wanted Nuno to lamp him for it.

'Why Barcelona?' she asked, wishing to throw Nuno a crumb of solidarity in facing a common foe.

'Because he's *from* bloody Barcelona,' Bett answered for him. 'And he thinks the whole bloody world revolves around it.'

Nuno shot back an angry look, but again swallowed whatever he had to say.

'It's as likely as Paris,' Jane admitted. 'You might as well get me to throw darts at a map. I don't have any priceless insights, trust me on this. And I'm starting to feel like an idiot for bothering to get myself here. The best chance of me being any use to Ross is if he phones for help, and in the highly unlikely event that he does, I'll be in the wrong bloody country.'

'I don't believe it's unlikely at all,' Bett said, again impervious to her rant. 'The fact that he'd not been in touch for three weeks before he ran will most probably make it more tempting to hear a friendly voice. No matter how self-reliant he is, he'll never have felt so alone. He's going to want to talk to someone, and my guess is, it'll be his mum. He'll call, Mrs Fleming, believe me. Eventually, he'll call, and what country you're in is irrelevant. We can get to anywhere within . . .'

'I'd say it's pretty bloody relevant if I'm not at home to answer.'

'If your mobile doesn't work abroad, I can get you a SIM card that will—'

'I don't *have* a mobile. Only the free gift I got at the supermarket, courtesy of Alexis here.'

There was a moment of complete silence around the table. Bett remained poker-faced as ever, but she could read the headlines in everyone else's reactions. He'd screwed up. That the odds were enormous would be scant consolation: Jane was probably the only woman in Lanarkshire between the ages of nine and ninety who didn't own a mobile phone, but for Mr Attention-to-Detail it constituted a howler.

'Does anyone at home know the number of the phone you're carrying?' he asked, remarkably no hint of anxiety in his voice.

'*I* don't know the number of the phone I'm carrying.'

'Have you phoned anyone with it?'

'Yes, I called Michelle, my daughter.'

'Then she should have it. You're still contactable.'

'She *may* have it. I wouldn't say more than that. I don't know whether international codes show up on Call-ID.'

'You're right. Call home. Now. Give your husband the number. Alexis has it. Alexis, write it down for Mrs Fleming, please.'

Jane took out the mobile and looked around at the circle of faces. This wasn't a conversation she wanted to share.

'Would you excuse me,' she said, and walked across the room to the fireplace. A silence hung in the air as she left, thick with unspoken recrimination. Ironically, despite her feelings of solidarity with the others, it was Bett who'd thrown his lot in with her, and right then it looked like they were both sinking.

She dialled her home number. It rang out. She looked at her watch, tried to estimate where Tom might be, asked herself whether he'd have gone to work as normal after Michelle told him his wife had absconded. Chances were, Tom would have gone to work as normal if Michelle had told him he'd twelve hours to live. He didn't operate well outside of defined parameters. 'Twelve hours? Okay, I'll put in a shift, have my tea and just hope the game tonight doesn't go to extra time.'

She dialled his mobile instead. A recorded announcement said it was switched off and invited her to leave a message.

She called Michelle. She answered so quickly, she must have been sitting with the phone cradled in her lap.

'Dad?' she asked expectantly.

'No, it's Mum.'

'Mum, thank God. I was hoping you'd call. Mum, it's about Ross.'

'You've heard from him?' Jane looked towards the table, her voice having risen unintentionally. All eyes were now fixed upon her.

'He called Dad last night, not long after you phoned me. He's in trouble, Mum. That's why they tried to grab Rachel.'

'I know.'

'You know? Why didn't you say something?'

'It's complicated. What did Ross say? Do you know where he is?'

'Yes. Dad's gone to meet him. He flew out first thing this

morning. Couldn't get a direct flight because they're all full, so he flew to Madrid and drove the rest.'

'Drove where?'

'Barcelona.'

Jane looked across at Nuno, unable to stop herself when she heard the word. She put her hand over the speaker.

'He *is* in Barcelona,' she announced. Nuno threw his hands in the air in a gesture of exasperation.

'Mum? You still there?'

'Yes, honey. Barcelona, you said. But what's your dad planning to do? He can't bring him home, it's too dangerous.'

'Dad said he knew someone over there who might be able to help.'

'Dad? Who does he know in Barcelona?'

'I don't know, he didn't tell me the name. He said it was someone with connections.'

'And is he there now, your dad? Is he with Ross?'

'Yes. Dad called about an hour ago. They had met up with this guy and they were waiting for someone he knew, someone who could help. Look, you shouldn't be talking to me about this. Call Dad. He's got his mobile, and—'

'I just tried him. It's switched off.'

'Must be the signal. Try him again.'

'I will, honey.'

'Mum?'

'Yes?'

'Where are you?'

'The wrong place. I'll tell you later.'

Jane disconnected the call and began dialling Tom's mobile again. As before, a recorded voice informed that it was switched off. She'd keep trying.

'He's with my husband,' she reported. 'My daughter said Tom knows someone there, but it's the first I've heard of it.'

'Rebekah,' Bett said with a nod. The girl got up from the table and made for the door.

Jane hit the redial button. Still no joy. She felt her heartbeat speed up, echoing the urgency she felt to get connected now that she knew Ross was also at the other end of the line. What she didn't know was how the hell Tom could have a friend in

Barcelona that he'd never mentioned, and why of all places Ross should choose to pitch up in that particular city in his time of trouble. It was quite a coincidence, as was Nuno having suggested it not five minutes ago.

She glanced again at the young Catalan. He looked pissed off rather than vindicated. Bett's stone-set countenance was showing cracks too.

'Why did you think he'd go to Barcelona?' Jane asked.

'I saw the photographs from his apartment. Posters on the wall. Celtic.'

'What's that got to do with Barcelona?' Bett asked.

'They're playing there tomorrow night. They bring thousands of their supporters. Los Verdiblancos. Where better to blend in, maybe find friends, get help.'

Bett's eyes flashed, anger now unconcealed. 'Well, why the bloody hell didn't you say this before?'

'I did say.'

'You didn't say *why*.'

'You weren't prepared to listen.'

'That's nonsense. If you had something to say, you knew it was your duty to—'

'Ah, bullshit,' Nuno retorted. 'You'd already made your mind up that *she* would have all the answers. She knows nothing. It's her husband we should have tailed. And the scariest thing is that maybe someone smarter *has*.'

'Ross phoned home last night,' Jane said accusingly to Bett. 'If you'd just let me be, instead of all this cloak-and-dagger crap, I'd be with him by now.'

'Mrs Fleming,' Bett replied, the control in his voice hinting at the anger it held back. 'If I hadn't dispatched Alexis and Rebekah to carry out this "cloak-and-dagger crap", as you put it, then the men who attempted to abduct Rachel would have returned last night, as they intended, broken into her home, kidnapped her from her bed and murdered everyone else in the house.'

She looked to Alexis, who was staring down at the table. Reluctantly, she lifted her gaze, and Jane saw the truth written there indelibly.

Jane kept redialling. Still she could not connect. Still the announcement said it was switched off. But Tom's mobile was *never* switched off.

'Oh shit,' she said.

'What?' asked Bett.

Celtic.

They bring thousands of their supporters.

Dad said he knew someone over there . . .

Jane lifted the phone and called Michelle again.

'Michelle, who is it that Dad was meeting in Barcelona?' she demanded, trying to keep her voice from trembling, though she couldn't tell if it was from anger or from fear.

'I don't know, Mum. The name didn't mean anything to me, I don't remember.'

Jane bit her lip, controlling her growing ire. Michelle had first lied to her when she was two, standing at the top of the stairs and announcing, 'I haven't done a poo in my nappy, Mum.' Two decades later, she was more sophisticated but no less transparent.

'Michelle, you said before that Dad didn't mention the name. Now you're saying you don't remember. Come on, the truth.'

'I'm sorry, Mum. Dad made me promise not to tell you.'

'Well, you've told me now, just by saying that.'

A man with connections who Tom knew would be in Barcelona right then for the Celtic game. A man who travelled to all the European matches, money no object, well-earned respite from the arduous treadmill of flogging drugs. And a man Tom was deluded and desperate enough to trust.

That said, looking around at who she'd run away to team up with, perhaps she shouldn't rush to judge. What was it they said about the devil you know?

Bhoys n the hood

Ross hadn't intended to tell his dad so much. He'd just wanted to speak to him and Mum for a while, to hear their voices and try to keep the emotion from his own. But he'd barely managed hello before his dad began babbling anxiously about what happened to Rachel, and about Mum taking off from under the police's noses before they could talk to her. He knew then there was nothing to gain from keeping his own story back: the fear, the worry, the danger had already made it home. Poor Rachel, poor Michelle. The kid had come through all right, but he felt sick that she should be targeted to get to him. This was about more than just his own safety now.

He told his dad the bare bones, that was all. He didn't tell him everything – he couldn't tell anyone everything – but he gave him the salient parts. What he divulged he did so with the proviso that Dad must not inform the police. Arms firms' security contractors – sneaks, spooks, fixers and enforcers – were rife with ex-cops, and the information trafficking back and forth was as constant as it was insecure.

His dad asked him what he planned to do. Beyond reaching his next intended destination, he had to admit he had no idea; he didn't know who exactly was after him nor who he could trust. He was reluctant to divulge what that destination was, but reckoned it was just a little too paranoid to believe they'd have the clout to organise a tap on his parents' phone.

'I'm going to Barcelona,' he'd said. 'Tonight. I figure it'll give me a few days' grace to think things through. Even if they tracked me down to there, it would be like finding a needle in a haystack, just one more Tim among thousands.'

There was a pause at the other end of the line. 'Dad?' he asked.

'Let me make a couple of phone calls, Ross,' Dad said. 'I know somebody who might be able to help. A guy who'll be out there for the game. He's got connections.'

'What kind of connections?'

'Dodgy connections.'

'Who?'

'Tony Connelly.'

'The drug dealer? Are you kidding?'

'I know the bloke, Ross. He's bent as a nine-bob note, but he's the kind of guy you'd want on your side.'

'And what would be in it for him? Why would he want the grief? These are dangerous people on my back, Dad.'

'He's one of us, Ross. And his people are pretty dangerous too.'

Ross slept a few hours on the first leg of the journey, which was just as well, because he was never going to get a wink on the train from Marseille. What had appeared a quiet carriage when he boarded, had piled up with Celtic supporters a few minutes before departure, and none of them had brought a book or a flask of cocoa.

From their noisy conversations he gathered that they'd flown to Marseille, finding as his dad had last night that all flights from the UK to anywhere near Barcelona were fully booked. Dad was heading to Madrid via Heathrow, then making the rest of the trip by road. With a fair wind he'd be there by tea-time, for a rendezvous with Connelly at his hotel.

Ross kept his head down, sitting by the window, occasionally flipping through a French newspaper to put them off the scent. It was tempting to talk to them, and even at that time of the morning he could have used one of the beers they'd doubtless have offered, but he thought it safest to avoid any entanglements. Glaswegians were as nosy as they were garrulously indiscreet. He didn't want to give out his name, nor was he confident of remaining consistent if he chose to lie about that or any other detail they asked for.

One hour and several beers into the trip, the songs inevitably started up, which was what banished all chance of kip. It was intrusively distracting enough to take his mind off other matters for a while, but there was only so much vicarious Oirishness he could stomach. By the time they were approaching Barcelona, Ross had heard *The Fields of Athenrye* so many times that he'd have happily swapped places with the poor bastard on the transportation ship to Oz if it meant he never had to listen to that fucking dirge one more time.

It was an aspect of supporting Celtic he'd never been able to identify with, and the source of not a few arguments in his time. 'It's wur roots, but, man,' was usually the gist of the justification offered when he suggested they were maybe over-egging the soda-bread. Roots, to his knowledge, did their job best when they remained buried. Tooth or tree, overexposing them was never healthy.

His main objection, however, was that they weren't his roots. You had to go back three generations to find any Irish blood in his family, and that was probably still closer than half the bhoys singing 'Soldiers are we' on that train. The reason it so set his teeth on edge was that it echoed what his dad had been trying to do since he was old enough to notice: shape him into something he didn't want to be, and in the face of this plainly failing, paint him as something he was not.

Arthur Koestler called it the Dual Mind: the ability of the religious to protect their faith by keeping their beliefs separate in their thoughts from the facts and practical knowledge that contradicted all of them. Thus a doctor could profess to believe Jesus rose from the dead when he knew, from the studies he had dedicated his life's work to, that this was complete mince. Or thus Tom Fleming could be in a shouting match about his son's – and indeed his daughter's – stated atheism, then ten minutes later describe them as 'a Catholic family'.

This was another reason Celtic had become such an important bond between them: it was one way his dad could pretend to himself that his son was still 'one of us'. That was what Dad meant about Connelly. Not that he was local, not even that he was a Tim, but that he was a Catholic. Ross couldn't picture him on his knees of a Sunday, but that wouldn't have mattered. To some people – to too many people – it was a pseudo-ethnicity rather than a belief system. Dad saw it as reason enough to trust this guy, despite everything else he knew about him. Ross wasn't so sure, but neither was he spoilt for options right then. Crooked help was better than no help, and maybe he could do with having someone scary in his corner. Being in the guy's debt wasn't something he was looking forward to, but right then it wasn't the worst problem he was facing.

When the train pulled in, he waited in his seat a while until the Verdiblancos had departed, then got up and made for the door. He spotted a scarf one of them had dropped beneath a table that was almost creaking under the weight of empties. He picked it up and draped it around his neck, figuring it would help him blend in.

About a quarter of a mile outside the station, he took it off and stuck it in his pocket, having been accosted four times to be asked: 'Any sperr tickets, big man?' The place was already hoaching with Celtic fans. They were wandering every pavement and spilling out of every bar, café and restaurant. He'd banked on the security of becoming a needle in a green-and-white haystack, but the sharper eye might yet pick him out as being conspicuously sober. At least his anxious expression wouldn't be unique whenever they got to seriously contemplating their chances in the forthcoming game. The biggest danger would be if they got a result and he was the only Tim in the city not kicking his height, but Barca's formidable current form didn't make that look very likely.

He made his way to Connelly's hotel on foot, stopping at a few places on the way to enquire after vacancies. The hotel receptionists did well not to laugh, he thought. It was a disadvantage of his home-from-home plan that he'd failed to anticipate. Well, if he couldn't offer anything else, perhaps Connelly might at least be able to sort them out with a bedroom floor to kip down on.

The place was called the Hotel Gran Havana, on a wide sunny thoroughfare running east-west just north of the city centre. He'd passed the Ritz a couple of blocks back on the other side, smiling momentarily at the thought that it just might be the one place in the city that had a spare billet.

Having located the Gran Havana, he took a walk around the block, found a pavement café with a view of the place, pulled up a chair and waited. He managed to string out two coffees to almost ninety minutes before he saw a blue Passat pull into the quarter-circle plaza in front of the hotel. Ross almost laughed out loud as he saw his dad step out of the vehicle and speak to

202

the approaching concierge. It was so typically him, same as on holiday: he always hired the same model car as he drove at home. 'It's safer driving something you're used to,' he'd explain. This time even the colour was the same.

Ross scanned the surroundings. He'd seen only very light traffic on the wide *vie* throughout the late afternoon, and was satisfied to note there'd been no vehicles following behind the Passat at any visible distance, nor any drivers suddenly deciding to park further back at the same time as Dad pulled in. It had worried him that his dad could have been tailed all the way from home, whether by an individual or by relay, but it looked clear. No one could have maintained line of sight unless they were half a mile back and carrying a telescope.

Ross watched the concierge give his dad directions, most likely to where he could safely and legally leave his car, then called for *la cuenta* as the Passat pulled away again.

He entered the lobby of the Gran Havana and looked around. It was cool inside, in every sense of the word. The walls curved around him in an elegant kidney shape, climbing dramatically to a glass ceiling to create a plunging well of light. There were sofas and tables dotted around a sunken area in the centre, before a short bar hosting a sturdy brass espresso machine and a host of brandies. Slightly spoiling the art-deco ambience was the sight of ten or twelve tipsy Tims in matching hoops, lounging around and sipping San Miguels. Nobody looked twice at him when he walked in. He didn't know what Tony Connelly looked like, but guessed none of them were him. A guy like that wouldn't be wearing a football jersey, no matter how much he loved the team. It made you look like a foot soldier, and he was bound to consider himself officer class.

From the corner of his eye, Ross spotted the concierge pull open the doors, and turned around to see his dad walk through them. They ran towards each other and hugged tightly, something they hadn't done since he was a child. He faintly remembered Dad moving to do so at Glasgow Airport when he was leaving for the job at Marledoq, and Ross stepping away in subtle rebuff. That day he had felt the old man was doing it because he reckoned it decorous in marking the occasion, like it was in the big Fishell Book of Catholic Family Conduct. Today, though, it was warm, genuine and mutual. They held each other for a long few seconds, then finally broke apart and exchanged the usual breathless greetings, Dad sniffing back tears. He always looked smaller and a little rounder than Ross was somehow expecting. This, he suspected, was because the image he kept in his mind was not of the most recent time he'd seen his father, but of a younger man he used to look up to.

He wore his business suit, like it was a day at work, and was even carrying his briefcase. Ross ordered him a drink while the old man called Michelle on his mobile to let her know everything was okay; at least as okay as it could be at that point. Ross took a shot on the phone himself while his dad went to the reception desk to ask for Connelly. There was no news from Mum, though he did get to hear Michelle re-iterate first-hand that she'd definitely been alone, wherever she was, when she called last night. Ross wasn't sure he didn't find this more of a worry than had she been abducted. He couldn't picture Mum going further than the Centre West shopping mall on her own, never mind away overnight or blanking the polis.

Connelly gave Dad the room number and told them to come on up. Ross urged him to have a seat and finish his tea first, but he insisted on going straight for the lift. Ross was as instinc-tively reluctant to bring this guy into the equation as his dad was nervously eager. In his dad's case it was because it was the only way by which he thought he could help; in Ross's, the fear that tying himself to one plan might close out all others.

The door was opened by a man-mountain in a casual suit and a white polo shirt underneath. He was easily six-four, broad in the shoulders and no doubt muscular, but carrying plenty of baggage around the middle too. Ross guessed it wasn't Connelly but a minder, and his cursory nod for them to go on through confirmed it. He noted the absence of hoops or other overstated Celtic regalia on Big Bhoy, he presumed at Connelly's insis-tence, the bodyguard's appearance unavoidably reflecting on the principal.

They found Connelly on a mobile phone, standing by the window on the other side of the room's king-size bed. Ross figured it a safe bet Big Bhoy had more modest quarters down the hall against ten billion to one that they were cosying up of an evening.

He waved hello while continuing to talk, like their arrival and its circumstances were barely incidental. He was Dad's age, Ross knew, but looked younger, mainly due to the designer threads, expensive haircut and wiry build. Big Bhoy handed them beers from the mini-bar, squeezing off the caps with his bare hands and passing them over without asking whether they wanted any. Ross was relieved to observe that they were twist-off tops. The minder noticed him examining the neck for this very feature and gave him a grin as if to say: 'Aye, but I could'.

Connelly finished his call and turned to greet them. He shook Dad's hand and patted him on the back familiarly. Ross didn't think they knew each other that well, and took it to be the kind of gesture gangsters enjoyed bestowing, knowing nobody would ever object to it.

'Thomas, good to see you. Pity about the circumstances. Shame it wasnae just for the game, eh? And you must be young Ross,' he said, offering a hand. Ross shook it tentatively. 'Sorry to hear about your troubles, son, but let's see if we cannae sort something out.'

He leaned back against the window and nodded to the mobile, which he'd put down on a writing desk next to the landline.

'I'm just off the phone to a friend of a friend. I've been makin' enquiries and sendin' up smoke signals since you called last night. The good news is, it looks like we've found somebody local that can help.'

'What's the bad news?'

'I was right about what I says to you last night, Tom. There's no' many Bob Geldofs in this game. Naebody works for free. How much did you get?'

'Five thousand,' Dad said, placing the briefcase down on the bed and opening it to reveal several stacks of tightly packed notes. 'I was on the mobile from the second the banks opened this morning. Got it wired through to Madrid. Comes out around seven thousand euros.'

'Seven thousand?' Connelly grimaced. 'These boys were talkin' aboot ten, for starters. I thought you says you had more.'

'That was the maximum transfer they would authorise in one go. I can get more, but not right away.'

Connelly let out a sigh. 'Hopefully they'll prefer seven thousand and a promise to nothin' for nothin'. We'll front it out anyway. See what they say.'

'And what does my dad's seven thousand euros buy us,' Ross asked, '*if* they accept it?'

'Somewhere to lie low, somewhere safe, where naebody can get to you.'

'A safe house? For that money I could rent a quiet wee place in the hills and get by for six months.'

'It's no' safety that really costs, Ross son,' Connelly explained. 'It's information. It's findin' oot who's on your case, to begin with. After that, the next stage could be a bit dearer, if you know what kinda services I'm talkin' aboot. But it might not come to that. There's a lot of ways to get somebody aff your back. But in the short term, the safety they're offerin' is a sight better than holin' up somewhere.'

'How?'

'You'll see. And you'll like it, trust me.'

'I don't trust you, Mr Connelly. You're a drug dealer.'

'Ross,' Dad started.

'Don't worry aboot it,' Connelly replied. 'I wouldnae trust me either. But it's not me you have to trust.'

'Who are these people?'

'You'd be better asking them, but you'll need to hurry up. They won't hang around forever. Time is money to these people, literally just now.'

'Literally? How?'

'Come on and find out.'

They followed the rental Mercedes in Dad's hired Passat, Ross having caused another moment of parental embarrassment by refusing to get into Connelly's car. Connelly seemed more understanding of it than Dad, perhaps appreciating the element of surrender entailed in climbing into a vehicle under the control of someone you didn't know enough to trust. The Merc led them south-east, past the new harbour development already teeming with early diners and ubiquitous wandering Tims, until they were driving parallel to the coastline. A right turn took them past some low concrete buildings, probably boathouses, and on to the approach to a long stone jetty, along which several yachts were berthed.

Ross got it now. Time literally was money – in mooring fees.

'It's not a safe house,' he said to his dad. 'It's a safe boat.'

And where safer, in fact? Nobody could find him, far less get to him, if he was secretly stashed out at sea.

Connelly's Merc pulled over and parked by a low wall. He and Big Bhoy, whose name turned out to be Charlie, got out and stood at the entrance to the quay. Connelly glanced along the jetty but Ross couldn't see precisely where he was looking or whether anyone was looking back. He beckoned them to come forth.

Ross and his dad climbed out of the Passat and walked slowly forward.

'Come on, don't worry,' Connelly said. 'We're just gaunny talk. If you don't like what they've got to say, we walk away.'

'What about the money?' Dad asked. Connelly hadn't removed it from the Merc.

'Aye, right enough. I'd better go and have a word about that first. Actually, fuck it. Tell you what, we'll offer them what you've got, and if it comes tae the bit, I'll front you the difference.'

'Thanks, that would be, you know ... I really appreciate it,' Dad said.

'Hey, I've got weans of my own,' Connelly replied.

He led them along the jetty. Once they had walked about a third of the way down, past the first couple of yachts, Ross saw someone emerge on to the concrete at the very end, a man dressed smartly in sandy-coloured trousers and a crisp white shirt. He looked like he'd stepped out of a restaurant rather than off a boat, which augured well for on-board comfort. From what Ross could see of the stern, it was more than a weekend pleasure cruiser. The man smiled and gave them a broad wave. It seemed a dispro-portionately large gesture considering they were now only about twenty yards away, not at the other end of the quay.

Then Ross sensed movement behind him and turned to have a look. The man *had* been waving to someone further away, though not quite at the end of the jetty. Two men suddenly appeared from the first vessel Ross had walked past, both of them carrying what he recognised as Ingrams Mac-10 machine pistols.

'What the fuck's this?' Ross asked Connelly. His failure to so much as skip a beat was too cool even for the most hardened and phlegmatic gangster. The bastard was in on this.

'Fuckin' slimy prick, you've sold us out,' Ross said. He balled his fingers and swung a fist, but Connelly saw it coming. He'd seen it coming since last night when Dad was daft enough to phone and tell him Ross was on the run. Connelly shifted his weight and sent a fist upwards into Ross's gut. He felt an explosion of pain and saw white as his breath burst from his lungs. Dad stepped to intervene and was immediately grabbed by Big Bhoy, who pulled him by the arm towards his oncoming head-butt. Dad dropped to the concrete, dizzy, on his knees, blood pouring from his nose. Big Bhoy knelt over him, patted him down and removed his phone. He went to place it in his pocket but Connelly overruled.

'It's traceable. Chuck it.'

Big Bhoy tossed it casually over the side of the jetty and into the water. Meanwhile, Connelly was frisking Ross, still paralysed as he bent double, reeling from a pain that was worse than a boot in the balls multiplied by raging diarrhoea. The three other men had arrived and surrounded them by this point. Connelly produced Ross's wallet, ignoring the lip-balm tubes. He removed all the cash and let the wallet drop to the jetty.

His dad looked up helplessly, confused. 'Why?' he asked, his voice trembling with shock and tears.

Connelly simply laughed, a short dry snort of dismissive derision.

Ross just about summoned up the breath to voice a defiance he knew to be as pointless as his rage nonetheless made it compulsory.

'I'll see you again, Connelly,' he vowed.

'Sure you will.'

'Think I won't? You don't even know why they want me. I'll see you again, and I'll shut both your mouths, ya two-faced cunt.'

Connelly shook his head. 'Charles?' he prompted.

Big Bhoy kicked Dad in the ribs, causing him to curl and writhe like a startled caterpillar.

'Felipe,' Connelly said to the man in the white shirt. 'I suggest you take *el papa* too. He'll make sure junior behaves himself.'

Vital away fixture

Bett got up and walked to the window again, having grown too restless for his chair to contain him. He prowled, a latent aggressive energy about him, like a static charge that would shock you if you got too close. Nuno, Armand and Alexis remained at the table as Jane spoke, leaning against an armchair a few feet away from them.

'A drug-dealer,' Bett muttered ruminatively.

'Yes,' Jane said, nodding, though she'd supplied enough details that she knew he didn't require any confirmation.

He stopped pacing and sighed heavily, staring out across the perfectly manicured lawns.

'Shit,' he stated, like it was the precise answer to a complex mathematical equation. He turned back to face the room. 'Armand, go and tell Rebekah to fold her wings.'

Armand got up with a nod and made for the door. Before he reached it, Bett had an addendum. 'She can continue with the refuelling but, other than that, we hold for now.'

'Hold?' Jane said. 'You can bloody hold. I'm going to Barcelona.'

Bett shook his head. Infuriatingly, he clearly inferred it as an order, not a comment. 'You're staying here,' he underlined.

'My son is in Barcelona. You've already whisked me away to the wrong place once, you're not doing it again. I even know what hotel they're in.'

'No, Mrs Fleming, you only know the location of the man who has just delivered your son into enemy hands.'

'How can you possibly know that? How can you be so bloody certain, sitting here hundreds of miles away?'

'Do you want to try your husband's mobile phone again?' he asked rhetorically. According to Michelle, the last time Tom called had been when he and Ross arrived at the hotel. Reception hadn't been a problem then. Was it possible they'd gone somewhere since where there wasn't a signal?

She knew her husband too well. If he was waiting on a call or he knew someone might need him, he was obsessive about checking his phone to make sure the signal was okay. When they'd been expecting Michelle to go into labour the first time, he'd stood in the street while Jane went into certain shops if the reception inside was poor. His phone was off. Jane tried to think of any circumstances under which he would deactivate it himself at a time like this, and finally admitted to herself that there were none that didn't involve duress.

She grasped for flaws, though it was a sign of desperation that her only hopes lay via the gaps in her understanding.

'Tom only phoned Connelly last night. How could a guy like that, a Glasgow drug-dealer, find out who was looking for Ross?'

'He may not have, yet,' Bett replied. 'But in the meantime, he'll be keeping him somewhere secure until he does. That or he'll deliver him to an intermediary for a quick and simple return. A finder's fee.'

'But how would he even know there was anything to be gained?'

'Simply because your husband told him, however indirectly. A man on the run is clearly valuable to whoever is chasing him. Add to that the knowledge that the man in question works for an arms company and the purse starts to look even heavier.'

'Christ, do these bastards have some kind of worldwide-web message board for villains to trade information on?'

'No, but only because their channels of communication have always been broader and faster than the internet. If they did have a webpage, it wouldn't be a bulletin board, it would be an auction site. Every item of information is potentially saleable. A guy like Connelly will have all sorts of direct or indirect contacts, not just in drugs. Smuggling is most likely the common conduit. People who move drugs know people who move other things: guns, explosives, illegal immigrants. That's you into human traffic and the arms trade in about two phone calls, maybe only one.'

Jane reeled at the words, realising she had until then only glimpsed the enormity of Ross's situation. She thought of the driver yesterday, that cold, dispassionate professionalism. She remembered Michelle's words on the phone last night. *It was on TV about two burned bodies being discovered out by Calder Glen.* The water was deep and sharks were circling everywhere. But surely one of the sharks had been tagged.

'If Connelly's got them, then what are we waiting for?' she asked. 'We know where he's staying for God's sake. Even if he doesn't have them any more, he knows who does.'

'He's not going to tell us over a quiet drink, Mrs Fleming,' Bett said.

'That wasn't what I had in mind, Mr Bett. Just give me five minutes with the bastard.'

'Connelly won't be alone. He'll have back-up. There are measures we can take, but not in a busy hotel, no doubt full of football fans. These things take delicacy, and planning.'

'Time, as you keep insisting, is of the essence,' Jane reminded him.

'As is timing,' he replied. He narrowed his eyes and looked searchingly at her. She felt suddenly naked to his gaze, but naked like a patient being scrutinised by a surgeon rather than under the gaze of a voyeur.

'You used to drive a taxi,' he stated. 'In this man's firm.'

'It wasn't his firm when I joined, but he'd purloined it by the time I left, yes. Why?'

Bett didn't answer, merely nodded to himself.

'Okay,' he announced to the room, a gavel-banging timbre to his delivery. 'Reveille six o'clock tomorrow morning. For now I suggest everybody goes home and gets an early night. That's all,' he added, raising his palms in a class-dismissed gesture.

'Ehm,' Alexis ventured quietly but firmly. 'You were planning on feeding your guest, I assume.'

Bett paused just long enough for Jane to guess the issue hadn't remotely occurred to him.

'Of course,' he said; more 'of course, thanks for reminding me' than 'of course, what do you take me for'. 'I'll have Marie-Patrice prepare something.'

'And where will Mrs Fleming be sleeping?' Alexis pressed. 'I mean, I know you normally offer our most special guests the Romanian Suite, but I wasn't sure you'd want to extend precisely that level of hospitality.'

Bett eyed Alexis with a look that would have withered spring flowers.

'I do have quarters prepared, Ms Richardson. Why don't you show Mrs Fleming to them. Upstairs, first floor. Turn right. Second door on the left.'

'Wouldn't you like to show her yourself, as the master of the house?'

Bett responded with a glare that made the first one look like something from a christening photo.

'Okay, okay,' Alexis said, getting up from the table. Jane spotted Armand offering his colleague a knowing, applauding grin, his back to the boss.

Alexis closed the door and led Jane back down the corridor towards the entrance hall.

'He's a whole bundle of fun,' Jane remarked.

'No, don't be fooled by the façade. Beneath that icy and impermeable exterior there beats a heart of pure, simmering evil. Some nights we just laugh and laugh,' she added grimly.

'I'm not sure I caught his first name. In fact, I'm not sure he gave one.'

'I'm not sure he has one. I find he usually responds to "Sir". You could try Fuckface.'

'Perhaps not while I'm a guest.'

Jane followed her up the broad staircase, conscious of the reverberations her footsteps made around the high walls and marble floor below. She lowered her voice to speak.

'I'm sorry if I've not turned out to be much help,' she offered meekly. 'I get the impression there's a bit of tension over me being here.'

'Don't sweat it, I'm sure you'd sooner you weren't. It was Bett's idea to bring you in, and not everybody was sold on it, but he's the boss, and they're used to that. Doesn't mean they like it, but he's got an infuriating, chronic habit of turning out to be right. They're used to that, too, it's just . . .'

'What?'

'Nothing. I've said too much. You've got enough to worry about without our squabbles.'

'You can't leave me hanging there.'

'Well, Bett's about as single-minded as it's possible to get, and on the whole you don't ask questions because, like I said, he usually turns out to be right. He knows what he's doing and he doesn't take chances.'

'But you think that's what he's doing with me?'

'Me? I'm taking the fifth. But it would be fair to say there's a concern that Bett's being more single-minded than usual, and nobody can work out why.'

'So me failing to supply many answers in there didn't make it any clearer.'

'Not much, no.'

Jane stopped on the first-floor landing and looked along the corridors in both directions. She dallied a moment as Alexis led off to the right rather more urgently than seemed necessary, even if Jane was in serious need of some rest. It seemed less a matter of hastening towards her destination than anxiety that she should be contemplating another. Jane stared along to the left a moment longer to test her thesis, prompting a beckoning gesture from her guide by way of confirmation.

'What's down there?' she asked.

'That's the west wing. Bett's private area. I mean, it's all his house, but, you know, that part's more his than the rest. It's where he hangs upside down or naps in his casket, or whatever, I don't know. But don't go there. Come on.'

They reached the door Bett had directed them to. Alexis opened it and stepped aside to invite Jane past her. She walked in to find an area boasting more square feet of floorspace than an entire storey of her house. The four-poster against the near wall meant it could technically be referred to as a bedroom, but to Jane it looked like a flat missing several walls. Four windows gave out on to the lawns, each three panes tall, each pane six feet wide and three feet high. There were antique wardrobes, a chaise longue, a mirrored dresser, a bureau, two armchairs, a low coffee table and just acres and acres of space.

'There's an en suite through there,' Alexis pointed out, indicating a half-open door to the right. Through the gap, Jane could see the end of a roll-top bath standing free upon a broad tiled floor.

'So is this the Romanian Suite?' she asked.

Alexis laughed rather darkly and shook her head.

'No, no, this is . . . this is the VIP suite. He's not the most communicative, so consider this Bett's big stab at courtesy.'

'I'd take this over a kind word, wouldn't you?'

'Sure. But you'll be a long time waiting to get both.'

As soon as Alexis had departed, Jane ran a bath, peeling off her clinging and less-than-fragrant clothes as soon as she'd turned on the taps. She laid her garments on the arm of a chair and stood in the doorway, watching the tub fill and listening to the splashing resound noisily about the tiled walls. It was cool in the room, but it felt good to be naked, to feel the air on her skin.

She lay and soaked for a while with her head half-submerged, closing her eyes and letting the water block her ears. She could imagine other circumstances under which it would be close to heaven, but for now it served only as respite. Nor did it last, her mind still too full and busy to let her relax. She lay only a few minutes then got on with her ablutions.

When she emerged, wrapped in a heavy cotton dressing gown, she found that a tray had been left on the low table and that her clothes were gone, but for the open plastic pack of under-wear she'd purchased last night at that twenty-four-hour super-market. The tray bore a plate of quiche, cheeses, cold meats and relish, as well as a baguette, a small bowl of fresh fruit, an earth-enware pitcher of water, two glasses and a bottle of wine.

Jane fell upon it ravenously, devouring the quiche and tearing into the bread before pausing to take a drink, surprising her-self with how hungry she was. Calmed a little by this glut, she examined the bottle. There was no label, nor any impressed markings, not that she'd have known a Cabernet from a Cranberry. Curious, she poured a little into the unused glass and had a sip. It was lighter than she was expecting, less bitter. It didn't have that diluted-perfume taste of the white stuff Catherine had insisted she try, nor the blood-like thickness she remembered from sampling a red before. She took a bite of Stilton and then had some more. The wine tasted sweeter in contrast to the cheese, pleasantly warming going down her throat. She could feel it right across her chest, in fact, and after another few mouthfuls, in her face too.

Jane almost giggled with a childish kind of pride when she

saw that she had actually finished a whole glass. She ate a forkful of carpaccio and poured herself another. Ten minutes later she was sound asleep.

She awoke to find herself stretched out on top of the bed-clothes, still wrapped in the bathrobe. The dinnerplates and glasses were gone and in their place there was a silver-coloured jug from which she could smell coffee. She looked at a clock on the wall. It said seven twenty-five. From outside she could hear a low chug-chugging, some gardening device being put through its paces.

Jane sat up and walked to the table. As she poured herself a mug of coffee, she spotted that there was a black lycra dress draped over the back of an armchair, roughly where she'd left her own clothes last night. She picked it up, causing a pair of black nylons she hadn't noticed to fall on to the upholstery. Jane shook her head. What age did they think she was? She couldn't wear that. She never wore skirts these days, never mind a dress. It was too small as well. She'd never get into it, let alone walk in the thing.

Faced with the alternative of going downstairs in only the bathrobe, she decided to try it on. As it turned out, it wasn't too small, though the hemline was six inches higher than any-thing she'd contemplated in a decade. Nor was it restrictive, the material comfortably snug and accommodating as it stretched and contracted with her movement. The colour did, however, serve to emphasise the grey streaks in her hair, though they were the least of her tonsorial worries at that point. She hadn't dried it before the wine zonked her last night, so she had that Bride-of-Frankenstein thing going on. She noted a brush and a comb on the dressing table, but there was little they might achieve that would improve upon tying the whole thing back with an elasticated scrunchie.

Her mane thus restrained, Jane had another swallow of coffee and ventured downstairs. The chugging sound got louder as she neared the open front door; it was powerful but still unex-pectedly muted. She wandered outside, where she discovered that this was because it was coming from the rear of the house, where the rotor blades of a helicopter were rhythmically chop-ping the air.

Walking around the building, she could see Rebekah at the controls, Bett and Nuno standing to the side a prudent ten yards away. Nuno noticed Jane's arrival first and tapped Bett on the shoulder. He turned, saw her and beckoned her forward.

'Good morning,' he hailed as she approached, calling loudly over the sound of the helicopter.

'I'm ready,' she said.

'Ready for what?'

'Anything it takes, remember?'

Bett nodded. 'Welcome aboard.'

Several hours later, she was in another set of someone else's clothes, once again a good enough fit, though this time a little more formal. The peaked cap was her particular favourite, accompanied by wraparound shades that she was supposed to wear at all times, indoors and out. They were for concealment and disguise, but she'd have been surprised if Connelly had ever paid enough attention to know what she looked like anyway.

They'd arrived in Barcelona by mid-morning. It took Bett less than an hour to organise the vehicles and Nuno little more to suggest and secure a suitable venue. The longest single stretch had been Jane's driving lesson, first getting used to the vehicle and then learning the route. She'd have liked more time to practise, given the thing had a turning circle of about a quarter of a mile, but them's the breaks. Somehow she didn't anticipate her driving being the biggest thing her passengers might have to complain about.

In the meantime, Rebekah had gone to the hotel and run a tail on Connelly, picking him up on his way to lunch and following him around a few bars until he decided it was time for a pre-match siesta. Jane pulled up in front of the Gran Havana at bang on four o'clock, Nuno in the passenger seat, Bett in a hired A6 just around the corner. The place was utterly swarming with guys in Celtic tops, waving and grinning stupidly to each other whenever they encountered another of their kind. Nuno opined that they wouldn't be smiling in a few hours, but Jane suspected he was overestimating the importance of the actual game to such a trip. Bevy and parties were going to be top of the agenda, win or lose. However, she did know of at least one Celtic fan who definitely wouldn't be getting the result he wanted.

Having seen them approach, Rebekah walked out through the glass doors and made her way to the Audi, while Nuno picked up the car phone and asked to be put through to Connelly's room.

'Señor Connelly? *Si*. Is just a call to say that your limousine is waiting downstairs whenever you are ready, to take you to Camp Nou. No, Señor, I eh . . . I *comprendo*, you no order, *si*. But is okay, you no pay. Is ordered by friend. He say is, how you say, gift, in interest of business, *comprendes*? *Siiii*,' Nuno nodded, grinning. 'That's right. A "wee thank you", *si*. Okay. Is . . . my driver, she is outside now, she take you, okay? But she not speak English, Señor. Only right and left, okay? *Si*. Okay. When you are ready. *Si. De nada*, Señor.'

He put the phone down.

'A wee thank you?' Jane asked.

'His words. Meaning he's already made the sale.'

She nodded, understanding. Their default gambit was to play it as a perk from a prospective buyer, Bett carefully phrasing 'in interest of business' to keep the tense neutral. Connelly had assumed who the gift horse was from, and instantly taken it as a gesture of gratitude. He wasn't looking it in the mouth. Too bad for him it was Greek.

'Time to go to work,' Nuno said. They both got out of the car, Nuno heading for Bett's Audi, Jane taking position, arms folded, leaning against the side of the black stretch limo.

Ten minutes passed, throughout which Jane was anxious that Connelly might be calling someone to acknowledge the gesture. In any eventuality, Bett had anticipated that both curiosity and flattery would get the better of him and he'd get in anyway, keen to discover who was behind the gesture and what opportunities they might have to offer. Bett had therefore reasoned that any caution on Connelly's part would be overcome by the sight of a lone and female driver, predicting further that the booze-lubricated back-seat conversation would be less circumspect if they thought she didn't understand a word of it.

Finally, the concierge held the doors open and Connelly

stepped into view, accompanied by a tall and heavy-set minder she recognised from her taxi days. Charlie, his name was, or Big Chick. She felt her chest tighten as they both looked at her, their stark familiarity making reciprocation seem inevitable. Now she understood why Bett insisted on the sunglasses; they were as much to hide her reactions as her appearance.

Neither of them exhibited the slightest glimmer of recognition. They were mainly looking at the car, grinning at each other with a nauseating self-satisfaction. From behind her shades she felt as though she was looking at them through a two-way mirror. She could see them, but they couldn't see her, and the membrane that protected her from their view was much thicker than glass.

'*Hola*,' she said, holding open the door and offering a thin, professional smile. Don't look too friendly, Bett had coached her. It hadn't been hard.

Connelly climbed inside, but Big Chick paused on the pavement, his expression looking suddenly uncomfortable.

'Eh, we want . . . we're hingmy, you know, no' wantin' tae go straight tae the gemme. No . . . football . . . yet? You understand?'

This was the guy's pitch at bilingual communication. Connelly's abilities were doubtless no better, but he had the seniority to leave making an arse of himself to his minion. She almost felt for him. The guy's face couldn't have looked more contorted or pained if he was straining for a jobbie.

'*No comprendo.*'

'Eh . . . hingmy, it's a restaurant we're after the noo. Restaurant?'

'Restaurant? Tapas?'

'Aye. *Si.*'

'Fuck's sake, Charlie, show her on a map,' Connelly called from within, where he was already removing the foil from a bottle of Cava.

'Huv ye got a map?' Chick asked.

'Map?'

He mimed unfolding and pointing, or at least that's what she assumed from already knowing what he meant. Marcel Marceau could rest easy.

'Ah, *mapa*?' she asked.

'Naw, map,' he insisted.

'Fuck's sake, man, mapa *is* map.'

'Oh, right. Aye, *mapa*, hen, *mapa*.'

Jane opened the driver's door and retrieved a map from the side pocket. It was handed through to Connelly, who pointed out a destination to Chick, who in turn demonstrated it to Jane. She pretended to examine it. '*Si, si*,' she assured, nodding her head. She'd no idea where the place was, nor did it matter. What did was that the big eejit climbed in and she was able to get going, Bett's A6 pulling away swiftly at her tail.

There was an almost giddy air of self-congratulation about them as they stretched across the back seats and guzzled the Cava. Connelly in particular was enjoying the chance to demonstrate how such complimentary luxury reflected upon his status and acumen.

'It's turning into a very successful wee trip,' he observed. 'Have to fancy our chances the night, the way everythin' else has been goin'.'

'Too right,' Big Chick agreed.

'Noo and again you get these wee gifts from the gods, but they mean fuck-all unless you're sharp enough to make the most of them.'

'Opens doors for the future as well.'

'Aye, you're tootin' there, Charlie. Wee touch of class fae that Felipe, sendin' this. It's aw aboot respect. Two days ago, we'd never heard of each other. But we do business, we deliver what we say we will, and he recognises he's dealin' with the real thing. We baith knew the boy was worth a sight mair tae him than he was payin', but we also baith knew he was worth fuck-all tae me otherwise. I could have asked for more, he could have offered less. Respect, Charlie. Nae need for him tae dae somethin' like this efter the deal's done. Touch o' class. And if he's ever in Glesga, we put the boat oot for him.'

'He's got his ain boat, but.'

'Figure of speech, ya tube.'

The restaurant they had pointed out would only have been five or ten minutes away in light traffic had they been driven there, but they were well into their second bottle of fizz before

219

Connelly began paying any concerned notice to what was passing outside the windows. They were speeding along a broad dual carriageway, medium-rise apartment blocks lining the route. In just about any city in the world, even after a few drinks, it would be clear that they were heading away from the centre.

He tapped on the thick glass partition and spoke through the narrow gap behind Jane's head. His mounting anxiety prevented him from deferring the task this time.

'Haw, Señora, where we gaun? This isnae right. We're away the wrang way.'

'*No hablo ingles, Señor*,' Jane told him.

'We are going the wrong way,' he enunciated. 'Restaurant, remember?'

'Restaurant, *mapa, si*,' she responded.

'Naw, haud on. Stop.'

'*Pardon, Señor. No hablo ingles.*'

He slammed the glass angrily with his hand.

'I says stop. Stop the fuckin' car,' he shouted.

Jane reached back and slammed home the sliding glass panel behind her head, locking it with her free hand while the other remained guiding the steering wheel. She briefly turned her hazard lights on and off, a signal to Bett that Connelly now knew something was up. She'd been briefed to pull over if it got hairy, at which point Bett would board the limo armed with a pistol, but she was only minutes from their goal. She was also enjoying the look on the bastard's face when she glanced in her rear-view.

It got even more satisfying when he tried the handle, Jane having engaged the child-locks before she shut them in so that the rear doors could only be opened from the outside. She could see the growing panic, the smug words about Felipe and his touch of class turning to ashes as he realised how credulously he'd walked into a trap.

Both of them began hammering at the glass partition, no longer to get her attention but trying to break it. It was a desperate act. Connelly wouldn't be able to fit through the gap, never mind his big pal, nor would they be able to reach forward far enough to even tug Jane's hair. It didn't deter them, though, and they kept at it until Big Chick finally succeeded in putting a foot through the pane. Unhappily for him, this co-incided with Jane swinging the limo hard right around the final corner, sending him sprawling sideways into Connelly so that the pair of them ended their journey in a heap on the vehicle's rear floor. Jane brought the car to a stop beneath the canopy of the disused petrol station that Nuno had appointed their destination, Bett's car rolling immediately into place alongside.

Connelly and his minder disentangled themselves and looked up hesitantly as the figure of Bett approached the limo. He pulled open the door and stepped back, Nuno standing behind him with his arms folded. The disused petrol station was on the outer edge of a run-down and largely derelict industrial estate, the kind of place Jane would normally drive through at high speed and with the doors locked. On this occasion, however, she knew the people on her side were far scarier than anything she'd ever feared meeting on such darkened straits in the past.

Connelly, despite having demanded the car stop and having made such desperate efforts to escape its confines, was no longer in any great hurry to get out, though not from any apparent fear. Jane eyed his expression in the rear-view mirror: anger and defiance burned beneath the surface, but he was determined to present an air of control. He wasn't jumping out of the door on anybody's cue.

Big Chick had fewer layers to his countenance. He looked psyched and aggressive, ready to bring his considerable weight to bear upon whoever incurred his boss's displeasure.

Connelly waited a measured few moments, then announced: 'Let's see what these cunts want.'

He had Chick step out first, bristling with underlying hostility, taking position, arms folded, then Connelly followed him on to the crumbling tarmac.

Connelly looked Bett and Nuno up and down, waiting for them to say something, or perhaps make a move. They didn't.

'Can I help you?' Connelly eventually asked, his tone exaggeratedly weary, like this was all a big yawn to him.

Nuno looked to Bett, who nodded. Nuno then began babbling in Spanish, asking incomprehensible questions, his tone increasingly aggressive.

'*No hablo español*,' Connelly stated flatly. 'We only speak

English. *Comprendes?* Now tell us what it is you want or fuck off. You understand that?'

Nuno renewed his bitter inquisition, still entirely in Spanish, and stepped forward, prodding a finger just short of Connelly's chest.

'Fuck this,' he muttered. 'Charlie, let's do these cunts.'

With that, he picked up a bottle of Cava he'd left just inside the door and smashed it against the wheel-arch, while Big Chick produced a stiletto blade with a brass-knuckle grip from inside his jacket. Jane watched anxiously through the window, expecting Bett and Nuno to draw pistols, or perhaps Rebekah to emerge armed from the Audi. Instead, Nuno tutted – she actually heard him tut – and shook his head just before Connelly came swinging at him, Big Chick towards Bett.

The expertise with which Bett and Nuno disarmed and dispatched their opponents was clinical; the ruthlessness with which they persisted coldly sickening. Jane winced as she watched Bett pick the big man from the floor again only to expertly inflict further damage. He and Nuno had guns, and the plan was to take the pair below, to the petrol station's disused underground reservoir, so why hadn't they just commanded their prisoners' cooperation that way?

As she watched the two beaten figures cower on the floor, utterly helpless in the face of further assault, she understood. Bett wanted them broken, wanted them to know they were hopelessly mismatched, not merely coerced by the advantage of weapons.

He signalled to her and to Rebekah to come forward from their cars. It was time to take them below. Once again, Jane was grateful for the sunglasses, which hid the revulsion she couldn't keep from her eyes. She held her mouth closed and her lips tightly pressed, and from the outside she must have looked coolly indifferent. Inside, she was concentrating on not throwing up.

She watched Connelly climb to his knees, trembling in fear that it was only the prelude to another kick or punch. Blood was pouring from his nose, spluttering from his mouth as he coughed, doubled over in pain. She remembered her remarks of the previous night: *Just give me five minutes with the bastard.*

What she'd witnessed hadn't even lasted one, and it was more than enough to turn her anger into disgust.

Then she remembered why she was here. The disgust remained, but it would not, could not, turn to pity.

Now Nuno drew a gun, Rebekah likewise, and gestured the two prisoners towards the petrol station's dilapidated office. There they would be led downstairs through a maintenance passage to the aluminium chamber where the fuel used to be stored. Jane had been taken down herself earlier so that it didn't freak her out when the time came. Despite its volume, it had looked pressingly claustrophobic in the low light of a single wire-muzzled bulb on an untidily snaking extension lead. What the chamber would look like with two bloodied casualties trussed up inside was something she was in no hurry to discover, but she suspected the view would be a lot worse from where they were sitting.

Bett waited for her to catch up as Nuno and Rebekah forged ahead.

'I'm guessing you're not so sure about having five minutes alone with him now,' he stated quietly.

'Correct,' she admitted, looking away before he could read any more of her thoughts. She gazed at the floor without focusing, just somewhere to direct her eyes.

'You're doing fine,' he assured her.

'I think I'm going to be sick.'

'That's normal. Go ahead. Just get it over with before you go downstairs to face them.'

'I'm not sure I can.'

'Well, like I said, he's not going to tell us over a quiet drink. But if you're feeling a little queasy, just consider how long it took him to decide to sell out your son when your husband came to him for help.'

Now Jane looked up, her insides turning to steel.

'My liberal estimate would be a heartbeat,' she said.

She waited outside the chamber, as instructed, after telling Bett what she'd overheard in the limo. From inside, she could hear Nuno continuing to rant in Spanish, intended to maximise their fear that there was nothing they could say, never mind do, to improve their situation.

Bett went in first. She heard him conferring with Nuno in an ostensibly private discussion that was in fact entirely for the benefit of Connelly and friend. Following this, Nuno withdrew, emerging from the chamber and thus providing her cue. He also provided her with Big Chick's chib, the blade-cum-knuckleduster, as a prop. She took it delicately, letting it hang from her index finger by one of the loops. This was initially because she was reluctant to take proper hold of the ugly thing, but as she stepped through the low hatchway and righted herself again, she realised it gave the appearance of a nonchalance that was far removed from what she was feeling. The shades helped too. Their affectation rating was now off the scale, but she had her orders.

She stopped just inside and surveyed the scene. Connelly and Chick were tied to two sturdy tubular aluminium chairs, secured by their feet, arms and necks with fine but strong cord. The muzzle-framed lamp hung from above, taped to the metal ceiling, the lead dangling limply to the floor, where it was plugged into an extension socket. Bett leaned casually against a wall, arms folded, gun tucked into his waistband. He looked so slovenly and unprofessional that she knew it had to be part of the script. Rebekah was putting on less of an act, Jane guessed, standing vigilantly to attention behind the two prisoners, feet slightly apart, pistol in right hand, pointed down, left thumb over the safety catch.

Nuno had done well. Connelly looked anything but defiant now: trying to hide his fear, but unable to conceal his confusion. Chick was less concerned with appearances. A big hardcase unused to being on the losing team, he looked like he was on the verge of tears. They both glanced anxiously at her immediately as she entered the chamber. She walked towards them very slowly, the blade still dangling from her finger, then she took a firm grip, feeding her digits through the rings before stroking the side of the blade with her left hand.

All four captive eyes remained fixed upon her, and in particular the knife, as she continued her sadistically slow progress. Connelly looked pathetic, even his attempt to put on a blankly neutral expression faltering with each inch she drew nearer. She'd moved forward slowly at first out of her own reluctance and apprehension, but as she observed the effect on him, she grew in confidence with every measured step.

When she was only a couple of feet from their chairs, she stopped and stood still, saying nothing for a moment, just looking back and forth between them with slightly exaggerated movements of the head. Now they were looking anywhere but at her, neither wanting to meet her shaded eyes lest they be chosen first for whatever was about to follow.

She sighed, tiredly, then reached up and slowly removed the peaked cap, her hair spilling untidily from it. Turning away, she brushed the strands from her face with her left hand, then very gently and deliberately took off the sunglasses, placing them inside the hat and holding it out with her right hand. Bett stepped away from the wall obediently and took it without a word.

Then she turned back and faced them.

'Anthony,' she said quietly, the walls absorbing and muting the sound.

Connelly's face registered puzzlement at first, the beginnings of recognition still scrappy while they awaited the more crucial details of why she was familiar and where he knew her from.

'I'd have thought you of all people ought to recognise a driver,' she said, helping him along. 'Though these days I'm less picky about dropping off wee bags of shite.'

And then, with a look of true shock and even greater confusion, he got it. She could see the processes whirring in his calculating little head, connecting points here, overlapping there, until he reached a verdict that ultimately appeared to give him some comfort. Now that he knew what this was about, or thought he knew what it was about, he could start to consider his odds, plan his strategies, evaluate the true nature of what he faced.

He even managed a smirk. It was a you-got-me smirk, but it was a smirk nonetheless. And as such, a very expensive self-indulgence.

'You sold out my son and my husband to this Felipe character,' she said. 'A wee bit of business. A quick deal. That's all it was to you.'

'Boo fuckin' hoo,' Connelly said. 'Big bad me and poor wee

225

you. So you've hired some muscle to find out where they went. If you'd a fuckin' brain you'd have saved the dosh and just paid me to tell you. That's how it works, hen, it's aboot money.'

She shook her head. 'You don't even have the first clue what it's about. I mean, do you even know why Ross was valuable to this Felipe? You're a long way from Lanarkshire and you're in a lot deeper than you bargained, Anthony. Don't flatter yourself, these people here aren't interested in you, and I didn't hire them. *They* came to *me*. Do you want to know why?'

'Not particularly.'

Jane smiled grimly and gripped the blade. She walked slowly around behind Connelly's chair, then leaned close to him and spoke in barely more than a whisper.

'You've got kids yourself, haven't you, Anthony?'

He said nothing.

'Two, I know. Kayleigh and Michael. They go to Saint Aloysius, don't they? Up in Glasgow. No rubbing shoulders with the lumpen proles. Oh, I'm not saying anything judgemental. You never know who they could be mixing with at the local comprehensive . . . there could be children of drug addicts there, for God's sake. And you'd do anything to protect them, wouldn't you? We're both parents, we understand these things.'

Still he said nothing, but she could see his Adam's apple bob as he swallowed.

Jane leaned even closer and placed the tip of the blade on his cheek, just below the right eye. He strained his head back and away, as far as the cords would allow, but there was no escape.

'So I ask you, Anthony. Do you think there's anything I wouldn't do . . .' She applied pressure, pushing the tip of the blade up under his lower lid until his eyeball could feel it through the skin. '. . . any line I wouldn't cross, to get my son back?'

He made to speak but no words emerged. He swallowed again, finding saliva to lubricate his throat. 'No,' he managed, in a whisper.

'No. So here's what's going to happen. My friend here is going to ask you some questions and you're going to tell him everything he wants to know. *Comprendes?*'

He nodded. It was barely a movement at all, so desperate was he to keep his head thrust back against the pressure of the

226

blade, but it was unmistakably there. She pulled the knife back and stepped away, Connelly slumping again with a jittery exhale.

'Nuno,' Bett called out, and a few moments later the Catalan reappeared, bearing a bucket of water, which he placed on the floor between the two prisoners. He went out again and retrieved two lengths of heavy rubber hose and a roll of thick silver tape, then a third time returned with a hefty car battery and some crocodile clips. All of this was laid out close to the prisoners, who eyed it with increasing agitation.

'What the fuck's this?' Connelly asked Jane.

'It's to make sure you're telling the truth.'

'Fuck's sake, I said I'll talk,' he spluttered, squirming in his chair.

'Talk then,' she advised.

He did.

'Okay, set it up,' Bett ordered, when he was satisfied Connelly had no more to tell him. Rebekah picked up the roll of tape and the lengths of hose, while Nuno knelt down and began attaching the clips to the battery.

'Jesus God, I've told you everything,' Connelly insisted, shaking and trying to jump the whole chair backwards, away from his tormentors. Big Chick expressed a typically blunt reaction to what he saw by simply passing out.

'As Mrs Fleming explained to you, this is to make sure you're telling the truth,' Bett reminded him.

'But I swear I mmmm-mmm.' He was cut off by Rebekah tugging a wide length of the tape across his mouth, his eyes bulging in horror as Nuno stood up, electric leads held in his right hand, dipping a length of hose into the bucket with his left.

'Oh for goodness' sake, calm down,' Bett said impatiently. 'It's not how it looks.'

Rebekah took the knife from Jane and cut a small hole in the tape, then attempted to feed the hose through it into Connelly's mouth. She was unsuccessful in the face of squirming and clamped jaws. Meanwhile, Nuno reached down to the floor and briefly plunged the chamber into darkness as he disconnected the lamp from the extension then reconnected it to a socket at the end of the leads running to the battery.

'Thank you, Nuno,' Bett said, as light was restored, though more dimly than before. Rebekah stepped across and began repeating the tape-and-hose procedure on Big Chick, who was too woozy to resist.

'We'll be going in a moment, Mr Connelly, but I'm afraid you and your friend won't. There's enough water there to keep you both hydrated for several days, maybe five at a pinch. We'll send someone to let you out as soon as we've recovered the two Mr Flemings. Clearly, the sooner we do that, the better for you. So in the light of this, would you like to change any aspect of your story?'

Connelly stared with renewed revulsion at his surroundings, joints testing the bonds and finding them sound, eyes scanning bare metal walls with no rough edges to use, and which would sound no clang beneath several feet of earth. His gaze alighted penultimately on the bucket of water, the only sustenance in the cell, and last on the lamp attached to a battery that promised maybe less than an hour of light.

He gulped and shook his head.

'Last chance,' Bett stated.

'I wizzit wyne,' he mumbled through the hole in the tape, looking pleadingly towards Bett and Jane. *I wasn't lying.*

'Good,' said Bett. 'Then with any luck we'll find what we're looking for before your water runs out.'

And with that he led them from the tank and closed the hatch.

They were airborne again within two hours, after a couple of errands, the latter of which was dropping off the limo along with a sum in cash to cover the damage. The cash itself had been acquired during their first detour, a search of Connelly's hotel room to see what material clues might be found to supplement the sparse details his interrogation had thrown up. Inside they found what Jane instantly recognised to be Tom's briefcase, containing close to seven thousand euros. It was Bett's guess that he not only sold out the pair of them, but that he got Tom to pay up front for the privilege, no doubt selling the credulous numpty a story along the way. She shouldn't be too hard on him, though. It was easy to believe in a lie if it gave you hope, as easy as it was to open your wallet if you thought it was the only way you could help your son.

Bett had spent much of the trip back to the helicopter on the phone, talking in a wide variety of languages and an equally broad spectrum of tones: sometimes officious, sometimes pally, sometimes appealing, sometimes turning the screw. The one word she could make out, common to all calls, was Felipe.

'Who have you been talking to?' she asked, after the chopper had made its initial, stomach-lurching vertical climb and reached a more comfortable cruising altitude.

Bett looked almost incredulously irritated by the impertinence of her query.

She'd been waiting in vain for someone else to ask some questions, hoping she could perhaps interpret from their threads of discussion. Perhaps they knew all they needed to, but from Bett's reaction she suspected it more probable they merely knew not to ask. She had no such qualms. She didn't work for the icy-arsed bastard and it had been his idea to bring her aboard. She might be a little overawed, thoroughly out of her depth and extremely scared for her son, but she wanted him to know she wasn't going to play the deferential damsel in distress.

'Is it the rotors, the engine, maybe?' she demanded, provoking a look of puzzlement along with the displeasure that she was continuing to pester him.

'What?'

'Too noisy: why you didn't hear my question. I'll ask you again. Who have you been talking to?'

Bett frowned. 'Contacts,' he said, the intention of his brevity starkly clear.

'And what were you asking them? Look, I know you like acting the Victorian schoolmaster with your wee gang here, but I'm not fucking playing, okay?' The swearie-word really annoyed him, she could tell. And it was meant to. 'My son and husband were taken away on board a boat more than twenty-four hours ago and could plausibly be anywhere in the entire Mediterranean by now. Meanwhile, despite your helicopters, your guns, your brutality and your, frankly, affected posturing, you have so far gleaned little more than the square root of bugger-all about what's going on, so please try and understand if I'm a little less reticent than you'd ideally like and ANSWER MY FUCKING QUESTION.'

Bett held her in the same impermeably cold gaze as before her outburst, and she feared for a moment that he would simply ignore it, which would have left her out of options and not a little humiliated. Across the cabin she saw Nuno hide a smirk with his hand, in a way that was actually intended to hide nothing. That tipped the balance. Bett could ignore it if he wanted, but the delighted onlooker's verdict was that he'd just had his arse kicked.

Bett took a breath to speak, then pressed his lips a moment, considering.

'Mrs Fleming,' he said at last. 'I'm . . .' then tailed off, another change of mind. Would the next word have been 'sorry'? She'd never know.

'I was speaking to a number of associates around the continent,' he recommenced. 'Mostly in law enforcement, but not exclusively. I gave them the name Felipe and as much as we know about him, and asked them to get back to me with some names, aliases and KAs. Chances are we'll get the phone book, but we might get lucky with a cross-reference.'

'KAs?'

'Known Associates.'

'And what can we cross-reference it with? This Felipe guy didn't even give Connelly a surname.'

'Well, I gave them Voormarten and Gelsenhoff, Connelly's initial contacts. We know one of those put Felipe on to him, even if Connelly himself had no idea which. To be honest, if Connelly had known more, he might not have been alive to question. He's small fry. When we showed up, he shat himself because it made him think what he might have gotten into. He had no idea what Ross could be worth, and it's my guess the price he asked for reflected that. Ten thousand euros, for God's sake. Felipe was happy to pay it. The guy had a yacht, men with machine guns. He could easily have killed Connelly and taken Ross for nothing, but it was a cheap deal so not worth it.'

'No price is cheaper than free.'

'Killing carries risks. Danger, noise, witnesses, disposal of bodies, to say nothing of drawing attention to yourself. It's a false economy to save ten grand if doing so jeopardises your main deal.'

'You think Felipe's going to sell him on again?'

'I couldn't say for certain until I know more about him and I know more about why Ross is so valuable.'

'Why can't you ask the people who're paying you?'

'Now there's a bloody good question. According to Deimos, the reason they are so keen to get him back is to prevent people finding out what he's working on. They're closing the door after the horse has bolted and they know it. But they're still clinging on to the hope that their secret is safe and there's some other reason Ross ran.'

'But that's nonsense. Surely it's the very fact that people do know what he's working on that's put him in danger, so it's self-defeating to suppress information from the very individuals they've hired to help them.'

'Well, you may think that, Mrs Fleming, but that's because you're not in possession of the full facts.'

'And what would the full facts be?'

'That Deimos are, like every arms manufacturer on the globe, paranoid, slippery lying bastards who fear we're as devious and untrustworthy as themselves. So for now we have to follow the leads we've uncovered and, in the meantime, hope that our own Alexis can work some magic with your son's home computer.'

Lex wandered blearily to the fridge and grabbed a bottle of Orangina while she waited for the coffee pot to boil. She gave it a shake, popped the lid on the fridge door's built-in opener and downed about half of it in one go. There was half a pizza in there too, left over from last night. She didn't remember eating any of it, but distantly recalled sitting waiting for it inside Andre's restaurant with a glass of wine. She slapped the box on to the worktop, rolled up a slice in one hand and took a bite. Tomato sauce, basil, mushrooms, Roquefort, all cold. Breakfast of champions.

She walked through to her living/working area in just her T-shirt, and sat on the edge of an armchair, surveying the dis-embowelled PC on the floor. The casing lay three feet from the exposed motherboard, ribbon cable spilling from the mobo like an umbilical cord, the other end of which connected it to one of her own machines. She'd set it up like that just in case Bett or anyone dropped in unexpectedly, so that it would look like she was hard at it. She glanced at the clock: just gone four. Yep, hard at it indeed.

Truth was, she'd been asleep all day.

Truth was, she'd been awake all night.

She booted up the big box, checked the lights on her router. It was getting on for decision time.

That son-of-a-bitch Willis. Why wouldn't he tell Bett what this was about and send him the files? It was ridiculous, particularly now that Bett had told him what Lex had heard from that French thug in Scotland. '*Everybody*'s seen the video files.' The toothpaste was out of the tube. What was there to lose in giving us a squeeze, what with us trying to help you and all?

'Then it shouldn't be so hard for you to procure a copy for yourself,' Willis had replied.

The inference, as far as Bett had interpreted it, was that it wasn't a good enough reason to proliferate – or further proliferate – copies of top-secret information. It was no more than an overheard remark, he said, second-hand at that by the time Bett was quoting it. It gave no indication of how much was really known or by whom. Lex reckoned it being overheard from someone who was trying to kidnap Ross Fleming's goddamn niece was a pretty big indication that whatever was known was known by some heinous motherfuckers, so how's about a heads-up for the home team? But no dice. How paranoid was this guy? And how big a secret was it that he couldn't trust Bett with it?

Okay, all things being known, the truth was Willis ought *not* to trust Bett with it, given that Bett's team was the conduit for it getting out there in the first place, but *he* didn't know that. The point was . . . Shit, she didn't know what the point was any more, of anything. Nothing had been straightforward since Marledoq, with the only thing making any direct sense being the blunt lesson to never, never again try and play both ends against the middle.

She had, however, given herself an out. A bluff, a piece of

inspired bullshit at Chassignan, had provided her with a new option. What she had to decide now was whether to take it.

She took another bite of cold pizza and gazed again at the charade laid out at her feet.

I can check for residual data from files that might have been erased, she'd told Bett.

You can do that?

Nope, but you don't know that, do you, smart-ass?

She didn't have the hardware or the software, never mind the know-how to recover erased data from Fleming's hard drive. She didn't even have the means to determine whether or not data *had* been erased from any sectors of it, and that was where the dilemma lay. She had opened up a way of secretly redeeming herself: she could retrieve the files from the remote storage FTP server and claim she'd recovered them. The mystical reverence with which her abilities were regarded by the computer-illiterate meant nobody else on the team had any idea how much she knew and, thank God, even less how much she didn't. Only Som had any kind of suss, but he didn't poke his nose too deep because he had Alpha-geek aspirations and close discussion of her work tended to show up the limits of his knowledge. Thus, she could engage in this sham: pretend she'd been in full-on deep-hack mode, working to sift and filter buried electronic secrets – while she was actually catching up on the sleep that wouldn't come last night, despite having spent much of the previous one awake also, parked outside Mrs Fleming's motel.

Insomnia wasn't a chronic problem. As a proto-hacker, her sleep patterns had seldom been regular, and certainly not dictated by the rise and set of the sun like normal, civilised humans. But there was a difference between deliberately staying awake throughout a thirty-six-hour para-meditative coding session and being unable to sleep while you lay in bed all night in the darkness. Funny what did it. For some people it was what they ate or drank; for others stress and tension. Not Lex. At times of anxiety, she had always been easily seduced by the merciful oblivion of zedding out: that sanctuary of the unconscious that unfortunately had to turf you out on your ass all too soon when morning came around. It took something headier than mere worry to keep her from her beauty sleep.

Shooting people dead at point-blank range would do it every time.

Her own personal headcount now stood at four. She used to think that repeating the experience would never be as bad as the first time, but that hadn't turned out to be the case. The first time had been when they took down Ilianu, one of the vilest specimens of humanity she'd ever encountered. One of his maggots thought he had the drop on her in that horrible farmhouse she still had nightmares about. She was only minutes past seeing the rooms where the bastards held the girls before moving them on to their buyers, so there was little compunction to restrain her trigger finger. There was even less when the lumbering son-of-a-bitch, assuming her to be unarmed, began advancing on her with that sadistically lascivious grin.

Oh yeah, baby, I got something for you. Come get it, big boy.

She'd unloaded half the mag into him, anger, hate and fear pumping away like the slider on the pistol, all the very things Bett had tried to teach her not to feel when she was in such a situation. And when it was over, all passion spent, she understood why. For one thing, it was undisciplined, reckless even. If you're out of control, then so is your situation, Bett had said, and he was right. When she stopped firing, she felt like she was waking from a trance, during which she'd had no awareness of her environment, her position, her colleagues, her parameters, anything: just her and the man she was shooting. Then as she watched him gurgle and twitch, it didn't take long for anger, hate and fear to turn to relief, then for relief to turn to disgust. A dead, slaughtered human being looks like just that, no longer the thing you feared or hated, stripped of everything that drove you to kill it.

The next time had been calm, controlled, dispassionate, professional. Zeebrugge harbour, night, a container ship, Lex standing fifteen feet from a Turkish mercenary toting a Kalashnikov: put him down or in about a second and a half, it would be her gurgling and twitching on the floor.

And then Scotland.

They were going to kill a whole family. There were two of them. She had a gun, they didn't. She had no choice, she knew, but that knowledge wasn't doing the cocoa-and-cookies thing for her last night.

She'd gone to Maison Bla for seven, as ordered, only to be told to go home and work on Fleming's hard drive while they went daytripping to Spain. It was a godsend. Faced with the dilemma that this task presented, she started to feel the kind of worry she *could* deal with, and thus procrastinatory oblivion finally beckoned.

Now that she was awake, however, it was time to decide whether to report that her day's work had struck gold or been valiant but vain. The dilemma lay in the potential that her 'out' could yet become the thing that unveiled her betrayal. She didn't know what had or hadn't been on this hard drive. Neither did Bett, but if they got the lab-geek back successfully and it transpired that the files she 'recovered' had never been on his home PC, then she was going to be wide open.

And then what?

Wasn't it about time she asked herself that, seriously? How scared was she of Bett? Answer: plenty. But rationally, soberly, what was she afraid that he would do if he found out? She had seen him do some horrible and merciless things – Ilianu's detention and interrogation in what henceforth became known as the Romanian Suite being a case in point – but did she honestly think he would kill her?

Or was she actually scared that he'd simply tell her to leave?

The saddest thing was that he, the team, this, was all she had. She resented what he had turned her into. She resented the things he'd caused her to see. Most of all, she resented what he had prevented her becoming. But for better or worse, this was who she was now.

She logged on to the FTP server, selected the Marledoq files and clicked Download.

Project fuckwit

'You know, son, it's just occurred to me, I think this must be the most time we've spent together in about seven years.'

'Is that supposed to sound like a silver lining?'

Ross looked across at his dad with a scowl and waited for the retort to register, before breaking into a smile which precipitated some welcome laughter from both of them.

It was the early hours of Friday morning. They'd been at sea now for, by his estimation, about thirty hours. The last seven or eight of these had been on a different, larger vessel with which they had rendezvoused somewhere in the Med, and the transfer had provided the worst moments since that wanker Connelly stitched them up. The first of these was in the onset of dread that accompanied the very sight of this other tub looming beyond the prow, as Ross assumed that it must represent deliverance into the hands of whoever had been on his tail from the start. Mere hollow dread, however, was a day at the fairground compared to their journey from boat to boat. Swirling winds and choppy seas dictated that no gangway could be safely deployed, so he and Dad had made the trip across the waves by breeches buoy, sliding along a cable suspended from a tiny pulley-wheel by a terrifyingly insubstantial-looking harness. It was, however, the only part of their treatment that he could reasonably describe as inhumane.

Their arrival on the other side was overseen from a gantry by a tall, relaxed, middle-aged man, elegantly dressed in a suit that probably cost more than Ross had cumulatively spent on clothes his entire life. He exuded an incongruous geniality allied to an underlying sense of power; good-natured because he was unused to being displeased. There was something almost dandified about him, supremely lacking in self-consciousness. He watched them swing aboard then made his way down to the deck to greet them.

After Ross stopped vomiting, his relief at remaining alive was enhanced by learning that he was still, for the time being, travelling. Not entirely hopefully, it had to be said, but not yet arriving either. The smaller boat, his new host explained, had been a charter, merely conveying them to his vessel where, he advised them, they would remain for as much as a week.

'Uncertainty breeds desperation,' he told them in lightly Euro-accented English. 'Uncertainty about the duration of detention doubly so. I do not wish you to do anything desperate, and given what I am informed about your intellect, I do not expect you to do anything stupid. I would like you to understand that I have nothing to gain from mistreating you, unless it becomes necessary to prevent your escape.'

'I understand that my dad's nose was broken bringing us here. Does that count as mistreatment? Just so that we can agree on terms.'

'Yes, Felipe told me. Mr Connelly does not work for me. These men do. They will show you to your quarters. Please, make yourselves comfortable. If there is anything you require, do not be afraid to ask.'

'Yeah, sure. Could you sort me out with a couple of Mac-10s and about two hundred rounds of ammunition?'

'I'm afraid not. I don't deal in small arms, Mr Fleming.'

They'd each been taken to a spacious cabin, one on either topside of the hull, into which they were not locked, and it was made clear that they were free to move around the vessel as they pleased, unless barred by secure doors.

'If we catch you anywhere we both know you shouldn't be, the pleasure cruise is over and you go steerage,' an armed guard explained.

In the hours since boarding, they'd been supplied with fresh clothes, towels, drinks and the best food Ross had eaten in days: a generous platter of grilled fish fillets, squid, prawns and taramasalata. One of the guards must have had some training as a chef, Ross opined, though this failed to encourage Dad to eat more than a few tentative mouthfuls, several times mumbling about rather having breaded haddock.

Following their repast, they were invited to follow a guard along to a spacious area near the stern, where several more of the troops were gathered. The deck boasted sofas and tables, a bar and an enormous plasma widescreen TV. It looked as though they were waiting on some kind of formal address from the boss, who was noticeably absent. However, shortly after Ross and his dad were invited to take seats, someone pointed a remote at the TV and brought the screen to life.

Despite the size of the thing and the clarity of the digital satellite picture, it took Ross a good few moments to realise he was looking at the Camp Nou stadium, where the Barcelona–Celtic game was about to kick off. It was only yesterday he'd been in the city, but the match had been the last thing on his mind then, so out here, wherever the hell here was, it was like looking at a transmission through a wormhole in time. This had happened years ago, hadn't it? Way, way back, and in another world. It couldn't be live tonight, beamed before them on this boat.

But it was. And thus he and his dad spent easily the most surreal couple of hours of their lives, watching Celtic grind out their most famous result in years, beers in hand, couched in the opulent luxury of a multi-million-pound yacht, in the company of several trained killers probably armed with enough firepower to mount a coup.

'You know, I'm actually quite glad of all the guns,' Dad said, as the match clock ran into the closing ten minutes, 'because they give me something else to worry about. If I was concentrating exclusively on the fitba, I'd have had a bloody heart attack by now.'

The final whistle was as bittersweet as any moment of victory could ever be. As the game ran into injury time, Ross allowed himself to be drawn fully into what was on the screen until the surroundings faded from thought and vision. All his hopes and anxieties became channelled into one thing: that Barcelona would not breach the Celtic defence. Then when the referee blew to end the contest, even as his dad stood up and hugged him, the meaningless mirage dissolved and reality broke upon him as mercilessly as waking from any perfect dream. It seemed to take his dad a wee minute longer to undergo the same effect, but he got there soon enough, and looked a little embarrassed for it.

It had been a false conduit for their emotions, but it had

channelled them nonetheless, and left them both a little drained. All but one of the guards dispersed soon after, though his remit appeared to involve clearing up empties rather than any great vigilance over the prisoners.

Unbidden, they made their way back to their quarters. No shepherding or prompting would have been required: Ross felt a need for some form of sanctuary, even one as illusory as his four-star jail cell.

They both paused at Ross's door. It didn't seem right to be alone, despite the temptations of somewhere comfortable to kip.

'I've got a kettle in here. I'll fix us up a cuppa,' he invited. His dad nodded with a sad smile.

They said little while Ross boiled the kettle and looked out the tea bags. Dad made a couple of tentative gambits about the game, but it seemed pointless. The very momentousness of the result served only to underline how irrelevant it was. His dad was markedly aware of that, but it sounded very much like he just didn't know what else to say.

It was in this growing silence that he ventured his remark about it being the longest they had spent together for a while.

'Some story, eh?' his dad remarked, shaking his head.

'At least you'll be able to top the lot down the pub when they start asking where everybody watched the Barca game,' Ross replied. They both laughed a little, but the unspoken caveat hung heavily in the air.

If you live to tell the tale.

'Aye, not too shabby,' Dad observed. He was indicating his immediate surroundings, but clearly meant the vessel in general. 'There's worse places to be held prisoner, I dare say.'

'True, but I can't help remembering *Dr No*.'

'Why?'

'He laid on plush surroundings and a first-class meal for James Bond. It was to ensure he'd be well-rested and fuelled up so that he'd be fit to endure the maximum torment before finally snuffing it.'

'Cheery thought, son.'

'Not one I'd entertain seriously, though. Whoever our man is, he's not interested in feeding us to his pet piranha. All of this doesn't come cheap, so he doesn't want me for fish-food. We're

240

being very well looked after because he doesn't want to damage the merchandise. I'm worth a fortune to him.'

'How? What does he want with you?'

'He doesn't want me at all. If he did, then I wouldn't have spent the evening watching the football. But he knows a man who does. In fact, my guess is he knows quite a few men who do. And when the time comes, he's going to hand me over to whichever of them pays him the most.'

'But why? What is this really all about, Ross?'

'I can't tell you, Dad. Just knowing about this could . . .'

'What? Put me in danger? Do you not think I'm there already?'

Ross couldn't help but laugh. It was, as they say, a fair shout. He stuck the kettle on for another cup and got talking.

He blamed his provenance. Scots just can't help inventing things. Leave one alone on a single-palm desert island and by the end of the week he'll have built a paddle-craft using every available resource, right down to hollowed coconut shells for a propeller. Maybe it was because Scotland was such a miserable place to live that the drive to improve one's day-to-day existence was utterly imperative. What the hell got invented in the Caribbean? Nothing. But Scotland? You name it. And Ross often would, with relish, particularly if some colleague or acquaintance made the catastrophic mistake of being in any way disrespectful of his country's standing in the modern world.

'Why don't you call me tonight on the telephone,' he'd say to the unfortunate offender. 'Invented by Alexander Graham Bell of Edinburgh. Chances are you'll interrupt me watching television, invented by John Logie Baird, of Helensburgh, and I'll tell you to get on your bike, invented by Kirkpatrick Macmillan of Dumfriesshire. You got pneumatic rubber tyres on that thing? Thank John Boyd Dunlop of Dreghorn. And you'll be riding it on a road surface invented by John 'Tar' Macadam of Ayr. What's that? You fell off and broke your leg? Don't worry, we'll fix that under general anaesthetic, pioneered by James Young Simpson of Bathgate. And no need to worry about infection, because we'll clean the instruments with antiseptic invented by Joseph Lister of Glasgow, and we'll be using antibiotics derived from penicillin, discovered by . . . Now what was that bloke's name again?'

He could also cite microwave ovens, adhesive stamps, cloned sheep, the decimal point, bakelite, iron bridges, logarithms, colour-photography, insulin, fingerprinting, radar, ultrasound scanners, paraffin and hollow-pipe drainage, these last two further supporting his assertion regarding the correlation between creativity and climate. At a more theoretical level, there was Colloid chemistry, geoscience, Brownian motion, chemical bonds, thermodynamics and, rather pertinently of late, James Clark 'Daftie' Maxwell's equations in electromagnetism.

But it wasn't all worth boasting about. Admittedly you couldn't pin McDonald's directly on Adam Smith, but as the father of modern capitalism he was without a cast-iron alibi. Scots were further indictable over other such misbegotten creations as the Bank of England, the US Navy and motor insurance.

There was also Captain Patrick Ferguson. In 1776 he invented a rifle that loaded via the breech rather than the muzzle, replacing the awkward and slow ramrod method, which restricted a soldier to three shots per minute and required him to fire only from an upright position. Captain Ferguson's rifle doubled that rate of fire and allowed greater versatility of posture. Then in 1809 the Reverend Alexander Forsyth invented Percussion Powder, which rendered the damp-prone flintlock obsolete and facilitated its replacement with a weatherproof hammer action.

After which we were all far more efficiently able to get on with killing each other.

Ross had always considered there to be something ugly and crude about guns: in their design, their method and, in particular, their purpose. They were machines for driving projectiles into living tissue. That's it. It was a principle that hadn't changed since the first musket. The muzzle velocity kept increasing, the accuracy kept improving and the rate of fire just kept accelerating (Thanks, Mr Gatling. Good work, Mr Thomson), but each new gun was simply a more sophisticated way of carrying out the same crude and brutal act: driving projectiles into living tissue. And talk about one size fits all! No matter your situation, we've got the solution. Soldiers, need to bring down your enemy? Drive projectiles into his flesh. Policemen, need to

242

restrain a suspect? Drive projectiles into his flesh. You there, angry, confused and alienated ghetto kid, want to avenge a minor slight and restore your status among your peers? Hey, guess what? That's right, you're getting it now.

Bang bang bang bang bang bang bang.

Too fucking easy. Too fucking moronic. Too fucking final.

Guns made killing remote, personal and dead, dead simple. To kill someone with your bare hands, or a blunt instrument, even with a knife, you've got to want it bad, because you're going to have to work for it. With guns, it was literally the same effort and almost the same action as switching on a light. You didn't have to want it that much, or for that long. You only had to want it for a moment, and then it was done – forever.

Thus the raging wee nobodies who weren't being paid enough attention could have their world-wrecking tantrums. Thus, 'going postal'. Thus Hungerford. And thus the most evil act perpetrated by an individual in Scotland's history.

Ross's disdain for guns went right back to the playground. They seemed needlessly unimaginative, especially in those days of make-believe.

Piaow, piaow, piaow. That's what he'd hear all over the place. Piaow, piaow, I got you. Naw ye never. Aye I did. Piaow, piaow.

'Zloopf.'

'Whit?'

'Got you. That's you frozen in my Displacement Vortex.'

'Your whit?'

'My Displacement Vortex. Noo you cannae move.'

'Nae chance. Anyway, I shot you afore you could set it aff.'

'You fired, aye, but your bullet never hit me. It got sucked into my Gravity Well.'

'Your whit?'

'My Gravity Well.'

'Fuckin' poof.'

Ross would contest the kiddy gospel according to Obi-Wan Kenobi. To his mind, there was no such thing as an elegant weapon, even one that looked as cool as a lightsabre. There were only lesser degrees of ugliness. However, where ingenuity could substitute for violence, where innovation could replace physical damage, then that device could be said to have something

243

close to grace. Even the Resin Cannon, which engulfed its target in a sticky, quick-setting gum, was a far more humane means of neutralising an armed opponent than blasting lumps out of him.

But no government in the world cared much about being humane, and even less about grace. Everybody needed guns – more guns, bigger guns, better guns – because everybody else had them. Which would have been a better argument if it could be supported by an example, from any place, in the history of the planet, where proliferation of weapons hadn't merely led to more deaths. Air Marshals: that was the latest. The possibility of people smuggling guns on to aeroplanes was dangerous, so let's make damn *sure* there's a gun on *every* aeroplane. Sheer fucking genius.

The more guns there were, it seemed, the more guns we needed for our protection. This kept the gunmakers rich and the market for non-lethal enforcement very marginal. Deimos knew this as well as anyone. The NLW research facility had always been little more than a side-project, motivated less by conscience or altruism than by the possibility that something developed there might find an application back in the plain old lethal sector. From almost the first day Ross got there, he'd heard gloomy mutterings that the bosses were thinking of shutting it down or selling it off, the latter merely meaning it would be shut down and asset-stripped by someone else.

He felt like he was farting into a thunderstorm. If it took little thought, even less skill and almost no effort to, ahem, 'neutralise' or 'restrain' someone by drilling them full of holes, then who wanted to take a chance on this vegetarian pussy stuff Ross was hawking? Resin Cannon? Sonic Blackjack? Automirmillo? No thanks, we'll stick to this machine here. It drives projectiles into their flesh, see?

The man with the gun always had the advantage, whether he was pointing it at you or merely selling it. There was no way of changing that.

Not without a Gravity Well.

It was a vivid testament to the role denial played in the human self-defence instinct that Lex had at any point even attempted

244

to convince herself that Ross Fleming's disappearance would turn out to be unrelated to the files she spirited away from his place of employment. Laughable, she'd admit, except that what she had retrieved from the server wasn't very funny. She was glad she'd watched the video clips on her own before taking them to Maison Bla. Everybody was going to look pretty shocked when they saw them, but she thought it unlikely any of them would run from the room and blow chunks, which would have made her own initial response uncomfortably conspicuous.

After redistributing her cold pizza around the toilet bowl, her next instinct was to check that the front door and all her windows were locked. She couldn't believe how much danger she had unknowingly – *negligently* – put herself in. Her shadowy contact, this nameless ghost with his ethereal promises and unspoken air of intimidation . . . God, what was she thinking? She should have run screaming, gone straight to Bett. And, looking back, her being part of Bett's team might well be the only reason she was still alive. Having seen what he hired her to procure, it was easily conceivable that he'd have murdered her to cover his own tracks, if it wasn't that he guessed doing so would bring a whole world of trouble down upon himself. There was also the consideration, immodest as it sounded, that nobody on Bett's team was very easy to kill. Instead, he'd relied on her own fears and self-preservation to ensure that Bett didn't discover her betrayal, and now that she had manufactured a reason for being able to produce the files, it looked certain he never would.

She was waiting for them when the chopper landed, having called around to make sure Somboon and Armand were there too. If you're going for maximum class credits on your homework assignment, might as well do the whole teacher's pet thing and look super-eager with it. She handed print-outs of all the documentation straight to Som, who began devouring the information while she set up a data-projector in the drawing room. There was a steady stream of 'What-the-fuck's and 'No-way's, as well as muttered ejaculations in Thai.

'If this shit's for real, then this Fleming dude is gonna be immortal,' he opined, as the away team entered and took their places around the big table.

245

'I'd be less worried about him if that was true,' said Mrs Fleming, pointedly.

'Sure, shit, sorry,' Som told her, before bowing his head to resume poring over the print-outs.

'So what's it all about, Alexis?' Bett asked. (He'd been typically effusive in his praise for her achievement in recovering the data. 'Okay,' he'd said, when she informed him she'd managed it. That kind of warmth and encouragement went a long way.)

'It's probably best if you just watch this,' she announced to all of them, then set the first video file to play.

It was a high-quality digital transfer, with a date stamp (14 October last year) and clock running along the bottom, beginning at quarter past midnight. It was a fixed-camera perspective, probably a tripod, filming from an observation area behind a thick glass screen. A control panel the size of a mixing desk was just in shot below the window, dozens of dials, switches, sliders and read-outs ranked along it, and at one end sat a formidable twin-spoked lever, like a cross between the altitude control on a jet and something from a mad-scientist's laboratory.

The observation area was in an elevated position looking at a slight downward incline into a white-walled octagonal chamber forty or fifty feet in diameter, a silver-coloured circle in the centre of an otherwise uniformly clay-coloured floor. Towards the left-hand side of the chamber, as the camera viewed it, there stood a life-size crash-test dummy, held upright by a narrow pole angled upwards from the floor to the small of its back. The dummy was anatomically proportioned, limbs and trunk fully shaped to accurately describe bone and muscle structure, with dotted lines and colour-coding delineating different parts. In car safety research, this was to catalogue and assess specific points of injury sustained during a crash. This dummy was more detailed than Lex had seen in any Volvo commercial, however, the arms industry being even more interested in knowing precisely how much damage their products could inflict.

At the opposite end of the chamber, there stood a low table, on which rested a pistol, a pump-action shotgun and a fully automatic rifle, magazines or cartridges stacked next to each as was appropriate.

It wasn't looking very good for the dummy.

In between, there appeared to be nothing but empty space, until a closer examination of the floor revealed that the circle in the centre, approximately six feet wide, was not merely silver-coloured, but actually metallic. Nor was it flat on the ground, but described a gently indented concave beneath the surface, like the lens of a telescope.

Into this sterile, geometric arena stepped a figure in yellow overalls, emerging from a door beneath the camera position and thus out of sight. The overalls covered him from neck to ankles, elasticated cuffs drawing the plastic material tight at the wrists and the tops of his boots. On his head he wore a pair of ear-protectors, but when he turned around he was recognisable as Ross Fleming.

His mother breathed in sharply at the sight of him, his image projected six feet wide across the blank wall. Her anxiety was palpable but a little misplaced. This had happened six months ago, so she didn't have to worry about the outcome. Only the aftermath.

He walked across to the dummy and briefly examined it, checking its support and making slight adjustments to its posture.

'Any last requests?' he asked it, his voice relayed by intercom from somewhere inside the observation room. It sounded quiet and oddly dampened. The chamber looked like it ought to generate echo and reverberation, but instead it had the muffling, still-air quality of a recording studio.

Someone laughed, close to the microphone.

Ross made his way to the table and stood behind it. He lifted the pistol and slapped a magazine into the handle.

'Okay,' he shouted. 'Fire her up.'

A hand moved into shot and reached for the big lever, pushing it slowly forward against no little resistance until it had arced through about one hundred and fifty degrees. When it reached the other end, a keening sound began growing, somehow high and whiny but deep and shuddering at the same time. It seemed to come from all around rather than any discernible direction, its note getting very slowly and gradually higher over the next few seconds until it plateaued, which coincided with a sudden

247

jarring of the image. The picture shuddered and then gently righted itself, like when Lex degaussed a monitor. Serious electromagnetic activity.

'Good to go,' said the voice in the control room.

'Roger that,' Ross acknowledged.

He pulled the slider to ready the gun, took position to fire, with his feet apart, both hands gripping the butt, the pistol held about eighteen inches in front of his face.

Around the table, every breath but Lex's was held, Som staring up open-mouthed from his documents. Even Bett's emotionless demeanour was briefly interrupted by a narrowing of the eyes normally only seen when he was in sight of an enemy.

Ross fired the pistol, the report dull and muted, the slider automatically chambering the next round as the spent cartridge was spat from the ejection port. The shell appeared as a brief flash of metal next to Ross's hands, then vanished from sight. By that time he had fired again. He fired repeatedly and steadily at one-second intervals until he had discharged twelve rounds. Used to her own habits, Lex had expected him to eject the mag and let it fall from the butt, but he simply placed the gun down on the wooden table.

Everyone looked to the dummy. It had sustained no visible damage whatsoever.

'What's the invention, a gun that doesn't shoot straight?' asked Armand. 'How could he miss every round? From that distance?'

Bett's face failed to revert to its familiar impassivity, his gaze held utterly by the screen.

Ross picked up the shotgun and loaded half a dozen shells into its side-entry port. He pumped it, levelled it and fired. Nothing hit the dummy. He pumped and fired again, three times, four times, five, six. Still the dummy remained intact.

'Your son isn't blind, is he?' Armand asked Mrs Fleming.

'No. He's a dead shot. When we took him to the fairground we always came home with half a dozen goldfish and a bagful of gonks.'

Flashing a wickedly knowing grin up towards the observation screen, he dropped the shotgun and lifted the rifle. He clipped in a mag, slid the bolt, flipped off the safety, hefted it against his right shoulder and let rip.

He sustained fire on fully automatic for several seconds; quite a volley but, Lex estimated, not enough to empty the mag. Everyone else's eyes continued to focus on the dummy, but hers, this second time around, were watching the spent shells and, more specifically, what happened to them as they poured from the ejection port.

'I don't get it,' Armand confessed, shaking his head.

Som giggled nervously.

'Look at the disc,' Bett said quietly, unable to keep a note of awe from his near-whispering voice.

'The disc?'

'On the floor.'

'What about it? I can't see, it's too far.'

'Okay, kill it,' Ross shouted, up on the screen.

The assistant's hand returned to the mad-scientist lever and hauled it back to its original position. The image shuddered again and the keening noise died away to nothing.

Ross walked around the table and proceeded to the silver circle in the centre of the chamber. He crouched down, bending his knees, and put a hand into the wide salver, grasping something in a balled fist. Then he lifted his hand and opened his fingers, letting bullets, shot and cartridges cascade from his palm like seashells on a beach.

'*Mon Dieu.*'

'Fuck me.'

'No way.'

'*Madre mia.*'

'Bloody hell.'

Bett said nothing, just continued to stare with unbroken concentration.

'Uh-uh,' said Rebekah, into the growing, breathless silence. 'Not possible. An illusion. Blanks. Gotta be blanks.'

Lex smiled grimly to herself, knowing what was next.

On the screen, Ross Fleming took position behind the table once more, picked up the rifle, unlatched the safety again and emptied the rest of the magazine. The dummy jerked and exploded in a storm of splinters, ripped to pieces by the bullets. Limbs came off, its head blew apart, and what was left was thrown back against the wall by the force of impact.

249

Another assortment of expletives and ejaculations ensued.

'Okay, that's clip one,' Lex told them.

'There's more?' Som asked eagerly.

'Just the one. Here it comes. That one was tagged "Normalpolarityvid". This one is "Reversepolarityvid".'

'What does that mean?'

'You'll see.'

The second clip showed the same chamber, a new, intact dummy in position, but this time no table. When Ross entered the arena he was carrying what looked like a shrink-wrapped clear-plastic parcel, which he placed on the floor at roughly the spot where the table had stood. This time he appeared to be working alone as there was a pause after he withdrew, and, a few seconds later, footsteps could be heard in the observation room. The camera then zoomed in on the parcel, which revealed itself to be a bomb: a nailbomb, to be precise. Plastic explosive, detonators, a receiver and several pounds of the local iron-monger's finest, all tightly wrapped in thick transparent film for purposes of demonstration.

Ross's hand pushed the big lever. Again, the keening noise grew, and again the picture shuddered as it reached its plateau. Meanwhile, Ross dollied out on the camera to show as wide a shot as the observation window allowed.

A few more seconds passed, then his voice sounded out a countdown from five.

He went right on zero. There was a dampened bang and a flash, followed by surprisingly little smoke – certainly not enough to obscure the view of the dummy, which remained upright and undamaged. The sight of it was less surprising in light of what they had already witnessed, and certainly less visually impressive than the picture painted by the nails. There were thousands of them, gathered against the walls and spread around the floor. However, there were none – absolutely none – inside a three-metre radius of the disc, the thousands of little black sticks denoting a shape like a keyhole on the floor. It was a perfect circle of exclusion, with a further corridor of safety extending from it, through where the dummy stood, to the rear wall behind it.

The clip ended, reverting the image on the wall to a projection of Lex's desktop. She switched the data-projector off, the absence of its hum accentuating the silence around the table.

Bett's response, when at last it came, was prefaced by a long sigh, after which he stated simply: 'Oh dear.'

He then turned to Som. 'Not a fair question, I appreciate, given the time you've had, but your thoughts anyway.'

'My first thought is wow. You know, not like wow, as in wow, check out the new Ferrari, but wow as in, like, WOW! Somebody just invented time travel or Wow!—'

'Som? Coherent thoughts, please: relevant, concise, minus the wigging?'

'Shit, sorry. Yeah. But we are talking serious—'

'*Som!*' Bett warned.

'Yes, sir. Okay, there's a lot of literature here, most of it informal, memos, lots of notes to self kinda stuff. This thing's in early Alpha, still barely off the drawing board, really. He calls it a Gravity Well. Lots of extremely heavy physics and electromagnetics stuff in here, equations, proofs, theoretical models – way, way over my head, man.'

'So it's essentially like some giant, super-duper magnet?' asked Mrs Fleming.

'No,' said Rebekah, before Som could respond, clearly thinking out loud. 'That would be impossible.'

'Why?'

Bett's features broke into a tiny, proud little smile as he looked to Rebekah for her answer, one which Lex suspected he already knew.

'Because lead is not magnetically susceptible,' Rebekah explained. 'Well, it's not zero per cent, but it's close. Bullets are made of lead,' she added, to further clarify. Lex knew this latter part, but would have to confess ignorance to the first, and had made the same assumption as Mrs Fleming about the nature of the device.

'So how the hell does it work?' Lex was therefore moved to enquire.

'As far as I can understand,' responded Som, 'it does generate electromagnetic forces – huge electromagnetic forces – but after that it gets, well, complicated, if not to say weird. The documents talk about creating a field of hyper-gravity that . . . hang

251

on until I find this here, oh yeah, got it: "exerts correspondingly greater forces upon objects with greater velocity". And again, here: "The Gravity Well harnesses and diverts the kinetic energy of subjects entering its field of influence . . ."'

'Which means what, in English?' Lex asked.

'It means the faster something is going when it enters the Gravity Well, the more it'll be affected. The docs say the ideal is that you'd be able to walk right across the thing carrying a steel tray, but if you tried throwing it . . . That's a long way off, however. Right now, in Fleming's words, "if you stood too close wearing a wristwatch, you'd end up minus a hand".'

'Which is why the shells are being drawn in too,' Lex suggested. 'They leave the ejection port at speed.'

'So it is still magnetic,' Rebekah observed. 'Why isn't lead immune?'

'Let's see, I read something about this back a page or so. Yeah. "Forces can only be exerted upon metals and certain ferr magnetic minerals, though in extreme low-temperature tests . . ." yadda yadda yadda, nah, that's a blind alley. No, here it is: "Resistance Paradox Effect". This phrase comes up a lot. My particle physics isn't really up to speed for this shit, so I'm only getting a broad-brush impression, which is that it's kind of similar to the earlier principle of greater kinetic energy being turned back upon itself. He's found a way to exert magnetic forces that make lead respond in a certain way *because* of its insusceptibility.'

'How?' Rebekah demanded.

'Fuck, man, don't ask me. You take a look at this shit. He's got correspondence and consultation papers from superbrains in electromagnetism here, these guys got more letters after their names than in them. But I don't think anything in this file would constitute a blueprint, or anything close. Not surprising. If I had something as big as this, I wouldn't keep copies of the secret formula on a PC in my apartment.'

Nor indeed, Lex thought, on his PC at Marledoq either.

'All this stuff,' Som went on, 'is kinda like the separate sheet of paper you do your working on. The exam answer must be written down elsewhere.'

'If it's written down at all,' mused Bett. 'If the key, the secret, is in the mind of the inventor, then that would explain why there is so much interest in acquiring him personally, rather than merely the data.'

'You certainly wouldn't be able to follow his work from this stuff,' Som observed. 'It's a scrapbook. Notes, theories, ideas, a lot of projections, too. Scale, for one thing. He talks about the ratio of energy to influence, size to effect. You notice both those tests we saw were filmed after midnight? That's because it took all the juice in Marledoq to operate it. He had to do it late at night while nobody else in the building needed any power. In developing any technology, the size-to-effect proportions always start at one extreme but, given enough time, they'll balance out and eventually invert. Thirty years ago, to generate the computing power in Lex's laptop would have taken enough hardware to fill this entire room. If the Gravity Well followed the same curve . . .' Som tailed off, letting their imaginations finish the thought individually.

Dad got up and walked to the wall, gazing out through the square porthole at blackness. There was nothing to see, but he needed somewhere to look. He was dazed, reeling.

'Bit of an ice-cream headache, isn't it?' Ross said.

'Bloody hell, you're not kiddin'. It's . . . amazing. It's astonishing. It could change the world, son. It's, it's . . .'

'It's early, Dad. Very early. We'd be talking decades of development. You've heard the phrase "Standing on the shoulders of giants"? Well, I'm no giant. I'm just . . . I'm just a wee guy who's waiting to give the first giant a leg-up, if and when he comes along.'

'Don't sell yourself short, Ross. What you've achieved . . . and on your own.' His eyes were beginning to well up. 'I'm so proud of you.'

Ross swallowed. He couldn't afford to succumb to the same.

'The Gravity Well,' his dad repeated. 'The Fleming Gravity Well. I like the sound of that.'

'I never thought of my name being on it, I just tend to think of it as Project F.'

'F for Fleming.'

'F for Fuckwit.'

253

'What, is that supposed to keep you modest or something?'

'No, it was a personal code, so that it wasn't so on-the-nose. Project Gravity Well became Project Fuckwit.'

'How?'

'The initials. GW.'

'The ini . . .' Dad smiled, then they both laughed, a moment of blessed relief from the pressure of burgeoning emotion in the cabin. But, when the moment was over, Ross knew he had to crank it back up a few atmospheres.

'I haven't told you everything,' he said. 'I've left one small technical detail out.'

'What?'

'I can't tell you. That's why I left it out. This really is for your protection, and for mine, and for the project's.'

'So why are you mentioning it?'

'It's kind of an insurance policy, or more like an "in case of emergency, break glass" deal.'

Ross went to the wardrobe where his jacket was hanging and retrieved one of the small, innocuous-looking tubes from a pocket.

'I want you to take this,' he said.

His dad held out a hand and examined what he'd been given.

'Lip balm?'

'Don't ask, just keep it safe.'

'What is it, Ross?'

'It's a key, of sorts.'

'To what?'

'Dad, I told you: you can't know. You're safer . . . everything I care about is safer. Just keep it secure and don't let anyone know you've got it, unless . . . Unless things get out of control.'

'You don't think this qualifies as out of control?'

'This is nothing, Dad. This is retrievable. That's for when it's not.'

'And how will I know that?'

'Because at that point you won't have any choice.'

'There could be one in every home, every building,' Mrs Fleming said, her voice breathy, like she was almost afraid to speak this aloud.

'It's goddamn bullet repellent,' suggested Rebekah.

'More like a force-field,' Som observed. 'One that can draw projectiles into its pull or deflect them around its sphere of influence.'

'Now I know what that asshole in my car meant the other day,' Lex said. 'We were talking about the video clips, and he made some crack about why he was carrying a knife and not a gun. This thing could make them obsolete.'

'More pressingly,' said Bett, 'I would remind you also of Mr Willis's analogy regarding the pharmaceutical industry. What would the other drug companies do if they knew you were developing a cure to an ailment for which they sold remedies?'

'Guns aren't a remedy,' Mrs Fleming argued. 'I'd say they were the disease.'

'Yes, and tonight we may have been looking at the first clinical trials of a vaccine. Mrs Fleming, I must congratulate you. Your son has conceived a device of unprecedented humanitarian benefit, something that could save millions of innocent lives. Unfortunately, there are a lot of very wealthy and influential individuals out there who are not going to tolerate that, and therefore he couldn't have picked a more effective way of jeopardising his own.'

'No wonder he ran,' Mrs Fleming said, tears forming. 'He could be making some of the world's most amoral businessmen redundant.'

'Believe me, arms firms wanting to stop him developing this device are just the beginning of his troubles. Those who'd want it for themselves will be just as desperate, and just as ruthless. What lengths wouldn't any government go to in order to have this technology before their enemies? And that could yet be what gives us our chance.'

Mrs Fleming's bloodshot eyes regained sharp focus, her body stiffening to attention like a parade-ground recruit.

'If the man who's got him, this Felipe, or whoever he is, has any idea what he's really holding, he's not going to play first come, first served. Even if he's working for someone specific, he's going to want to renegotiate his price to reflect market value.'

'And how does that help us?' she asked.

'Serendipity,' Bett replied.

Mrs Fleming wrinkled her brow in puzzlement. Lex had no idea what he meant, either, but he said it with a thin, nasty little smile she had long since learned to interpret as 'Fasten your seatbelts.'

The perfect apprentice

In retrospect, Jane interpreted it as a subconscious sign of security that when she woke up on that third morning away from home, she was thoroughly woolly-headed and had, for several seconds, no idea where she was or what she could possibly be doing there. No bouncing straight into her stride, as had happened in the motel, no instant recognition of her surroundings and what that context signified, like how yesterday morning had greeted her, but a churning, disorientated, reluctant dragging herself to consciousness and a hazy coalescence of details and memories.

The need to get up was significantly less imperative than before. Her body was making a strong case for remaining where she was, warm and comfortable, relaxed and regenerating after sustained ill-use. Don't go out there, it was saying. Things will get no better than this today.

Her first lucid, motivated thought was of Ross. It tugged at her inside, but it didn't grasp and twist like before. She knew he was safe, for now at least. Well, secure was maybe the word, but either way it was a lull she had to take advantage of now that she understood it was a long game they were playing.

'I can't ask you to banish your fears, your anxiety or your anger,' Bett had said to her. 'But don't let them use you up. In time you're going to need to use them.'

It had been his way of closing business for the day – a very long day, admittedly. His patronising sentiment had failed to disguise a utilitarian diktat intended to dismiss her and her inconvenient feelings, but, as Alexis had warned her, the bugger was usually right.

Her second lucid, motivated thought was of coffee, the absence of which by the bed on this occasion probably accounted for many of the morning's documented symptoms. She settled in the meantime for a shower, during which she discovered that her body had been laying it on a bit thick about the need for more recuperation. As the jets hit her and the events of the previous day became sharply focused, she realised she was feeling as robust as she could ever remember.

She stepped out of the bathroom and saw the black dress draped across the chair where she had left it the night before. In her less awe-struck and disorientated condition, it occurred to her to wonder why this particular item had been selected for her. It had proven surprisingly practical for climbing in and out of cars and indeed helicopters, but no more so than the less figure-hugging combination of a pair of trousers and a blouse, and the only garb necessary to yesterday's pursuits had been the chauffeur's uniform. So what was with the little black number? Was it for his amusement, somehow? Or was she flattering herself to think so? Such questions, however, failed to alter the fact that it remained the only thing available to wear, so she donned it once again and ventured out of the self-importantly commodious room he had allocated her.

In contrast to the previous day's ferment, there seemed no evidence of activity, or even habitation, as she stalked the upstairs corridor. No rotor-blades, no tyres on gravel, not even any voices. She reached the landing above the entrance hall, intending to descend in search of company, or at least breakfast, but the stillness and silence caused her to consider other temptations. Dead ahead, another corridor beckoned, irresistibly as it turned out, because Alexis had warned her off it when she first showed Jane to her room. Nothing made a place more alluring than being told it was forbidden, as illustrated by the illicit draw of a long corridor ostensibly identical to the one she'd just left.

Jane walked along slowly, her feet soft on the floor tiles, the quiet all around and the thought of Alexis's concerned face making her even more aware of what sound she did make. She passed closed doors, a table bearing dried flowers in a clay pot, landscape paintings along either wall: rural Van Gogh, maritime Turner, urban Ernst. Anger and turmoil, she thought, looking at the prints. Storm and stress. Beautiful chaos. Longing and loss. She felt suddenly most uncomfortable, like she had stepped into someone else's uneasy dreams. The privacy of this place was unmistakable, something she was immediately concerned not to violate. She turned around again, intending to retreat, and was racked with a violent shudder as she found Bett standing in her path.

'Exploring, are we?' he asked, his voice low, the tone of accusation cutting through her.

Our little crimes only seem wrong once we've been caught, Jane reflected, contrasting how guilty she felt with how lightly she had considered her actions only moments before. The corridor was dim, Bett's shape somehow magnified by what illumination there was being behind him. She felt a second shudder, less jolting but just as involuntary, and realised that she was terrified. Here in the forbidden corridor, the light was poor but a veil had lifted from her vision. She had blinded herself to just how frightening she found this man because until then she hadn't seen what he looked like through the eyes of someone who had crossed him.

Fear helped her focus on the search for mitigation. As far as he knew, she might not be aware it was off-limits. He didn't know what had or hadn't been said by Alexis when she was showing Jane around, and the subject hadn't been brought up voluntarily by the girl, only in response to Jane's stare.

Tell it to the judge. There was no point compounding the sin by playing daft. She imagined any defence invoking ignorance or personal stupidity would play particularly badly. Bett placed the initiative upon his charges; he expected them to know things without being told. By extension, there would be things he expected them to communicate too.

Rather oddly, then, he proceeded to spell out the nature of her transgression.

'This is my home, Mrs Fleming,' he said. 'A grand home, a privileged one, I would concede, but that grandeur does not render it an exhibit. I attempt to extend whatever hospitality makes my guests most comfortable, but I do ask that they respect my personal privacy.'

'I'm sorry,' she said, as contrite as she was embarrassed, but that more defiant and calculating part of her was wondering at this rare show of sensitivity. There couldn't be a chink in his armour, could there? Her apology certainly didn't quell the hurt.

'Perhaps you find your accommodations insufficient, restrictive,' he suggested sarcastically. The tone of scorn and implicit snobbery dispelled Jane's fears and replaced them with an outrage of her own, which she chose to voice with exaggerated articulacy.

'No. My accommodations are, as you know, beautiful, and, I would wager, purposely ostentatious. I am under no misapprehensions about the levels of hospitality you enjoy it being in your gift to dispense. However, given the way I was peremptorily summoned here, I must say I feel more like a prisoner than I do a guest.'

She stared him down, not attempting to kid herself that he wouldn't know it was all front. His eyes narrowed slightly as she dared to put him on the back foot, and she was sure she saw a twitch in his cheek at the 'purposely ostentatious' remark. He knew when he was being called out.

'I have no prisoners here,' he said, stepping to one side to unblock her path. It might even have appeared chivalrous if it wasn't so demonstrably self-righteous.

'No. Not since the Romanian, I gather,' Jane replied.

'You came here of your own free will, Mrs Fleming. The Romanian did not. You know where the door is. You walked right past it on your way to play nosy parker. If you leave, no one will stand in your way.'

'What, you were so anxious to get me here, but you wouldn't blink if I just upped and left right now?'

'Were you to leave, my task would be harder, much harder, but I'd still carry it out. It would be harder for you too, I'd expect, from the sidelines. Which is why we both know this conversation is moot.'

Jane rolled her head to one side, a gesture of acknowledgement.

'You'd carry out your task,' she agreed. 'No doubt. So what's in it for you?'

'You know what's in it for me. You want a figure for what my client is paying to save your son's life? In euros?'

'No, I just . . .'

'Oh, I see,' he said, smiling like a shimmer on black metal in twilight. 'Perhaps you're looking for the hidden message of

260

hope, harboured somewhere in this darkest human heart, is that it? There is no hidden message, Mrs Fleming. This is what I do, for money, and I do it very well, so it's a good thing Willis hired me and not someone else.'

'And what if someone else had hired you ...' she paused, her mouth dry as she searched for the words and the nerve to say them, '... *not* to save Ross's life? What else do you do for money, Mr Bett? What did you do to the Romanian for money?'

Bett laughed, bleak and hollow.

'I could use a coffee,' he said. 'How about you?'

'Aren't you going to answer my question?'

'Not without caffeine, no.'

And with that, he turned and walked away, annoyingly sure she would follow, and even more annoyingly spot on.

He led her to the kitchen, a cavernous and handsomely fitted affair, dominated in the centre by a rustic table: vast, old and formidable enough to have been made from reclaimed drawbridge. She ignored the chair Bett pulled out for her, preferring the less subjugated posture of leaning against a slate worktop as he busied himself in front of a brass espresso machine that might well have cost more than her car. He filled two small cups and handed one to her. He didn't ask whether she took sugar, nor did she see any around. She didn't, but she didn't think the lack of offer was because he had taken pains to ascertain her tastes.

'You have quite a house,' she said. 'And my remarks about purposely ostentatious quarters notwithstanding, it is all rather exquisite. Which continues to pique my curiosity as to how you pay for all of this.'

'Back to the Romanian already?'

'You've got your coffee.'

'I have. How is yours?'

'Needs sugar,' she lied.

'You're sweet enough. At least, you were yesterday when your spoon came back from breakfast unused, and when you drank your espresso neat after lunch in Barcelona. But if you require, it's in that cupboard behind you.'

'You don't miss much.'

'I wouldn't say that, but I do pay attention. You have to in my line.'

'Tell me about it. Tell me *all* about it: apart from security consultancy, fake assault exercises and high-end missing-persons retrieval.'

'You didn't get the hidden message of hope, so now you want to know how dark this human heart really is.'

'Never mind how dark it is, is it big enough to own up to itself?'

'I've done nothing I'm ashamed of, Mrs Fleming, let that answer your question. No, I'm not a hired assassin and no, there are no circumstances under which I could be hired to, as you diplomatically put it, *not* save your son's life. But there have been lives I have gladly not saved. Sometimes we ... I have been retained by individuals, by organisations, by *governments*, to do things that legitimate, official forces cannot or will not do. Ilianu, for instance, was legally untouchable, protected by a cocoon of deniability, hierarchical removes and loopholes. He was trafficking girls for prostitution, and when I say girls, I mean girls. He catered to paedophiles in high places, which bought him even more protection, and not just through direct influence, but through the lengths these people would go to cover their own crimes and secrets. His contacts, his supply lines, were key to an entire network of white slavery around the Black Sea, but no court, no policeman, could get near him. Even if he could have been indicted, he would have been murdered before he could possibly name any names. So my team were engaged to bring him in.'

'By whom?'

'Client confidentiality forbids me from saying. But going through us bypassed extradition issues and any number of other legal impediments.'

'But if you did that, how could he be tried?'

'He wasn't,' Bett said, his face expressionless. 'But he did name names. Eventually.'

Jane gulped her coffee, her mouth suddenly dry.

'And what happened to him after that?' she just about managed to ask.

Bett looked directly at her, his eyes as dead as a shark's.

'Client confidentiality forbids me from saying.'

Silence fell upon the kitchen for a while after that, punctured only by the sound of coffee being sipped and cups placed down on the table. Bett didn't seem the type to be bothered by it. He was used to dealing with higher stakes than personal awkwardness. She knew that part of her should be glad someone of such mettle was in her corner, but couldn't miss the wider picture, in which she, Ross and Tom were now caught up in a game played by men like him.

Knowing she would be waiting a while to be offered, Jane got up and opened the fridge in search of some breakfast. She found some croissants, bread, some confiture, cheeses and cold cuts. It occurred to her to fill a single plate and make a point of eating it herself, but that was unlikely to register as a protest. Better to contrast her own example by serving enough for him too. She placed the breakfast items on the table and retrieved two plates from a rack on the wall. She put them down on opposite sides of the table and took a seat.

'Thank you,' he said, a tiny note of surprise in his voice.

'Don't thank me. It's your stuff.'

'Thank you anyway.'

She stopped herself saying, 'You're welcome', though she wasn't quite sure why. Perhaps she didn't want the exchange to conclude like it was merely a ritual of politeness.

'So,' she said, swallowing a mouthful of croissant. 'Serendipity. You're unco fond of these elliptical pronouncements, aren't you? Drip-feeding tantalising titbits to your underlings without letting them near the fridge themselves. Is it to remind them who's boss, because believe me, pal, they're under no doubts about that. Or do you just enjoy reminding yourself?'

Bett smiled as he chewed on a hunk of bread, amused in that patronising way she was already learning to recognise and resent.

'Underlings. Something about that word makes me think of gnomes or smurfs or Oompa-Loompas. Does anyone really consider themselves to have "underlings"? Or is it merely a term used in envy or spite to impugn the respect a person has for his employees?'

He fixed Jane with a scrutinising gaze, his tone markedly less amused as he phrased this last question.

'Coming from me?' Jane responded, meeting his stare.

'Definitely the latter. You like playing the big I Am, and you control information so that your underlings don't know which way is up without you telling them.'

'I think you're grossly underestimating a number of brilliant individuals, and that you're only doing it to insult me is the reason I'm not taking great offence on their behalf. They are not underlings, but I *am* – there you go, is that "I am" big enough for you? – I *am* their leader. No, I don't always tell them all I know about a situation, because if I did, there is the danger that they would assume it was everything there was to know about it. If I tell them too little, then they will assume there is more to find out, and find out they will. Information, yes, I control it, and they work to discover it. Information is the greater part of what we are about, me and my . . . crepuscular little company.'

'Crepuscular?'

'Beings of the twilight, Mrs Fleming.'

'Scurrying around in the shadows.'

Bett nodded. 'Legal shadows, political shadows . . . moral shadows.'

'Well, I'm not in your company. I'm sitting here in the daylight. Serendipity. What are you on about?'

Bett rolled up a slice of cooked ham and popped it into his mouth. He gestured with a slight wave of the fingers of his right hand, indicating he would answer when he was finished. He chewed, swallowed, then went to the fridge and poured himself a glass of orange juice. Even when put on the spot, this guy really loved to tease it out. He was about to close the fridge door again when something struck him and he turned back to the table.

'Juice?' he asked.

'Yes, please. *All* the juice.'

He poured out a glass, handed it to her and then stood, leaning against a worktop as she had done before. Jane took the body language to be a good sign: he was shaping up to hold forth.

'I got a call a few hours ago, around five a.m., from one of the contacts I fed our information to yesterday. He got a cross-match against Gelsenhoff for a Juan-Felipe Saleas. He's a smuggler. Runs supplies to the Balearics, mostly Ibiza: ecstasy, cocaine, crystal meth. He's comparatively small-time, which is why he's still trading.'

'The Spanish cops let him get on with it so they can follow his trail.'

'Correct. He's the criminal equivalent of a barium enema.'

'Lovely image.'

'Appropriate, don't you think? They've got him flagged up so that they can track his progress through the murky depths.'

Jane made a deduction and felt her heart quicken with anticipation.

'They know his boat. They can find out where he is,' she suggested, though even as she said it she realised it had to be over-optimistic. Whatever serendipitous connection Bett had referred to had been something he knew last night. The news about Felipe had only come in at five this morning.

'They know where his boat is. It's back in Barcelona.'

'So can we, can they . . .'

'Ross won't be on it.'

'How can you be so sure? Isn't it worth—'

'He won't be on it,' Bett stated firmly, and she knew he was right. Why would they take their prisoners out to sea only to return to their port of origin?

'Saleas handed him over to someone else,' she suggested. 'A bigger player.'

'Saleas is known to service some high-end clients as well as his bread-and-butter runs to the hedonist havens. His boat does little trips to Portal Nous, Puerto Banus, San Trop, Monte Carlo.'

'Marinas. Yachts. The super rich.'

'Private supplies, select gatherings. Clients who want the good stuff and can afford to pay a premium for convenience, discretion and the knowledge that they're getting it far enough up the supply chain to be uncontaminated. He's got a lot of exclusive mobile numbers. We can't plot exactly who called whom in what order, but from Connelly telling Gelsenhoff, word would have made it through Saleas to someone who knew what Ross was worth. Then, same as Connelly passing him to Saleas, Saleas passed him up the chain, for a fee, to a real player, with the clout and the connections to move the merchandise.'

'Who?'

'I don't know.'

'Well, can't someone lean on Saleas to tell us?'

'That was the first thing I asked. Unfortunately, my contact informed me that Saleas being left unhindered is just too important to a number of ongoing investigations. Incidentally, you should be aware I informed my contact that there were two gentlemen in need of assistance at a disused petrol station, now that Mr Connelly's information has been verified. He said he was very busy, but he'd send someone to look into it. I told him there was no hurry.'

'I wasn't losing sleep over Connelly.'

'No, I didn't think you were.'

'So if we can't talk to Saleas, what's so bloody serendipitous?'

'The fact that I *do* know where Ross's new captor is going to set up his medicine show.'

'Medicine show?'

'Well, he won't roll up in a covered wagon, but he'll be hawking his wares nonetheless, just like any number of other unconscionable shills.'

'Where?'

'There's a "European Defence Exhibition" taking place next week. Orwellian euphemism for an Arms Convention. All the toy manufacturers will be there, showing off their latest ways of defending the hell out of anyone who pisses you off. Displays, demonstrations, exhibits, stalls and conferences, just like any other trade fair. And like any other trade fair, all of this will be a sideshow to the real purpose of bringing the major players together in one place, where business can be done: offer and counter-offer, barter and trade, off the record, away from the boardroom, unofficial, unaccountable. The biggest deal in town will concern the opportunity to acquire the Gravity Well, for development or . . . discontinuation. We will be there, amid the shadows, watching and listening unseen. Track the buyers, we find the seller. Find the seller and then there's the small matter of armed assault and hostage rescue, but let's cross that bridge when we come to it.'

'Let's,' Jane said, glad to defer the thought. 'So where is the Air Bett helicopter headed? Frankfurt? Milan?'

'No. That's the truly serendipitous part. It's on the Côte d'Azure: Cap Andreus. Just down the road from here.'

He picked up his glass and downed the last of his orange juice.

'Now,' he said, 'any more questions, or can I get back to being the big I Am?'

'Just one,' Jane replied, toying aimlessly with a piece of croissant that had gone a little hard and which she had no intention of eating. Her fingers needed something to occupy them, a sign that she was unexpectedly nervous about this final, rather trivial query. 'This dress,' she began. 'It's not exactly lounge-wear. Is there a particular reason it was left out for me yesterday morning?'

'Yes,' he stated. 'It was the only thing in the house in your size. Apart from fatigues, and of course what you came in, but those were in a bit of a state.'

'Oh,' Jane said, somewhat taken aback by how much his answer had disappointed her. Even though it would have pissed her off no end, she realised she'd actually have preferred if it *had* been for his amusement. What was it about indifference that drew you to seek reaction, to seek approval? He was an arrogant, callous, manipulative bastard. More than that, he was a brute, a killer. And yet she wanted to believe he saw her as more than a piece on his meticulously controlled board or another chattel to commandeer.

'I'll get Alexis to take you shopping for some new clothes if we can fit it into your schedule,' he went on.

'My schedule? What schedule is that?'

'Your training schedule. You didn't believe you wouldn't have to sing for your supper here, did you? The Defence Exhibition starts on Tuesday, which doesn't leave us a lot of time, so it's going to be pretty intensive, but I'm sure you can handle it.'

'Handle it?' she enquired, bemused. He really was straight back into his elliptical drip-feeding. 'And what exactly are you expecting to train me for?'

'Espionage, Mrs Fleming. What the bloody hell else?'

She was glad her mouth had been empty when he told her, as she would surely have choked otherwise.

'*Espionage?* Me? I'm a housewife, a *grandmother*, for God's sake.'

'And as such, you've served the perfect apprenticeship, according to one expert.'

'The perf . . . what numpty said that?'

'Stella Rimington. She was the head of MI5. In truth, she said being a mother, so you're more than qualified.'

'How does being a mother prepare me for being a spy?'

'For a start, you're a woman, and therefore more naturally suited to this kind of thing.'

'Is this where you imply my sex are naturally sleekit and two-faced?'

'No, it's where I concede that you have evolved over millennia to outwit men because you cannot compete with their brutality. Men dominate through their physical strength. It's a contest women can't win, so women entice them to play different games.'

'So you *are* saying we're sleekit and two-faced.'

'You are more intuitive, psychologically aware, subtly manipulative, and, most crucially of all, more attentive to detail, this last for the simple reason that women listen. You see, the greatest skill of intelligence is to sit quiet and let everyone else talk.'

'Around men, that's not necessarily a choice.'

'Quite. Men dominate conversations: they love to beat their chests and are less discreet about what they say because they are often less concerned by what they may betray than by how they are perceived – by their peers and especially by women. It's a vulnerability women are therefore well-equipped to exploit. Take Alexis, for example. Her computer skills are valuable, but her true talent lies in simply getting people to talk. In fact, she's the best at it I've known. I trust you heard what she did on Tuesday, with the man who tried to abduct your granddaughter?'

'The gist of it, yes.'

'She stepped in at a moment's notice, improvised, postured, got the guy to trust her, *instantly*, and thus got him to divulge secret information even though she'd only met him minutes before. I confess, I'd hate to be in the position whereby she sought to deceive me. She's one of the few people who I have no doubt could manage it.'

'Yeah, well, just like all men aren't necessarily much cop at the brute force and roadmap-reading, it doesn't follow that I could do what she does just because I'm female. And I really don't see what being a mother has to do with it.'

'Being a mother instils a ruthlessness of mind, a linearity of purpose.'

'No, being a mother muddles your mind and gives you a meandering *loss* of purpose. If you'd seen me around my children, it would soon cure your delusions.'

'What if I'd seen you face down a trained killer and allow no pain or peril to stand between you and rescuing a child? Would that suggest a linearity of purpose to you?'

'Needs must when the devil drives, Mr Bett.'

'He's saddled up, Mrs Fleming. But so are you. Being a mother makes you adroit at partitioning areas of your life, of your mind: adult-to-adult, adult-to-child. Putting on a happy face for the baby even though you feel like shit, putting on a stern one to admonish even though, inside, you're pissing yourself laughing at what the kid has just done. Don't you think all those years of playing a one-woman good-cop, bad-cop to get the little buggers to cooperate would make you adept at maintaining a deceit in order to procure what you need?'

'There's a big difference between deceiving a toddler and deceiving an intelligent adult.'

'True. You probably never had to burst your own nose in order to deceive a toddler. Mrs Fleming, in the space of a few hours on Tuesday, you stole two cars and a passport, then successfully violated border security at an international port. Yesterday you kidnapped two hardened criminals and earwigged their conversation before priming them for interrogation with a convincing performance of ruthlessness bordering on the sadistic. I've been in this game a while. Trust me when I tell you, you've got what it takes.'

The litany sounded like he was talking about someone else, and, at the time, much of *doing* it had felt like someone else, but Jane knew it would now constitute only self-indulgence to go on thinking that way. *You have evolved over millennia . . .* That thousands of years older woman. It was her. And that nineteen-year-old with everything to look forward to was still her too.

'Okay,' she said. 'I'm sold. What now?'

Bett looked her up and down appraisingly.

'Are you slim because you eat nothing or are you slim because you keep fit?' he asked.

'I go to the gym a couple of times a week, when I can manage.'
'Good. That should make it easier on you.'
'Easier? Why? What has fitness to do with espionage?'

Jane was woken by an old-fashioned wind-up alarm clock on her bedside cabinet, which brought her to consciousness with a heart-racing jolt, partly from the insistent cacophonous racket and partly from the shock of it not having been there when she went to sleep. She flapped blurrily for it with her right hand and succeeded only in knocking it over, which served to amplify the din as the ghastly device fitted violently upon the wooden surface. She sat up and tugged the chain on her bedside lamp, then lifted the clock in both hands, placing it in her lap as she searched for the switch to shut the thing up. Having succeeded, she turned it over and read the dial. No chance, she thought. Obviously wrong. She picked up her wrist-watch to find out the right time, only to discover that the clock had been correct and it really was five a.m.

'You have got to be kidding,' she mumbled, dropping the clock on to the duvet and flopping back to the horizontal.

She spent a few moments trying to decide which part of her hurt the most. Not her legs, definitely, because they had been amputated by some lunatic and replaced with fossilised tree-trunks incapable of any flexibility, far less weight-bearing or motile properties. The same bampot had also employed some super-torqued racking device to tighten her buttocks so that they felt taut enough to repel steel. His name was Nuno. He had spent four (was it five? Felt like twelve) hours with her in Bett's gymnasium as an introductory lesson in effective ways to hurt people. It was early days, she knew, but she reckoned she was off to a flyer given how much she had learned to hurt herself. Boxercise class had never been like that. She had never kicked or punched anything so hard or so often as that hanging bag, though it had proven a doughty opponent, easily inflicting more damage on her than she had landed on it.

He had done horrible things to her arms too, but that damage was light compared to what Rebekah had wreaked upon them and her poor shoulders, downstairs in the basement shooting range. She'd heard people say that your first time riding a horse made you hurt in muscles you didn't previously know you had. Well, she now knew the same was true of firing fully automatic machine guns, especially after warming up with about five hundred rounds of pistol shooting. The pain went right down to her fingers, already mashed by sustained bag-pounding, and thoroughly finished off by an hour's supervised repeated disassembly and reassembly of both weapons.

Groundwork, Bett had called it. Foundations.

'And just how does this provide a foundation for harnessing those feminine wiles you were waxing lyrical about?' she had asked. 'Whatever happened to using guile and intuition to entice men to play a different game?'

'You don't need training for that, Mrs Fleming, you're a natural. However, while deceit and pretence can get you into many places, they may not get you out again. One of the first rules you will learn here is never to walk into a situation without knowing how you intend to exit, and to be ready for that way to suddenly change, or be closed altogether. When that happens, your guile and intuition may not be enough, in which case you need to be able to play the men's games too. Little as you'd like to, I'm sure you can imagine many circumstances in which you might need these skills.'

He'd looked at her, demanding acknowledgement.

'Yes,' she conceded.

'Good. But mostly you're learning them for the circumstances you *can't* imagine.'

It had been early evening before she moved on to anything related to intelligence gathering, and that hadn't spared her physically either. Her eyes and ears had felt the strain from so much of Somboon's gadgetry, but the ultimate winner, she decided, the grand prize for the sorest anatomical component, went to her brain, which felt thoroughly swollen with overload, strained from the logic flips and psychological contortionism she'd been instructed in by Bett and his Canadian protégé.

She'd crept into bed around midnight, having been told she'd 'probably done enough for day one'. Five hours later this, this bloody alarm clock had gone off and she just knew that any minute someone would be in to haul her out of bed and begin the torture all over again. She couldn't say whether they could turn her into a trained assassin in three days, but she was pretty sure that by the end of it she would definitely be ready to kill someone.

Jane had never been convinced of the maxim that whatever doesn't kill you makes you stronger, but that morning made her a true believer. It was Nuno who came to escort her, via a light breakfast, back to the rigours of the gymnasium, where, instead of suffering a cumulative fatigue, she found to her surprise that her limbs actually felt better able to repeat what they had taken on yesterday. She felt looser, lighter and, yes, stronger, giving her the sensation of building on foundations rather than drawing from a dwindling reserve.

She even, she had to concede, began to enjoy it, and took a girlish delight at what she discovered herself able to do.

'I can't teach you a lot of things in a few days,' Nuno told her, 'but I can teach you to do a select few things very well.'

Any scepticism she retained about their respective abilities to achieve this was dispelled come the end of their second session, when he got her to execute a deflective block that involved a perpendicular step and a redistribution of her bodyweight, using the strength of the attacker's own blow to force him off-balance. It didn't feel like much while she was doing it, but that was before he demonstrated exactly what she was deflecting when he repeated the blow on a flat wooden target dummy and shattered it into splinters. Her surprise at this was then trumped when he got her to repeat the strike on a fresh dummy and she sent her own hand through its wooden face too.

Down in the basement, Rebekah moved her on to more skilled use of the guns, after the previous day's mere 'familiarisation and demystification exercise', which, she explained, had been about 'boring the hell out of you and making these suckers seem as mundane and functionary as a vacuum cleaner'.

Rebekah would never know how unintentionally inspirational her choice of words had been.

Jane thereafter took up her arms with gusto, and learned to her delight that she was, in Rebekah's opinion, an 'outstanding' shot. That was what she exclaimed after each firing exercise: 'Outstanding', an unmistakable military cadence about it. It shouldn't have come as so much of a surprise, had she thought about it. Remember Ross and those bloody fairground shooting galleries. The boy couldn't miss. It had to have come from somewhere, and it was natural to assume such traditionally masculine talents were inherited from the father. However, Tom had usually had a go at those rifle ranges too, and, as Ross once put it, he couldn't hit shite if he fell down a stank.

Less intimidated by the whole of what she was embarking upon, she then found it easier to unshackle herself from her natural technophobia as she was reintroduced to Somboon's plethora of hardware. Rebekah's wisdom about demystification and her jewel of a metaphor served Jane well among the electronica, though she suspected Som would be less sanguine about his creations being considered mundane and functionary.

By the time she got around to Alexis again, her appetite for this previously arcane knowledge remained such that she was actually sorry computer hacking wasn't on the agenda. She was also, she would only reluctantly admit, a little sorry that on this occasion Bett was not around to supervise, busying himself elsewhere for the evening. It was, she decided, a healthy sign of her being more comfortable with all that she was taking on, that even his brooding presence was no longer something to put her on edge. Another sign was that she was starting to talk to her instructors like they were people, rather than jailers or even fellow inmates.

Alexis was the most open, though perhaps only because she was the one Jane was around when she started feeling comfortable enough to talk much herself.

'So how did you get to be a hacker?' Jane had asked, genuinely curious about what she considered a true netherworld of almost alien intellect.

'I'm not a hacker,' was Alexis's surprising and rather indignant reply.

'I'm sorry, I'm not quite "down" with the argot. Is "hacker" pejorative these days?'

'Oh, no. Hacker is what I aspire to be, not what I would call myself. It's a misused term in mainstream culture. When most people talk about hackers, they really mean crackers, and that's closer to what I am. A cracker is someone who breaks into other

273

people's computer systems, and true hackers figure that's a pretty lame use of your abilities.'

'It's come in useful for you, though, hasn't it? It brought you to Bett's attention, anyway.'

Alexis laughed, a bitter edge to it.

'Fair to say it sure did. But, to be honest, I'm not even an especially good cracker. That wasn't why Bett came in for me. It was more because he figured I was predisposed toward getting into where I'm not supposed to be and tinkering with shit that isn't mine. I've got hacker aspirations but a cracker mentality.'

'So what's a hacker?'

'A hacker is someone who really knows their shit when it comes to programming. The hackers' own definition is, and I quote: "Someone who enjoys exploring the details of programmable systems and how to stretch their capabilities, as opposed to most users, who prefer to learn only the minimum necessary."'

'From what I've seen and heard so far, that sounds like you.'

'I know some tricks, but they're cracker tricks, mainly; script-kiddie stuff. I'm like a kid punk guitarist who can play a lot of cool-sounding riffs, but can't read a note of music. Truth is I can play better than a lot of classically trained people, but even more than music, computers are about structure, protocols, formalities. My learning process has usually been a matter of cumbersome and sloppy reverse-engineering. I was supposed to go to college to learn how to read the music, you know? But it didn't happen. Things got in the way.'

'What things?'

'Let me put it this way . . .'

When Jane walked into the firing range the next day, she found Rebekah wrestling with a human dummy far more substantial-looking than the target figures Jane had been shooting so far. They'd been wooden, no sturdier than the kind of cases fruit used to come in at the supermarket, with gun-toting figures painted on them, or sometimes merely concentric circles. This dummy was fully three-dimensional and heavy, constructed of similar material – and certainly similar bulk – to the punchbag she was rapidly succeeding, according to Nuno, in 'making her bitch'. Rebekah was hauling one upright, while another two lay on the concrete floor.

'We reckon you're ready for some hot-dogging, to use a hideously American phrase,' said an unexpected, disembodied voice. Bett. She looked along the barrier and saw him step out from one of the corrals.

'Hot-dogging?'

'Yes. Ghastly, isn't it? Anyway, you've seen the movies, right? Guys firing guns with just one hand? Firing bloody *machine* guns with just one hand!'

'Yes. I'd assumed it was nonsense even before I felt one of these things.'

'It *is* nonsense. If you're going to use one hand to fire a gun, you'd be as well having a gun in *each hand*.'

He held out two matching Hechler & Koch nine-millimetre pistols, presenting the grips. Jane took them, a little dubiously, as Rebekah hitched one of the dummies to a hook and reeled it ten yards back down the range. It was closer, by at least ten yards, than the standard targets, but Jane didn't fancy her chances of hitting it with more than the first shot if she was firing, as normally instructed, in quick succession.

She pulled on her ear-protectors and took position behind the barrier, her now comfortable firing stance impossibly encumbered by the second gun.

'Okay, let him have it,' Bett commanded.

She fired on order. One of the first pair of shots hit home, but after that the bullets went zinging into the walls and ceiling around an embarrassingly wide radius.

Jane looked to Rebekah and pulled an Oops! face. Rebekah grinned and shook her head. Then Bett came up behind her and put his arms beneath Jane's oxters, pulling her hands into position. She felt one of his biceps brush her right breast, his own taut chest pressing into her shoulder. They'd never touched before, never been this close. He smelled freshly of outdoors, like clean washing on the rope. Her body tensed a little at that brushing contact, though she didn't think the locus of his touch was intentional. His hands felt firm and callused, like her father's had been, and, like her father's, they were a confident and steady guide.

275

'You have to cross your hands,' he explained, a gentleness to his voice despite the volume required to penetrate her ear-protectors. 'That way the recoil has something to play against. And don't pull both triggers at once. You want an alternating pattern of shots.'

He stepped back and she tried again, firing four rounds from each pistol. She managed only two hits from the eight shots, though the radius of the missed rounds was considerably less erratic.

'I don't see the point,' she complained. 'I could hit that target with every shot if I was firing one pistol.'

'It's not just about accuracy,' Bett said.

'Not much point firing the bloody thing without it,' she countered.

'It's about fields of fire.'

He vaulted over the barrier and into the range, where he and Rebekah proceeded to hang two more dummies from moving overhead trellises. The three of them dangled and swung, side by side, less than two feet apart and ten yards back.

As they did, Jane ejected the spent magazines and quickly slapped in replacements. It already felt a practised action, as natural and familiar as assembling the liquidiser at home in her kitchen.

'Okay, so you can hit a human-size target from twenty yards no problem,' Bett said, climbing back behind the barrier. 'If we need a sniper, you're our girl.' He stepped towards the target controls, his hand hovering over the panel. 'But look, what do you know, you're in a confined space, nowhere to retreat, three men bearing down on you, two hundred pounds each, ten yards away, and one little bullet isn't going to drop them unless it's right through the centre of the brain. What do you do?'

He slapped the panel. All three targets began advancing the short distance towards the barrier. Jane crossed the guns and fired, the hammers beating rapidly in syncopation as her wrists fought the recoil, to describe a narrow arc across her automated assailants. Bullets thumped into the padding, rocking all three dummies back on their hangers and in one case blowing a head off completely.

Bett slapped the button again, stopping them five feet away.

'Congratulations,' he said. 'You live to fight another day. Step over the three corpses, mind you don't trip on the severed head and you walk out alive.'

Jane flipped on the safety catches and put the guns down.

'You're revolting,' she told him. 'I don't think I've ever met anyone so callously brutal.'

'It's not me that's revolting, Mrs Fleming, it's the nature of the game. I didn't make it callous and I didn't make it brutal. I'm just teaching you how to play it.'

'Bollocks. You made this game. Men made this game. Don't tell me you'd rather it was different. It's too bloody obvious you enjoy it.'

'Watching you deploy your skills and maximise your abilities, yes, I do quite enjoy it. Knowing you're equipped to handle yourself if it all turns to chaos next week, yes, that gives me satisfaction too. But beyond that, Mrs Fleming, don't presume.' Bett stood close to her, almost toe to toe, and as he was less than an inch taller than her, eye to eye too. 'You're shooting at stuffed sacks. You've no idea what I've witnessed when the targets bled more than straw, and I can assure you I enjoyed none of it.'

With that, he turned on his heel and walked out towards the stairs, a spoor of high-minded huff in his wake.

Jane and Rebekah looked at each other in silence for a moment. She wanted to say something like 'touchy touchy' but it would have sounded petty and shallow. She reckoned she'd find Rebekah on her side in sorority against the big bad boss, but was wary of making any assumptions.

'He likes you, you know,' Rebekah said after a while; quietly, almost as though she was concerned he might still be in earshot.

'He likes me? I'd hate to be in his bad books, then.'

'Who wouldn't? But believe me, he's been a ray of sunshine since you showed up. All things being relative,' she added, with a smile.

'You're havering. I've given him nothing but grief.'

'Yeah, but I think he digs that. It's probably been a long time since anyone spoke to him like you do. We're all sure enjoying it.'

277

'Glad I've been of *some* benefit to you, then. I've nothing to lose; nor do I have anything to gain from pulling my punches.'

'True,' Rebekah agreed, though her coy smile preceded an equivocation. 'But I think you kinda enjoy it too.'

'That's ridiculous,' Jane protested. 'I'm not playing *games* with this bloke. I'm a married woman and I've got enough on my mind right now without . . .' she tailed off, reining in her growing indignation.

'Okay,' Rebekah said, making a backing-off gesture with her palms. 'You ain't playing games.' She was still grinning; more so, perhaps, in response to Jane's overreaching display of ire. 'But when you're ready to talk, I'm here,' she added.

Jane stared at her for a moment in sustained outrage at the implication, then couldn't stop herself bursting into laughter. Rebekah responded in kind, and the two of them soon found themselves breathless with it like a pair of schoolgirls. Pity help them if Bett chose this moment to make his reappearance.

'So, does Bett have . . . women?' Jane enquired, once she had stemmed her giggles long enough to know this wouldn't set them both off again.

'He has women, yeah,' Rebekah replied. 'I'm not sure he has relationships, but he has women. I'm not really the one to ask, to be honest. All I know is through Alexis, and a lot of what she knows is through the housekeeping staff. They're here more. They see more. I mean, we're not hanging round this place all day normally.'

'And these women, what are they like?'

'Teenage-fantasy stuff, according to Lex.'

'*Teenagers?*' Jane asked, horrified.

'No, though they do tend to be half his age. Male teenage-fantasy figures, I think Lex meant. You know: pretty, young, nubile. I think she was being polite. She meant his appetites were immature.'

'Younger women are less . . . complicated,' Jane said.

'Easy come, easy go too. I'm sure they're impressed when they see his crib, but they know they ain't getting their feet under the table. In fact, here's a thing. According to Lex, and that probably means according to the housekeeper, the women he brings home sleep . . . well, in the room you're in.'

'It's certainly built to impress.'

'I'm not saying he's lining you up,' Rebekah added hastily, with a giggle. 'What I'm saying is, they don't get taken to the west wing. *Nobody* gets into the west wing.'

'Not even the housekeeper?'

'Well, yeah, sure, she gets in. I don't think he's got his dead mom in there and her clothes to dress up in or anything. But it's his domain, and his alone.'

'Have you never been tempted to, you know, sneak a peek if you were sure he wasn't around?'

Rebekah looked at her as though the question was absurd.

'Nu-uh,' she said, 'Two things. One, I'd never be sure Bett wasn't around. And two, I don't want to know what's in his rooms like I don't want to know what's in his head. But I'm not so sure you can say the same.'

Jane thought she might begin giggling again, but merely found herself blushing instead.

Lex was sitting at the edge of the swimming pool with her jeans rolled up, dangling her feet in the water. It was chilly, but there was something irresistible about doing it when the spring sun was shining on her shoulders. It was one thing she knew she'd miss if she left this region. Back home there would be weeks and weeks of merciless winter to endure before the mercury got over its vertigo. Sure, it might turn rainy again in a couple of days, but for now she was seizing the moment. Armand was out there too, though with a more industrious purpose. He was checking air tanks and regulators, servicing the kit ahead of possible deployment. Feeling warmth on her skin, cold on her feet and watching the rays on the ripples, she felt absolutely no compunction about not helping.

However, the moment was brought to an all-too-sudden end as Bett emerged from around the side of the house, walking with a briskness of pace that usually meant he was in a real hurry to kick someone's ass. She got to her feet instantly, seriously hoping it wasn't hers.

He said nothing, though, just paced around next to the water. He had this look on his face that she'd never seen before. At first she thought it was anger, but, looking closer, it was clearly something else, something he could neither contain nor express. It was as though he did not know where to put himself, unaccustomedly lost.

Armand looked up from where he was kneeling in the shade.

'Is the trainee having difficulties?' he asked solicitously.

Bett shot him a glare that seemed more irritated at being roused from his uneasy brooding than at the question itself.

'What? Oh, no, not at all.'

'You sure? You were going to try her on the triple-target test, no? Did she handle it okay?'

Bett snorted, a hint of scorn far more resembling his normal self.

'She ripped the lot of them. Blew one of their bloody heads off. She has the makings of a very bad girl.'

'So . . . all is well, then,' Armand suggested, clearly indicating otherwise.

'Not quite. It's fine, really, it's just . . . well, I think it would be easier if she didn't give the impression she fucking hates me all the time. Christ, you'd think it was *me* who'd kidnapped her family.'

Lex and Armand shared a look that they were doubtless both glad Bett never saw. It said: are you getting this?

'Your happy-go-lucky demeanour not getting through to her, then?' Lex said, instantly astonished and horrified that she had done so aloud. However, the anticipated thunderous reaction never came. Instead, he seemed to be mulling over what she'd said and looked . . . surely not hurt, not him.

'I suppose she's . . . under a lot of stress,' Bett ventured uncertainly.

Maybe he had eaten something that disagreed with him. He definitely needed to go lie down, and soon. This was freaking Lex out.

'Dinner,' said Armand.

'What?'

'You should invite her to dinner. You have this beautiful house, a magnificent dining room. You have the services of Marie-Patrice . . .'

'Yeah,' Lex agreed, figuring she might as well ride with this. 'She's only eaten in her room, or grabbed a slice of pizza with some of us down in the kitchen.'

280

'She has had a very hard time recently,' Armand added. 'Perhaps it would benefit if she saw a more . . . sympathetic side to you.'

Bett pondered this. It was like watching some philosopher wrestle with a concept he had never known existed before.

'I think . . . you're right. Yes,' he decided. And then, weirder still: 'Thank you. Thank you both. Excellent suggestion.'

'*De rien*,' Armand shrugged.

Bett nodded to himself. 'Alexis,' he said. 'You've spent the most time with her, I think she's quite comfortable with you. Would you please ask her if she'd care to join me for . . .'

'Oh, no,' Lex interrupted. 'Uh-uh.'

'I'm only asking you to . . .'

She folded her arms, standing her ground.

'Sir,' she stated, 'you can order me if you want, but this is not a matter for delegation. Trust me. I've hacked into systems for you, I've broken into buildings for you. I've even killed for you. This is something you have to do for yourself.'

It was the first time she had seen Bett look truly daunted.

'But what . . . what if she says no?' he asked.

Lex caught a glimpse of Armand out of the corner of her eye and immediately tried to banish the image of his shoulders convulsing with muzzled laughter.

'She won't,' Lex assured him.

'How do you know that?'

'Between another plateful of cold cuts alone in her quarters and *haute cuisine* in your grand dining room, it's a no-brainer, no matter who the company is. Ask and she'll be delighted.'

'If you're wrong, I'll be holding you responsible.'

'It'll be fine. Just as long as you make it sound like a request, not an order.'

Lex saw the beginnings of indignation glimmer in his eyes, then he nodded his head as if to say: Yeah, good call.

He wandered off towards the house, his gait less pointlessly meandering than before, but still hardly his familiar confident strut. Lex looked across to Armand. He put a hand over his mouth: I'm saying nothing.

*   *   *

281

Jane heard a knock at the door and prayed it wasn't him. She checked the clock and confirmed that dinner wasn't for another hour. Thank God. Stay of execution. Time to get herself together, get her head together. Time to pack a bag and plan an escape. What was she doing, agreeing to this? It had sounded very tempting at the time of asking, but that was mainly because she hadn't had any lunch by that point and the prospect of food had obscured all other considerations. It was now five or six hours since then, in which time she'd only eaten half a baguette, but she was feeling less hungry by the minute. Why was she so apprehensive? Why was she in such a bloody tizz? All the insanity she'd phlegmatically dealt with in the past week and she was in this state over dinner.

There had to be some kind of transference going on, or perhaps guilt. No, definitely not guilt. It was only a meal with her host, a mutual courtesy. It wasn't any kind of betrayal of Tom, and in any case her loyalty towards him could better be measured by what she was undertaking to assist in his rescue. Well, yes, okay, there was an element of guilt then, in dining with another man in some fairy-tale mansion while he was held prisoner on some hulk, but it was mainly to do with their comparative circumstances and very little to do with fidelity.

This wasn't a date, for Christ's sake. Fidelity was not, nor would be, an issue. Point one: he liked glam little nymphets half his age, not greying grannies. Point two: he was a monster. That pretty much covered it from both sides. Neither could possibly be interested in the other.

So why was she starting to wish he'd never asked, and what had changed since he did?

Owning up time, girl: she'd been flattered.

He'd come back downstairs to the firing range and sent Rebekah off on some spurious errand, conspicuously engineering a moment's privacy. He shuffled his feet rather listlessly, impatiently watching Rebekah's departure and clearly waiting for her to be gone before he spoke. When he did, it was as direct as ever, though lacking his customary authority.

'I'd like to add a little something to your itinerary today, if that's all right with you.'

'Sure, what?'

'Dinner. Marie-Patrice's finest. Shouldn't be all work and no play, should it?'

'No.'

He'd started a little, and it was tempting to watch his consternation fully develop, but Jane opted to clarify her position.

'No, it shouldn't,' she said. 'That would be lovely.'

She managed to keep the grin off her face until he turned his back and walked away. At that moment, her thoughts were not of mutual courtesy, and she had convinced herself that his couldn't have been either. She still wasn't sure why she wanted him to like her, but she knew it felt good when he indicated that he did. Perhaps it was because it provided further independent evidence that she wasn't quite the frumpy old hag she recently feared she'd turned into.

Alexis had provided the first of it when they'd squeezed in a hit-and-run clothes-shopping trip the previous evening at an enormous two-storey supermarket-cum-department store. While Jane wandered around, unsure where to find anything and trying to remember how European sizes corresponded with those back home, Alexis was swiftly picking up garments and slinging them over her arm. At first Jane assumed Alexis was buying them for herself, until she got Jane to hold a shirt against her chest for size.

She was about to state her objections, but held her tongue. Out of her normal environment, out of her normal self, she was able to step away and hear how truly tedious her protests would sound. Insistent frumpery, she could suddenly see, was a self-indulgence. The girl wasn't choosing anything inappropriate and nor was she making any statement: she was just grabbing a few things by way of suggestion because they didn't have long before the place closed. What took Jane a revelatory moment to absorb was that Alexis was choosing clothes for the woman she was looking at, and that woman was a lot younger than the one Jane had got used to picturing.

The following morning she had caught her reflection in the gym as she swung kicks at the hanging bag, barefoot in her loose khaki fatigues. What struck her most was not the sight of what she was doing – her agility, the power with which she was delivering her blows, the sweat running obliviously off her face on to fatigues already dark with it in places – but how natural she looked. *This* was her, and it didn't look wrong.

However, the closer it came to dinnertime, the more her old self threatened an ambush from behind the full-length antique mirror. She stood there in just her bathrobe, surveying her sartorial options for the evening, her old self insisting nothing she wore could disguise who she really was. That's why she was having second thoughts. Monster, brute, killer, no matter, when Bett looked at her in that dining room, she wanted him to see someone who belonged there. She wanted him to see her as an equal, and if she couldn't make that happen, then she didn't want to be there at all.

She walked to the door and slowly opened it an inch to see who was outside. It was Rebekah.

'Brought you these,' she announced, holding up a pair of hair straighteners. 'I'm not exactly a beautician – too much of a tomboy all my life – but I thought I could lend you moral support.'

'Could you ever,' Jane said, welcoming her inside with a smile.

Lex had called it a day and was heading for her car when curiosity got the better of her and she decided to head out via the kitchen. Whatever magic spell had turned Bett into a human being was unlikely to last, so she wanted another glimpse of its effects before the enchantment wore off. She stuck her head around the door, ostensibly to say goodbye, though she knew this would have been utterly transparent given that neither of them had ever sought the other out for such a salutation before. In truth, she was still half-expecting to have that head bitten off, spell or no spell, but instead Bett beckoned her inside and began showing her the intended menu. Marie-Patrice was conspicuous by her absence, but this was because she had been dispatched on shopping duties with the kind of budget Bett normally only spent on ordnance.

'What do you think?' he asked.

'I think you should be careful not to overwhelm her,' Lex replied, casting an eye over the list of extravagant dishes he had planned.

'That's what Marie-Patrice said, too.'

'But you overruled her.'

'Well, yes. Armand was right. The woman deserves a bit of the good life.'

'Yeah, but if you overdo it, it could be intimidating, like you're trying to show her you're lord of the manor when you should be trying to make her feel at home, right?'

'Er, right,' he said, trying to disguise the fact that he had just been called on his true intention. The poor bastard. He really was a beginner at this normal-human-relations thing.

'And is this the wine you've chosen?' she asked, indicating the bottle sitting in pride of place in the centre of the kitchen table.

'Yes,' he said, smiling eagerly. 'Margaux, 1982. It's the last of three I got as a gift from the French minister for—'

'Then don't waste it,' Rebekah told him.

'What?'

'Save it for someone who'll appreciate it. Put it back and open some Ruby Cabernet.'

'It's *Shiraz* Cabernet. Ruby Cabernet is marketing-speak nonsense, and anyway, I'm not going to serve Mrs Fleming some inferior plonk. What would that say about my hospitality?'

'Mrs Fleming doesn't drink wine very much. She's only getting started, though she is getting to like it. She won't like your Margaux. She will like some Ruby Cabernet. There's some nice Australian—'

'*Australian?*' he asked, appalled.

'Australian. Like I said, she's new to it. If you want her to enjoy herself, give her a bottle that will make her think wine is great, not a bottle intended to make her think *you*'re great. You copy, sir?'

Bett sighed. This was all very confusing for him.

'I think so,' he said. 'Will I have to drink the same stuff?'

'Only if you don't want to look like an asshole.'

'Copy that,' he said, a glowering rumble in his voice telling her this was probably a good time to cut and run.

Bett was waiting for her in the drawing room, where they'd first met those long few days ago. He smiled a little stiffly by way of welcome, standing by that window he was so fond of gazing from. He had that incredible self-confidence when there

285

was a multitude to be ordered and addressed, but he seemed less assured now that it was just the two of them, and markedly less so than their first one-on-one, when there was the demarcation of roles between them: the man of shadow and the woman he had mysteriously summoned. That said, he still had a presence that filled the room, and it had to be borne in mind that a less assured Bett still presented a more commanding countenance than the majority of the male population at their most cocksure.

She stood just inside the doorway and they both sized each other up for a wordless few moments. She was looking at him a while before noticing that he hadn't gone to the same pains and stresses as she with regard to dressing for the occasion. The reason it took a few seconds was that her immediate impression was simply that he looked good, he looked right, with issues of code or formality only factoring into her assessment as an afterthought. He wore a crisp pair of pale green chino pants and a sandy polo shirt. Jane had opted for a peach dress that Alexis had picked out at the supermarket. It was a light and airy garment, and the feel of it against her newly-shaven legs, without tights, made her think of holidays.

Given the grandeur of her surroundings, she'd had uncomfortable visions of Bett fronting up in a DJ and making her feel like a taffeta-deficient poor relation. However, when she saw him, she felt precisely that anticipated anxiety of being underdressed, despite the relaxed informality of his chosen attire. There was something intimidatingly formidable about his appearance that would have had that effect no matter what she'd been wearing. The short sleeves of his polo shirt hugged taut muscle, an unflinching sturdiness about him that made her picture someone hitting him with a crowbar and the crowbar bending, like in the cartoons.

'Hello,' she managed nervously, once they'd been smiling awkwardly at each other for one nanosecond longer than she could possibly tolerate.

'Good evening,' he replied. 'Can I get you a drink?'

He stepped across to a table by the wall, which bore eight or nine bottles of spirits and some glasses. She stared at them, wondering how bad it would sound to admit she wasn't very well versed in the whole aperitifs thing, or the whole drinking alcohol thing in general.

'Gin and tonic, perhaps?' he suggested.

'Yes, please,' Jane assented, simply to disguise the fact that she didn't have a clue.

'Tanqueray, Bombay Sapphire?'

She looked at the bottles and opted for the blue one. The stuff she'd tried once before had been from a green bottle, so maybe the blue stuff didn't taste like bleach.

Bett poured two and handed her a glass.

'Your health,' he said, subtly tilting his glass.

'Which is . . . strangely as good as I can remember, though I'm left wondering whether that's in spite or because of everything else in my world falling down about my ears.'

'It's times like these that show you what you're really made of. In your case, sterner stuff than you perhaps suspected.'

'I'll drink to that,' she said, and tried not to wince as she raised the glass to her lips. She took a decent mouthful, having learned from wine that you taste nothing but bitterness if you only take an apprehensive sip.

She smiled in mild surprise. It tasted quite refreshing, and barely like bleach at all. She wondered whether it was the circumstances, her surroundings or the quality of the drink that made the difference, but, given that it was easily twenty years since her last go at the stuff, it was fairly possible her palate had matured a little.

Bett invited her to take a seat opposite him, having positioned two armchairs either side of his favoured window. They traded small talk as they drank, mainly about her training, and avoiding the subject of why she was undertaking it. It was safe, neutral stuff: common ground, in fact the only common ground they had, given that she knew next to nothing about him. Jane was already starting to worry how they would fill the gaps between courses when Marie-Patrice appeared at the door to summon them to dinner.

Bett walked behind her, carrying her drink, while Marie-Patrice led the way, holding the door open for them when she reached the dining room. Jane gaped. The table could comfortably have seated twenty, but only two places were set, down at the far end, at ninety degrees to one another. The conversation position, she remembered Michelle explaining it, as opposed to the more confrontational aspect of sitting face to face.

The ceiling hung sufficiently high above for her to imagine clouds obscuring the elaborate cornicing on a rainy day. Around her the walls towered to meet it, replete with coverings that looked luxuriant and expensive enough for Derry Irvine to have blanched at spending other people's money on. Jane found herself concentrating on the two carved chairs and the place settings, trying to zone out their wider surroundings, as they were giving her something she imagined was akin to stage fright. She would come in here again, alone, in the morning and have a look around, then she could merge the decor details into her memory of the meal.

Bett poured them each a glass of wine and some water from a pitcher as Marie-Patrice brought their starter. It was, she explained, brik: a deep-fried egg in the lightest filo pastry, stuffed with spinach, and accompanied by some tiny merguez sausages.

The churning sensation in Jane's stomach, which she had assumed to be trepidation, revealed itself to be hunger as soon as she got a noseful of the aroma. A sense of etiquette restrained her from just scarfing the lot in between exquisite mouthfuls of velvety wine, while discussion of the dish's constituent ingredients and their coalescent deliciousness further eased the pace.

It was followed by a spicy and aromatic lamb tagine served with couscous: rough chunks of meat and root vegetables bobbing in a large casserole from which Marie-Patrice ladled the portions, steaming, to their plates.

'This is Marie-Patrice's speciality,' Bett informed Jane almost conspiratorially once the cook had left the room. 'Family recipe. Her mother is from Tunisia. Do you like it?'

'It's wonderful,' Jane enthused.

'Isn't it. Though I have to confess it wasn't my first choice for the menu. I had planned something a little more . . . a *lot* more elaborate, but I was advised by young Ms Richardson that it might seem somewhat grandiose.'

'I'd still have eaten it, I'm sure.'

'How's the wine?'

Jane swallowed the sip she'd been savouring.

'Habit forming.'

'She was right about that, too.'

'Handy girl to have around, in any number of ways.'

'Indispensable, is the word I'd use.'

'And for her to end up in your service,' Jane remarked. 'More serendipity, would you say?'

'Only if we discount the notion, which I don't, that you make your own luck. But of all the luck I've made, finding Alexis has been among the best of it.'

'And did all of your company arrive by such, what was your word, *crepuscular* routes?'

'She told you how she came to be here?'

'Yes.'

'That's quite a confidence so soon. Bodes well for your ability to elicit more vital information.'

'Well, this one didn't require any subterfuge. I've developed the impression there's a lot of people around here missing their mother.'

Bett nodded sagely, staring into his plate.

'Somboon's the only one who's still a little shy of me, but he's getting there.'

'Somboon's naturally shy of everyone, at first,' Bett said. 'If he starts wittering away, it's not necessarily because he's decided he's comfortable with you; it's usually just a more nervous manifestation of his shyness.'

'I noticed. He'll get past that too.'

'Perhaps. But the last thing he's going to talk to you about is how he got here.'

'Did you come to his rescue, too?'

'Only in as much as I saved him from himself.'

'How?'

'I'm not sure he'd want me to tell you. They're all a little skittish when it comes to . . . certain matters. I'm never quite sure who knows what or how much about whom, and it's kind of an unwritten rule not to ask.'

'Okay, that covers why he might be reluctant to tell me. It doesn't stop *you* telling me.'

'No, it doesn't,' he agreed. 'But it's also my choice not to.'

'Hmm,' Jane said, sensing a weakness. 'You know, in the UK

289

these days, your decision to remain silent can be used against you in court. Thanks to those crazy liberals in New Labour.'

'What are you getting at?' Bett asked, slightly suspicious.

'It means you're giving up your right to prevent me drawing my own conclusions.'

'And why should I care what those conclusions might be when I know the truth?'

'Because you do care. You care about them. You're not as impervious as you like to make out. I've seen you. You're protective of them, you're *proud* of them, and you care what I think of them. You chewed my arse off the other day for selling them short.'

He smiled rather shyly. Found out.

'Can I trust you?' he asked. 'Can they?'

'Other than that you're teaching me to be devious and deceptive, I think you can.'

'I think I can too.' He took a swallow of wine and washed down a last forkful of couscous.

'Somboon is an orphan,' he said. 'But don't tune up the violin just yet. He's from a moderately wealthy background and the sob part of his story only began four years back. His parents were murdered in a bomb attack while on business in Indonesia. Islamic fundamentalists.'

'They were targeted specifically, or just . . .'

'As much as those fascist psychopaths specifically target anyone. They were part of a trade delegation at a tourism conference. It was attacked because of pandering to the West, encouraging immorality, something vague and ill-defined like that. You know how well thought-out their ideological motives tend to be: pick an insane bigotry and run with it.'

'And Somboon?'

'Somboon was home in Bangkok. A bright kid, as you know. Resourceful, inventive, intelligent, and now very lost and very, very angry. To cut an extremely long story short, he began dedicating himself to vengeance. He was planning to become a one-man, or one-boy, counter-terrorism assassination unit. I couldn't tell you exactly what he was planning, but the least worst scenario would have been him ending up only killing himself.'

'So how did he come to your attention?'

'Another very long story. But the punchline is I was in Bangkok and caught him trying to steal a potentially catastrophic quantity of plastic explosive. I offered him an alternative path, a way of channelling his anger.'

'Alternative just to vengeance, or would I be right in guessing an alternative to jail?'

Bett gave a thin and knowing smile.

'It's good intelligence practice to recognise the recurrence of a pattern,' he conceded.

'You offered alternative paths to Nuno, Rebekah and Armand too, then?'

'Not Armand. He's an old friend, we go back a long time. When I planned to set up this enterprise, he was the first person I called.'

'Nuno?'

'A promising, ambitious and idealistic young police officer. Too promising, too idealistic and way too ambitious for his own good, as it turned out. He made enemies of some powerful senior officers, went sniffing around too close to their slush funds. They were setting him up to take the fall for a police corruption scandal. He'd have ended up in jail and then been looking at an exciting career as a security guard if he hadn't been brought to my attention.'

'By whom?'

'Contacts.'

'Okay. What about Rebekah? My instincts suggest a military background, and, given her particular talents, I'd guess the US Air Force. How the hell did *she* come to your attention?'

'That's a little more sensitive,' he said, his voice lowering though only they and Marie-Patrice were left in the building, and even she had to be at least fifty yards away. 'Rebekah was actually in the US Navy.'

Jane smiled sadly to herself at the mention of it, as it made her think of Ross, who could not hear the US Navy discussed without pointing out that it was founded by a Scot.

'It's little-reported enough in the US,' Bett went on, 'and therefore barely at all overseas, but the US Air Force has had some serious problems with regard to the training of its female recruits. Still too much of a macho culture among the fly boys who reckon just because women have been allowed in doesn't mean they have to make it easy for them. This has taken all the petty forms you might imagine, but also far less petty forms too.'

'Are we talking about . . .'

Bett nodded solemnly. 'At times, near systematic sexual abuse, using seniority and the chain of command to keep the victims silent. But the real scandal of it has been that the ones who spoke up and said *J'accuse* have ended up being punished or even discharged. It's been covered up on a disgusting scale, but there's been a snowball effect among victims in recent years: the more who speak out, the more who come forward.

'The same problems were believed to be less manifest among the navy pilots, but Rebekah's experience suggests it's merely that the story has yet to be told. It also illustrates how far they're prepared to go to ensure that it won't be.'

'What happened? I mean, spare me the details for the sake of the girl's dignity. Just the end result.'

'Rebekah was being "groomed" by a senior officer. He had got her to do certain things, sexually, but not . . . Anyway, he demanded she meet him after curfew one night, at a location on the base where she had no authorisation to be. She knew the set-up, guessed what was coming. This was how the bastards shielded themselves: the victim can't say where she was because she wasn't supposed to be there. Either she's lying or she's in serious breach of base discipline. The location was high-security, a maintenance hangar. He had clearance, she didn't.'

Bett took a long, slow sip of wine and sighed.

'He had a side arm in case the weight of all his other means of coercion wasn't enough. He underestimated Rebekah, though. She's a strong girl, in lots of ways. There was a struggle. He lost.

'So there she is, standing over a dead senior officer in a hangar in the middle of a US Atlantic Naval base, thinking what the hell do I do now? Nobody's going to believe her about what happened; too many senior figures can't afford her to be believed. Her career is over and she could be looking at decades in jail. There is, however, a fully-fuelled Harrier jump jet sitting about twenty feet away.'

'She stole it?'

'Flew right out of there and headed east. Those things have a flight range of about twenty-five hundred nautical miles. She came coasting in on fumes and landed in Brittany.'

'Where you became aware of her through "contacts".'

'Quite.'

'What did the US Navy do about it?'

'Their principal concern was keeping the whole thing under wraps, but they were also understandably put out at misplacing several million dollars' worth of aeroplane.'

'What happened to it?'

'I brokered a deal, through diplomatic backchannels, to return it to them. So you can officially call me an arms dealer, to add to my other crimes and shames.'

'How much?'

'Money did change hands, but the greater part of my price was an assurance that they forget about Rebekah. I sold myself short – I should have anticipated they'd be only too happy to. Got themselves a bargain. She disappears and so does their embarrassing tale. So their nasty little secret can stay under wraps a little longer.'

'But you used their plane as a bargaining chip to save her. That was ... pretty selfless.'

'Don't let's colour me too altruistic. I cleared a few euros from it, more than enough to buy that helicopter.'

'Complete with fully trained pilot.'

'Yes, and a good deal more besides. I didn't take her on because I reckoned I could use a flyer. I took her on because she had what it takes, what I need. When it came down to the moment, face to face with the enemy, when she was looking him in the eye, she pulled the trigger, and that's a lot harder than you might think.'

'No, I think it would be extremely hard. But not as hard as facing up to what would follow.'

'Sometimes you can't afford to think about that. Especially when you know your enemy won't.'

'True, but that still doesn't make it easier to live with yourself afterwards.'

'It makes it easier to live than if you're the one getting shot,' he retorted impatiently.

'But it's not always you or them, kill or die, is it?' she asked.

Bett narrowed his eyes, his posture stiffening.

'You and Alexis really have been talking, haven't you?' he said tersely.

'She's just a kid,' Jane protested. 'Not everybody's cut out for this stuff. Not everybody's *got what it takes* to kill people.'

'Some have it, some learn it,' he said. Jane thought she detected a hint of sorrow in his tone, but maybe she was giving him too much credit for anything north of glib.

'Don't you think nineteen's a bit young to learn? And don't you think it should be a choice?'

'Nobody has a choice about when they discover the world's harsher realities, Mrs Fleming,' he fired back with a barely suppressed anger. 'And Alexis discovered them a lot older than . . .' he sighed, swallowing something, shaking his head, labouring to calm himself. 'A lot older than some,' he finished quietly, this time with real sorrow in his voice.

Jane looked at him, kept her eyes trained so that he knew he couldn't hide from her gaze no matter how long he stared at his empty plate.

'What happened to you?' she asked softly.

He said nothing, but regained that iron countenance. The shutters were up.

'We've talked all evening about where everyone else came from, but what about you? How did you get here?'

'Military Intelligence.'

'Which country's?'

'More than one.'

'Where are you from?'

'Lots of different places.'

Jane nodded. It was going to be like this, was it? Good practice, perhaps. Get anything out of him and tapping the weapons hawkers would be a doddle.

'Originally. Childhood.'

'A small town. Just an ordinary small town. The name is on the front gate.'

'Rla an Tir?' Jane asked. He smiled at her pronunciation. 'Where is it?'

'By a river.'

Jane sighed, loudly communicating her exasperation, though she knew it signalled acceptance of defeat.

'What is it you're afraid of?'

'In my experience, the more people know about you, the more ways they can find to hurt you. I've made a lot of enemies.'

'And so that means you can't afford to make any friends? Nobody gets in, do they? Into your sanctuary. I don't even know your first *name*.'

Neither she nor Bett spoke for a few moments, both of them simultaneously reaching for their glasses, as though otherwise occupying their mouths would excuse or disguise the absence of conversation. Jane's silence was a stubborn one as she was feeling there was nothing left she could say and that the ball was in his court anyway. Bett's seemed more reflective, as though she had at least given him something to think about.

Covering the gap, but accentuating the awkwardness, Marie-Patrice returned at this point to take away their plates. They thanked her heartily, but were once again left with their impasse after she had departed to fetch dessert. They sat for a few more wordless moments and then Bett finally spoke.

'It's Hilary,' he said.

'What?'

'My first name. It's Hilary. And if you tell anybody, I'll have no choice but to kill you.'

A tale of a tub

Another few days of this and Ross would have to start checking himself for barnacles. The longest he'd ever spent on a boat before had been about an hour on the pond at Rouken Glen with his mates, and the longest he'd spent on a boat with his dad had been half that, on a pedalo in Lanzarote when he was about eleven and their relationship was, to put it politely, less problematic. He wasn't sure how much more he could take. The only upside was that it made his need to escape all the more imperative, if that was at all possible. So far, escape itself most definitely wasn't.

It was what, six days now? Five? Seven? He was starting to lose track. Certainly enough time for his dad to have muttered, 'Water, water everywhere but not a drop to drink,' at least a couple of thousand times. He probably wasn't even aware he was saying it, or at least not aware that he had said it again and again and again and again just about every time there was a lull in conversation long enough to have a look over the gunwales or through a window.

Not that Ross didn't have his own unconscious verbal tick, right enough. He couldn't remember when it had started, but he was aware that he was constantly singing snatches of *Friggin' in the Riggin'*, and this awareness was not proving the first stage towards cessation. All the bloody time, in his head, under his breath; whenever he wasn't talking or following a sufficiently engaging train of thought, there it was.

Give it some bollocks! Indeed.

It was a big yacht, its size and opulence a constant reminder of the stakes being played for and the resources at the enemy's disposal. It had to be at least a hundred feet long, and maybe thirty tall from the flybridge to the waterline. Price, he knew too little to gauge; two million, five, ten? However, the longer Ross spent on it, the smaller it got. It may have dwarfed the vessel

297

they were ferried to it aboard, but it was still a confined space, a limited environment hemmed in by – thank you, Dad – water, water everywhere. Ross walked the decks constantly, round in circles and figures of eight, each fixture, each polished rail, the tesselation of the wooden floor becoming more familiar, the spaces between them shorter. He climbed the stairs between decks to give his routes the variation of a third dimension: some-times taking in the saloon bridge on his way to the main helm, other times the galley, until he had surely exhausted every con-figuration. For some reason, he often felt compelled to keep moving, perhaps because most of the time the boat wasn't.

There was no actual rigging and, unlike in the song, there was far from fuck-all else to do. There was the big plasma screen and a wide selection of DVDs, plus the satellite telly option, the free drink and a passable library, the owner's tastes – or at least the tastes he wished to project – tending towards the classics. The boat was built and equipped for pleasure and for hospi-tality, not as some modern-day prison hulk. However, the plea-sure and hospitality properties were nonetheless being deployed to make its prison hulk role more securely effective. Idle hands, and all that. Captives with, ahem, truly fuck-all else to do would more diligently turn their minds and energies towards escape.

That was why Ross preferred to walk the decks. That and to get away from his dad, who was steadily doing his head in with his apologetic sincerity and ceaseless underlining that 'at least we're getting to spend some time together' – even if it seemed Dad would gladly spend most of it stretched out in the saloon bridge watching Sky Sports, like he'd never left home.

He had been a good dad when Ross was a wee boy: atten-tive, calm, playful, dutiful, reassuring, all the things wee boys need their dads to be. He wasn't one of those fathers whose kids might sketch a picture of a newspaper with feet sticking out if they were asked to draw a portrait of him. He always had time for Ross and Michelle, time and patience. It was only on Sundays that there was ever tension.

Sunday. Mass day. He and Michelle never wanted to go. Kids, huh? Who can figure their funny little minds, that they'd not want to go along to a laugh-riot like that of a weekend morning? It was always a struggle, always a fight, huffs, anger, shouting, tears, threats, sighing and tension, tension, tension. Not just between Dad and the kids, either, but between him and Mum too. Ross didn't understand it at the time, just thought that Dad was in a bad mood with everyone, but looking back it was easy to see where the pressure was coming from. It was the one time in the week when she wasn't being the dutiful wife he needed. Oh, sure, she'd play her part in the chivvying along, the dressing of reluctant weans, promises of a big fry-up awaiting when they got home, the physical bundling into the car, but then she would be heading back through the front door. After that, he was on his own, dragging the weans into the chapel where he'd be conspicuous as the only father there unaccompanied by his living wife, because she was, you know, one of *them*.

None of them knew it at the time, but those aggro-ridden Sundays were merely the early marker-buoys denoting the collision course they were rigidly set upon, when those kids, who he had brought up to be smart and enquiring, began supporting their reluctance by asking awkward questions. An early one Ross remembered was: If it's a Mortal Sin not to go to Mass, and a Mortal Sin means you'll go to Hell if you die without it being absolved at Confession, then doesn't that mean Mummy will go to Hell, as she's never been to Mass *or* Confession?

The answer, if it could be called that, was Ross's formal introduction to the Roman Catholic Church's theological goalpost-mobilisation technique, a system of pseudo-logic and undefined terms that prevented any argument taking a foothold in anything so base or vulgar as fact, reason or consistency. For Ross, scientifically evidence-minded from a precociously early age, this was never good enough, always resulting in a tenacious pursuit of the issue that ended, familiarly, with his dad losing the place, outraged and offended by his son's temerity in questioning these matters *at all*. That truly was the thing Ross couldn't relate to, and the reason Dad couldn't relate to Ross: he was so unquestioningly accepting of the way things were. He *liked* sitting in his armchair, flipping channels. He *liked* having the same boring stuff for dinner all the time. He *liked* routine. He *liked* order and paradigms.

Dad was a boring old fart, and Ross had just been too small to notice at the time that Dad had been a boring young fart, too.

'If it ain't broke, don't fix it.' 'I know what I like and I like what I know.' Two of his most-used phrases.

Water, water all around . . .

There were also eyes all around. Ross was being watched, not invasively, but constantly. He and Dad had freedom to roam the decks, but he seldom found himself in a spot where at least one guard didn't have line-of-sight. They stood off, almost respectfully, keeping their distance and not attempting to be ostensibly intimidating, but their presence was for all that even harder to miss. The only place where nobody was looking at him was in his cabin, which made him think that it might actually be the place where he was being monitored closest. He hadn't found a camera yet, but he feared trouble if he was caught looking too hard, and there were plenty of places – ventilation grates, built-in speaker panels, mirrors, smoke alarm/sprinkler units – where such a device might be concealed. There could be audio bugs too, though Ross had his doubts about that. For one, he hadn't noticed any of the guards looking soul-crushingly bored, as would surely single out the poor bastard whose job it was to monitor the less-than-riveting content of his and Dad's conversations. For another, nobody had come looking for the lip-balm tube he'd given Dad on the night they did talk about something worth listening to.

As well as being unobtrusive, the guards were also coolly polite, in varying competencies of English. This had further encouraged his dad's slide into slothful embrace of their situation's silver lining – we're sailing for hell, but we're sailing there first class – but to Ross it was the opposite of reassuring. Simmering menace and casual brutality would have marked them out as mere thugs and hard-cases, whereas these guys were controlled, utterly disciplined professionals. They wouldn't be easily manipulated, panicked or misled. They couldn't be played off against each other or tempted into self-seeking errors of judgement. And cool as their politeness might be, their execution of harsher commands would be far colder.

Their boss was seldom to be seen, and definitely not to be approached. On the rare occasions Ross had spotted him on one of the outer decks or other more public areas, there was always a guard blocking the path, saying nothing but making it plain that visitors would not be made welcome. Consequently, the bloke hadn't said a word to him since their first meeting, which Ross had found odd, not because he imagined himself a fascinating conversationalist, but because he assumed the guy would want to pick his brains about the project. He also, Ross would have to confess, expected him to lord it over his captives a little, maybe engage in a bit of Bond-villain moral-philosophical discourse. But no. To this arrogant motherfucker, Ross was just cargo, a commodity to be bought and sold. He'd no sooner pop by for a blether than talk to a crate of munitions down in the hold.

This business was full of people just like that. They might talk about defence, they might posture about developing technology, but they were just about the money. Even doddery old Willis, for all his solicitous attempts to appear interested, struggling manfully to at least look like he was following Ross's explanations, didn't really care. None of them did: not about how it worked, not about what would be done with it, not about the people who'd be killed by it, not about the wars that would be fought with it. Just the money. It wasn't the arms trade, it wasn't the arms industry. It was the arms *business*, and don't ever forget it. A business where blood was money, and to buy a boat like this from it meant enough had been spilled to float the fucking thing.

Ross climbed to the fly-bridge and had a look around. That he was allowed up there was advance notice that there'd be nothing to see, as it was off-limits at times when they were in sight of land. The boat had put in somewhere that morning, or close to: they had halted outside a harbour and someone had gone ashore in the speed launch that was usually cradled above the lower transom-deck platform – always, always, *seriously* off-limits – at the stern, next to the jet skis and an outboard-fitted dinghy. By process of elimination, he deduced that it had been the boss and two guards. Ross's picture had been taken on a digital camera before they left, of him holding a print-out from the online edition of *Le Monde* to verify the date. Proof of life, they called it. Proof also that time was running out. He and Dad had been ordered to their cabins for the duration, only allowed above decks once they were well on their way out to sea again.

He'd seen land for the first time in days through his cabin's small window, but had no idea where they were. Just some Mediterranean port: leisure rather than industrial; lots of jetties, rows of yachts.

Right now, however, there was nothing to see. Just water, water . . . The most effective component of his imprisonment encircled him as far as his eyes could see. To the stern he could just make out the edge of the lower transom deck, a good thirty feet below where he stood. The cradle was empty, the speed launch not having returned from where they had put in, leaving the jet skis and the dinghy. That platform was the heart of all temptation, and there was no one aboard who didn't know it, which was why there was no way of accessing it. The doors leading to it from either side were kept locked, and in all the miles of circuits Ross had clocked, he failed to notice any indication of where or on whose person the keys were kept. The only other means of approach was via a twenty-foot drop from the rear of the helm-bridge two decks above, which could not be accessed without a guard being in full view. In fact, Ross found it hard to even look at the platform without his interest being noted. But something on this tub had to represent hope, otherwise he might as well join his dad on the saloon bridge, watching Clint Eastwood westerns and Spanish football re-runs.

Before all this had engulfed them, Ross had been concerned, as perhaps most men were, that he didn't really know his dad, had never sounded his depths, looked for the finer explanations beneath the obvious. The most disappointing thing about this enforced solidarity and its ample opportunity for cross-generational soul-searching was that it had taught him he knew his dad just fine. What you saw really was what you got. The only thing he had actually learned from his father's well-intentioned candour was that the person Ross really didn't know was his mum, and with each conversation it had become patently clearer that Dad didn't know her very well either.

The constant repetition in his head of *Friggin' in the Riggin'* had reminded him of an aspect of her he'd often wanted to know more about, but had seldom been encouraged to ask. His mum had seen the bloody Sex Pistols. She'd been a punk, in there when the real thing happened, first wave, not *new* wave, the Jubilee, safety pins, bin liners and England's dreaming. And Ross knew almost nothing about it, mainly because it wasn't something she ever seemed comfortable discussing. He'd never understood: surely having been in the midst of an era as exciting as that would provide a pool of nostalgia you'd never get fed up wallowing in. But most times it was brought up, she got coy, evasive, bashful, as though they were discussing something that made her very self-conscious, like an early career as a topless model. There were also times when she simply shook her head and seemed intolerant of the intrusion. When Ross got a little more mature, he began to suspect that perhaps something bad had happened to her during that period. Then, with a little more insight, he realised that something bad did happen – *he* came into being.

Given this unprecedented access to his dad's memories, the punk days were one of the first things he asked about, figuring if they'd met back then, he must have been ringside for some of it too.

'Didn't mean much to me,' Dad said. 'It was just the music of the time. I liked some of it, but you like whatever's playing when you're that age, don't you? Not really my scene. Folk made out that it was like some kind of cultural revolution, but half the folk . . . no, three-quarters of the folk, were at those gigs and those clubs because it was Saturday night and that's what was on. There wasnae even that many of them dressed up like you see in the photos. It's all exaggerated.'

'But Mum dressed up, I'm sure I heard.'

'Oh, aye.'

'What did she look like?'

'Nothing she'd be proud to recall, I'm sure. But I could see beneath the eye make-up and the dyed hair and the scruffy gear that there was a decent, normal, sensible girl in there.'

Decent, normal, sensible, Ross thought. What girl doesn't dream of a man who'll one day call her all those things?

'Ach, to be honest, her falling pregnant was the saving of her, son. It was a dodgy crowd she was in with, some right ne'er-dowells.'

'Falling pregnant?' Ross asked blankly, feigning ignorance. 'What are you telling me?'

His dad looked both confused and uncomfortable, it being the first time he had actually acknowledged to Ross that he'd been conceived 'out of wedlock'. It was a little cruel, but he couldn't resist, payback for years of pointless sham and denial, including Mum and Dad having an 'official' wedding anniversary on which the rabidly Catholic Granny Fleming came round and made show of presenting a card, months ahead of the real one that they celebrated just between themselves with a meal out and the kids packed off to Gran Bell's for the night.

It never occurred to him growing up, just how young Mum must have been, because kids accept their parents as they find them, with no notion of what other age they ought to be. Other boys at school, especially Secondary, used to bait him by saying they wanted to shag her, and though he was faintly aware she was younger than a lot of the other mums, she never seemed very young to him. Young was cool, young was trendy, young was carefree. Mum was just Mum, and he couldn't see her in fishnets and an Anarchy T-shirt any more than he could imagine her having sex.

There were too many assumptions he'd made, questions he'd never asked, and not just about her past. Even latterly, with her abortive return to education, her voluntary work at the Asylum place, her stint driving a taxi. What had she been looking for? Where the hell had she disappeared to after saving Rachel from the kidnapper? Who was this mysterious woman with her projects, plans and ambitions? And how many of these hidden parts had been passed on to him?

He and Michelle had grown up with the notion that Dad was the brains of the household, and thus the source of their own academic prowess. He was out doing his surveying, all briefcase and paperwork, while she was home cooking the tea and ironing shirts. In scientific terms, this conclusion had been arrived at superficially and without sufficient data, and subsequent, more extensive evidence superseded its findings. If it was the essence of Ross to explore, to question, to challenge and, most crucially, to create, then that sure as fuck hadn't come from Tepid Tom. As neither was its source merely a decent, normal, sensible girl, then he really wanted to meet the female he *had* got it from.

To do that, however, he needed to get the pair of them off this fucking boat. He took a seat on the fly-bridge, in front of the secondary helm and its auxiliary control desk. A guard, Stefan, took note with a glance. All of the controls could be overridden at the main helm below; the glance was a warning, just in case Ross didn't know that. He placed a hand on the tiller and looked at the polished wood fascia, housing a speedometer, compass, echo sounder, radar, GPS monitor, tachometers, oil-pressure gauges, battery indicators and even a sea-temperature read-out. The engines were off. The echo sounder and the radar showed that the boat was drifting gently. They were too far out to drop anchor, but neither did they have anywhere to go. They were just waiting for the boss to conclude his business ashore, waiting at sea because doing so securely contained his prisoners and prevented any interested parties snapping up the merchandise at a bargain rate. Ross looked down at the waves, listened to them lapping the hull, the only sound audible out here other than the faint mumble of Spanish football commentary. Then he looked to stern and realised that there was in fact one other way of reaching the transom deck.

I, spy

Jane allowed herself a lingering look in the full-length mirror. She felt the need to familiarise herself with what she saw, and to confirm that those were her own eyes staring back at her. This mirror didn't have that Residual Image Sustainment function like the one at home: it was next generation. It didn't show the woman she'd been even as recently as last week. It showed another woman she could have been; another woman who, today at least, she was *going* to be. Her wedding and engagement rings lay across the room on the dressing table, accoutrements of a life willingly shed.

It would be inaccurate to say she looked a million dollars, but, factoring in the materials, the expertise and the personnel involved in bringing it all together, she did look six figures, minimum. She had more new clothes, and not from another grab-and-run trip to the supermarket with Alexis. This time Bett had brought in specialist help: one 'dresser', one 'buyer', and, given that they were about forty minutes from the French Riviera, the clothes were not from some local corner boutique either. She had been scrutinised, measured, made to walk up and down, made to stretch and contort. Notes were made, mutterings issued. The buyer was dispatched, returning in a couple of hours. Then followed adjustments: pins, chalk, more walking, more stretching.

And all of this was being accommodated around the lengthy ministrations of two hairdressers also brought on-site: one stylist (male), one colourist (female). There was much muttering in French and the occasional referral to Bett, such discussion making Jane feel excluded to the point of superfluous all points south of her scalp. For some reason she had convinced herself they'd make her blonde, which, against her Scottish pallor, she feared would only make the dye-job conspicuous, and was considering whether and how to politely communicate such a reservation to sensitive artists, in particular wondering what the French was for 'peelly-wally'. However, as cloths and towels

307

were removed and her hair expertly dried, it was revealed to have been transformed to a chestnut shade that not only looked plausibly natural, but was a near pantone-match for the material of her meticulously bespoke trouser suit.

'I can't carry off sophisticated,' she'd warned Bett when he told her the remit.

'You've read too many airbrushed magazines,' he replied. 'As long as you're wearing enough money, you'll look sophisticated.'

'You've obviously never been out to lunch in Bothwell,' she opined.

Bett stared, slightly impatient, like she wasn't telling him anything he needed to know right then.

'I don't have time for false modesty or even for genuine self-consciousness,' he told her. 'It's a self-indulgence.'

'It's not a self-indulgence. It's a concern about whether I can carry this off. I've never been much of a glamour girl.'

'It's not who you are, or who you've been. This is an act, Mrs Fleming. A performance. Remember that if you ever feel like it's the clothes that are wearing you.'

And so here she was, in costume, taking a last moment in her dressing room to prepare. The hair stylist had returned this morning for some running maintenance after she'd slept on the new coiff, and after that, one last consultant had pitched up to supply and advise with regard to make-up. After a surprisingly sparse application of powder and paint, she had moved on to the accessories, which were each probably more expensive than any of the other components, tonsorial or sartorial, even the shoes.

There was a camera in her mobile phone. Sure, these days everybody had a camera in their mobile phone, but not like this; not full-motion video, infrared imaging and 8X magnification zoom. Her diamond earrings were also audio transmitter/receivers, the top bar of the tension settings that held the jewels in place slightly overlapping her lobes so that tiny speakers could project communications inaudible to anyone standing right next to her. Her pendant was a camera too, suspended on a chain of eighteen-carat gold, nestling in cleavage she'd never before dared wear a bra capable of creating, far less exposing. Her instinct now was to do up another button, but her orders and Somboon's rationale had been clear. It gave the camera maximum scope and protected it from unwanted scrutiny. If guys were looking down there, it wouldn't be the pendant their eyes were on, and it would also provide plausible cover should she seem concerned that they were staring.

Her style consultants had also fashioned her with a bag – or purse, given its petiteness – on a long shoulder strap, just enough room inside to accommodate a few essentials, such as lipstick, hankies, her exhibition accreditation and half a dozen minute bugs. It completed the outfit, but she had also donned one final, hidden accessory: a Walther PPK 380 pistol, secured by a holster around her left ankle.

Bett had presented it in a neat little box like it was a gift. Perhaps, in his universe, it was.

It was a neat, almost delicate little thing: only three and a half inches long, blue with black plastic grips on the side and a red dot sight at the delivery end of the barrel. It took eight rounds per clip, two spare magazines secured by a strap around her right calf.

'Walther PPK,' she observed as she accepted it. 'Now all I need is a casino to visit and a sports car to get me there.'

Bett said nothing, just twitched his brow knowingly.

Jane had assumed that spying must principally be about being inconspicuous, but as Bett explained, that didn't always involve melting into the background. There were many more effective ways to hide in plain sight.

'Being physically awkward and clumsy, for instance, while making your actions stand out, can paradoxically all but render you invisible. People write you off as no threat, and won't pay you any attention in case you come and bother them. And if you are bothering them, you can ask them anything if they think you're an idiot. You, however, will not be awkward or clumsy, and certainly won't be playing an idiot.'

Her mission therefore – initially, at least – was to be as visible as possible, to be seen and to be noticed. The clothes, however, were not enough. To enhance the impression of her status, she was to be accompanied by Nuno, ostensibly as her bodyguard. This, she happily extrapolated, meant they'd be going in Nuno's Beamie Z4, over which she had cast a few longing glances whenever it sat outside on the gravel. Better

309

still, Bett had stated that she, and not Nuno, must do the driving.

'A real bodyguard doesn't double as a chauffeur or PA, or anything else. And a woman of your status would not let the hired help play with her cherished automobile. The privilege of owning such a machine is the privilege of driving it. The *exclusive* privilege of driving it.'

'A privilege I will relish,' she assured him, walking out of the front door and on to the steps, placing an in-character, near-proprietary hand on one of the stone sentinels as she passed. 'I've never driven a BMW before, never mind a convertible.'

She heard Bett tut behind her, and turned around to see him and Nuno share a look.

'Nuno's Z4?' Bett said. 'You won't be going in that heap of shit. You want to make an *impression*.'

Bett pressed a button on a remote control he produced from a trouser pocket. Jane looked to the side of the house, where the steel door on one of the outbuildings was ascending slowly, accompanied by a deep metallic grind and an electric keening. Sunlight streamed in through the widening gap, reflected back in glinting silver. It was like the doors of the mothership opening, an effect further enhanced by the vehicle within's resemblance to some form of spacecraft.

'Mrs Fleming, your carriage awaits.'

The door had opened fully now, but Jane still wasn't sure what she was looking at. Other than that it was open-topped and on four wheels, it still looked more like a starship than a car.

'What the hell is it?'

'A Lamborghini Diablo Roadster, Millennium edition. V-12 engine, light-alloy block, longitudinally mid-mounted. Dual overhead cam shafts, chain drive, four valves, intake variable valve timing, electronically controlled. Five hundred and thirty brake horsepower and a maximum speed of two hundred and ten miles per hour.'

Bett drove it from the garage, climbed out and handed her the keys.

'There were thirty produced,' he said, 'so, strictly speaking, it isn't *quite* irreplaceable, but I am rather fond of it, so do drive carefully.'

*   *   *

'I think he's insane, giving me this thing,' she said to Nuno as she edged it out of the main gates, checking each direction several times before even thinking about pulling out. She felt like she was on her driving test, or maybe her first lesson. 'I don't care how it fits in with my cover. It's got to be worth more than my house. Twice my house. Three times. I don't know.'

She eased it very delicately on to the main road, driving slower than had she been in her own ageing Civic. It felt even slower than the speedometer said, due to the awareness of colossal latent power, but she wasn't anywhere near ready to unleash it.

She drove a hundred yards or so at this tentative pace before Nuno calmly reminded her she ought to be on the right.

'See? It's got my head messed up. I drove fine on the right getting here, and in Barcelona.'

'It's got your head where Bett wants it,' Nuno said. 'And he's not insane.'

'He wants my head messed up?'

'No. But he'd rather you spent the journey to Cap Andreus worrying about denting his paintwork than worrying about what you'll be doing when you get there. And maybe he reckons that if you can learn to relax and enjoy this ride, you might relax and enjoy the next one.'

Jane thought back to a Lanarkshire living room, rain against the windows, school looming in the morning, lying with her elbows on the fading carpet, eyes riveted to the TV screen, transporting her somewhere else. The French Riviera, espionage and intrigue, posh togs and sleek gadgets, sports cars and casinos.

She smiled, gunned the engine just to hear it growl, then let the clutch out properly.

G-forces ensued.

'It had to be sunny, didn't it?' Lex rued, as Air Bett cut through clear blue skies, Cap Andreus hugging the coastline ahead, their target a distinct tower next to the 1920s and 1930s hotels and terraces.

'It's sunny, we're going to the seaside, and you're complaining?' Somboon replied. Lex gave him the finger, underlining the reason for her complaint by the digit, and indeed her entire fist, being obscured under the billowing sleeve of the red

311

nylon overalls she and Som were wearing. Underneath those they were fully kitted out in Hotel Reine d'Azur staff uniforms, comprising trousers, shirts and blazers. Armand was spared the outerwear, but was also kitted out in official hotel toggery, in his case as a security official.

'You'll be complaining too when your ass starts chewing your underwear,' she told him.

'You think heat bothers me? I'm from Bangkok.'

'And when was the last time you went tooling around Bangkok dressed like this? Actually, scratch that. I don't want to hear about your fetishes.'

Rebekah's voice interrupted, breaking over the intercom from the cockpit.

'ETA minus two minutes,' she informed them. 'A-fag everybody.'

'A-fag,' they all acknowledged, cutting the chat and getting ready for the drop. They'd been toiling several days on the groundwork for this, beginning with Lex hacking the hotel's system to find out who was booked to stay and, when available, what rooms they had been allocated. They had each been inside the hotel a few times already too, when they weren't required for training Bett's new kid-prodigy, as they had begun referring to her. So far, however, they had restricted their activities to public areas. There was nothing less conspicuous than leaning against a wall in a bar, for instance. But when Som leaned off those walls again, he left a brass light switch matching the real fittings. It didn't turn anything on or off, but it did contain a camera, transmitting a composite fish-eye image generated from four lenses housed where the screws would normally be.

However, they needed to hit the roof today, because this was work they couldn't carry out until the penthouse suites' exhibition occupants had taken up residency, which would only happen after their own security people swept their respective accommodations for bugs.

They had figured that the biggest players would take the biggest suites, and Lex's leeched booking information bore that out. Some of the major firms would be off-site, basing themselves at rented villas or harboured yachts for the duration of the exhibition, but there was little they could do about that; they had to settle for what was local, initially at least.

The good news was that the main lead they had at this stage, Ordinance Systems Europe, was taking a suite in the penthouse. Bett's exhaustive contacts had led him to identify the firm from merely the two names Lex had picked up in Scotland: Lucien and Parrier. OSE had a Pascal Parrier in senior management and their deputy head of security was named Lucien Dirlos, a former cop, reputedly as brutal as he was corrupt. He and OSE were a good match, it appeared. The company, which made short-range anti-tank and anti-aircraft missiles, as well as assault rifles and tripod-mounted field guns through a wholly owned subsidiary, had been at various times indicted for – or at least implicated in – just about every form of corporate intimidation and corruption there was a law against. Naturally, they had a bigger legal budget than most courts could muster against them, especially when OSE had sufficient politicos in their pockets to hamstring the prosecutions from above. They were, in that respect, 'just your typical arms firm,' according to Bett, who had therefore surmised that under a threat such as Fleming posed, they'd have few reservations about unleashing the jackals, even if that entailed child abduction and murder.

The stand-out question at the briefing was why OSE, more than anyone else, had such a hard-on for Fleming and his device. The most plausible explanation was simply that they knew earliest, and thus got saddled up quickest to do what they felt was needed. This thought had prompted a return of that tight, cold, this-is-it feeling in Lex's gut. Whoever knew about this first knew about it through her nameless conspirator, and thus through her. She thought of her meetings, the phone calls, talk of contacts and influence. For all she was aware, it could well have been this Lucien guy. She'd have to keep her eyes open real wide in case the pair of them ended up face to face in some hotel corridor.

With OSE already having gone to great and ruthless lengths to acquire Fleming, it was a shoe-in that they'd be in the forefront of the bidding when whoever had him made his position known. The plan was to spread their surveillance as wide as was practical, but initially the closest eye had to be kept on the OSE principals, to see who came a-hawking. Once they knew who was holding the geek, it would be a different game, the game Bett played best.

The Hotel Reine d'Azur was an Eighties-built high-rise in black, chrome and glass, abutted on three sides by two-storey extensions housing the exhibition and function halls. It was intended to look high-tech and ultra-modern in its time, thus rendering it swiftly dated when culture and architecture both inconveniently failed to stop in their tracks. According to Armand, it was a fitting, iconic landmark for Cap Andreus, a harbour resort forever in the shadow and in envy of its coastal neighbours such as Cannes, San Tropez and Monte Carlo. In its attempts to compete with their status and prestige in attracting the tourism and conference dollars, its burghers and investors had attempted to outdo its rivals in terms of opulence and ostentatious expenditure. The result was a sink of flash-trash vulgarity, a kind of Vegas-sur-la-Riviera, its ill-starred excesses crowned by this graceless, three-toed monolith. To Armand, it was no surprise that this so-called 'defence exhibition' was taking place in this town and in this building, as the more self-respecting resorts and hotels would have told them to fuck off. Up the coast, they didn't need the business any more than they needed the hassle that went along with it, such as having their premises predictably picketed by protesters, as was going on down at ground level right then.

The helicopter barely came to a halt on the landing pad, its wheels touching down for less than ten seconds, and not quite coming to a stop even then. Armand, Som and Lex bailed out, backpacks strapped to their fetching red overalls, and quickly scurried for cover as Rebekah lifted the chopper clear and away again.

Lex scanned the flat rooftop. There was no one around. Landings on the H-pad were supposed to be prearranged, so there was no official greeting party, and nor, she hoped, would there be an investigating party, given that any observers would only have seen their chopper cursorily buzz the building then whiz off again.

Armand went straight for the door leading to the main roof-access stairwell, for which he had a cloned swipe card, fruit of early reconnaissance work. He'd be riding the elevator all the way to the sub-basement, a destination only accessible by punching in the aforementioned plastic. His work lay with the hotel's internal telephone exchange, all lines of which were routed through a junction housed in the bowels of the building. Once he accessed it, he had two tasks. The first was to run relay taps on the voice lines serving the top-floor suites, the second to clone-phreak the data lines serving the same rooms. The first part he'd done a thousand times before. A few minutes with cable-strippers and miniature croc-clips, some cosmetic work with electrical tape and plastic sleeving, and it would be over, the resulting evidence indistinct from routine maintenance. The clone-phreaking was a bit trickier, involving the installation and concealment of some Som-spawned hardware. This particular box of goodies intercepted the traffic in both directions and duplicated it, restoring the original signal to its particular line, while sending the cloned data out on another. From there it got bounced around a few servers – so that the cloners couldn't be traced in the event that the hardware hack was discovered – and ultimately sent *chez* Bett, where Lex would analyse it later.

Meantime, she and Som were preparing to pursue a matter of conscience, protesting demonstrably about the evils of the arms trade and the amorality of the Reine d'Azur in playing host. Before that, however, they had to site two receiver/converters on the roof, attaching one to each of the hotel's twin mobile-phone masts. The devices were identical, duplicating each other's work in case of malfunction. They picked up the short-range transmissions of the many bugs and cameras they had secreted – and were about to secrete – around the premises, and converted the signals from analogue to digital before sending them to base across a raft of mid-band cellular connections.

That was priority number one. The task completed, they moved on to the reason for their ridiculously conspicuous garb.

There were no balconies on the building, just sheer faces of glass and steel, but there was a ring of aluminium balustrades around the penthouse level, which was inset from the rest of the building by about three feet. It was also fifty per cent taller than any of the lower storeys, with its ten-foot windows slanted at about fifteen degrees, an architectural conceit that was supposed to represent a crown atop the hotel.

Lex and Som stood close to the edge, near an emergency-access stair leading down to the narrow platform between window and balustrade, and began removing materials from their backpacks which they had laid down on the concrete. There were four suites, each with dual aspects, and they had a decoration for all of them. With Lex holding his legs in case he leaned out too far, Som reached down to the window below and attached the top end of a red paper banner to the glass, the remainder tightly rolled up on the roof. The banner was held in place by two black rubber suckers, each of which contained a video camera and transmitter, now pointing straight into the suite, with infrared capability for when the blinds were closed. They placed all eight before unfurling any, as the moment the first one was spotted, they were on injury time to complete the rest of their work: the old unseen clock that could stop any second. The banners displayed a selection of slogans copied from a website set up by the genuine protesters who were downstairs on the sidewalk. They would be torn down by hotel staff within minutes of being unveiled, hopefully with maximum haste and minimum care. They were fragile, designed to rip free easily in order to leave the cameras in place. No doubt a few of the suckers would come loose, hence the superabundance, but it was unlikely busy and harassed staff would go to the bother of removing these. Their orders would be principally to tear the banners down – some window cleaner or janitor could worry about the rest.

All eight banners attached, Som clambered hurriedly down the access stair on to the platform, clutching his backpack, while Lex stood with her foot on the first roll. Upon his signal, she kicked it loose. It uncoiled, buffeting slightly in the breeze, covering a four-foot width of penthouse window and dangling a further twenty feet over the side. On the platform, Som pressed home two more suckers at waist-height to further secure the banner to the window, then got busy – now hidden from any occupants – replacing a half-metre stretch of plastic bird-spikes at the foot of the balustrade with ones of his own. His were near-identical in appearance and would work just as well to prevent pigeons or seagulls from roosting, but were an improvement on the originals in that every alternate spike was in fact a supersensitive directional microphone pointed at a different angle into the suite.

Som worked fast. The longest part of the operation was the journey along the narrow platform to the site of the next banner,

Som understandably not hurtling flat-out and quite definitely not looking down. He was just completing the final stretch of spikes when they got word in their earpieces from Nuno, down in the lobby, to warn that there was much running and pointing going on among staff. Time to wrap it.

Som ascended to the roof again and they both stripped off the overalls. They stuffed them quickly into the backpacks, which they stowed out of sight between ventilation ducts before briskly heading below.

Three men in hotel security uniforms came bursting from one of the lifts as Lex and Som made it to the foot of the access stairwell. The new arrivals took in their uniforms and breathless, hurried faces and came to precisely the conclusion intended.

'*L'autre ascenseur, l'autre ascenseur*,' Lex shouted angrily at them, indicating the closed doors of the other lift. '*Allez, allez*,' she demanded. The three of them didn't stop to confer, just barged back into the lift and descended in hasty pursuit of their quarry. Lex and Som meanwhile waited calmly for the other elevator to return from the twelfth floor, where it had by this time stopped.

Lex got the okay from Armand in her earpiece and looked at her watch. It read 11:34. They were due to be complete by 11:35, which meant that any second now ...

She and Som shared a smile as her mobile began to ring. She pressed the talk button and Bett's voice was instantly audible to both of them in the confined seclusion of the lift.

'Status?' he asked, all small talk and solicitousness as usual.

'Status is we own the building,' she reported.

'Damn, you people are good,' Bett replied.

Som looked at the phone, like it might be malfunctioning.

'I don't say that enough,' Bett went on. 'I think it a lot, though.'

'Thank you, sir,' Lex said, trying not to giggle at Som's bewildered expression. Bett hung up.

'What's wrong with him?' he asked.

'I think you'll find the answer somewhere on the ground floor right now.'

Jane found herself glad of the intensive training she'd been put through, as much for the small things as the more major, such as not starting at the sounds of disembodied voices in her ears, and suppressing her instinct to reply whenever anyone could see her. She had simply walked the floor at first, around the lobbies, the stalls, the exhibition halls, to see and be seen, her 'bodyguard' a deliberately ostentatious adornment. She was supposed to look bored, tediously underwhelmed, which would have been difficult in her state of nervousness and excitement, but found disapproval a close and easy substitute as she perused the exhibits and displays. It was all extremely tacky; expensively so, but tacky nonetheless. The problem was the unresolved tension between the need to glamorise the products while maintaining the façade of a moral sobriety that could never, *I say never*, consider these *tragically necessary* devices glamorous. Thus there were several nubile models in business attire dotted around many of the stands, retained in a meet-and-greet capacity, handing out leaflets and catalogues, as opposed to draped over field guns, wearing bikinis, as the exhibitors would doubtless have ideally preferred. They all looked young and, as she had suggested it to Rebekah, *uncomplicated*. Great pick-up potential for Bett, she thought. Miaow.

And yet there had been as many gazes alighting on her as on the professional eye-candy, starting with her exit from the Diablo and the unseemly scrum of valets competing for the keys. It was slightly disconcerting, slightly flattering and slightly laughable. She was turning heads because people saw money and were fascinated by who owned it. Sure, she looked good in her professionally selected finery, but who wouldn't? She'd have been embarrassed by her own affectation if it wasn't for another thing Bett was right about (she was learning it was true what the girls said, that he was right irritatingly often): she was merely playing a part. She was enjoying it too, though she had to guard against the Brechtian technique of passing comment on the character through one's performance.

She had just about relaxed enough to start thinking this spying carry-on was a doddle when, at eleven thirty and thus right on schedule, Bett announced that the transceivers were in place. This meant he could now see what all of their hidden cameras were showing, including the view from her pendant. That was when the running commentary had really begun in earnest: brief CVs of the men she was standing near – names, companies, positions, history – and descriptions of the ones Bett wished her to gravitate towards.

Conversations were struck up, small talk, petty enquiries, all the while Bett informing her whether the speaker was worth persisting with or to be let down at the politest convenience. She spoke in a neutrally English accent, as clipped as she dared without it beginning to sound put-on. Then, after less than an hour, he gave the order she didn't realise she'd been dreading so much until it came.

Though she'd practised the moves until they felt second nature, it was the most nerve-racking moment of the day the first time she pinned a bug to someone. The lucky recipient was one Dieter Raulf, sixty-three-year-old vice chairman of German munitions firm Gieselcorp. He had taken a seat at an adjacent table in one of the hotel lounges as she waited for the waitress to return with her coffee. The lounge was busy, but not so busy that there weren't free tables further away. Raulf and his younger subordinate made their way past several of these, the older man affecting a distracted air as if to make out he had randomly chosen his table without even noticing who or what was nearby. And the reason she could be so certain he was affecting it was that Bett was giving her a running count of how many times the old letch's eyes had zeroed in on her cleavage throughout his approach.

He struck up a conversation. Mostly the usual – who was she with, what market was she in – but with a few unsolicited contributions from himself intended to convey how rich and important he was. She smiled but played it coy and reticent, as instructed. Then when she rose to go, he stood up also, extending a hand and a card. She took it with her right hand, the adhesive plastic wafer of a bug palmed in her left.

'I have to know, where did you buy your suit?' she asked, pretending to be suddenly taken by it. 'I love the material. Do you mind?'

He proudly told her the name of a tailor in Dortmund as she stroked the lapel, placing the bug high up, near the collar. Part of her was astonished that he didn't immediately rip it away and demand that she be apprehended, but as Bett assured her, 'you're doing fine'.

She placed six more throughout the day, mostly instances

following déjà-vu-inducing reprises of the same routine. Ageing execs, drawn as though hypnotically by her enchanted jewel, or rather the tits either side, so intent upon impressing their credentials upon her that she very soon knew more about them and who they worked for than Bett's homework could have revealed. She gave away little about herself, dropping only ambiguous replies intended to provoke further curiosity, and she asked very few questions.

She only had to use the 'nice suit' gambit once more. The place had heated up as the day wore on, jackets being hung on the backs of chairs in the lounges, bars and restaurants, so she was able to slip a few fingers under collars on the pretence of resting against them as she stood up to leave. It felt easier each time, as all crimes and deceptions do.

The last two she executed over dinner, having been 'rescued' from dining with her bodyguard by an invitation to join a table shared by delegates from British Defence Engineering and their counterparts at an Italian firm, CMK. Wine was flowing, and she let a glass be poured for her, but didn't touch it beyond one sip to smear the glass authentically with lipstick. Thus it looked in use but wasn't topped up. She stuck to mineral water and ate lightly, her appetite largely diminished by her adrenaline level, excusing herself before it was time for coffee. Her own instinct would have been to enquire after her share of the bill (at which point, she was sure, she really would have wanted a drink) but she didn't need Bett's prompting to know not to bother. Free to those who can afford it, as they say.

Bett congratulated her on a prodigious first day on the job, and advised that it was time for Nuno to escort her to the main entrance while a valet very carefully returned her car. She felt relief tinged with a slight disappointment as she walked back through the expansive and thoroughly over-opulent lobby. She'd got through the first test, but she would regret coming out of the role. Just as long as the Lamborghini didn't turn into a pumpkin.

However, before Nuno could approach the concierge's desk, Bett announced that there was a sudden change of plan.

'I've got a positive ID on Pascal Parrier,' his voice informed her. 'He just walked past our light-switch cam in the casino. There's a credit line of seven thousand euros in your name –

320

your op name – at the desk. Lift two grand in hundred-euro chips and go play.'

Jane walked in through the archway that formed the entrance to the casino from inside the hotel. There was another way in directly from the seafront avenue outside, the approach covered by a canopy. She noted the position of that door and two other exits, details she'd never have considered a week ago, but that were now a matter of routine, almost of reflex. She paused at the top of the short stair leading down four steps to the casino floor. It was a good spot for taking it all in, for Bett's benefit as well as her own. Her first impression was that it was small, far smaller than she had ever imagined lying out of shot in those old Bond movies. There were maybe only ten or a dozen green baize tables, themselves surprisingly tiny and neat. Even the roulette wheel and the dice table seemed like they were three-fifths scale, but as the hotel's decor was otherwise striving to make an aesthetic of excess, it was unlikely these weren't the real deal. Nonetheless, she felt like she was looking at a mock-up, a stage set, which was fine, because she was here to act.

She looked around, but not directly at anybody. Bett was doing that part for her, and didn't want even cursory eye contact between Jane and her mark until they were seated at the same table. Even then, she was to let him make the first move, let him notice her. If he didn't, she was to finish her game and walk. No chances were to be taken. He was the guy they most wanted a bug on, but he was also the last person they could afford to alert to their agenda.

Jane scanned the gathering. She recognised some of the women as the models from the exhibition area, perhaps still on duty as hired adornments for the execs they were with. There were no bored millionairesses in cocktail dresses at the tables, pissing away tens of thousands to while away a dull evening, mainly just men in suits, perhaps playing out as much of a fantasy as Jane was. But somewhere in the place there *was* a scheming millionaire with evil on his mind.

'Blackjack table,' Bett directed, to Jane's relief. Pontoon. She knew that one. 'Bet big. Play risky but not stupid. You don't care about the money but you like to beat the odds.'

She walked slowly among the tables, relaxed, like it was as familiar as the supermarket. Nuno hung back on the raised area in front of the arch, hands clasped in front, back straight. She was surprised to find the table empty, no Parrier, but took a seat anyway. The dealer, a skinny and awkwardly tall female, asked her something in French. Jane didn't reply, blanked her as though she was talking to someone else. She hated doing it, but it was the role, and her blank, ignorant indifference was definitely a near-Brechtian comment on the type of woman she was playing. Receiving no reply, the dealer tried again in English. Jane smiled patronisingly and the game began.

She played a few hands, soon forgetting what each of the blue plastic chips represented. She was ahead for a while, then got knocked back to half her starting pile by twisting on seventeen. Her only response was to take another sip of the G&T she'd ordered. As she did, she was aware of a figure crossing the short distance from the roulette table nearby and pulling up a chair alongside her.

'Payout,' whispered Bett. Parrier.

'Seventeen,' Parrier said. 'This must be the only place we're not wishing to see it again.' The voice was low and confident, lightly accented French.

Jane took a breath, preparing herself to look him in the eye, this man who wanted her son dead, who had unleashed hired killers upon her grandchildren. Ca' canny, she advised herself.

She forced a thin smile, one that was politely indulgent of the interjection but let him know he was still a long way off making a good impression. He was younger than the others, around mid-fifties, though maybe it was just that his better looks and air of cockiness made him appear so. He had the arrogance of a man who had not been told to fuck off anything like enough in his life, and yet something about his expression suggested he wasn't quite so sure of himself as he'd been a few seconds ago. She'd noticed it almost as soon as their eyes met, this tiny change in his features like he'd composed his best chat-up face, then hadn't quite seen what he was expecting when she turned around.

Conflicted as she was, she found it hard to believe he was truly ruffled by any suppressed contempt he'd detected in her coolness. This was something else.

322

She went back to her game, the croupier dealing him in this time. He threw down some chips and picked up his cards, but she could tell he was looking at her more closely than he was his hand.

'We've met before, haven't we?' he asked.

'Is that your best line?' she replied, not meeting his eyes, but her tone sufficiently playful as to suggest he was being invited to improve.

'It's not a line. We've met, but I can't place you. You have the advantage of me, Miss . . . ?'

Jane turned again slowly, sipping at her drink, buying time as her mind raced. It wasn't a line. He'd seen her photograph: he'd have seen photographs of her whole family, proof of how deep he was in, how much he knew of what was being done on his behalf. That was what had derailed his casual chat-up: when he got to see her properly, he realised he knew her face, though she'd wager he'd never place it in a million years. She wanted to crush him, wanted to spit in his face, but knew she had to mask her anger, *use* her hatred, channel it into the game, the better to leave him defeated in the end.

She smiled again.

'Bell,' she said. 'Jane Bell.'

'And I am . . . none the wiser.'

'That is because we *haven't* met before,' she informed him, her tone demure but enigmatic. 'We have seen each other, but not met. I've thus far been too careful to allow it . . . *Monsieur Parrier.*'

She returned her attention to the table, letting him chew on that one for a moment.

'Allow it?'

'Bad for my reputation to be consorting with someone of yours.'

Parrier took a beat to recompose himself, looked like he was sorting through faces for a safe one to wear. He opted for a knowingly bashful visage, brazenly aware he was fooling nobody.

'And what reputation do I have?'

Jane played her hand, found herself looking at seventeen again, the house holding nineteen, Parrier eighteen.

'You're a rogue, Monsieur Parrier,' she said, smiling but not looking at him. She didn't have to to tell he loved it.

He stuck, too intent on her to be bothered with the game. She transferred his attention to the table by putting down all her chips, by this point back to around two grand, and indicating she wanted another card.

The croupier turned over the top card. It came up four of diamonds. Jane's expression betrayed nothing.

'You like to live dangerously,' Parrier said approvingly.

'I like risk,' she replied. 'But not games of chance. I'd rather be betting on myself than on sheer fortune. Besides, the stakes here are too low to be genuinely exciting. Good evening, Monsieur,' she concluded, getting to her feet and walking away.

Parrier called after her. 'What about your winnings?'

Jane turned around and picked a single chip from the pile, lifting it with her right hand, the plastic wafer of a bug between two fingers. She placed the token in Parrier's outside breast pocket, pressing the bug into the interior lining.

'Buy yourself a drink,' she said. 'The croupier can have the rest as a tip.'

And with that, she did leave, the faint sound of Bett's applause pitter-pattering in her ears.

They had been on the autoroute only a few minutes when Nuno checked the right-side wing mirror for the umpteenth time and announced: 'We have a tail.'

'A tail? How exciting.'

'Call it a vote of confidence in your performance. Somebody's intrigued. Dispatched a drone to check you out, wants to know where you go after the lights go down.'

Jane looked in her rear-view.

'Where are they?'

'Three cars back. Toyota SUV.'

'Poor choice,' she said with a grin. Nuno laughed and checked his seat belt, knowing what was coming next.

'The car in front is a Lamborghini,' she said.

Further G-forces ensued.

The house looked all but deserted as Jane guided the Diablo carefully up the drive. Travelling slowly along the gravel felt like the final stretch of a rollercoaster ride, after the swoops and turns; still in the carriage, still moving, but you know the fun's over. It had been quite a ride, and she didn't just mean the motor. She let Nuno put it back in the garage, concerned she might clip a wing mirror on the doorframe, or super-calamity, prang it off of some other equally exquisite vehicle inside.

She walked on alone through the front door, all but the vestibule in darkness, no sounds echoing around the hallways. The place appeared sleepy and tranquil, but she knew it to be anything but. She made her way downstairs to the basement level, where the corridor lights were on. She turned right, opposite the entrance to the shooting range. Still there were no voices, but she could hear the clack-clack of a keyboard from the open door of Bett's operations centre.

Inside was like the control room of a TV studio. There were two banks of monitors, each arrayed in two rows of eight, hanging from the ceiling on black aluminium frames. The banks were angled slightly downwards and set at about a hundred and twenty degrees from each other, presenting two aspects to the long central desk at which Bett, Armand and Rebekah sat, each wearing headphones. The desk itself was flanked by multi-tiered electronic fascias, signal lights and LEDs blinking and flickering, and between these towers sat a control deck that wouldn't have looked out of place at Cape Canaveral. In front of each seat was a keyboard, mouse and flat-screen monitor, presenting a user interface considerably less intimidating than the prospect of messing about with the NASA knock-off in the middle.

The monitors showed a plethora of images from inside the Reine d'Azur, frequently changing as Bett, Armand or Rebekah switched to a different view. Some showed only orange-yellow blobs, infrared traces recognisable as human only when they walked across the screen. One of the penthouses didn't have its blinds drawn, affording a nightscape view to the CMK chief as he lay back on a sofa and enjoyed a blow job. His obliviousness of being watched was reassuring, but Jane felt bad for the girl, and thus it served as a reminder of the intrusive nature of what they were about.

Separate from the main desk, Alexis sat at a smaller console, five computer monitors arced around her field of vision, her fingers playing busily back and forth across three different keyboards. Jane saw screeds and screeds of code scrolling up the central screen, occasionally slowed down by a movement of Alexis's hand on a mouse, after which a click or a key press would cause an email or text document to appear on one of the peripheral monitors.

Jane stood in the doorway a moment, not wanting to interrupt. No one seemed to notice her, she thought, but after a few seconds Bett beckoned her inside without taking his eyes off the monitors. She approached the empty chair next to him and sat down, looking up at what was holding his attention. She could just make out one of the execs she'd bugged, sitting at a bureau in his suite, talking on the phone. He hung up, at which point Bett took off his cans and finally turned around.

'Hi,' he said, his voice little above a whisper.

'Where's Som?' she asked, for the sake of something to say, feeling a little self-conscious for the first time that day.

'Grabbing some kip. He'll be doing the late session, when most of our subjects are asleep. Good job, by the way,' he added. 'You put in quite a shift.'

'Thanks. So what next?'

'Next? This. We look, we listen.'

'I'm not going back?' she asked, trying to keep the disappointment from her voice.

Bett shook his head.

'But didn't you say the best source of intelligence is just getting people to talk? I'm sure I could get more out of those people.'

'It's a risk/benefit issue. You did well today, played it smart, sat back and let the subjects make all the moves. But your cover story won't hold up under deep scrutiny. You get too close, and they'll start to get suspicious very quickly.'

It wasn't what she wanted to hear, but she knew he was right. He was always bloody right.

'Can I do anything?' she asked.

Bett nodded towards a pair of headphones and then showed her how to alter the channels using the computer. An information panel appeared with each change, denoting whether the source was a bug, a directional mike or a phone-tap, as well as stating the name of the company or individual it had been applied to.

'That red bar flashes underneath the panel if someone else is already listening to the channel,' Bett informed her, before placing his cans back on and leaving her to it.

326

She toggled through a babble of voices, a Babel of languages. She eventually found someone speaking English, one side of a conversation, and deduced that it was the subject talking on a mobile. Mobile traffic was, Bett had explained, too prolific to tap, with no way of identifying worthwhile signals amid the hundreds emanating from just the hotel. More importantly, none of the people they were surveilling would be daft enough to say anything indiscreet over such an easily monitored medium.

She listened for a while, inconsequential business talk. Figures and jargon. Speculation about some board-level vacancy. Chat about football. She barely knew what to be listening for, only that she wasn't hearing it. So much noise, so much static. Low-bandwidth conversations, as she'd heard Alexis disparage such inconsequential discussion. What were they ever going to deduce from it?

Her expression must have betrayed her, because Bett leaned across and gently tugged the headphones away from her ears.

'You have to pan a lot of muddy water before you find any gold,' he said. 'You've had a long day. Get some sleep.'

She didn't argue.

Jane rose early and grabbed a croissant and a mug of coffee to take down to the basement. When she arrived, she found she was the last on the scene, though not the first to bring breakfast.

'Anything . . . come up?' she asked Bett nervously.

He nodded but didn't elaborate, merely wheeled his chair along to make space by way of inviting her to take her place. She pulled on her cans and got comfortable in the free seat.

Hours passed. The river flowed, fast and muddy. Dross threatened to engulf them, but surely and gradually, the gold did accumulate, often in precious little specks that came perilously close to being missed; and occasionally in jaw-dropping chunks.

By early afternoon, they knew of four bidders: Ordinance Systems Europe, British Defence Engineering, Gieselcorp and a Dutch/Belgian firm named Industries Arutech. There would be others, it was fair to assume. They knew the auction floor was set at fourteen million euros, and that two of the parties – Gieselcorp and Arutech – were prepared to go to at least twenty. The bidding would be conducted by video-conference at eleven o'clock

327

the day after next, with only the winner's connection retained after completion, meaning none of the losers would know who won.

They knew that the vendor would be arriving in Cap Andreus later today, with proof of what he held, and that bidders wishing to examine it would be picked up by car and taken, alone, to an unspecified location to do so. They knew also that the vendor would be accompanied by a formidable personal security staff and was taking various measures to prevent any attempts on the part of the bidders to discover where they might more directly acquire their target.

But crucially, they still didn't know the one thing they needed most: the name of who was selling. Nobody had referred to anything more specific than various languages' equivalents of 'the vendor', seemingly just as cagey about identifying him as they were about what they were bidding on, which was itself usually alluded to only in euphemistic terms.

'Do you think they don't know?' Alexis asked, voicing a fear Jane had been too scared of to enquire herself. 'Like, he's concealed who he is somehow?'

'No,' Bett said, much to her relief. 'He needs credibility to make the pitch. You can't just phone up and say, "Hey, you don't know me and I'm not telling you my name, but I've got Ross Fleming and I'm open to offers." They'd need to know they were dealing with someone of reputation before they took it seriously, and my guess is that his reputation is taken *very* seriously. Seriously enough that you don't go dropping his name all over the place because you never know who's listening and you don't want it common knowledge that you're doing business with him.'

'In which case we're wasting our time,' Jane argued. 'Ross's time.'

'Nobody's that discreet,' Alexis offered in an attempt at reassurance. 'Someone will let it slip eventually.'

'We don't have until eventually,' Bett said. 'We have less than a day, and after the auction we're into injury time. So . . .' He turned to Jane, who was, for once, ahead of him.

'So the risk-benefit ratio has changed,' she stated.

'The ratio, not the risk.'

Jane switched to her English accent.

'*I like risk*,' she reprised.

Oil and water

Ross feared that Dad might take some convincing, either of the viability of his plan or of the wisdom of pissing these people off, but, in retrospect, Ross was overestimating the comforts of the saloon bridge even for a seasoned couch-potato like him. Travelling to hell first class might have its perks, but that didn't mean he wanted to reach his destination. Ross told him what to do and he nodded eagerly, it uncharitably flashing through Ross's mind that being told what to do was pretty much always how Dad liked it. Besides, the plan entailed Ross doing the improvisational stuff, and even required Dad to sit on his arse and watch the telly for a while, thus harnessing what each was best at.

With no indication of how much or how little time they might have, they went for it that same night, after dinner, which Ross opted to have in his cabin so as to conceal how little of it he was eating. He flushed the rest, then made his way to the saloon bridge where his dad had, as ordered, cued up *Die Hard* on the DVD player. As ever they were helping themselves to drinks, Dad slowly sipping a bottle of San Miguel while Ross made more frequent trips to the bar, reaching each time for a bottle of vodka but pouring mineral water into his glass below the gantry, out of sight of Guillaume and Kurt, the two guards present. He became gradually more belligerent with each round, starting by mouthing derisory comments about his dad's choice of film, and working his slurred way up towards more bitter mutterings about Dad's role in bringing him to this station in life. This provided a reason for Dad repeatedly jacking up the volume on the plasma TV, and culminated in a stand-up argument in which he was roundly told he'd had his last drink and ought to go sleep it off. Dad even gave an appealing glance to Kurt, who stepped forward to escort Ross away, but didn't get there before Ross beat his own staggering retreat. He kept up his pretence all the way to the cabin, unsure who might be looking on, even sounding out a plausible volley of retching noises from the toilet. The dry-boak complete, he went to bed and killed the lights, waiting for his eyes to become accustomed to a darkness that would still obscure his subsequent activities if there really was a concealed camera. As he lay there, he could hear *Ode to Joy* ringing triumphantly out into the moonlit maritime night, beneath it a voice unintelligible from this distance, but Ross knew from memory whose it was and what was being said.

'You ask for miracles, Theo. I give you the F . . . B . . . I.'

It was almost time.

Ross unstrapped the small but solid fire extinguisher that was fixed to the cabin wall at knee-height near the door. He placed a few personal effects and a rolled-up T-shirt inside a ziplock plastic bag salvaged from the galley, and stuffed it into his underpants across the top of his buttocks. Then he took position beside the window and waited, barefoot like Bruce Willis would be right then on the plasma screen. Very soon Alan Rickman was conveying this detail to Alexander Godunov and thus heralding the loudest sequence of an already noisy soundtrack. This was his cue. Ross drove the fire extinguisher into the thick, sealed pane as, upstairs, the faux-German hijackers unloaded thousands of rounds into glass office partitions to create their own miniature *Kristallnacht*.

It took four good wallops, but when it went, it turned out to be shatterproof, turning into a pliable opaque sheet that could be pushed right out and into the drink below.

Ross squeezed out after it, having to manoeuvre head-first through the narrow gap, his arms pinned at his sides. He inched forward, face-down, and realised, as anticipated, that the point when his arms would be free would come only at the same moment as his centre of balance passed the edge. He delayed there a second, psyching himself, then took a breath and wriggled that last decisive few inches.

He was in free fall for about half a second, just long enough to extend his arms and palm his hands above his head to break the water. It would take him deeper under, but it would also lessen the splash. Ross felt a convulsive shock rip through his

330

entire body, the shuddering most violent about his trunk, as the temperature of the water bit through his skin. He'd never felt cold like it. He had looked at the sea temperature read-out, but had either failed to acknowledge what it was telling him or merely blanked it out as something he couldn't afford to worry about. The physical jolt of the cold cleared his mind of all other thought, including his spatial orientation, which was potentially disastrous. He'd closed his eyes out of instinct as he broke the surface, but opening them made no difference, except admitting the sting of the salt water. Now he was floating in blackness, unsure which way was up, and fast running out of time to reach the surface.

He felt movement, a sudden buffeting as the water shifted him like helpless flotsam. He struck out with his arms but felt no air. Panic threatened. He had to still it. Until he was oriented, he shouldn't be trying to move, as his efforts might well only be driving him deeper under.

His breath was tightening in his chest. He could hold on a little longer, but it seemed harder as long as there was no relief in sight. Then he realised he had a solution. He placed his hands around his mouth, one on top, one below, and let slip some air. Bubbles burst against the fingers and palm of his right hand. He estimated he was at about forty-five degrees from upright. He kicked out and hauled his arms through the water, then broke the surface with a gasp of relief.

His open mouth was instantly filled with water as a wave slapped against him, knocking him backwards. Another followed it, bumping him against the hull. The wind had picked up a little as evening fell, something else he'd noticed but failed to consciously acknowledge. He wasn't exactly being tossed in twenty-foot breakers, but it wasn't a millpond either. He'd imagined treading water, gently and quietly bobbing his way around the boat, one hand on the hull for guidance and support, but that was never how it was going to be, just something he'd fed his mind to get it to cooperate. This was the open sea, at night, miles from land. Just because it was the Med didn't mean it was the same as diving off the back of a pedalo in Puerto del Carmen.

Still, his body was getting used to the temperature; not liking it much, but over the shock and able to operate. He kicked off against the hull, swimming away from the boat at first so that the next wave didn't just slam him into it again. It was incredibly hard going, a real effort just to stay above the surface in this chop, and that he made it to the stern was far more to do with good fortune that the waves were pushing him that way. The hardest stretch, therefore, was negotiating across the current to reach the short ladder leading up to the lower transom deck. It felt at times like that dream where he was running but getting nowhere, but eventually he did manage to get an arm around the first rung, and just hung there for a while, recovering, the drag against his dangling legs telling him how easily he might have been swept away for good.

He looked up towards the deck of the main bridge. He could see the glow of lights, but no bodies. Gunfire and screams sounded out from above. Bruce was freeing the hostages. Any second now, the roof of Nakatomi Plaza was going to blow, and his dad was about to announce he was away to the toilet.

Ross hauled himself on to the lower transom deck and unlashed the dinghy, which was rested on its side against the bulkhead. He untied all of the ropes and then secured one of them to a brass cleat. He didn't know any knots, but figured a tight figure-of-eight looping ought to do the trick. Just in case it didn't, he kept hold of one end as he eased the dinghy to the edge, letting its own weight tip it aright on to the surface of the water. The waves tugged it immediately, but the mooring line held. He lifted the two short oars and chucked them on board. Ross looked up again. Still no sign of movement. His dad ought to be appearing on the main bridge deck any minute, glancing down enough to confirm that they were good to go. Just as well it was an exciting movie, as it would provide a plausible explanation for why he might look pallidly anxious, knowing his wee boy was intending to take a header into the briny deep.

Ross crouched close to the starboard bow. Opposite him were the jet skis, the most immediate means of pursuit once they were discovered to have gone. He scuttled across to them, staying low, and took hold of the one nearest the edge of the platform, intending to drag it over the side. As soon as he pulled at it, the other two leaned across in concert. He looked closer and saw that they were chained together and padlocked at the back. Shite. Still, it meant it would take the guards all the more time to get going. If he and Dad could make some headway in the meantime, it would be enough. They could kill the engine and drift in the darkness, wait until the sounds of the jet skis were long silenced before revving up again.

Ross heard footsteps on the boards, above and to his right. He looked up and saw his dad. They exchanged a thumbs-up. Ross climbed into the dinghy. Timing was everything now. He untied the mooring and made his way to the rear bench, hand on the engine, feeling the dinghy float free of its master vessel. He became aware his teeth were chattering and that he was shivering. It reminded him to pull out the bag from across his arse-cheeks. There was no time to change into the dry T-shirt, so he stashed the bag under his seat for now, before lifting the oars and sliding them into the cradles on either side. He then began quietly paddling towards the port bow, where Dad would be taking position on the lowest of the open decks. Somewhere above, Bruce Willis was down to two bullets but laughing.

Yippee-kiyay, motherfucker.

Dad's head appeared as soon as Ross rounded the stern. He was waiting and, Ross hoped, preparing himself for what was next. Ross pulled in the oars and reached for the starter-cord. He looked up and saw his dad vault over the grab-rails, a circular life belt clutched to his chest, snatched moments before from the port bulkhead. It made a hell of a splash, but wasn't as noisy as the outboard engine, which screamed into life first time, Ross hauling at the cord with all the strength his anger and desperation could summon. He let out the throttle, a little too much at first, which caused the boat to leap forward, the prow rising unnervingly and obscuring his view of where Dad was gasping in cryo-shock above the waves. A flick of the wrist brought the speed under control, and he was able to bring it to as near a stop as possible next to where Dad was kicking and thrashing. Ross resisted the temptation to look up as he leaned over to help haul his dad over the side and aboard the dinghy. It took an agonisingly long time, mainly because Dad had forgotten – or ignored – Ross's advice about stripping his trousers and sweater off before making his leap. He eventually slumped aboard in an ungainly heap, causing Ross to fall

333

backwards also as the dinghy rocked violently in compensation for having been tipped to one side. As they both sprawled on the floor he noticed that his dad was still shod in his trademark Hush Puppies.

'You didn't take your fuckin' shoes off?'

'These cost me nearly fifty quid.'

'Jesus fuck.'

Ross clambered back on to his seat, this time compelled to look up. He saw three of their guards staring back down, two from the lower deck, one other above them. Orders were being shouted. He knew they couldn't shoot him because he was worth too much alive, which explained why they weren't reaching for their guns. Less explicable was that they didn't seem to be in a pronounced state of urgency about their pursuit, which confirmed his impression of calm and highly confident professionalism. Still, he and Dad were off the boat and had a head start into the darkness. Game on. He flicked his wrist and let the throttle out in a controlled acceleration. As he did so, the moon began to emerge from cloud cover, easing his natural reluctance to give it maximum thrust as he headed into blackness. He took this to be a good omen until two things happened. The first was that he remembered how the increased visibility would be more of an aid to the pursuers than to the fugitives. The second was that the engine began spluttering as a brief prelude to cutting out altogether.

The boat continued to drift silently forward, moonlight reflecting on the waves around them. Ross felt a growing dread, an awareness that this wasn't turning on an unlucky quirk of fate. He looked briefly to the oars but knew it was hopeless. The reason the dinghy wasn't chained and padlocked like the jet skis was that they had kept the petrol tank all but empty, just enough in it to prime the engine so it didn't get choked when they did fuel up. It was a precaution against precisely this kind of escape attempt, and that's why they weren't scrabbling around with any great haste when they saw what was in progress.

From not so far away, he heard the sound of jet skis as a searchbeam began swooping across the waves from the flybridge of the yacht.

*　　*　　*

They were towed back between two of the jet skis, lines run through a fibreglass loop on the front of the dinghy. Upon reaching the yacht, they were hauled aboard, dripping and shivering, by Guillaume and Stefan, while a third, Gilbert, paced behind on the transom, his ear to a mobile, presumably reporting this business back to the main man on shore. The hierarchy of the crew had not made itself apparent thus far, through lack of occasion, but now it was obvious he was the ranking officer. He said nothing to the others, but made his intentions known with looks and nods as he listened to whatever was being said on the phone.

'*Deux?*' he said into the cellular. '*Trois? Deux. Oui.* Okay.'

They were escorted back to the saloon bridge, to the lounge area where the plasma was now austerely blank. On the bartop, there stood the vodka bottle Ross was pretending to drink from, as well as the water bottle he was really quaffing and the glass central to this subterfuge. Gilbert clocked Ross noticing it and nodded at him, then briefly fanned out a sheaf of computer print-outs in one hand. Ross didn't get a close look, but saw enough to recognise that they were low-res infrared images, bodyheat picking out a single figure in white against indistinct grey: him in his cabin, breaking the window.

Gilbert nodded again.

He was letting them know they'd only got as far as they did because he'd allowed them to, merely to demonstrate how futile their actions were. The bottle was left out to indicate just how early the alarm had been raised, underlining all the points at which the guards could have intervened, but the kicker was that ultimately they knew they didn't have to.

'Sit,' Gilbert ordered.

A folding chair was placed behind Ross, while his dad was allowed to take his familiar place on one of the sofas.

'You were warned, were you not?' he asked quietly.

'You can't shoot a man for trying,' Ross said. He wanted it to sound winning and amiable, but it just came out tremulous and nervously hoarse.

'No, we can't shoot you at all, Mr Fleming. That's why we need other sanctions to guarantee your discipline.'

Gilbert blinked, his gaze switching from Ross to the guard

nearest Dad, the stocky and expressionless Guillaume. He reached down, took Dad's left hand and hauled back his index finger until it broke at the knuckle. Dad's screams cut the night sky but failed to obliterate the sound of the snap resonating in Ross's head. He went to stand up, but immediately felt hands on his shoulders. They were firm but not violent, underlining the message: they weren't going to hurt him, which, no doubt intentionally, worsened the pain he felt over Dad.

Dad was squirming on the sofa, his body racked with agony but unable to cradle and protect his injury because Guillaume still had an irresistible grip on his wrist. That was when Ross remembered Gilbert on the phone. *Deux? Trois? Deux.*

Guillaume reached down again and this time snapped the middle finger. Again Dad's howls tore into the night.

'Okay,' Gilbert said, and they were soon left alone, he and the other guards withdrawing quietly and calmly like extras from a stage. Ross had expected to be hauled away to some grotty hold and locked in, but perhaps Gilbert wanted to stress that further measures of restraint were redundant. They were already as securely imprisoned as it was possible to be.

Ross helped his dad back to his cabin, where he fed him some Ibuprofen; not exactly diamorphine, but still better than nothing. He helped him get his wet clothes off, a torture in itself around that mangled hand, then wrapped the fingers together in a makeshift splint rendered from torn hand-towels and a comb. All the time, Ross was apologising, trying to hold the tears back but failing utterly.

He knew that as bad as he felt, as helpless and as guilty, it would be nothing compared to what his dad was enduring over and above the physical pain: humiliated and impotent in front of his son. That in itself made Ross feel even worse about his role in bringing it about, and pretty soon the two of them were just sniffing and weeping on the cabin floor, in the throes of the most profound misery they'd ever known.

'I'm so sorry, Dad,' he kept saying, his throat swelling and choking the words.

'It's me should be sorry,' was the repeated return volley, the rally going on for a few minutes until they gave up the stalemate and Ross did the most constructive thing he could imagine under the circumstances, which was boil the kettle.

They said nothing for a while, just drinking the warm tea, glazed-eyed and welcome of the heat it brought. Then after about half a mug, Dad broke the silence.

'I really am sorry, son.'

'Oh, let's not start again, Dad.'

'Naw, seriously. It was me that . . .' he shifted uneasily, wincing, but Ross couldn't tell if this was prompted by his fingers or what Ross realised he was about to mention. 'Connelly,' he confirmed, his shame at this disastrous misjudgement etched heavily upon his features. 'I'm so sorry, son.'

'Just leave it, Dad. It's not you that's to blame. You're not responsible for the actions of a prick like that.'

'Nah, you don't know the half of it, Ross,' he said, shaking his head. 'I knew what he was. I don't know how I managed to fool myself . . . I let him trample all over your mother before, and now . . .'

'Mum? How?'

'Her taxi job. Remember I told you she gave it up. Well, ach . . . The truth was he bought over the firm and he muscled her out because she wouldn't run drugs. And I let him do it because I thought she was well off out of it, characters like that running around. But he saw me for a mug back then, and so when I came calling . . .'

'She *was* better off out of it,' Ross assured him, aghast at what his mum might have been caught up in. 'Christ, what if there'd been a turf war, or if she had delivered a package and the polis got involved? God knows what kind of mess she could have ended up in.'

'I know, I know that. But to her it was a betrayal. I never stuck up for her. In fact, she saw it as me siding with him, and I don't think she's forgiven me. She definitely won't now. But I was just trying to do what I could to protect her. Your mother, she needs me to look out for her. Especially these days.'

'Why especially these days?' Ross asked, unable to remember any time his mother gave the impression of needing anyone to hold her hand.

'Well, you maybe wouldnae be aware, not being around much.

337

I'm not having a go,' he assured. 'Just saying. But the two of us . . .'

'You're not exactly love's young dream. I'd noticed. Even from afar.'

'I don't know what it is. Nothing's changed as far as I can see, but your mother, well . . . she seems a wee bit lost. This taxi business being a case in point. You've got to ask what a woman's doing, taking up something like that at her stage in life.'

'You make it sound like she's a pensioner, Dad. She's in her mid-forties.'

Dad shifted his balance, about to transfer the empty mug to his right hand to put it on a table but arresting the movement and gingerly getting to his feet instead. He put it down next to the kettle as he spoke, still grimacing every so often as the pain continued to pulse.

'Aye, but you know what I'm saying,' he continued. 'She's a grandmother, for goodness' sake. A mid-life crisis, I said it was, and I was only half joking. She doesn't know what to be doing with herself.'

Dad sat down again, very gently, as though every movement or impact could give his fingers a nasty jolt. He looked across with an expression of apprehension and determination, and Ross could tell there was some soul-searching in progress. He steeled himself to charitably receive something he suspected he wouldn't like.

'Now, I know you don't think much of the Church, but you're young, too young to understand when you really need it.'

Ross let this go, but only because he thought his dad was talking about himself. He was wrong.

'See, your mother . . . I always hoped she'd come around, and this is why.' Come around. Dad couldn't bring himself to say it, maybe because he knew how ridiculous it would sound if it was spelled out. 'She doesn't see where she fits in, she's lost sight of the point of her life. If she'd come around, her life would make more sense.'

Ross swallowed a last mouthful of tea, bitter and a bit nasty from going cool. He hoped it provided adequate cover for his expression. His guilt and general anguish reined him in, but he was pissed off, figuring his dad was playing the situation more than a little, banking on not getting the usual both barrels in response. He'd never have dared come out with this kind of shite under normal circumstances, and broken fingers or no, he wasn't getting away with it.

'Maybe she doesn't fit in,' Ross suggested quietly.

'What do you mean? We've been married more than a quarter-century,' Dad responded, his vehemence proof that he knew *exactly* what Ross meant.

'I mean maybe you're not the same people you were more than a quarter-century ago. When I'm home I don't hear you talk much. In fact you seldom give the impression that you even like each other.'

'Ach, rubbish. It's not flowers and chocolates all the time, but what marriage is? Especially after all this time. But I love her, Ross, I always have.'

Ross bit his lip, though he knew he was going to say it anyway. He felt like a thousand kinds of shit already, so it wouldn't make much difference to heap on a little bit more. It might seem callous, but he'd been watching his dad build these delusions around himself his whole life, based on fallacies, undefined terms and unchallenged assertions. And now here he was, doing it again, using Ross's guilt to stave off the truth.

'Love is just something people say, Dad,' he stated regretfully. 'When to mean anything, it should be something people do. You and Mum have been drifting apart for years. It's nobody's fault, but please don't tell me you love each other. You hardly know each other.'

'I do love her,' Dad protested, and Ross could see tears in his eyes, making him feel that bit closer to a dysentery-bearing amoeba. He did love who she'd been, love his kids, love all that they'd come through, the family they were. Ross could see that. But neither Mum nor Dad had any time for the people each other were now. And through his dad's tears Ross could see he knew that too.

'If she'd come around,' he stumbled, shaking his head. 'I don't know, we don't have much in common any more apart from you and Michelle and the kids.'

'That's what I'm saying. If Mum's taking taxi jobs to stay out of the house half the night, then it doesn't sound like she enjoys being around there very much. And that would make me concerned she might not be around there much longer.'

Dad smiled sadly, with a faraway look. 'No, no. If I get out of this mess, we'll be together for life. Don't you worry.'

'Why, because Catholics don't get divorced? It takes two people to stay married, Dad.'

He shook his head.

'You don't understand. It's not about that. That would never even be an issue, believe me. She needs me, Ross. That's why we'll be together. As long as she needs me, I'll be there. And that's what's got me awake at night as much as your situation, to be honest. She's always had me to look out for her, and I really fear for how she'd get along if I wasn't there.'

Decent, normal, sensible girls

Lex glanced up from her monitors to have a look at the video feeds. Bett sat a few feet to her left, glued to the screens, toggling between cams in an unusually fidgety manner. His attention was focused mainly on two: the moving view from Jane's pendant and a fixed angle across a smoky bar where, now out of shot, Parrier had recently entered with another man, identified by Bett as Lucien Dirlos. They'd got a good look at him via the sucker-mounted cameras outside the OSE suite, where he had arrived a couple of hours back. Lex had been relieved not to recognise him, but her relief was tempered by the corollary knowledge that she still didn't know who her duplicitous contact was.

Jane and Nuno had been in a holding pattern, driving around the outskirts of town while they waited – and hoped – for Parrier to leave his suite. He and Dirlos had seemed frustratingly settled there, making calls and sending emails, but eventually Parrier announced his intention to go downstairs for a drink. Dirlos had mentioned jokingly that they had plenty of booze in the suite, but he clearly knew what Parrier meant, even before he pointed out that 'there's nothing to fuck in the suite apart from you'.

The pendant view swept through the building towards the piano bar where the light-switch camera had spotted the OSE pair. Nuno was instructed by Jane to wait outside in the lobby, his presence not being conducive to intimacy, then she pressed on into the lions' den.

Lex watched Bett swallow, his eyes fixed upon the monitors. She'd never seen him so nervous; in fact, she wasn't sure she'd ever really seen him nervous at all. It was little wonder, however. They were sending in a barely trained operative with a fragile cover story that was not designed for longevity, but truth was they had no choice. Jane did have this connection with

341

Parrier, everyone had seen it. There'd been an energy between them, even if only one side knew it was the crackling static of hatred.

'She's going to give me a heart attack before this is over,' Bett said, his finger muting the microphone so that Jane wouldn't hear. 'Whose idea was it to bring her into this?'

'That would be yours, sir,' Som informed him.

'Remind me to fire myself when we're finished.'

Jane had barely sat down at the bar before Parrier made his move, inviting her to his table where she was briefly introduced to his enforcer, Dirlos. Dirlos smiled politely as he shook her hand, but his eyes were cold, evaluative. She detected a twitch about his brow as he surveyed her, reminiscent of the moment when she had first presented her face to Parrier. However, they weren't given time to make any further impressions upon each other, as Dirlos understood the introduction to also contain his marching orders now that his boss had female company.

Parrier ordered them drinks and made small talk, idle flim-flam about the exhibition, stuff both of them knew to be meaningless preamble. The chatter was stemmed by the arrival of their drinks, and did not resume. They each sipped, glancing across the table, sizing the other up like combatants. A knowing, flirtatious grin shaped Parrier's lips, heralding the start of the bout.

'Am I to take it that you are not so troubled by my reputation any more?' he asked. 'I mean, here you are, drinking with the roué, in full public view.'

'I believe I said rogue.'

'I have more than one bad reputation.'

'Perhaps I have decided I might learn from you, Monsieur Parrier.'

'Call me Pascal.'

'Pascal, then. I'm a rich woman. But if I had the nous to get away with half as much as you've done, I'd be a lot richer still.'

'What have I gotten away with?' he asked, feigning hurt but bursting with smug pride.

'Officially nothing. Barely a blemish on your copybook. That's what's most impressive.'

She played with an olive on her cocktail stick, letting him bask.

'Who are you?' he asked. 'Who do you work for?'

'I represent a collection of interests, whose identities it is *not* in their interests to disclose.'

'You *represent*?'

'A polite term. You could say I work in acquisitions, in as much as I get them what they want.'

'And what do they want here this week?'

Jane looked him in the eye and smiled.

'Nothing I've seen on the market floor.'

He mugged back, responding to the signal.

'And do you think I might be able to offer you anything of interest?'

'Possibly. Not merchandise. Underhand business skulduggery consultation services, perhaps.'

'He's loving it,' Rebekah commented. The sound feed from Jane's earrings was being routed through the speakers, nobody scanning any of the other channels. Tonight, this was the only show in town. 'She'll have him on a leash barking like a dog before she's through.'

'Never make assumptions about who's playing whom in this game,' Bett grumbled. 'Parrier's an experienced womaniser, and there's girls half his age in there, easily impressed by a Platinum Amex and the key to the penthouse. What's he really after?'

'Perhaps he's really after a woman who isn't half his age and isn't impressed by a Platinum Amex,' Rebekah countered.

Ouch, Lex thought, and the thunderous look on Bett's face confirmed the strike. Lucky for Reb he had other shit to worry about right then.

'So I'm wondering,' Parrier said. 'Is it only my business reputation you find yourself less troubled by?'

Jane said nothing, hitting him with a blank look that demanded elaboration on his part.

'I mean, would you make certain assumptions if I was to suggest we continue our conversation somewhere a little more private? Somewhere with a better view, perhaps.'

'I wouldn't make assumptions if you didn't,' she replied.

Parrier grinned and reached for his drink.

Bett's voice immediately sounded in Jane's ears. *'Don't do this,'* he commanded flatly.

'I believe I would be a fool to make any assumptions of you, Miss Bell.'

'Then you may suggest a change of view.'

'D'accord.'

'Do not *do this,'* Bett repeated, as Jane downed the last of her G&T. *'We can't control this environment. He's got a security guard outside his door up there, he's got Dirlos prowling downstairs, God knows who else in tow. And he is making every assumption you can think of.'*

She got to her feet and let him lead her out of the bar towards the lifts.

'Jane,' Bett appealed, voice low. It was the first time he'd called her anything other than Mrs Fleming. *'Nobody's asking you to do this.'*

Jane let out a laugh inside the elevator as she watched Parrier swipe his keycard to access the penthouse level.

'What's funny?' he asked as the lift lurched into movement.

'The people I work for. I was thinking they might not be best pleased if they knew I was heading to a penthouse suite with you. They can work themselves into such a tizz about some of the things I get up to.'

'I know what you mean,' Parrier replied, understandably assuming it was him she was talking to. 'But in my experience they're not so concerned once they see the bottom line.'

'Just salving their consciences, I think. None of us are under any illusions about the nature of the game. The reason they took me on is because I told them I'll do whatever it takes to get what I want.'

'And what do you want tonight?' Parrier asked.

She put a hand around his neck, pulled him closer and kissed him.

The monitor displaying the pendant-camera feed went all but blank, showing only a blurred view of Parrier's jacket. There was a deadly silence around the room, other than the occasional amplified slap of mouth on mouth. Lex barely dared to breathe.

Bett looked frozen in time, unmoving, his finger muting the microphone lest the tiny speakers in Jane's ears give themselves away.

The kiss broke off as a chime sounded to announce that the lift had reached the top floor. Parrier let Jane step out first, then gestured left along the corridor.

Nuno's voice broke the silence, coming through the speakers.

'Sir, it's Dirlos. I tailed him when he left the bar. He had a drink in one of the lounges, but he did not look like he was about to undo his tie and start crooning. Very, very unrelaxed. Anyway, he made a call on his mobile and now he's hovering around the front desk like a kid needing to pee, keeps going up and bothering the receptionists. Gut feeling, sir: I don't like it.'

Bett didn't respond for a long couple of seconds. When he did, his voice was low and throaty, like he'd had to delve deep to find it.

'I don't either,' he said. 'Rebekah?'

'You got it.'

'Champagne?' Parrier asked.

'Why not,' Jane answered, staring out through the full-height, full-width windows that lined the suite on two sides. An L-shaped open area curled around the enclosed bedroom and bath-room in the centre. She stood close to the bureau, upon which sat two laptops, a sheaf of faxes and hard-copy emails fanned untidily between them next to a portable printer. The laptops were both blank and silent, impossible to know whether in sleep mode or fully closed down.

Parrier stood behind the breakfast bar of the kitchen area, having removed the wine from a quite unnecessarily large fridge, just one of many monuments to self-importance incorporated into the suite's extravagant design. There was even a singularly hideous piece of free-standing modern sculpture next to one wall, or so Jane thought until she spotted the letters OSE etched upon it at regular vertical intervals, at which point she belat-edly realised it was actually a stack of heavily insulated black fibreglass cases.

Parrier poured two flutes of champagne and walked slowly across the floor to hand her one.

'*Salut*,' he said. They clinked their glasses. Jane had a tiny sip, Parrier a more lusty gulp. He put his flute down on the bureau and placed his hand on the stem of hers, running a finger along the glass, along the back of her palm and slowly up her arm.

'It has been said of me,' he said softly, looking at his hand as it made its progress along her sleeve, 'that I am an arrogant man. That I have a very high opinion of myself.' He looked into her eyes, his hand reaching her shoulder, the skin of his fingertips then brushing her neck. 'I *am* an arrogant man. And I do have a high opinion of myself. But not so high an opinion as to remain unsuspicious when what I want comes too easily.'

His hand spanned her throat, gripping but not quite squeezing.

'You see, it's been troubling me that I can't place you, and yet you know so much about me and my . . . reputation.'

Jane didn't react other than to look towards the door. Parrier noted it.

'He won't help you,' he told her. 'Denis is here to protect me, in whatever way I deem necessary. So maybe it's time for you to get something off your chest. Such as a wire.'

Jane's gaze never left his, nor had her hands moved to protect herself. Still staring into his eyes, she transferred the champagne to her left hand and with her right undid two buttons on her jacket.

His hand relaxed, left her neck and drifted down, the backs of his fingers brushing across her chest. Parrier slipped two digits beneath her bra-strap and delicately tugged it down her arm, exposing her left breast. Then he reached to cup it with his palm, but she intercepted him, gripping his wrist tightly with her right hand.

They stared into each other's eyes at point-blank.

'Forgive me,' he said. 'You'll understand that in this business it pays to be paranoid.'

'Don't mention it,' she told him coldly. 'But now that we're that bit more intimate, perhaps we can cut the flirting shit and talk about why we're both here.'

She took a step away and stood against the back of a settee, doing up her buttons. Parrier remained where he was next to the bureau and had another drink of champagne.

'Why are we both here?' he asked.

She stared at him, letting what was unsaid hang in the air between them a moment. Then she sighed deeply.

'I don't know, Pascal, maybe it's because I just had my tit hanging out a minute ago, but I'm suddenly all through being coy. I'm talking about what you're here to buy. I'm talking about the auction. And I think we might be able to help each other.'

He put the glass down and folded his arms. *Now* they were talking. 'How?' he asked, intrigued.

'I believe we could improve our chances by combining our bargaining power. In fact, I'm not sure you're in with any chance otherwise. I know for a fact that Gieselcorp and Arutech are both ready to break twenty million.'

'How can you possibly know—'

'It's my business to know. The people I represent can go higher, but a combined bid would cost both of us a lot less. *If* our interests can be demonstrated to be compatible. How much were you planning to offer him?'

Parrier bit his lip for a second, then coughed up.

'We can go as high as anybody, but above twenty it's not worth our while.'

'All the more reason to consider a joint bid. *He* wouldn't need to know, either: we'd be a silent partner. We both understand what the greedy bastard's like: if he found out you had a bigger reserve to draw from, he'd raise the auction floor.'

'So what's your end?' Parrier asked. 'How would this partnership work?'

'I'm not sure it would, yet. That's what I'm here to ascertain. I'm guessing, unlike the other bidders, you're not particularly interested in acquiring the technology. OSE doesn't have the investment or the infrastructure to spend twenty years and hundreds of millions on development. I think you're interested in stopping it.'

Parrier said nothing, just grabbed his glass and took another gulp. He sat himself up on the bureau, scattering some printouts.

'Clearly that would be in your interest,' Jane went on, 'but it would also be in the interests of a great many people in this industry. Now, I know you're not averse to a bit of unilateral action, but your previous attempt only cost you a couple of men.'

Parrier's eyes widened. He just about managed to stifle a response, understanding that she wasn't going to tell him how she knew this. Hopefully his busy little mind would now be making few assumptions about what else she did or didn't know.

'Shelling out twenty million, however, strikes me as a very generous piece of unilateral action to be taking. So I'm guessing there's something else.'

She folded her arms and offered him a smile, intended to suggest she knew what it was but that she wanted to hear it from him.

'Stopping the technology is not our only motivation,' he confirmed. 'It's Deimos we're after. More specifically, Marledoq.'

'Shit, she's good,' Lex whispered, now sitting between Bett and Armand as they watched the two-hander unfold. Jane was bullshitting with aplomb, dangling a nebulous temptation before someone as greedy as he was curious, just to keep him talking. 'She's real good.'

Bett nodded sincerely, his finger still muting the mike.

'I'll be more impressed if he ever mentions *the name*,' said Armand.

'She's not just after the name,' Bett told him. 'The name might save her son today, but she wants to keep him safe tomorrow too.'

'She's going after the leak,' Lex realised with a gasp. She hoped it merely sounded like she was impressed, as opposed to suddenly terrified.

Parrier's voice resumed from the speakers.

'We wanted an underground facility for our own research and testing, and we were preparing to table a bid for Deimos, lock, stock and barrel, in order to get Marledoq. Deimos was idling, costing Phobos too much money. I knew Nicholas Willis's patience with the non-lethal research was running out. He's a tired and disillusioned old man, and I knew he was ready to sell up. We'd done some sounding out, estimated he'd accept a bid of forty million euros just to be rid of it. Comparable facilities elsewhere would cost us twice that.'

'By sounding out . . .'

'We put out feelers, found ourselves a willing contact inside.'

'Poker being easier if you can get a look at the other guy's hand.'

'Indeed. But not all of the cards had been dealt. Segnier—'

'Segnier?'

'Our man on the inside; there's always someone willing to suck up to his potential new bosses, especially for a decent kick-back. Segnier warned us there was something in the pipeline that could change the game. It was top-secret, and he wasn't even sure himself what it was at the time.'

'But he sure found out, didn't he?'

Lex held her breath, staring at the screen, forcing her eyes to stay there and not look at Bett, who was sitting two feet away. One fleeting reference now and she'd be lost.

'Oh yes. He managed to get some computer files smuggled out. There was a *window*, an opportunity, I don't know what, but I do know we paid top dollar for them.'

'You and everybody else.'

'Indeed. Once he knew what he had, the bastard sold the files all over the place. Suddenly everybody knew what Deimos was developing.'

'And Deimos's value just as suddenly went stratospheric.'

Nuno's voice broke across the speakers again. Armand automatically pulled on his headphones to continue following Jane and Parrier's conversation.

'Sir, it's Dirlos. Someone from reception just handed him a piece of paper. I couldn't see what it was, but I'm guessing it had to be a fax. He took one look at it and now he's dialling his cellular.'

Bett turned a dial on the audio console and jacked up the volume from the OSE suite. The phone sitting next to Parrier on the bureau began to ring.

'Shit,' Bett muttered. He lifted his finger from the mute button, but as he did so, Parrier pressed something on the keypad to silence the ringing and continued talking, unwilling to be interrupted mid-flow.

Bett switched channel on the mike, transmitting only to Nuno.

'What's Dirlos doing now?'

'He's giving the piece of paper back to the receptionist with instructions and he's waving to someone down the lobby. Big guy on his way.'

Bett switched channel again.

'So now everybody wants to acquire Deimos,' Parrier said. 'Not just to be first with the new technology, but to have a head start on developing weapons that will circumvent it. Willis could name his price. Two hundred million, three hundred, who knows? But as everything in the files was pertaining to one man, to this Fleming, we guessed it was some solo genius rather than a team effort we were dealing with.'

'*Get out of there,*' Bett's voice stated, calm but insistent. '*Now. Dirlos knows something's wrong.*'

Jane held her position, two things keeping her from obeying. One, the secondary consideration, was that there was a guard outside the door. The primary consideration was that she still didn't have the name, and if she ran now, she wouldn't get a second chance.

'I figured: take him out and the project dies too,' Parrier went on with a shrug, the planned murder of her son merely a logical transaction to this prick. 'Deimos's price tag drops back down to what we wanted.'

'*Jane, get out of there. Dirlos is heading for the lifts. He's got another OSE security officer with him. You are out of time.*'

She had to get him to say it.

'But before you can get to Fleming yourselves,' she prompted, 'he ends up in the hands of . . .'

'Our mutual friend,' Parrier replied. 'So now we're back in the same situation: everybody bidding up the price.' The phone rang out again, but on this occasion only once. Parrier looked at it, clearly this time not required to take any action. Alongside him, the printer hummed into life. 'The problem for us,' he went on, 'is that if someone else gets it, they'll want Marledoq too, otherwise they'd be recreating the project from scratch. And that sucker Willis will sell it to them despite everything, because he'll have nothing left and whoever it is will be offering a decent price. Nothing like what it would have cost them if Deimos still had Fleming, but still cheap to the bidder, even

350

factoring in whatever they end up paying out to that thieving asshole R . . .'

He stopped, his lips forming the first letter of the name he was about to speak. His eyes had fallen upon the sheet of paper that had just glided out from the printer on to the desk next to his thigh. It was upside down, but Jane was only four feet away, close enough to recognise her own photograph, a head-and-shoulders crop from a shot Ross had taken of her posing with Rachel.

Parrier's gaze lifted from the paper and alighted once more on Jane, his mouth now slack, that crucial word melted away. Then his eyes suddenly narrowed as it all fitted together.

He took a step forward and swung an open-handed slap at Jane's face.

It didn't connect. She had repeated certain movements thousands of times in the past few days, a process of 'retraining reflexes'. It nonetheless surprised her how automatically her response came, though it was made easier by how early Parrier had telegraphed his strike. He was a man used to having someone else do his fighting for him. Jane blocked with her left hand, her torso rotating at the waist, before recoiling as she drove her right fist into his throat, aiming as she'd been trained to, at a point two feet behind him. He buckled, clutching his neck, breathing in with a strangulated gasp, but somehow managing to utter a cry of 'Denis' as he exhaled.

The door opened almost immediately, but Jane had already drawn the Walther from her ankle. She stepped behind the dazed and reeling Parrier, and pulled him off-balance towards her with an arm around his neck as Denis came through the door, pistol in hand. She got off three rounds, hitting him with two, both in the chest. He fell backwards against the door, the gun tumbling from his startled grip, but not before firing one desperate shot, which hit Parrier in the stomach. Jane released her arm from his neck and let him fall to the carpet, where he curled up in the embryo position, clutching his wound.

In the brief moment of silence that followed, Jane could hear the chop of rotor blades outside.

'The roof,' Bett's voice insisted. '*Get there now. Dirlos is in the lift.*'

But she still didn't have what she'd come for.

She placed a heel on Parrier's shoulder and dug down, spinning him around so that he was looking up at her.

'Stings a wee bit, eh?' she said. 'Not such a big fan of guns now, are we?'

He grimaced, trying to roll on to his side. She kicked him on to his back again and pointed the Walther at his face.

'Who is the vendor?' she asked.

He looked baffled amid the racking pain. She was worried for a second that Bett was wrong and somehow the name had remained secret, but realised the source of his confusion was that until very recently Parrier had been under the impression that the vendor's identity was something she already knew.

'WHO IS HE?' she shouted. 'HIS NAME. NOW.'

Parrier looked towards the door. Denis was lying motionless, blood pooling beneath him, but more help was on the way. She swung her arm a few short degrees and shot him in the right thigh. He bucked and howled in response, trying to turn, trying to grab at the source of the pain, but her foot kept him pinned.

'His name,' she repeated. 'Or I keep shooting.'

Parrier spluttered, snot and tears exploding from his nose.

'Roth,' he gasped. 'Marius Roth.'

'I don't believe you,' she told him, angling the Walther to point at his other thigh.

'I SWEAR,' he screamed. 'It's Marius Roth. Marius Roth.'

'Ring any bells?' she asked Bett.

'More than Quasimodo. Now get the fuck out of there. Dirlos will be up any second.'

Jane stepped off of Parrier, who immediately curled up on his side like a poked woodlouse. He was squirming and helpless but, she realised, he was also still a threat.

'He could warn this Roth, couldn't he?'

There was a pause.

'Not could. Will. There'd be money in it.'

Jane looked into Parrier's face, now staring back up, eyes wide in horrified realisation as he deduced what her last words meant. She feared she'd see all the things Alexis had told her about, and that it would stay her hand, but instead she saw Ross in the same position, Michelle, Rachel, Donald, begging for their lives from this man and those he sent to do his bidding.

She emptied the Walther, firing the remaining four shots into his chest, then reached to her right calf for a change of clip. As she slotted the new magazine home, she looked around the suite but couldn't see which, if any, of the windows slid open. From outside in the corridor she heard the chime the lift made to herald its arrival moments ahead of its doors opening.

Dirlos, plus one.

She ran across the room and picked up the pistol that lay on the carpet next to Denis's dead hand, switching the lighter Walther to her weaker left. She tried not to look at his face. She'd only seen it twice before she'd killed the guy, but now wasn't the time to get philosophical.

Jane threw the door open to the wall and peered around the frame as she heard the lift slide open at the far end of the corridor. Dirlos emerged, drawing a handgun as he did so, a second man at his back. She crossed her wrists and leaned into the gap, opening fire with both weapons. The two men dived to the floor, Dirlos scrambling for the nearby stairwell and the other back into the lift. She didn't fancy her chances of taking down two armed pros, especially not at that distance, but she did think she might buy herself some time to escape. It was Bett's technique but it was as much Nuno's psychology she was banking on, something he'd told her as he was teaching her a particular blow. 'Make your first strike very hard, very fast and very controlled, and most opponents will fear they're beaten already.' These guys weren't likely to throw in the towel, but they'd be that bit more slow and careful about approaching this door.

She withdrew on swift feet but waited for the return volley to cover her intentions. When it came, after a long few seconds, she levelled both guns at one of the windows and tore it away in a million twinkling jewels, the sound of the helicopter becoming immediately louder.

'For Christ's sake, hurry. Rebekah's waiting and the entire hotel security staff's on its way up there.'

Jane stepped through the gap and found herself only three feet from the edge. She tried not to look down, but she had come out on one of the inland-looking sides, where the play of

353

street lights and the glow of distant buildings conveyed an unavoidable sense of altitude. She looked to her right, saw the access stairs about twenty yards away, only a low balustrade, barely waist-high, hemming her in from the drop. There was no further gunfire from inside. Bad sign. They were on the move. She got her head down, focused her gaze on where she was putting her feet and concentrated on putting one rapidly but carefully in front of the other.

The access stair was more like a ladder, just an inclining column of steel steps. Jane was almost at the top of it when Bett warned her that Dirlos's accomplice was about to step out on to the ledge. She turned around and loosed off three shots as he emerged through the aluminium frame. He was spun by the impact, his feet slipping on the treacherous carpet of glistening shards, before he tumbled over the low barrier, his falling cry swallowed by the sound of the chopper.

Jane hauled herself over the edge and on to the roof. Air Bett was ahead, the cockpit door beckoningly open. She saw Rebekah looking anxiously towards her, both hands on the controls.

Jane noticed the wheels drag as she ran towards the helicopter, its weight not quite borne by them as the blades strained impatiently to lift the craft away. It lurched a couple of feet as she reached to climb in, causing her to take a step back. Then she turned and looked behind, figuring that this close to the noise, she might not hear Bett's warning if Dirlos was on his way up the ladder. Facing forwards again, she threw herself at the gap and clambered aboard.

'And she's outta there!' Lex exclaimed with delighted relief. However, when she looked to Bett for his reaction she found him still concentrating on the monitors.

'Not yet,' he stated gravely.

They watched Dirlos open a black case, one of a pile lying on the floor of the suite, and pull a long black tube from within. He removed another object from the container – cylindrical but tapered at one end – and placed it inside the first.

'Oh, fuck,' was Lex's revised opinion.

Bett's voice screeched from the cockpit radio.

'Dirlos is on his way to the roof with a Sam. Acknowledge: Incoming Sam.'

'Incoming Sam, acknowledged,' Rebekah replied, lifting the chopper away from the concrete.

'What's a Sam?' Jane asked.

'Surface-to-air missile.'

'Jesus Christ. Get us out of here.'

'I can't.'

'You *what*?'

'We can't get out of range. We fly off right now, we're an easy target.'

'So what the hell are we going to do?'

Jane felt her stomach lurch as the chopper swung around, barely moving in space but turning to face the access stairs she'd ascended. She looked at the automatic she'd taken from Denis. It would be more effective than the PPK from that range but she couldn't remember how many rounds she'd fired and she wasn't feeling lucky. Nor could she remember how many she'd fired from the Walther, but at least she did have spare ammunition for that. She pulled her last spare clip from her calf, ejected the current mag and reloaded.

'I'm getting out,' she announced. 'Put us down. I'll wait until he sticks his head up and blow the fucking thing off.'

'Go for it,' Rebekah hailed, gently lowering the aircraft.

Jane reached for the doorhandle, estimating ten feet from touchdown, but as she looked out through the side window, she saw Dirlos dead ahead, already emerging from a different access stair on the coastal side of the building.

'Oh shit, we're too late,' she shouted. 'What do we do?'

Rebekah looked too. Dirlos was getting to his feet, picking up the missile-launcher and hefting it to his right shoulder.

'Turn on the wipers,' Rebekah growled, hauling at the joystick.

The helicopter banked sharply and suddenly, swinging at speed towards Dirlos as though on a pendulum. There was a disturbingly minor variation in the hum of the rotor and a feather-light sensation of impact, a fraction of a second before the windows were sprayed with red.

Rebekah picked up altitude and velocity, taking them out to sea and out of sight, though not before turning on the wipers.

A Basque tale (old as time?)

Rebekah flew them out low over the blackness of the Mediterranean to disguise their direction, before banking to follow the coastline for a few miles and finally heading back inland. The journey took ten, maybe fifteen minutes, but Jane was barely aware of it. She was still back in that suite, back on those steel steps, back on that rooftop. She was aware of her pulse only now in the aftermath, the same as often happened at the gym, the thumping syncopation only noticeable now that what caused it had ceased. There was something else coursing inside her too, an energy that made her feel tiny pinpricks over every inch of skin, tingling in her fingers, lifting hairs from her scalp. It was like a heightened state of being, not something you came down from easily. No drink and no drug was going to let her sleep tonight, she was sure.

When they landed back at Maison Rla an Tir, Rebekah had to give her a nudge to bring her personally back to earth. She didn't know how long she might have sat oblivious in the cockpit otherwise, disconnected from her immediate surroundings.

As she hopped down on to the grass, the sight of her reception committee reconnected her fast. Bett was standing waiting on the gravel, arms folded, wearing an expression that might be familiar to anyone who ever worked monitoring dials at Sellafield or Dounreay. Alexis stood close by him, offering Jane a look that implied her attendance was an act of solidarity. Rebekah was still busy in the cockpit, flicking switches and ticking boxes on a chart. It was no doubt an important procedure, but Jane couldn't help wondering whether she was merely hiding out until this confrontation was over.

Jane stood her ground, facing off wordlessly with Bett for a few seconds.

'I'm fine, I'm doing all right, thanks for asking,' she eventually said, underlining that he hadn't.

'More by luck than judgement,' he countered. 'I told you directly not to—'

'I got the name. I think that says my judgement wasn't too far off.'

'You abandoned all protocols, all safeguards. You took enormous risks that could have seen the entire mission—'

'I had one chance and I took it,' she insisted, controlling the volume in her voice but powerless to repress the indignation. 'Risk/benefit, remember? I was the one who was there. It was my call, my risk.'

'You disobeyed direct orders, repeatedly. I told you—'

'And I told you, I'm not one of your subordinates. I don't take orders from you, Mr Bett.'

Rebekah finally emerged from the cockpit and stood a few yards off, she and Alexis uncomfortable but compelled observers.

'When you're in the field, yes, you do take fucking orders from me, because the moment you set foot inside that hotel, you did it as part of a team. In the field, you respect the chain of command, because when you don't, nobody knows where the hell they stand. When you went off the reservation tonight, it wasn't your risk to take, because what you did could have got you *and* Rebekah killed.'

Jane looked to Rebekah, who was biting her lip apologetically, like she was sorry to have been used as the trump card in Bett's argument. But if Jane had to lose, she decided she wasn't going to do it with grace.

'Don't forget about your expensive helicopter,' she said. 'You could have lost that too, another of your possessions. And that really *would* have been a tragedy.'

'Jesus Christ, do you honestly think . . .'

Bett let his words falter and looked from Jane to Rebekah, then lastly, perhaps longest, to Alexis, these three women ringed around him beneath the night. The rage seemed to fall from his face like a retreating wave, revealing a sadness beneath it. Jane thought she noticed him nod to himself, the smallest of movements but the involuntary outward signal of some resolution within.

He turned and walked away, saying no more.

Rebekah allowed him a respectful distance and then headed for the house also. 'I seriously need a drink right now,' she announced.

Alexis stayed where she was, turning to watch Rebekah leaving as though to underline the fact that she wasn't. When she turned back, her expression was troubled, indicating 'we need to talk' but clearly not looking forward to it.

'You okay? Really?' she asked quietly.

Jane nodded. 'I'm okay, my head's clear. I don't think it's ever been so clear, in fact. If there's any personal demons going to haunt me about what I did tonight, then they're in a holding pattern right now. I should probably apologise to Rebekah, though. Old grumblebaws is right about that. Always right and never satisfied with what you do. You must love working for him.'

Alexis looked away towards the house for a moment, that strained expression still tugging at her features when she returned her gaze to Jane.

'He's not right, not tonight,' she said. 'You did great in there. Your judgement calls were bang-on and they were your calls to make because you were the one on the spot. You made the plays and you got the name. More than the name: you got the Marledoq insider too. You can say thanks to Rebekah for getting both your asses out of there, but you've nothing to apologise to her for.'

Alexis's voice became quieter, as though to stress a humble meekness to her subsequent suggestion. 'But maybe,' she said, 'if your head's as clear as you say, you might find a conciliatory word to offer Bett.'

'Bett? Why?'

'Well, if it wasn't that I considered it such an improbable concept, I'd be tempted to say I think you just hurt his feelings.'

Jane pictured his face, that look around at the three women, the anger subsiding, the nod of . . . what?

'You're not telling me a guy like that's going to take a piece of petulant nonsense to heart.'

'I think it was the sender, more than the message.'

'What does he care what I think? He doesn't even trust me. He was telling me to bail out before I'd even left the bar tonight.'

359

'You're new to this. He was trying to protect you.'

'Ach, rubbish. You know fine that Bett uses people without concerning himself about what he's getting them into. He was worried I'd blow the mission by getting into something I couldn't handle.'

Alexis nodded. 'Okay, that was bullshit,' she conceded. 'He wasn't trying to protect you, but not because he doesn't care and not because he doesn't trust you. He does trust you: he had no doubts that you knew what you were doing or about how far you were prepared to go. That was the problem. He was protecting himself: he was the one who couldn't handle it.'

'Handle what?'

'What he might have been forced to watch.'

'Oh, don't be daft. I can't see Bett getting suddenly squeamish about being the voyeur when—'

'I was with Bett in the operations room,' Alexis said. 'And believe me, when you kissed Parrier . . .' She left the sentence unfinished, a memory tapering off into the half-light.

Jane sighed. 'I should have a wee word,' she said.

'Better leave it a while. He'll be off sulking in the forbidden zone.'

'I killed people tonight, Alexis. The word "forbidden" doesn't mean a hell of a lot to me right now.'

Jane marched up the stairs, intent on taking the proscribed left turn, and feeling more defiant than she was conciliatory. It seemed absurd that this man could be so commanding, to the point of tyrannous, and yet run off to feel sorry for himself because he didn't like something that was said. Quite simply, she wasn't having it. If he had issues with her, he should be big and scary enough to have them out.

She walked along the corridor, her footfalls not cushioned like the last time, but echoing off the tiles and plaster, intended to draw him forth and to hell with his self-important ire. All of the doors remained closed. When she stopped walking, stilled the clatter of her steps, she heard no sound from behind any of them, though light was visible from beneath two. It reminded her of Ross in his teens. When he was in cream-puff mode, he tended to brood in self-indulgently contemplative silence. Michelle opted

360

more often for slamming doors and cranking up the record player.

The thought made Jane that bit less defiant about the prospect of barging in, remembering how counterproductive any confrontational action tended to be. With a light touch learned from calming a thousand tantrums, she delicately twisted the nearest doorhandle and slowly inched it forward. Provoking no response, she pushed it open just wide enough to pass, and stepped inside.

She found herself in a room lined with bookshelves, hundreds of volumes filed along two sides, tall three-paned windows dominating the outer wall. She wasn't sure what she'd been expecting; perhaps something as gloomy and austere as the corridor. Instead she saw a place of solitude and reflection, somewhere she could imagine sitting on a rainy afternoon, losing herself in infinite lives. But she had need of escape to a more exciting life when she picked up a book; who would want to escape from Bett's? Did he read tales of being a housewife, complete with Tom Clancy-style technical details of the latest state-of-the-art vacuuming hardware?

She ran her eyes along the spines, found many of them to be in French. There were English ones too, the mix of titles so eclectic as to defy any attempt to draw even a shallow impression of taste. It was a collection testifying only to decades of a life.

In the corner, beneath one window, there was a cabinet, three sides glass, standing a little less than waist height. It drew her eye but she caught only a glimpse of its contents before forcing herself to look away. She saw a toy car, grey metal, missing one front tyre; a model aeroplane, perhaps a Spitfire or a Hurricane, green on one side but scorched on the other as though it had come through a real dogfight; and a dog-eared paperback copy of *Kidnapped*. It was tempting to examine them closer, but Jane felt reluctant to look again, like it was some kind of sin, much worse than reading someone else's diary. They were remnants of a childhood, frozen in time behind glass, preserved but untouchable.

Far more than Bett's previous wrath or admonishments, the cabinet made Jane feel she was trespassing somewhere she instinctively knew she ought not to be. She withdrew quietly, crossed the hall and gently opened the other door beneath which light could be seen. Once again, there was no reaction from within. She stepped inside, just to be sure Bett wasn't doing what Ross used to, blanking her intrusion and pretending she wasn't there.

He wasn't, but the room – his *bed*room – seemed sufficiently infused with his presence for her to feel a little nervous about being there alone, uninvited. It was sparsely furnished and simply decorated compared to her own quarters, and though this made it seem spacious, it was a good deal smaller than her room. There was a brass-framed double bed: large, sturdy and, she guessed, antique, but not quite the king-sized, carved-oak four-poster with billowing silk canopies she had half assumed the master's bedroom ought to boast. Nor was there a coffin to lie in or a rail for him to hang upside down from, so that was two more notions out the window. The only concession to the possibility that he was a member of the night-walking undead was an absence of mirrors, but there was an imposingly large wardrobe against one wall, that could well contain a full-length pane on the back of any of its doors.

There was no dressing table here, nothing so frivolous or girly, but there was a low chest of drawers next to the windows, upon which sat a few grooming essentials. It also supported a narrow vase containing a single red rose, and a pewter frame, inside which there was a black and white photograph of a smiling woman holding a baby. She looked young, Jane thought, maybe twenty at most. She remembered a time when twenty seemed old, but that was long before she reached it herself. By the time she had, she felt a lot older than she would ever have believed.

She took a few steps to have a closer look. The photograph wasn't recent, going by the condition, but whether ten years old or twenty or even fifty, she couldn't have said. The woman's long dark hair was swept back behind a band, in a style that had drifted in and out of fashion since Jane could remember, and of her clothes, all but a glimpse of a penny collar was obscured by the child: a podgy and baffled-looking thing, no more than a month old.

Drawn to it, Jane reached to pick up the frame, but never got there, a voice from behind causing her to shudder in startlement and turn around.

'Mrs Fleming.'

Bett was standing in the doorway, leaning against the frame with his hands folded.

Jane's earlier defiance was all drained away, her appetite for confrontation diminished utterly.

'I'm sorry, I thought you were up here,' she offered rapidly.

'I was working downstairs,' he said, his voice subdued, as though he didn't have much fight left in him either. 'Putting out Marius Roth's name to a few resourceful acquaintances. I've already got the name of his boat, and with any luck, in a few hours I should have a whole lot more.'

'Good,' Jane said. 'Great.'

She couldn't think of anything more to say. For all that she'd done tonight, this was the first time she felt truly vulnerable.

Neither of them spoke for a while, another stand-off like outside, but without the aggression. She felt less uncomfortable while Bett was looking silently at her, because when he looked elsewhere it served to emphasise where she was standing. His gaze alighted on the chest of drawers, specifically upon the portrait, then significantly returned to Jane. There was no accusation in his face, but she knew a confession had been extracted from her own eyes.

She glanced at the portrait again by way of coming clean. 'Who is she?' she asked, her voice softer, drier than she'd anticipated.

He simply stared back at first, long enough for Jane to think he wouldn't say. His face was impassive but there was a lot going on behind it, she could tell. His mouth opened and closed, a final false start, then he answered.

'My mother,' he said.

'And you?'

He nodded solemnly.

'My father took it. I don't have any of him, though. He died when I was one, killed on active service. Nothing heroic, it was a bloody motorcycle accident at an army base in Germany. My mother was left to raise me and my new-born sister alone.'

363

'Poor woman,' Jane said sincerely.

'Strong woman,' Bett replied. 'And courageous. Too courageous.'

He swallowed. Jane looked at his face, saw eyes that would never be permitted to cry; trained and disciplined but suffering in their denial.

'She died too,' he said flatly, the absence of emotion in his voice strangely conveying more than a volley of baying sobs, for sobs were a noisy trickling stream and this seemed the placid surface of a pool whose depths of sorrow might never be known. 'I was eleven. A house fire. She got out with my sister and she'd have been fine, but she went back in for me.'

He ceased, offering no more details. None were necessary. She pictured a child's ash-smeared face, stricken and disbelieving, pictured the salvaged toys, a favourite book she'd read to him, saved by a lost eleven-year-old for their connection to a world gone forever. Childhood abruptly ended; love, care, certainty replaced with a fight for survival, the first scarring battles taking place on the inside.

'I'm sorry,' Jane said, her voice crumbling to a whisper.

'That's the reason I sought you out, why I knew how far you'd be prepared to go. I was certain there was no risk you wouldn't take, no sacrifice you would refuse. And that's why I didn't want you to go to Parrier's suite. I was scared of what I might end up watching.'

'If it had come to that, I'd have insisted we go to the bedroom.'

Bett shook his head sadly.

'No, Jane. Don't you understand? I was scared I'd end up watching you die.'

And now Jane did understand, though a little too late to undo certain hurts. She took an involuntary step towards him.

'I'm sorry for what I said about the helicopter,' she told him.

Bett put out a hand, though whether to halt her approach or halt her apology was not clear. He closed the door behind him and half sat, half leaned on the near end of the bedstead.

'Don't worry,' he said. 'It's hardly as though I've earned the right to be offended. In fact when you said it, I found myself looking at you, at Rebekah, at Alexis, and realised what you were all looking back at. I thought about what I'd done to each of you: the situations I'd placed you in, the things I'd made you do. And I understood why you said what you did. I realised none of you could possibly see me as anything other than a monster.'

'Don't be daft, nobody—'

'I am a monster. I've turned kids into assassins, press-ganged runaways . . . I've stolen innocence, Jane. Stolen it from youth like it was stolen from me. They hate me for it and it's right that they should.'

Jane took a cautious step towards him and, not being waved away, took another until she was standing against the brass frame, a foot to Bett's right.

'Whether they should or not, the fact is, they don't hate you,' she told him. 'Oh, sure, you piss them off, probably more than any living soul, but they care about you. The reason I came up here was that Alexis thought you might have had it pretty rough tonight.'

'Alexis,' he said, managing a sad little smile. 'I don't know what I'd do without her.'

'Well, that's a question I think you'd better start to seriously consider soon, because you can't keep her.'

'She wants to leave? She never said anything to me.'

'She never dared. Though perhaps she might have if she thought there was anywhere she could go. But she could go anywhere, couldn't she? With the help of a man with . . . contacts.'

Bett nodded solemnly.

Jane reached down and very slowly, very tenderly, touched his hand, placing her fingers on the backs of his, then interlocking them.

'You're not a monster, Bett. You're a lost wee boy. I should know. I came here looking for one. And I wouldn't have had a hope of finding him without you.'

She lifted her other hand to his face and turned it towards her, then placed her lips against his. Bett's mouth remained still, unresponsive. He turned his face away, briefly closing his eyes.

'I'm sorry,' he said.

'No, I'm sorry,' Jane insisted, flustered and catching a glimpse of how embarrassed she was going to feel about this in the very near future. 'I'd better go,' she said.

Jane went directly back to her room and ran herself a bath. Reckoning she'd never felt quite so in need of one, other than post-labour, and given that she had such a capacity at her disposal, she decided she both required and deserved the biggest, deepest one of her life. She ran the taps, balancing them to regulate the temperature, until the water reached a level that she estimated would just about accommodate her without spilling over the top. Then she undressed, got in and lay back. Her estimate was way out. She closed her eyes and listened to the splash of water pouring down on to the tiles, concentrating on that and the sensation of warmth in order to keep a thousand other, more complicated thoughts at bay.

She lay with her neck resting on the rim, her hair hanging over the side. Every tiny movement, even the rise and fall of her chest as she breathed, caused a further displacement and resultant downpour, the trickling sound echoing around the tiled walls. That, perhaps, was why she didn't hear him approach. Or perhaps she did hear him, but pretended to herself that she hadn't, for she certainly didn't jump like she ought to when she felt his touch, and no bath was relaxing enough to so anaesthetise the reflexes.

She did start a little, moving her neck off the edge and thus pouring another volume over the rim, but his hands steadied her head.

'Shhh,' was all he said.

He pulled her hair to one side and kissed the back of her neck, the sensation sending a charge all along her spine. His lips remained there, his tongue gently brushing the tiny hairs on her skin, all of which seemed to be standing up, stretching and competing for the privilege. Bett's hands rested upon her shoulders, gently pressing and cupping his fingers to describe their shape. They moved slowly down along her upper arms, the pressure light, firm, exquisite; then they moved inwards. Jane felt as though the skin on her chest was rising to meet his fingers, until she realised she was arching her back, impatiently bringing the moment forward.

She sighed, even the outrush of breath feeling like part of a caress.

He continued fondly kissing her neck, but its very tenderness, its affection, made it no longer enough. She turned her head to pull his face to hers, and this time met no indifference. He kissed her deeply, thirstily, like they were lovers long denied.

She broke off eventually, but only to get to her feet, in order to climb out.

'I need to hold you,' she said. 'Skin to skin.'

He pulled his shirt over his head and stepped out of his trousers, leaving them to soak up some of the puddles on the drenched floor. Watching him undress, Jane caught a glimpse of herself standing naked before him, involuntarily prompting images of the young women Bett had entertained here. She swiftly banished them again, dispatching the harpies as clinically as any of the evening's other foes. She'd always been fairly tall, fairly skinny, and even after two kids there had never been that far south her B-cup breasts could have gone. So she was forty-six. So she had stretch-marks and cellulite. She was through being self-conscious, through being too old, through being not good enough.

She pulled him to her, burying her face in his neck for a moment, just relishing the sensation of his body pressed against hers. His arms clasped her, taut and powerful but holding her so gently. She could feel his cock stiffen against her stomach, and that was how she thought of it: his cock. There'd been so many coy, infantile terms between her and a man whose sexuality had been so damaged by religion that he couldn't directly refer to his own penis, but that was in the past, that was *so* in the past.

She reached her right hand down and took hold of it, this *cock*, thrilling to the feel of it, how it reared in response as her fingers encircled it. Bett's lips met her own again. He tipped her head back with his hand and began kissing the front of her neck, followed by her breasts. He almost slipped on the soaking tiles, causing them both to laugh. He said 'shh' again, placed his hands on her bottom, and knelt down in front of her. He kissed her navel, her stomach and the tops of her thighs. Then he pulled her legs slightly apart and did something she'd just about resigned herself to dying without getting to experience.

367

She didn't experience it for long, for, heavenly as it felt, it soon ceased to be all she wanted, at which point she took his hand and led him through to the bedroom. All the shutters and drapes were open, beckoning in the night. That felt right too.

Jane heard a knock at the door as she lay on her side, one arm and one leg stretched across Bett, her fingers tracing circles on his chest. It gave her a moment's pause – some residual memory of her mum walking in on her and a teenage boyfriend, blouse unbuttoned to the navel – and in the time it took her to assure herself she had no one to answer to, Bett called out to the visitor to enter. He clicked on a bedside lamp and sat up as Alexis walked in, carrying a folder. Jane stayed horizontal and pulled the sheet higher to cover herself.

'Sorry to disturb, sir. You weren't answering the phone in your room, and . . .'

'It's fine, Alexis. What is it?'

'Plans and photographs of Roth's boat, *Corsair*.'

'At least the bastard has a sense of humour.'

'It was a commissioned build,' she said, handing over the folder, 'and it's over a hundred feet, so if it's waiting out there, it shouldn't be too hard to ID.'

'It's waiting out there,' Bett insisted, flipping cursorily through the high-definition computer prints. 'They said he was "arriving" yesterday. Most of the buyers assumed he was flying in from somewhere, but he'll have come ashore in a motor launch. He'll stay on land until it's done – won't go back to his boat in case someone tails him to the prize. However, Roth will want the exchange complete and the money in his account as soon as possible, which means he'll want the goods safe but handy. It's out there,' he reaffirmed.

He handed back the folder to Alexis.

'Give these to Rebekah. Tell her to fly at first light. And tell her to see Som before she goes: he's working on something for her.'

'Yes, sir. Goodnight, sir. And goodnight, Jane.'

'Goodnight,' Jane replied bashfully, just before Alexis withdrew.

368

Bett killed the light and snuggled down alongside her again.

'I guess nothing's ever likely to stay secret for long round here,' she said.

'You bothered?' he asked.

'Not really, no. I don't care that they know. But I don't want it to change anything, either. That goes double for you, understand? If you treat me different because of this, I'll tell them all that you could only manage it the once.'

'That would be a lie.'

'I know, but I'm a bitch when I'm crossed.'

'I won't treat you different. But I will be watching your back.'

'That's okay. You had a pretty good view of it twenty minutes ago, and I liked what you were doing then. You can do it again if you like.'

'Tomorrow's going to be a long day, Jane. You ought to get some sleep.'

'I've been asleep for twenty years.'

Stolen glimpses

There was an image of the *Corsair* projected across ten feet of blank wall as Jane took her seat for the briefing, as if the boat could loom any larger in anyone's thoughts. A second laptop sat in the centre of the big table, showing a map of the coastline intersected by a grid. A tiny boat-shaped icon lay amid the blue, an information panel displaying its coordinates just above it like an outsize flag.

'This is where you spotted the boat?' she asked Rebekah.

'Just about. Unless it's moved since.'

'And what if it has?'

Rebekah was about to answer, but Somboon eagerly beat her to it.

'The coordinate read-out is coming from a GPS tracking device attached to the hull. I used a modified version of the kind of sensor employed in heat-seeking missiles as the guidance system, controlling a miniature propulsion engine, and housed the lot in a magnetised aluminium casing. The whole thing was the size of a grapefruit. Once Rebekah ID-ed the boat, she just had to drop my baby out of the window into the water and it made its own way to the target.'

'You had to ask,' Alexis said wearily.

Bett called them to order by changing the projected image to a photograph of an expensively dressed middle-aged man flanked by two younger men in sunglasses.

'This is Marius Roth,' he said. 'He's a multi-millionaire international broker, fixer and facilitator, operating usually just inside the cusp of respectability but generally understood, especially by those who do business with him, to be dirty as hell. He's got his finger in a lot of pies, mostly arms related, and has a lot of political connections too. He's acted as a go-between in a number of major international covert weapons purchases, most notably the illegal sale of helicopter gunships to Sonzola that almost brought down the Dutch government two years ago.'

Bett hit the keyboard and changed the image to a top-down plan of the boat.

'We won't be seeing him again today. He's not our concern. He's on dry land to control the sale, and away from his captives in order to protect his deniability. He isn't an obstacle and as far as bringing him to justice is concerned, Nicholas Willis hasn't put that on the job-sheet yet. What is our concern is his security personnel. According to reliable intelligence, Roth keeps a permanent personal staff of six, supplemented according to circumstance. Reports vary as to how many. He's made it known he has four with him at Cap Andreus, which could of course be bullshit. The real question is how many are on the boat, and it's a question I'm sure we'd all like answered before we hit it tonight.'

'No kidding,' Alexis opined.

'Unfortunately, I'm not interested in answers that come at the expense of letting them know we're on to them. The *Corsair* has full radar capability, so if anyone has any suggestions regarding how we can take a closer look at them without being noticed, now's your chance. Otherwise we start looking at worst-case scenarios and move to prep accordingly.'

'What sort of thing would you be hoping to find out?' Jane asked.

'Well, apart from numbers, what weapons they have, the command structure, and, ideally, where they're holding the prisoners so we're not running around opening every door on the tub.'

'And how could you find all that out, even if you were right alongside them?'

'You'd have to ask Som . . .'

'Please don't,' Alexis interrupted.

'. . . about some of that, but basically the closer we could get, the more we could find out.'

'Except that you can't afford to be caught looking,' Jane confirmed.

'Exactly.'

She looked again at the *Corsair* up on the wall, her head filling with thoughts of luxury yachts, marinas, riches, privilege and glamour. One image in particular stuck in her mind: of a doomed princess and a playboy billionaire's son, blurred and distant, a private time intruded upon by a world greedy for voyeuristic gratification.

'Shoot me down if this sounds daft,' she said.

'Don't worry, he will,' Alexis assured her, at least one person who was confident Bett wouldn't be treating Jane differently.

'But what if they thought you were looking at something else?'

'Out at sea?' Bett asked. 'What the hell else could we be looking at?'

Jane turned her gaze to Alexis and then Rebekah.

'So where is this yacht moored?' Jane asked.

'San Raphael,' Bett told her. 'Half an hour from here. Nuno chartered it three days ago and it's been kept on standby ever since. He's on the phone right now: we'll have a second boat hired and ready by the time we drive down there.'

'Which one will I be on? With the girls or . . .'

'Neither,' he replied flatly.

'You can't exclude me from this,' she warned him. 'You promised you wouldn't . . .'

'Can you scuba-dive?' he asked.

Jane's heart sank. It was worse than if he was excluding her; it was that there was no way of *in*cluding her. This was the situation she feared most, one of the things that had driven her to come this far: sitting it out while Ross's fate lay in other people's hands.

'No,' she admitted. 'I did it once on holiday about, God, ten years ago.'

Bett looked at his watch.

'In that case, it looks like you've got roughly eight hours to learn before tonight. Go on, Armand is waiting for you by the pool.'

'I swear,' Lex said, 'if there's any film in those things, I am *not* gonna see the funny side.'

'Goddamn right,' Rebekah agreed. 'I only went for this

373

because it was Jane's idea. If it had been any of the guys, I'd have told them to forget it. Even Bett.'

'There's no film in mine, but I do have about a gig of memory down here,' Somboon called out from below.

'And that's where it better stay,' Lex warned him. 'You stick your head above deck right now and I'll strangle you with my bikini top. It's not like I'm getting any other fucking use out of it.'

'The things you have to do to make a living,' Rebekah sighed. 'Though I guess I shouldn't complain too much. Under other circumstances this would be a pretty pleasant way to spend some time: the open sea, luxury yacht, cool drink, sunshine, to say nothing of posing as glam young starlets on the lam from the paparazzi.'

'Under other circumstances, yeah. For me, those would have to include genuine solitude and for it to be about ten degrees warmer too. My nipples are starting to pick up AM radio.'

They were, as Rebekah described, on the open sea, under spring sunshine (somewhat cooled by a maritime spring breeze), sunbathing topless on the foredeck of a yacht as it bobbed gently on the waves, only a few hundred yards from the *Corsair*. Their approach had been noted by the larger vessel, as Som reported – observing and listening from the cabin below through an array of zoom lenses, infrared scopes and parabolic mikes. The first response had been to hustle two people below decks out of sight, then pairs of binoculars had been produced by a couple of the crew in order to get a closer look at their visitors.

Rebekah had been manning the tiller at that point, Lex lying up front on a lounger, tossing back dire threats if her colleague didn't make good with her promise to take her top off also once they were in range.

She did, and played it cute too, waiting for Som to confirm that they were being surveyed, then giving a big wave to the boys with the binoculars before losing her T-shirt. So there they were, with the bad guys too busy looking at them to notice that Som was looking back. But that was only half the subterfuge. The clincher arrived after about half an hour: Nuno and Bett a quarter of a mile away on a smaller motor launch, posing as paparazzi, massive zoom lenses in plain view for the guys with the goggles to get a load of.

They reacted less hospitably towards the faux photographers, one of them firing a flare across their bows to demonstrate that they had been noted and were not welcome; as well as to alert the sunbathing starlets that they were being snapped. Thus alerted, Lex and Rebekah reached (gratefully) for towels and T-shirts, covering up in a fussy show of righteous celebrity outrage. The flares having drawn their attention, the photographers turned their lenses towards the *Corsair*, where the man who'd fired it held up a different kind of gun, intimating what would be the next shot across their bows if they didn't get lost. They did, turning their motor launch around and zooming off with an angry buzz of the engine.

Lex and Rebekah responded to this development by standing up to applaud, throwing in a few 'my hero' gestures, hands clasped to chests. Then they stripped off again and resumed their places on the loungers.

Throughout all of this pantomime, Som was shooting, listening, noting, recording. He got the number of guards (five), even caught some of their names, sussed the approximate chain of command, noted who went to which position when each boat appeared, and got a rough fix on where the prisoners were being held that they could later cross-check against the vessel's plans.

Then, once he'd garnered everything he usefully could, Lex and Rebekah gave their admirers a farewell wave, got dressed again and headed for shore.

Twilight and dark water

Bett cut the engine and let the yacht drift silently as far as its momentum would take it. It was the cue for one final weapons and equipment check, as well as for a sharp tightening in Jane's gut. There was no stopping this now, no going back, but it wasn't what she might be facing that was making her apprehensive: it was what was at stake.

She'd heard Tom's voice, old Margaret's on the checkout, asking who she thought she was, what she thought she was doing, but they were mere echoes, addressed to some other woman.

The rest of the team were getting nervous too, but its manifestation was also its therapy. They talked nonsense, wound each other up.

'Do you think I look fat in this?' Alexis asked, indicating the bullet-proof armour she had on under her T-shirt.

'Kevlar is very slimming,' Armand assured her, kneeling down by the gunwale and making some final preparation to his kit. 'Trouble is, how are they going to recognise you if they can't see your nipples? I mean, you don't think those guys with binoculars were looking at your face, do you?'

'Maybe if I stick two bullets in front, here, I can . . .'

Bett held up a hand and cut her off. 'A-fag, everybody. A-fag. Armand, it's time.'

'A-fag?' Jane asked. 'What is that, like "smoke 'em if you got 'em"?'

'No, it means cut the bullshit, it's time to get serious. It's an abbreviated acronym.'

'For what?'

'All fun and games until somebody loses an eye.'

Jane nodded. 'I hear you.'

Alexis turned to Bett.

377

'Hey, you guys do know this boat is on fire, right?'

'I said A-fag,' he told her.

'You still got that wee tube stashed somewhere safe?' Ross asked.

'Aye. The sea air chapping your lips?'

'No, just checking.'

'I was afraid they'd take it off me seeing as they must have seen it on camera.'

'Maybe they weren't watching at the time, or maybe they didn't consider it a threat. Which it isn't, not to them. If I'd palmed you a flick knife, maybe . . .'

'Do you want it back?'

'No, just thinking aloud. I'm not so sure it's going to matter. When I gave you it, I was thinking there'd come a time when I'd get taken off to . . . wherever, and they'd let you go, but I think we're in this together for the duration. The bad news is the duration might not be very long.'

'You going to tell me what it is, then?'

'No. That part hasn't changed. It's still best for both of us that you don't know, even if we do get sold as a job lot. Maybe especially if we get sold as a job lot.'

'Can't see it happening any other way,' Dad said gloomily. 'For one thing, they cannae just let me walk away if I can identify them, or if I can raise the alarm about whoever's bought you.'

'You're also needed to ensure my cooperation,' Ross added, unable to prevent himself glancing at his dad's bandaged fingers. The pain had kept them both up half the night, Dad unable to sleep for the discomfort, Ross for the storms in his head.

The atmosphere on board today had been very tense, particularly in the morning, the first time they'd faced their tormentors since. Gilbert and Guillaume had mostly kept out of their way, though this was unlikely to be out of any sensitivity or regret. Every time Ross did lay eyes on either of them, his mind filled instantly with hatred and thoughts of retribution, and both of them knew that. They also knew they could take him in a second, but it was a situation their professionalism warned them to avoid: Ross was potentially irrational, and the last thing they could afford was some livid and desperate gambit on his part that ended with him dead.

'So how would that work?' Dad asked. 'I mean, once the gavel's down and the winner gets his purchase.'

'Basically, they'll lean on me by leaning on you until I tell them everything I can about the Gravity Well, enough for their own developers to begin work.'

'But that can't go on forever, can it? You and me locked up in a secret cell feeding out technical titbits in exchange for staying alive.'

'No. The developers would be guys like me – they'd never be allowed to know the source of the information. This would give them two choices. One is to buy me out: buy my expertise, buy my silence and yours, make me a legitimate employee. But that's a lot more risky, a lot more expensive and a lot less convenient than just shooting us both in the head once I've given up the goods.'

'Cheery thought.'

'I'm just giving it to you straight, Dad. And what's worse is that's only the scenario if the buyer wants to develop the technology. If they just want to stop it . . .'

'Then the duration, as you said, won't be very long.'

They both found themselves staring out of the cabin's small window, it being an easier place to look than at each other. They were sharing his dad's quarters, Ross's own now out of bounds, presumably in case he took the desperate option to swim for it, or perhaps, in still greater desperation, to throw a seven. There were other cabins free, but not, he guessed, with in-built surveillance.

It was dark outside; not as black as it would get, but the last of the sun was failing. However, there was something to look at for a change: a small flickering light, its distance impossible to gauge. Some small vessel, tantalising proof that they weren't so far from the coast. It was the third sign of the outside world since daybreak. The first had been a helicopter, flying high overhead early this morning. The sight of it caused a heaving in Ross's chest, a surge of optimism like the old sailors must have felt at the sight of the first bird heralding landfall. Then it had passed indifferently, about its own business, leaving him feeling like a marooned wretch on a desert island, unable to signal to a passing ship.

The second sign had been another boat, initially only glimpsed on the horizon. Ross and Dad were ushered below decks before it came fully into sight, sent to Dad's cabin and watched over there by one of the guards in case they made any lame attempt to signal for help. The cabin being portside, however, they did at least get to see it: a pleasure cruiser not exactly crewed by hardy mariners and thus evidently not far out of port. It was a good couple of hundred yards away, maybe more, but he'd been able to make out two women sunbathing on deck: a blonde and a brunette. It looked like they were topless, but that might have been his mind wishfully filling in details unverifiable at that distance. What was verifiable, what was utterly certain, was that they were oblivious to what was happening aboard the bigger vessel. He had fantasies of telepathy, wished they had X-ray vision to see inside the hull, see the men with guns and their prisoners, but what were two spoiled bimbos going to do about that anyway?

After a while, he had decided resentfully that he hated them, and that was before they started waving to the guards like self-satisfied prick-teases. Shortly after that they had sailed away again, blithely leaving the scene of a crime-in-progress. It seemed to emphasise the hopelessness, the insurmountable barriers preventing even contact with the outside world, never mind escape.

'We're on borrowed time,' he admitted gravely.

'We've been on that since Barcelona,' his dad reasoned.

'Aye, but I mean the ref's looking at his watch, Dad. The heid bummer went ashore yesterday morning, and that bastard Gilbert's mobile was going off all day today, far more often than normal.'

'With his bloody Marseillaise ringtone.'

'Aye. The words, "love, love, love," keep popping into my head afterwards. Couldnae think of anything less appropriate.'

They both tried to laugh, but it was dry and bitter. They were running on empty and they both knew it. The flickering light across the waves kept drawing their eyes, a place for their gazes to retreat. It seemed to be getting larger, which couldn't be right, unless it was getting closer. The flickering was more pronounced, too, less like the blinking of distant lights than like fire, which *definitely* couldn't be right.

'Look, don't lose heart, son,' Dad said. It sounded a lot like, 'there, there,' with as much intrinsic value as an offer to kiss something better. There was some buried part of Ross that it soothed a little, ancient memories of a time when that voice alone, even saying, 'there, there,' could make him feel better. But that same part of him, in responding to this tiny droplet of balm, awakened his greater need for another source of healing. He tried to swallow it back, tried to spare his dad the hurt, tried to stem the tears, but lost the self-control to prevent any of it.

'I want my mum,' he said, sobbing.

He looked at his father, who was nodding gently, his eyes filling too. Unable to take it, Ross stared out of the window again, where the flickering light was now leaping and dancing, now something unmistakably aflame.

'Here, is that something on fire?' Dad asked curiously.

About a second and a half later, it exploded.

Jane felt the dinghy rock and a wave pulse through the sea as the blast ripped into the night somewhere above the surface. She heard a boom too, but it was muted by the water and the sound of her own breathing. She had her left hand on the keel of the fibreglass vessel, gripping a cord that dangled from the bow, while her right hauled her forward, her legs kicking for further propulsion. She saw by infrared, the *Corsair* a smudge of light green against enveloping darker shades, tiny streaks of white moving within it, getting larger as the dinghy progressed. She was clad from ankles to neck in a black wetsuit, a single air tank strapped to her back, the regulator clamped as snugly to her mouth and nose as the airtight goggles were sealed around her eyes. A Kevlar vest was strapped to her trunk, negating the need for diving weights to keep her below the surface. She did have a belt, but the only lead it contained was in the automatic pistol and spare clips zipped securely inside various pockets along its circumference. Flanking her on either side, Bett and Armand were swimming a few yards clear of the vessel, out of range of the oar strokes. And topside, charcoal-smeared, soaked black T-shirt over her armour, was Alexis, rowing her lifeboat away from the burning wreck of her pleasure cruiser – recently and expertly destroyed by Armand – towards the only succour to be found upon these waves.

'Isn't there some kind of moral taboo, something really low about killing people by taking advantage of the fact that they're coming to your rescue?' Alexis had asked, when Bett outlined his new plan, adapted in response to the day's previous success.

'They won't be coming to your rescue,' he assured her. 'They'll be salvaging some T&A they can abuse with impunity because they can burn the body after they've had their fun and nobody will ever know. They can't afford to let any strangers on board; or rather, they can't allow any to ever get off again, which means that if they're too disciplined to indulge themselves in the distraction of gang-rape, when they come down to the stern platform, it might simply be to shoot you.'

'I'll bear that in mind. And I'd ask you and Armand to keep it pretty prominent in your thoughts too.'

A digital gauge on the night-sight told Jane what distance they were from the *Corsair*, her pulse quickening more from the ever-diminishing numbers on the read-out than from the exertion of her strokes. Her job would be to stay with Alexis and keep the platform secured while Bett and Armand took on the more dangerous point-work of proceeding inside in search of Ross and Tom. However, she was under no illusions about what she was involved in tonight, even without Bett repeatedly restressing it. It was an assault, approaching from below, against a team of armed professionals. Real guns, real bullets, and with the enemy enjoying an elevated angle of fire. The element of surprise was crucial, though it wasn't the only thing giving them an edge.

They were twenty metres out when the waters above became suddenly illuminated: a searchlight from above. Bett and Armand immediately dived deeper and drifted wider in response. Jane, out of sight beneath the dinghy, remained close to the surface, close enough to make out shouting and Alexis calling back in response. Stretching her head forward, Jane could see upwards to the platform, which remained unoccupied, but not for long. As the range-finder read twelve metres, Jane saw two white shapes appear on the transom-deck platform. They were slightly distorted by the water, but as she got used to how the infrared rendered them, she could make out more and more detail. They appeared to be conferring, one of them holding an object to his mouth: some kind of walkie-talkie.

Eight metres.

'Help me,' Alexis was calling. 'Please. There was a fire. My friend . . . Oh God.'

Walkie-talkie down. More conferring. A nod.

Four metres.

Any second now Jane's view upward would be eclipsed as the dinghy reached the *Corsair*'s stern.

Two metres.

Just before it was, she saw one figure reach into his jacket, the other taking a step back. Jane looked to her side, saw Bett break the water, pistol held in two hands. She heard the shots ring out as she let go of the cord and lunged with her left hand to grip the short ladder descending from the platform. The dinghy was kicked backwards and clear of her head by the force of Alexis climbing off and aboard the *Corsair*.

She felt Alexis's hands grip her arm and yank her quickly forwards, yelling 'Get down!' as the searchlight swept across the platform from the flydeck high above, a heartbeat before a hail of bullets did the same thing. Jane dived headlong across the floor and joined Alexis in crouching against the bulkhead, far enough in to be out of sight from the decks above.

A few feet away, two bodies were lying flat on their backs and twitching. At this range, the infrared goggles made facial features distinguishable, and what most distinguished this pair was that they were missing many of theirs.

Jane looked back as Alexis helped her discard the air tank. Bett and Armand were still in the water, out of sight. The search-beam swept back and forth across the platform and the waves, its operator now enjoying a clear shot downwards at anyone who tried to climb aboard.

'The window is closed,' Alexis put it, pressing the transmit button and speaking into the boom mike of the comms earpiece she had just removed from her belt. Jane heard the voice crackle in her left ear as well as hearing it live through her right, and remembered to lever down her own boom mike now that her regulator had been discarded.

Alexis pulled a gun from a holster strapped to her back,

prompting Jane to remove her weapon from inside her utility belt. Alexis shuffled back a few feet and fired up towards the flydeck, holding the pistol with both hands as she unleashed four rounds. One of her shots took out the searchbeam, but a lift of Jane's goggles revealed there was still plenty of light bathing the platform from other sources. This time, when fire was returned, it was fully automatic. Alexis huddled back against the bulkhead.

'Motherfucker,' she spat, aiming a look astern, where Bett and Armand would not be climbing aboard any time soon.

Bett's voice sounded in their ears, it being safer for him to surface now that the searchlight was dead. She couldn't see him, probably having swum around to one side of the hull so that no one else could either.

'Roger that,' he acknowledged. 'Window is closed. I'll see if Nuno can reopen it, but meantime you have point. You can wait for Nuno or you can proceed to locating the prisoners. It's your call.'

Alexis looked to Jane, who simply nodded.

'Proceeding, sir,' she reported.

'Roger that. Rebekah, you are now Go for approach. Nuno, we are pinned down by suppressing fire from the flydeck. One hostile, automatic weapon. Please deal.'

'Wilco,' Nuno replied.

'Somboon, you are Go too, but keep your boat outside the agreed perimeter until the vessel is secure.'

'Roger.'

Alexis tapped Jane's goggles, which she interpreted as a reminder to take them off. Instead, when she went to do so, Alexis restrained her hand and gestured instead to Jane's belt, where she was carrying Alexis's pair.

'But all the lights are on,' Jane reasoned.

'Lights don't let you see through walls.'

They proceeded on quiet feet, taking it in turns to run forward to the next point of refuge – a corner, a doorway – while the other stayed in place, ready to offer covering fire should anyone appear. The view through the goggles was unnervingly dim, turning what Jane knew to be brightly lit corridors and walkways into a low-contrast haze. She felt as though she'd be more aware of her environment and thus safer if she just took them off, but knew that the one thing they rendered sharply distinct was also the one thing she most needed to see coming. In these tight passageways, the slightest moment's advantage could be decisive.

They knew where they were headed, Som having triangulated roughly where the prisoners had been while the sunbathers and the paparazzi played out their little tableau. However, there was a big difference between seeing a location on a plan and finding it in three dimensions, especially when the guards were used to the layout of the real thing.

They were, by mutual estimation, one deck below where they needed to be. Alexis paused at the foot of a staircase, a tightly raked helix that would bring the climber around to face the opposite direction upon reaching the level above. Somewhere beyond the vessel, the sound of rotor blades approached. Alexis held up a fist, meaning hold. Jane understood what she was waiting for: they both knew that at any moment there'd be a major commotion to say the very least, hopefully enough to provide sufficient distraction to anyone waiting upstairs.

Alexis made her move as the gunfire erupted from somewhere above, Nuno shooting through the open side door of the chopper with a tripod-mounted assault-rifle. If the guard on the flydeck got off any response, Jane didn't hear it. She ascended gun-first up the stairwell, in front of which Alexis was now crouching, training her pistol back and forth. They were close to the front, at the axis where two corridors curved around to meet near the prow.

'Hostile is down,' Nuno reported. 'Repeat, hostile on the flydeck is down. Clear to board, I am covering the stern platform.'

Jane's head had barely emerged before she instinctively ducked it under again in response to Alexis opening fire. Alexis discharged short controlled bursts, a few rounds at a time, aiming down the corridor to the right. Keeping the gun trained with one hand, she gestured behind her back to Jane with the other.

'Come on,' she ordered, her voice an insistent hiss.

Jane resumed her climb but ducked briefly again when she

385

fully cleared the stairhead and saw two white shapes somewhere ahead of her, one far larger than the other. Alexis was firing at the smaller, keeping him crouched somewhere around the curvature of the corridor where he was restricted to loosing off the odd blind shot; with no target to aim at, it was just noise. Each time the blob on the right moved forward, Alexis unleashed another couple of rounds. The blob on the left, thus being ignored, was, Jane realised, behind a wall, and according to her rangefinder, twelve metres away to the smaller's six.

'Need a clip,' Alexis warned.

Jane handed Alexis her full pistol in exchange for the empty, then ejected the spent magazine and quickly slid home a replacement. Alexis gave her an okay gesture with her free hand, then stabbed a finger three times in the direction of the left-hand corridor.

Jane got the message: she had this guy pinned down – go go go.

She proceeded slowly. As she followed the curved corridor around, she realised that from the apex at the stairhead she hadn't been viewing the larger blob through one wall, but three: it was in a cabin abutting the ship's outer hull. And as she progressed, reducing three walls to one, the target gradually clarified, expanded and changed shape until she could distinguish that it was in fact three people.

She walked as lightly as she could, now only a few metres away from the cabin. Through the wall, the figures were blurred: recognisably human-shaped but indistinguishable from each other. A very simple process of elimination told her who these three people were, but the life-or-death question remained: which was which?

Behind her, Alexis's suppressing fire continued to ring out. So far she'd fired four rounds from the fresh pistol. That left six more before she'd need to reload, which would require her to fall back and let her opponent make a move. Jane edged forward until she was right outside the cabin, the three figures only feet in front of her through a thin partition wall. Two were standing, one seated, but there was nothing to identify the guard.

She raised her gun in both hands and breathed in deeply.

* * *

386

Guillaume stood by the wall nearest the door, his Glock clutched to his chest, Dad at the opposite end of the room, sitting on the bed. They were all utterly silent, utterly still. Guillaume had appeared briefly after the explosion, ordering them to remain in the cabin, then returned for keeps shortly after sounds of gunfire broke out: repeat rounds from the stern, full-auto volleys from above. They'd heard a helicopter too, preceding further, higher-calibre ordnance amid panicked radio signals and an increasingly sweaty look of anxiety on Guillaume's face.

Ross hadn't yet dared believe it was a rescue. Who could know what enemies these people had, what other nefarious shit they were up to their eyes in? Plus there was always the possibility that some motivated buyer had found out where the goods were stashed and decided to cut out the middle man. Whatever it was, his jailers were getting their arses kicked. They were armed, they were disciplined, they were trained, but they'd been blindsided, and now they were being outgunned. Airborne assault tended to skew the odds that way, and from the ongoing sound of chopper blades, the gunship didn't have any imminent intention of leaving.

They'd heard Guillaume make his frantic call-outs, requesting check-in responses, getting fewer each time. Then the shooting had started just along the corridor, at which point he'd flipped the safety and put a finger to his lips. Guillaume said nothing, *could* say nothing, but the message was made clear by him briefly pointing the gun at Dad: either of you do anything to let them know we're in here, and I'll have nothing to lose by shooting him.

Outside in the corridor, the firing continued at irregular intervals; mostly nearby, with occasional replies from elsewhere on the same deck. He heard a slider being pulled, a round being chambered after reload, the sounds following almost immediately after the most recent brace of shots from the nearer gun. Ross could see in Guillaume's face that the guard's trained ears had made the same deduction as he had: the reload was too soon after the last shot to be the work of the same pair of hands, and they both knew it couldn't be Guillaume's colleague who had back-up. There was someone else out there, close by, free of the stand-off, moving, searching: if not for the prisoners then for any remaining guards.

Guillaume repeated the finger-to-lips gesture in the lull after the next exchange of fire.

Dad looked over, an expression of determination setting across his face. Ross read it: he was ready to defy, ready to take a bullet if it might save his son. Ross shook his head, eyes bulging in silent pleading: *Don't do this.*

Guillaume read it too. He fixed Dad with a look of direst threat, then extended his arm full length to level the Glock at him.

Ross swallowed, shaking his head faster: *Please, Dad, don't do this.*

Guillaume cocked the hammer, sweat trickling down his forehead. Dad's nostrils flared, an unmistakable *Fuck You*, then his lips formed.

Please no, Ross wordlessly implored.

'WE'RE HERE!' Dad shouted, the words barely out before the first gunshot sounded.

Ross couldn't close his eyes before the hammer fell. He witnessed Guillaume's arm rear up as five bullets ripped through the walls and into his chest. Their jailer was knocked back like a reeling boxer, matter exploding from his body with each blow, then he fell backwards to the floor.

Dad was down too, howling 'Ah, Jesus,' as he clutched his right forearm, where Guillaume's single erratic bullet had lodged.

The door flew open from a kick and a black-clad figure filled the frame: some futuristic cyber-soldier; black goggles around the eyes, stick-mike and earpiece wired to the mothership, wet black hair swept behind the night-scope, black Kevlar armour hugging the trunk, black rubber covering the skin from neck to toes. The figure stepped forward into the cabin, both hands extending a nine-mill, advancing to stand over Guillaume. The gun fired twice more, two to the head, end of.

Four more shots reported from the corridor, then ceased.

The figure turned to survey the prisoners, staring for what seemed an age.

'Who . . .' Ross began to ask, but was stopped by the figure – he now thought, surprisingly, that it might even be a woman – holding up a hand and hissing, 'Shh'. He thought he heard a crackle of transmission in the earpiece, confirmed when she said: 'All the way around. Roger. On it.'

She knelt rapidly and picked Guillaume's gun from his dead fingers, then positioned herself in a crouch, looking towards the far end of the room as though there was someone standing there.

'Get down,' she told him. 'Now.'

Ross didn't argue. He dropped to the floor and watched her cross both weapons at her wrists, her gaze and her guns tracking along the wall like she could see through it. Then she opened fire again and he realised that this was because she *was* seeing through it. She directed ten or twelve rounds upwards through the partition in a mercilessly rapid syncopation: fingers gripping, hammers alternating, kickback compensated by the crouch and the cross-over. Somewhere amid the final shots of this salvo he heard a thump from beyond the wall. She paused, held her pose, guns still pointed but now silenced.

Ross was in awe. The men who'd held him had been the real deal, not some bunch of minimum-wage security guards with a Mussolini complex; but *these* guys, whoever they were, were something else entirely; and this woman, this cyber-assassin, was just the baddest of the bad.

'Hostiles four and five eliminated,' she reported. 'Prisoners secure but Tom has been hit. Somboon, we need that boat here soon as.'

Her accent was Scottish, her voice just about the most reassuring sound he'd ever heard; reassuring, in fact, to the point of familiar, unnervingly so when she said Dad's name. No. Slow down. Knowing names meant nothing. They'd have been briefed. His emotions were running away with him. He didn't even know yet whether he could trust these people. But there was something about . . . no. Get it together, man.

She stood up again and turned to face the two of them.

'It's okay now, Ross, it's over,' she said. 'Tom, are you all right? Is it just your arm?'

'I'll be fine as soon as I get off this . . .' Dad's reply petered out in confusion, perhaps down to his pain and disorientation, as *surely* he couldn't be entertaining the same bizarre delusion that he knew that voice.

'Who are you?' Ross asked, his register falling to a bewildered whisper. 'Why are you here?'

She seemed to start at this, as though surprised by what he considered the most natural questions he could possibly have asked at that moment. Then she muttered 'Oh, the mask,' and took off her goggles, at which point very little in Ross's world continued to make much sense. For a horrible moment he thought this meant he was about to wake up in the same cabin and find himself still a prisoner, but the smell of cordite and the thumping in his chest were unmistakably real.

'You were out playing past your bedtime, son,' his mum said, tears in her eyes. 'I had to come and get you.'

One last bullet

Jane gave Ross a tight, lingering hug of the kind she'd reliably embarrassed him with down the years, and then finally let him go to board the chopper. Nicholas Willis was already on board, having completed his business with Bett. He looked tired and rather ruffled, like he hadn't had the quietest time of it of late either, but he seemed, for all of that, very calm. There was something of the eccentric but absent-minded schoolmaster about him, and Jane found it hard to imagine him playing hardnose with the types she had encountered at the Reine d'Azur. Willis had flown to Nice in person to escort Ross back to Marledoq, a touch she had admired, but perhaps further evidence that he was, sadly, a bit of a walking anachronism.

Alexis was on board too, up front with Rebekah. She'd seemed a little jumpy since they got Ross back to 'Maison Blah', as she called it, more so when Willis arrived this morning.

'This job began at Marledoq, and I won't feel it's done until it ends there too,' she'd explained when Rebekah asked why she wanted to tag along.

'It began at Chassignan,' Rebekah corrected. 'That's where the apartment was.'

'Whatever.'

Ross climbed aboard, then Alexis hopped out and slid the cabin door closed. Alexis stepped back into the cockpit and a few minutes later they took off.

Jane watched the bird shrink towards the horizon, wishing she could have had a little longer with her son, but aware that there would be time – there would be plenty of time.

She made her way back inside the house and eventually tracked Bett down to the kitchen, where he was making coffee with his grand contraption.

'Any chance of a cappuccino?' she asked.

'Certainly, Mrs Fleming,' he answered, opening the fridge and pouring milk into a stainless-steel jug.

'You can knock that off now. Ross is away and Tom's going to be in the hospital another couple of days.'

'And then what?' he asked, his voice becoming quiet to the point of timid.

Jane looked away, didn't answer, didn't want to.

'How did your meeting with Mr Willis go?' she asked, self-consciously changing the subject. 'I take it everyone's satisfied they've plugged the leak, otherwise Ross wouldn't have gone back.'

'Following up your lead, Willis uncovered a slew of emails between this man Segnier and OSE.'

'Ross had never heard of him.'

'He works for Phobos, the parent company, based at their premises in Lyon. That was why he didn't have direct access to the data. I should say, "worked" for Phobos. He's been fired and a criminal investigation is pending.'

'Still, the information is out there. What steps are they taking to ensure someone doesn't just kidnap Ross all over again?'

Bett placed a wide mug of espresso in front of Jane and poured frothy milk into it until it reached the brim. He left the jug on the table, handy for a top-up.

'That game is all but over. With Ross no longer up for grabs by underhand means, it's been back to business for the companies interested in the Gravity Well.'

'And they all just act like nothing happened?'

'Officially, nothing did. The auction never took place, and all of the evidence we garnered about who was bidding was illegally obtained. But the bottom line is, Willis has secured a more than adequate compensation for what they were attempting. He's concluded a highly lucrative arrangement with British Defence Engineering and their Italian partners CMK.'

'Phobos is selling off Deimos, then?'

'No. It's an investment deal. The Brits and Italians will put, or should I say torrentially *pour*, vast sums into Deimos's research and development, in exchange for a share in all resulting technologies, though obviously there's only one resulting technology they're really interested in. Deimos is in the money, and not a moment too soon, considering the size of invoice I'm about to hit Willis with.'

'You're worth every penny,' she said, placing a hand on his.

'We've got a temporary apartment organised for you,' Willis told him. 'I wasn't sure you'd want to go back to the old one, and it's your choice, but given everything that's happened, it might be best if we kept you somewhere under wraps until this deal is finalised. I'm so sorry about what happened, I really am.'

Ross looked across the cabin at the old man. It had taken him a while to recover from the mind-buggering jolt of his mother having turned into Carrie-Ann Moss, but once he had resumed accepting what was before his eyes as fact, certain of those facts had started to form a pattern.

The first clue was that it was this guy Bett and his people who were behind the rescue, the same outfit as Willis contracted for the Tiger Team exercise and security overhaul. The second, as he'd suspected all along, was written all over the face of that girl Alexis, who'd been insinuating herself into every room, every conversation and who was even now on board this flight. She was the one who stole the files, but Bett didn't know, and she was shitting herself in case Ross made mention of it; hanging around him so that if he did tumble her, she'd at least know when the cat was out of the bag.

And then the big one, the thing that pulled everything into focus: Willis nailing BDE and CMK for a combined investment of nearly two hundred million euros.

'You leaked it, didn't you,' Ross said, a statement rather than a question.

Willis gazed out of the window for a moment, procrastinating. Then he turned back to Ross and nodded.

'I did.'

'There is no Segnier.'

'No.'

'And you never really asked Bett what that girl Alexis was doing with my computer that night, did you?'

'No.'

Ross shook his head.

393

'If I hadn't seen enough violence of late, I'd be kicking your fucking head in right now, you know that?'

'I do, and I am truly sorry, Ross. I had no idea it would work out this way.'

'They came after my family, for Christ's sake, not just me. That's what you exposed me to.'

Willis nodded, taking his licks, but Ross didn't have the energy to dole out too many of them. They sat in silence for a while, listening to the muted sound of the rotorblades and the engines. Then Willis sat up straighter and folded his arms, the penitence erased from his expression, replaced by a piercing stare of which Ross would never have imagined him capable.

'You're right to be angry, Ross, absolutely right. But I'm not the only one with a confession to make, am I?'

Bett pulled his hand away rather stiffly, using it to lift his mug as an attempted disguise for his discomfort.

'How is your husband?' he asked, by way of emphasising the source.

Jane sighed, folding her arms.

'He's okay. They had to operate to remove the bullet. The operation went fine, but he was still unconscious when I left. They're going to keep him there for observation.'

'You speak to him much before he went under?'

'Yeah, as much conversation as I'd normally have out of him in a month; once he was convinced he wasn't hallucinating from the pain, that is. Shit, that reminds me, he gave me something to give to Ross and I forgot about it.'

'What?'

'Weird. He thought he was hallucinating and I thought he was delirious. He said it was something Ross had given him to be used as a last resort, which he wouldn't be needing any more.'

'And what was it?'

She paused, realising how crazy it was going to sound.

'A tube of lip balm.'

Bett's face remained admirably free of mirth. He seemed curious, in fact.

'Lip balm? Can I see it?'

'Sure,' she said, and reached into her jacket pocket. She handed it to him. He examined the tube as it lay flat on his palm, then opened it and twisted the end to project the pearly white shaft.

'As I said, Tom could have been havering; after all, he . . .'

She broke off as Bett snapped the soft cylinder and revealed something metallic to be concealed underneath. His fingers pulled the clinging balm away in chunks until they were left holding a solitary bullet.

'Tom said Ross wouldn't tell him what it was, for both their protection. I don't get it. It's just a bullet.'

'Less baffling than lip balm, granted,' Bett said. 'But I must confess I'm at a loss.'

He placed it gently upright on the table, pinched between his thumb and forefinger. She saw a tiny twitch furrow his brow, then he lifted his hand. The bullet jumped from his grasp of its own accord and hit the milk jug with a clang, eliciting a small shriek of fright from Jane.

Bett picked the bullet off of the side of the jug, exerting some force to do so, then looked at it closer. 'It's magnetised,' he said, sounding perplexed. 'Except, as we discussed the other day, you can't magnetise lead. This slug is made of steel. Wait a second. I think . . . Come on,' he said, getting up.

'Where?'

'The firing range. I've got a hunch about something.'

She followed him, the pair of them all but running to get to the basement. Bett selected a pistol of the appropriate calibre and slid the bullet into the breech. He flipped a switch on the controls and sent the target dummy in front of him all the way to the back of the range. Then he held the gun in both hands and fired.

Bett nodded as soon as the shot went off – unusually quiet, Jane thought – then hurdled the barrier and began walking towards the target. Once he reached the dummy, he bent down to pick something up. When he stood upright again, he was holding the slug in his right hand.

'It didn't even penetrate the cloth,' he reported. 'Barely enough powder in the jacket to get it across the range. He must have had these specially manufactured, maybe even made them him-self. I'm betting the dummy he used in the video was made of balsa, something you could rip to splinters with a pea shooter and a healthy pair of lungs. And that nailbomb – it wasn't held together by cellophane just because it's transparent, it was because cellophane wouldn't need much of a charge for the magnetised nails to rip through it.' Bett grinned, utterly delighted. 'Your boy is even more of a genius than I thought.'

'Why?'

'Because he's pulled off a two-hundred-million-euro fake.'

'It wasn't always my intention,' Ross told Willis. 'In the beginning, when I first had the idea, I genuinely did believe it might be possible, that there might be some way, even if the technology was decades off. But by the time I'd accepted it couldn't be done, I'd already envisaged the knock-on effects. I'd imagined how merely the knowledge that it was in the pipeline might scare people in the industry into thinking about other technologies, make governments, make *everybody* think about ways to defend ourselves that wouldn't involve blowing holes in people. And in the short term, I'd envisaged how the project might make Phobos think they had a reason to keep Deimos as a going concern. There were always rumours that they were pulling the plug on us and you were going to retire. I thought if I could make you believe in the Gravity Well, it would protect all the other projects we've worked on.'

'They were more than rumours, Ross. I *was* thinking about retiring; I still plan to, and soon. I've grown to hate this business. A little late in the day, you might argue, but I got there in the end. Once upon a time, perhaps it was diff . . . no, once upon a time, perhaps *I* was different. In recent years I've not been so easy with what we're about. That's why I created Deimos. It was my brainchild, or rather the salve to my conscience, to back the parallel development of non-lethal enforcement weapons. Do you want to know how cynical this business really is?'

'I think I spent the last couple of weeks finding out.'

'In a nutshell, it can be summed up by the fact that when you mention non-lethal weapons to most people in this game, they understand it as a euphemism for torture devices. Truth is, I was kidding myself. I was never going to be able to persuade my fellow directors at Phobos to keep pumping money into Deimos, not the kind of investment it really needs. But then came your Project F.'

'When did you suss it was a fake?'

'Oh, fairly early, Ross,' he said with a laugh. '*Resistance Paradox Effect?* You're an inspired engineer and a brilliant designer, but a rotten physicist and an even worse liar. Our visions weren't too far apart, however, or our methods: scare the industry into investing in new technologies – and that's exactly what we've done.'

'But once they've got access to Marledoq, it won't take them long to find out the Gravity Well is just a fucking big magnet. And then they'll close us down and asset-strip the place, not to mention suing Phobos out of existence.'

Willis was smiling, that newly revealed hardened edge to his apparent happiness.

'No they bloody won't. I've been negotiating this deal for weeks now, with several interested parties. OSE were never really in the frame, incidentally. They just thought they were, but I was using Parrier because I needed someone sufficiently greedy and corrupt to take the bait in the first place. I was never going to sell Deimos. BDE/CMK offered less than most but they got the nod because they agreed to the terms I was offering: an investment, not a purchase, and a ringfenced investment at that. They are investing in our development of non-lethal technologies. They get a corresponding share in the rights to those technologies and a very generous share in the back-end, but we retain control. Of course, the technology they're really interested in doesn't exist, but nor are they ever supposed to have heard about it.'

Ross smiled back, couldn't help himself laughing. 'Because the files were stolen,' he said.

'The Gravity Well was never mentioned in any discussions, negotiations or documents. For them to have done so would be to admit complicity in industrial espionage and latterly a whole raft of more serious crimes. We've got our investment, Ross. Deimos has a bright future. Well, as bright as it gets down a big hole under a mountain.'

*　　　*　　　*

'Willis,' Bett said, shaking his head, 'that fly old bastard.'

'You said it to me yourself,' Jane reminded him. 'Act awkward and clumsy and people write you off as no threat. He plays the bumbling old fool . . .'

'And no one sees him coming until his knife is in up to the hilt. They thought he was there for the taking but he played them all, even me.'

'He played *you*, how?'

'Oh, a small but crucial role. The real con was in making people believe in the technology, which he did by making it the most jealously guarded secret. Expensively guarded, too: he contracted me as consultant to overhaul Marledoq's security, and my recommendations weren't cheap, nor were my services. But that was all crucial to the deception.'

'If he'd paraded them around at an exhibition, people would have been more sceptical,' Jane surmised. 'But instead they believed the videos were real because they thought they'd been stolen, and stolen with some difficulty. This Segnier – whoever he really is, and if he really exists – gave Parrier the impression that he didn't even know *what* the big secret was. I suppose it might have set off alarm bells if he just handed over the files, so not only did he make out a third party got hold of them during some one-off opportunity, but he got everyone to pay through the nose for them too.'

'People are always more valuing of things that cost them dear, and information is no different.'

'Any guesses who this third party might have been?' Jane asked.

'Oh, I'm starting to get an idea.'

'You okay, girl?' Rebekah enquired as Air Bett prepared to touch down inside the Marledoq facility's recently electrified perimeter fence. Lex had been staring transfixed at the compound throughout their approach, this place the occasion of an unease that had never quite left her. She'd been on tenterhooks the whole time Ross Fleming was around Maison Bla, but her fear of what he might say wasn't the sole reason she'd felt compelled to take this flight. Having been the fool whose betrayal set this whole thing in motion, she needed the closure of seeing him returned, safe and sound, where it all began, the scene of the crime.

'I'm good,' she said, as the wheels gently took the chopper's weight.

'You looked kinda spaced.'

'Just weird being back here, you know?'

'Yeah. This was my first real exercise. Looks different in the daylight. Less threatening – though I guess we constituted the real threat that night.'

You got that right, Lex thought.

It did look different, and not just because of the time of day. Bett's recommendations had all been implemented, such as the removal of the above-ground, sabotage-friendly electrical sub-station and the construction of a high-security tamper-proof housing for the facility's previously vulnerable ventilation intakes, pumps and filters. (Bett had opted against pumping the place full of sleep agent during the Tiger-Team raid on the tri-partite grounds that it was too expensive, too easy and 'just no bloody fun'.) Inside the deliberately innocuous-looking warehouses there were now retinal scanners controlling the lifts, with inter-level access (and even certain individual rooms) also protected by optical-recognition equipment. If they were to stage a raid on this place again, somebody really would have to lose an eye.

Lex jumped out of the cockpit door while Rebekah killed the engines and reached, vigilantly as ever, for her maintenance paperwork. With the rotor sound dying off, she heard a keening noise from behind and looked over her shoulder to see someone approach in an electric buggy, coming to pick up the VIPs. She slid open the cabin door and offered both passengers a hand down on to the tarmac. They both looked pretty pleased about something. Willis emerged first, Fleming at his back. The lab-geek stopped in front of her and kept hold of her hand a moment.

'Thanks,' he said. 'For everything.'

'Don't mention it. Can I just say, your mom's an incredible woman.'

'You're telling me.'

He walked off towards the approaching buggy, which was now only yards away, close enough for her to see the driver.

'Oh shit,' she muttered to herself. She was looking once more into the face of the nameless man who'd seduced her all those months ago with his talk of influence, of contacts, and his bullshit promises. He got out of the buggy and shook hands with Willis and Fleming, laughing, ushering them aboard. All pals. Then, before he got back into the driver's seat, he turned to look at Lex, smiled and put a finger to his lips.

'Son of a bitch.'

Lex watched the buggy drive off. She heard the slam of the pilot-side door, then Rebekah appeared alongside her.

'What the hell was that about?' Rebekah asked.

'What?'

'That finger-on-the-lips deal? Who was that guy?'

Lex was about to plead ignorance when her cellular began ringing. She fished it out of her pocket and looked at the LCD, saw the name scroll across the panel.

Bett.

She pressed talk. 'Sir?'

'I know,' he said simply.

She swallowed, tried to think of a response, felt as though her throat was swollen, blocking her words.

'Fool me once, shame on you, they say. Fool me twice, shame on me. You're about the only person I believe *could* fool me twice, Alexis, and I can't afford to let that happen. You're fired.'

She gasped, the sudden intake of breath about the only sound she felt capable of making. A thousand thoughts rushed around her head, none of them lucid.

'Okay, fired is a little harsh. But definitely suspended. Or rather, indefinitely suspended. Mrs Fleming has informed me you're under the misapprehension that there's something you could still be taught about computers if you went to college. As I believe the only way you could be disabused of this notion is to actually go there, I am prepared to facilitate it in any way I can. And given that I now understand you're not quite as adept as your "data salvaging" achievement suggested, then who knows?'

Lex felt her eyes fill up. Her throat was still swollen, but she managed three weeping, whispering words.

'Thank you, sir.'

'There is a condition.'

'Uh-huh,' she managed.

'Stay in touch. Because once you've gone back to Canada, got your degree, worked in an office for a while and generally acquainted yourself with how tedious normal life actually is, there will still be a job waiting for you here.'

'Sure,' she sniffed. 'You'd always be able to find me anyway.'

'This is true,' he said, and hung up.

'Is everything okay?' Rebekah asked.

'Yeah,' Lex replied. 'Everything's okay.'

Jane found Bett in the drawing room where they'd first met, standing by those huge windows and looking out upon the gardens in the twilight. A call had come through from the hospital, which he had transferred to her in her bedroom where she was getting ready for dinner. A final meal here, a time to say thanks, a time to say goodbye. His voice had been soft but a little stiff as he informed her of the call, much as he'd sounded any time the subject of Tom came up. She knew then that he'd be in that room, knew that he would be by those windows. He had his sanctuary upstairs, but that was where he retreated to be alone; this was the place he felt most robust in dealing with others.

'Tom's awake,' she reported. 'I'd better go in and see him. I know we're supposed to have dinner, but . . .'

'Not at all. I understand. I'll drive you.'

'No, no, never bother. Best that I go myself,' she suggested.

'Of course, whatever you think. But before you do, before you see him, we have to talk.'

Jane wanted to procrastinate, tell him she had to go right away and that they could talk later, but she knew neither of them would buy that. She took a seat at the big table. 'Okay,' she said.

Bett walked over and sat down next to her.

'You've taught me a great deal this past week or so, Jane,' he said.

'I've taught *you*?'

'Yes. And I've very much enjoyed having you around. Which is why I have to ask, before you see your husband, whether I might yet be able to tempt you to stay.'

401

Jane thought this sounded as desirable as it sounded insane, and her self-defence mechanisms went into operation upon reflex.

'We were two people thrown together in extremely emotional circumstances,' she said, thinking aloud. 'I don't believe in fairy tales, Bett. I can't see a happy ever after for the two of us here in your mansion.'

'I don't believe in fairy tales, either, and you should know that. What happened between us meant a lot to me, but I'm not kidding myself. Neither of us is exactly naive.'

'Then why are you asking me to stay?'

'Because I just let my most talented protégée go and I need a replacement. I'm offering you a job.'

'Oh come on, Bett. I survived what we did but I don't think I'd be so brave or daring when it's not my nearest and dearest that's at stake.'

'Neither do I, and I believe your judgement and discipline would be the better for it. You're a natural, Jane. You were born for this.'

She looked at his face, realised he wasn't kidding. Bett was never kidding. That, of course, left deluded, but he was never that either. And she knew the only reason she was trying to convince herself that this idea wasn't viable was that she wanted it so much. It was like all her life she'd had dreams she could fly, and every morning she woke up and found her feet stuck to the ground; but this past couple of weeks, she had flown, she had soared, and now that she knew what that felt like, she wasn't coming back down again if she could help it.

'You can stay here until you find a place of your own. I can offer good wages, foreign travel, company car. Not *that* company car. Though, if that's what it takes . . . Name your terms.'

'I have only two,' she stated. 'One, plenty of time off to see my family.'

'Not a problem. What's two?'

'The firm does a wee "homer" for me before I start.'

Jane let him off with the offer of the Diablo and instead borrowed his other car, a Porsche Carrera, to get to the hospital in San Raphael. She stopped it at the end of the drive, watching the gates slowly open, her eye caught again by the name etched amid the iron creepers and thorns, and then it hit her. Maison Blah, she'd heard Lex say, assuming she meant as in blah blah blah, but it wasn't, and nor was it Maison Rla. She'd misread the curlicued caligraphy: it was Maison *Bla*.

Bla an Tir. Gaelic.

She laughed as she put it together, where he was from: a town by a river, sure enough, but not one you'd want to grow up in if you were a boy called Hilary. No wonder he'd learned how to fight.

She remembered when Ross was wee, how Tom used to tick him off if he left his bike lying outside rather than storing it in the garage: 'If you don't look after it, some bad boy from Blantyre will come and take it away.'

Pity he hadn't heeded his own lesson. Now a very bad boy from Blantyre was taking away his wife.

They had a wedding photo sitting on top of a nest of tables in one corner of the living room, dwarfed now by larger portraits of Rachel and Thomas. A full-sized print of it had hung in the downstairs hall for several years, until the glass had smashed when it got knocked off the wall by Ross during a misadventure involving a bow and a rubber-suckered arrow. It was sun-faded by that time anyway, and should have been taken down long before. Jane's admonishment of Ross for his carelessness masked her gratitude to be rid of it, and, truth be told, she'd been reluctant to look out even the smaller print she had by way of a replacement. Something about it had always bothered her. She looked good enough in it, hair and make-up immaculately (and unaccustomedly) administered by professional hands, her dress so delicate, and Tom beside her, so smart and undeniably handsome. But while he was staring into the camera, uncomplicatedly happy, she had this far-off look about her, dreamy but not quite smiling, disconnected.

It had been on the photographer's instruction. He'd told her and Tom where to look, composed the frame. 'Look like you're already thinking of leaving,' he'd joked to her. But down the years, even when things were better, that far-off look unsettled her. Yes, it was posed, but she couldn't help wondering whether the photographer saw something and acted upon it, whether she was already looking far away on the inside. His direction notwithstanding, it wasn't where her eyes were pointed that haunted her about the portrait: it was how distant she seemed from her newly married spouse.

She found Tom sitting up in his hospital bed, reading the *Daily Record*. He was in the south of France, but there was some alchemy by which West-of-Scotland males could always procure a copy of that awful rag no matter where they were.

'Catching up on the Celtic?' she asked.

'Aye. I'd forgotten all about the UEFA Cup. We ended up watching the Barcelona game on that bloody boat, can you believe that?'

'After the past fortnight, I can believe anything. Who do they have in the next round?'

'Ach, some mob called Villareal. Never heard of them. It'll be a skoosh. Shooty-in.'

'Good, good. How's the wing?'

'Well, we've Agathe down the right and . . .'

'I meant your arm, Tom. Sore?'

'A wee bit, but I've got this patient-controlled thing for analgesia. I just push a button when it starts to hurt.'

'So you're sitting comfortably, then?'

The homer

He stood with his back to the bar, a bottle of lager in his hand, and surveyed his men: assembled around him and awaiting his command. It was half past midnight and they had a lock-in, the landlord turfing out all but his crew when the time came. But this wasn't for a bevy session. This was for business. *Serious* business.

They had all answered the call: Tommy, Deek, Panda, Jai, Goggsy, Wee Flea, Fat Paddy. All, that was, except Big Chick, who wasn't expected to be answering any calls for a while. The poor cunt was cooped up in his bedroom back at his mammy's house, a quivering wreck who couldn't get to sleep at night because he went mental if the lights went off.

Two days they'd been chained up in that basement, in the dark, in complete blackness. Two fucking days. Pishing where they sat, drinking water through a tube, starving hungry and all the time having no idea when or if they'd ever get out.

But one thought had sustained him throughout it all, and now it was time for that thought to be made flesh.

The bitch had been seen again, at last. She was back in EK, arrived just today. He knew, because he'd had somebody watching the house for a week. She had returned, stupid or arrogant enough to think she could just waltz back into town and forget who ran the fucking show, forget the liberties she'd taken. He didn't care who she thought she was or who those bastards in Barcelona had been. The point was, they fucking well weren't with her now, were they?

The way he saw it, she'd left him no choice. This wasn't just about revenge, it was about reputation. So far, nobody else knew what had happened in Barcelona, other than that it had left Big Chick greeting like a wean every night, but it was only a matter of time before the rumours started. He couldn't afford that, and he really couldn't afford the truth to get out.

So tonight was a simple necessity, and one he was sorely looking forward to. He'd soon see how *she* liked being tied up and knocked fuck out of, how she enjoyed all the things he'd been dreaming up for her while he rotted for two days in that stinking hole.

'Right, boys,' he announced, calling them to order.

Which was as far as he got.

The lights went out and, a fraction of a second later, there was a deafening crash of glass, like every window in the place had been simultaneously smashed. He heard panicked shouts, soft impacts, groans and heavy thumps, sensed movement all around him but saw nothing. Then he felt arms about him, struggled in vain as he was pinned and twisted, violently hauled off his feet and brought down, hard and horizontal, on the pool table.

The lights came on again. He sat up and looked around. All his men were unconscious, lying on the floor where they had fallen, the coloured-fibre tails of tranquilliser-darts jutting from each of their chests.

But they were not all he saw.

There were three figures standing before him, dressed all in black, each holding a pistol, their faces masked by some kind of goggles, presumably for seeing in the dark. The one dead ahead began walking slowly towards him, the other pair moving in again to hold him as the figure approached. Some craven sensation of fear told him he knew that walk, a woman's walk, that he'd seen it before in Y-pishingly familiar circumstances.

The woman put a hand to her forehead and removed the goggles.

Oh shite.

The other two sat him up to face her. She stared at him, coolly contemptuous, then reached into a pocket and pulled out a piece of paper. She unfolded it and handed it to him.

'Read it,' she said. 'Aloud.'

He looked at the sheet, his hand trembling as he held it. It looked like a blown-up photocopy, the type oversized and slightly distorted.

'READ IT,' the woman demanded.

He read.

'Retribution,' he began. 'Noun. Punishment or retaliation for an insult or injury.'

'Very good,' she said. 'You see, Anthony, it occurred to me that following our last encounter, in your juvenile wee mind you may believe you've some account you need to settle with me and mine. So I ask you: Retribution. Do you know the meaning of the word?'

'Aye,' he told her. 'I just read it to you.'

She shook her head and took back the paper. Then she scrunched it into a ball and the other two gripped him as she stuffed it into his mouth.

'No, Anthony, that was just the dictionary definition. You come anywhere near my family again and I'll teach you the fucking meaning.'